Contents

London Borough of Tower Hamlets

91000008163622

Funny
Folk Tales
for children

Allison Galbraith

Illustrated by
Lucinda M. Wilson

Foreword by
Taffy Thomas MBE

The History Press

To Ethan

If laughter is the best medicine, then this book is for you. And to every child who has spent time in a hospital. May love and laughter flow from these stories to you.

First published 2023

The History Press
97 St George's Place, Cheltenham,
Gloucestershire, GL50 3QB
www.thehistorypress.co.uk

Text © Allison Galbraith, 2023
Illustrations © Lucinda M. Wilson, 2023

The right of Allison Galbraith to be identified as the Author
of this work has been asserted in accordance with the
Copyright, Designs and Patents Act 1988.

All rights reserved. No part of this book may be reprinted
or reproduced or utilised in any form or by any electronic,
mechanical or other means, now known or hereafter invented,
including photocopying and recording, or in any information
storage or retrieval system, without the permission in writing
from the Publishers.

British Library Cataloguing in Publication Data.
A catalogue record for this book is available from the British Library.

ISBN 978 1 80399 104 7

Typesetting and origination by The History Press.
Printed and bound in Great Britain by TJ Books Limited, Padstow, Cornwall.

MIX
Paper from
responsible sources
FSC
www.fsc.org   FSC® C013056

Trees for Life

About the Author

Allison Galbraith loved listening to her mum and dad tell stories when she was young. In her first job as a community librarian in Wolverhampton, England, she read stories to children. This was the best part of the job. Allison learned that reading a story out loud creates magic – the characters in the book come to life and the story leads us on adventures together. After that, Allison worked as an actress, a dancer, a theatre maker and a drama teacher.

One day she realised that these jobs were different ways of telling stories. So Allison put all her performance skills into one funky hat and became a traditional storyteller. Over many years she has told and collected hundreds of folk tales and written some of them in books, like this one.

Allison lives among the orchards of the Clyde Valley in Scotland with her partner and many animal friends.

About the Illustrator

Lucinda M. Wilson is a Scottish artist. She lives and works in the beautiful and vibrant city of Glasgow, where she draws and writes about all sorts of things. You might see her work online, or in little magazines, or maybe even in video games! She grew up in the countryside of Ayrshire, where her parents taught her all about the local plants and animals that live in the wilderness. You can see lots of different animals and plants in this book. How many of them do you think she learned to draw while she was out adventuring in the woods and fields?

Thank Yous

Many thanks to Nicola Guy at The History Press for her support and for publishing this book. After the Covid-19 global pandemic, Nicola and her team agreed that a collection of funny stories was just what everyone needed.

Much gratitude to Taffy Thomas MBE – the UK's first storytelling laureate – for kindly permitting me to retell his story about 'Why Dog Lives with Man'. Also, tremendous respect and thanks to Taffy for finding time to write the foreword.

Thank you, Lucinda M. Wilson, for the fantastic pictures and being so much fun to work with.

Thank you, Patti Keane, for being one of my oldest friends and helping me with this book.

Thank you, Judy Paterson, for all of your wise words. Your talent and experience as a storyteller and writer are extraordinary.

The greatest respect to Judy McGuire, who gave me my first storytelling work in Glasgow Libraries in 1992. Your consistent championing of books, reading, storytelling, and community is astounding. Your keen librarian's eye and unwavering friendship are greatly appreciated.

Thank you George MacPherson – the Great Bard of Skye – for allowing me to retell your story about the changeling cow.

This story is, without a doubt, one of the best tales I've ever heard.

An enormous and heartfelt thank you to Dr Margaret Read MacDonald, the most talented librarian, doctor of folk tales and storyteller I know. Your help with tracing back the origins and sources of some of these tales was enlightening and entertaining in equal measure – you are a folk tale oracle, Margaret!

Thank you Julia Henrikson for advising me on popular names for cows in Norway. ☺

Thanks to Donald Smith for your continuing support and for making the Scottish storytelling scene so vibrant. Thank you Teresa Lowe for organising the best storytelling events in Scotland!

And many thanks to my storytelling friends, who gladly shared their favourite funny stories. These include, Daniel Serridge,

Tony Bonning, Lesley O'Brien, Lea Taylor and Lari Don. You are all generous, witty storytellers who use your talents to spread happiness wherever you go.

Huge thanks to Finlay Stevenson for your unwavering support and making me the best hot cocoas in the world.

Finally, a thousand thanks to all of the storytellers who've kept these stories alive, and to the listeners who have helped me retell them.

Foreword

When it is the best of times and the worst of times, we may be in danger of raising a generation of children who are losing the ability to laugh and know joy and have an increased chance of mental health problems. It may be that storytelling and story listening can help with this. Storytelling and story listening in the company of a trusted adult or family member is integral to the rounded development of any child. Stories can develop a child's vocabulary and emotional literacy. If a folk tale takes us to a dangerous place, the actions of a hero/ role model deliver the listener or reader back to a safe place. One of the things that can make us feel good in the safe place is a chuckle or a good laugh. Allison Galbraith understands this and in putting together this collection of funny folk tales for children has produced a book that can help carers, grandparents and siblings build the feelgood factor in youngsters.

Professional storytellers will probably not find a wealth of new material in this book but will find a fresh way of repurposing some valued 'chestnuts', reminding us why they have survived so long and continue to delight. The stories are short, pithy and witty.

I commend this book to all who wish to encourage smiles through stories and help children to feel happier in a safe place.

Taffy Thomas MBE, 2023

About this Book

A Riddle

It's the best present you can give.
It never breaks, and it doesn't wear
out.
If you give it away, it gets better every
time.
If you don't give it away, it's worth
nothing at all!
What is it?

The stories that make people happy, are
the ones I like telling best. When we

smile and laugh, our worries vanish and we enjoy life to the max! That's why I've collected my favourite funny folk tales and put them in this book.

The stories come from all over the world. Reading them helps our imaginations travel to exotic places, supernatural dimensions, and fantastical worlds. Every story contains at least one grain of truth, a pot full of wisdom and a barrel of laughs.

I hope you like them and that they make you smile, chuckle, and laugh out loud.

If you find a story that you really like, share it with someone, because a story is the best present you can give.

(And that's the answer to the riddle!)

1

Monkey See, Monkey Do

Pedro made hats. Fabulous woven straw hats. He lived with Maria and their five children in a tightly packed house in a little town in Ecuador. Nearly everyone in the town made hats. Some were like Pedro's, woven out of special straw reeds; others made their hats from wool and felt. People travelled from everywhere to buy hats from the town. During the winter, fewer people visited, so Pedro sold his hats at the big market in the city.

One cold morning, Pedro was up early, ready to go to the market to sell hats. He filled saddlebags with Maria's knitted woollen hats and a selection of his straw hats. With the saddlebags over his shoulders, Pedro placed a dozen new hats on top of his own head. Maria gave him a bean burrito for his lunch and kissed him goodbye. His children shouted for things they wanted from the market, like a puncture repair kit, shoelaces, nail polish, comics, coloured pencils and sweeties. They all stood on the front porch and waved him goodbye. Maria said he must get to the market as fast as possible to find the best spot to sell the hats. She told him he was not to sit down for a nap along the way!

Pedro smiled and waved back at his family, shouting, 'Yes, my lovelies, I will get your presents, and I will not stop for a nap.'

He walked out of town, along the dirt track, up and over the hills. He turned off the main road to take the shortest route through the forest. The sun was beginning to warm the air, and halfway along the forest track, Pedro decided to sit down for a quick rest. His saddlebags were heavy and his stomach had already forgotten about the fried eggs he had eaten for breakfast. He nibbled a corner of his burrito and rested his aching shoulders against a large tree trunk. It still had a few leaves that fluttered in the breeze, high above his head.

Pedro relaxed and enjoyed the winter sun's gentle warmth upon his face.

He closed his eyes for a moment. Before he knew it, Pedro was fast asleep beneath the tree.

Sometime later, he was woken by an unfamiliar sound – burring and chattering. Above his head, he could hear squeals and grunts. Pedro looked up. To his surprise, he saw something moving. Pedro could just make out the shape of a monkey leaping through the branches above him. Then he felt a swish and a woosh of air as his hat was lifted off his head. Pedro put his hand on top of his head and felt … hair. The hats that he had been carrying on his head were gone! He jumped to his feet and yelled into the tree, 'Who has taken my hats?'

The noise of monkey chatter grew louder. Pedro could see many monkeys above him, and they were … wearing his hats! Each little monkey had at least one, and some, two hats on their heads.

The monkeys squealed wildly as Pedro began flapping his arms and yelling at the creatures.

'These are my hats! All of them are mine! They're for selling at the market – GIVE THEM BACK!'

The monkeys stared down at Pedro. Then, they flapped their arms about just as Pedro was doing. They jumped up and down on their branches and squealed and chittered loudly. Pedro was flabbergasted. These monkeys were thieves, and they seemed to be laughing at him.

He shook his fists at them and yelled out even louder, 'My hats, GIVE THEM BACK NOW!'

The monkeys watched Pedro closely and they jumped about with glee. Each of them copied Pedro, forming their paws into little monkey fists, which they shook at the man below them.

Pedro was ready to burst; he was so angry with these naughty creatures. Then he stopped, realising it was pointless losing

his temper and yelling at the monkeys. Pedro took a deep breath and had an idea. He searched his saddlebags. At the very bottom of a bag was one woollen child's hat. Pedro took it out very slowly. He turned it round, admiring the brightly coloured patterns that Maria had knitted. Then he put it carefully on his head.

The monkeys watched him and chirruped excitedly. Pedro walked away from the tree to get a good view of the monkeys. The monkeys watched as Pedro jumped up and down, holding tightly onto the little hat on his head. The monkeys in the tree copied him, each holding onto their hats and jumping up and down. Next, Pedro leaped high into the air, grabbing the hat on his head and throwing it down onto the ground. The monkeys did the same – each leaping up from the tree's branches and throwing their hats to the ground.

Pedro ran around the tree, gathering up all of the hats. He put them into his saddlebags and fastened them tightly. The monkeys bounced up and down in the tree and screamed with delight. They watched as Pedro ran along the path and out of the forest as fast as his legs would carry him.

After a good, busy day at the market, Pedro set off for home, laden with gifts for Maria and his children. He took the long path home, avoiding the forest and the trees full of cheeky monkeys.

That night, as he enjoyed supper with his family, he told them about his day and the story of his monkey adventure. Everyone laughed and laughed at their dad's story. From that day on, Pedro's family called his monkey tale, 'Monkey See, Monkey Do!'

Pedro and Maria's children told the story to their children, passing it from one generation to the next.

Who knows, maybe the monkeys passed the story on to their children too! I hope that you will pass this monkey tale on as well.

2

Why Dogs Live with People

Many moons ago, dogs did not live with people. They lived out in the wild on their own.

One morning, a dog woke up, stretched his paws and yawned.

'Yowww, it's a bit lonely being on my own all the time. I think it would be nice to have a friend to talk to. Okay, where can I find a friend?'

The dog stood up and looked around. The first animal he saw was a hare. Dog ran over to the hare and said, 'Hello, big bunny. Can you and I be friends? I'm kind of lonely and would love to have a friend like you to talk to.'

The hare scowled at the dog, 'I am a hare, not a big bunny!' The dog apologised to the hare.

'Well, Dog, we could give it a go. You may hang out with me today, and let's see if we get on well enough to be friends,' said Hare.

The dog was delighted and rolled over and over in the grass to show how happy he was. After that, the two animals went out into the hills and spent the whole day looking for food together. At the end of the day, Hare hunkered down in some long grass. Dog lay beside his new friend.

As the moon rose in the sky and night crept all around, Hare and Dog closed their eyes and dozed off to sleep.

But the dog woke up in the middle of the night, raised his head to the sky, and howled at the moon, 'Ow, ow, ow, aw-owwww,' cried the dog.

Hare woke up in a panic, 'What are you doing, Dog? Oh no, stop making that noise. Shhhhh, be quiet! If you make all that noise, you will wake up Wolf, and Wolf will come here and eat us for his supper. Shh, stop it, Dog!'

Dog stopped howling and settled back down to sleep.

In the morning, as Dog woke up, it occurred to him that if the hare was afraid of the wolf, he should go and make friends with the wolf instead of Hare. Dog trotted off to look for Wolf, leaving Hare asleep in the grass.

When Dog found a grey wolf sunning herself, he asked her politely, 'Would you like to be my friend, Wolf? It gets kind of lonely on your own, doesn't it?'

The wolf gazed calmly at the dog, 'I suppose we could give it a go, Dog. But just for a day, to see if we like each other enough to be friends.'

Dog wagged his tail enthusiastically and scampered along, following the stealthy wolf. The two animals spent the day together, hunting for food in the woods. At the end of the day, Wolf and Dog settled down among old tree roots to rest. The wolf and the dog fell fast asleep as the moon climbed up through the clouds.

Dog woke up in the middle of the night. He looked at the moon and began to howl, 'Ow, ow, ow, aw-owwwwww.'

Wolf jumped up in fright and hissed at the dog, 'Stop that, you dopey dog. Stop making that noise! If you do that, the bear will hear you and come here and eat us. Now, shhh!'

Dog's mouth snapped shut, and he stopped howling at the moon. He turned around and around and settled back to sleep next to the wolf's warm body.

In the morning, the two animals awoke. Wolf stretched her front paws and then her back legs.

Dog gave himself a good shake and had a thought, 'If the wolf is afraid of the bear, then maybe I should go and make friends with the bear instead of Wolf!'

And with a cheery wag of his tail, Dog trotted off to look for a bear.

Dog found a huge brown bear scratching her back on a pine tree.

'Hello, Bear; I was wondering if you and I could be friends?' Dog asked with a big friendly smile.

Bear kept right on scratching her fur on the tree. 'Mmm, I suppose we could give it a try, Dog. You should try this tree; it's the best scratching post in the woods. Let's spend a day together and see if it works for us.'

Dog rubbed his bottom on the other side of the tree. It did feel good. Then Bear and Dog set off into the wild to look for food. All day long, they fished in rivers and munched berries from bushes.

At the end of the day, when the sun had set, the two friends went to Bear's cave, high in the hills. They lay down on the soft, earthy floor of the cave. Side by side, the creatures fell fast asleep, and together they snored. But who woke up when the moon shone down into the cave?

Yes, Dog!

Dog blinked his eyes, stared at the moon, and began to howl, 'Ow, ow, ow, aw-owwwww!'

Bear sat up and put her paws in her ears.

Dog kept on howling, 'AWOWwwwwwwwwwwwwww!'

Bear put a big brown paw over the dog's mouth. 'Shhhhh, you daft dog. Stop that noise at once! If you do that, the people down in the valley will hear you and come here and hunt us. Be quiet!'

Dog and Bear went back to sleep.

The following day, the bear slept in, grumbling about being woken in the night by the noisy dog. Dog stretched and thought to himself. 'If the brown bear is afraid of the people in the village, maybe I should go and make friends with them instead.'

Dog trotted quietly away from the grumpy bear and headed to the valley where the humans lived.

Dog sat outside the village and sniffed the air. He could smell woodsmoke, chickens, children, horses, goats, and pancakes. Two children spotted him as he approached the human village and ran to meet him.

'Hello, Dog!' they called.

Dog wagged his tail and rolled over and over. The children giggled and rubbed his tummy.

'Can we be friends, please?' asked Dog. 'I'm fed up with living alone.'

The children said, 'We will take you to meet our parents. You must ask them.'

They went into the village, with Dog walking beside them. When the adult people met the dog, they were cautious, 'Let us spend a day together, Dog. If we all get along, then we can be friends.'

That is just what they did. All day long Dog went hunting with the people. He helped them to catch a plump deer. In the evening dog played with the children. A great feast of food was cooked around the campfire. Everyone ate their salad and stew, and Dog was given a chunk of deer leg to chew on. When the people went to their houses to sleep, one family invited Dog to join them in their home. As everyone settled in their beds, Dog lay on a straw mat next to the children's bed.

When the moon had risen bright and full in the night sky, you can guess who woke up and howled at the moon.

That's right, DOG!

He barked and yowled as loud as he could, 'Ow, ow, ow, AWOWWWWWWWwwwww!'

All of the people woke in fright. They sat up in their beds and listened to the dog howling at the moon. Then the man and woman spoke to the dog, 'What a clever dog. That is such an impressive howl. If you keep that up, you will scare away the big brown bear, who frightens our horses. You will frighten away the sneaky wolf who kills our goats and chickens. You will even terrify the pesky hare who eats our vegetables. You can be our friend if you can howl like that every night, Dog. You may come and live here with us.'

Dog was over the moon to hear this. He ran to each of his new friends and licked their faces with his tongue. They laughed and patted their dog friend.

'Why,' said the mother, 'if you come and guard our home Dog, we will give you a bed by the fire and a bowl of food for your supper every night.'

Dog wagged his tail happily, barking and howling for joy.

From that day on, the dog lived with people, which is why dogs are our best friends.

3

Sausages for Supper

Have you ever fancied working in a woodland or forest? This is the story of someone who did just that. His name was Hans, and he was a forester. But there was a big problem – he hated cutting down trees!

Hans lived in a cosy cottage with Hilde, his wife, in the Black Forest. His job was to find mature trees and fell them with his axe. But as the years passed, Hans found it more and more difficult to cut down trees. Hans liked trees. He admired their strong trunks, some tall like young warriors, others bent and wrinkled like great-grandparents. He adored their sticky buds and fluffy catkins in spring, their fragrant flowers of summer, and fruits and nuts in autumn. Every tree was so beautiful that he simply could not cut them down. His wife noticed he no longer brought big tree trunks home to chop into firewood. Hans brought only a few fallen branches and sticks home daily.

'Hans, why are you not bringing back big logs?' asked Hilde, 'These sticks are only good for our own fire.'

Hans would mumble and make excuses, like, 'The wind was blowing so strongly today. I couldn't fell a tree and have it land on my head!'

As time went by, the kitchen cupboards became empty, until one day, there was no food left at all. Hans and Hilde had nothing to eat!

'Today, Hans, you must chop down a big tree and bring us back firewood to sell. If you don't, we will starve. No more excuses, Hans – bring back a tree!' Hilde demanded.

Hans knew Hilde was right, so he grabbed his axe and trudged reluctantly into the forest.

He walked and walked, looking at each glorious tree. Hans walked so far that eventually he found himself in a part of the forest where he had never been before. Deep in the middle of the forest was the most magnificent tree of all. It was very old and exceptionally large.

Sadly, Hans apologised for what he was about to do. He raised his axe high and swung it towards the tree's trunk. But a high-pitched squeal filled the air as the metal blade struck the ancient tree. Hans stopped chopping and looked up. He couldn't see anything unusual, so he carried on. Raising the axe, he brought it down sharply into the enormous tree with a thwack. Once again, a strange cry pierced the air – the sound of something in pain. Hans looked all around and called out, 'Who's there?' But no one replied.

Uneasily, he picked up the axe and swung it at the tree for the third time. A loud scream came from high in the tree's crown of leaves. Startled, Hans dropped his axe. He put his hand on the chopped bark and said, 'Is it you, old oak tree? Have I hurt you?'

The tree did not reply, but a tiny clear voice called down from a branch above, 'No, it is I who calls you. Look up, Forester.'

Hans peered up into the tree's dappled canopy. To his astonishment, a tiny creature was sitting on the edge of a branch. The little thing had rainbow-streaked wings, an elfin face, and an acorn cup hat upon her head. She twitched her wings and buzzed down from branch to branch – landing just above Hans's head. Hans rubbed his eyes and stared in disbelief.

'I am the spirit who guards this tree. I've been here for over two hundred years. If you chop my tree down, then I will be homeless. Please stop.'

Hans didn't know what to do; his mouth hung open … Then he spluttered an apology, 'I'm very sorry. I didn't know … I mean … err … I'm sorry to have hurt your tree… I … I'll find another tree to cut down.'

The fairy creature smiled. 'Will you? Would you do that for me? Why, thank you!'

Hans nodded and fumbled with his axe. 'I don't want to make you homeless. In fact, I don't really want to chop any trees. They are all home to somebody – squirrels, bees, birds, bats, and … you. A real live tree spirit! The problem is, my wife and I have no food or money, and we don't want to starve.'

The little tree sprite looked thoughtful. 'I see; you need some help then. Well, I can give you three magical wishes. After all, I am a supernatural being!'

Again, Hans stood with his mouth open, too surprised to say anything.

'How about a deal then, Hans?' she smiled cheekily at him.

Hans didn't know what to say. He thought, 'She must be supernatural because she knew my name without asking!'

'If you leave my beloved oak tree alone and don't destroy my home, I will give you three magical wishes.'

Hans found his wits and accepted the offer. 'Okay, tree fairy. Yes, please, I'll take the wishes and leave you and your tree alone.'

'Good choice Hans, you are clearly a clever man,' she said triumphantly, 'But go straight home with your wishes before the magic wears away. Take them to your wife and use them wisely.'

With that, she shook her wings, and sparkles of coloured light glimmered and floated through the air. They landed on Hans's hat and his shoulders. The tree sprite flew back up into her tree, disappearing into the sunbeams that danced among the leaves.

Hans picked up his axe and tracked his way back through the dense tree avenues until he reached his cottage. He sat down at the kitchen table, calling on Hilde, 'Hilde, come quickly, my darling, for I am covered in magical dust.'

Hilde came in from the garden and looked at Hans. She saw no chopped tree or firewood in the yard. Hans was beaming from ear to ear. 'Sit down, Hilde, for the story I am about to tell you is unbelievable.'

Sitting down, she noticed the cobwebs stuck to his hat and shoulders, 'Where on earth have you been, Hans? You're covered in cobwebs.'

'Not cobwebs, my darling Hilde, but real fairy wish-dust.'

She had never seen her husband so excited before. 'What is going on, Hans? Why have you not brought us wood, and what is this nonsense about "wish-dust"? Have you had a bang to your head or something?'

Hans smiled lovingly at his wife and told her what had happened. He told her about the deepest part of the forest and the majestic old oak tree. Then Hans told the story of the tree spirit and the gift of three wishes for promising not to chop her tree down.

Hilde listened carefully. She stared Hans hard in the eyes and said very calmly, 'You have clearly spent too much time in the sun, my dear. Drink some water and lie down in the shade.'

Hans realised it was too much to expect Hilde to believe his story.

'Okay, my wonderful wife, I know it sounds too fantastical, but let your imagination run wild for a moment. Think, dearest Hilde, what would we wish for if it was true?'

Hilde sighed, 'Oh Hans, we should wish for some food, for we have nothing to eat, and I would love to have breakfast. Eggs and ham, buttered muffins, fried tomatoes, or even a simple bowl of porridge would be better than nothing.'

Hans grinned, delighted that she was beginning to soften towards the idea. 'Exactly, my love. We could wish for our breakfast. But, all this talk of delicious food is making me incredibly hungry.'

Hans's empty stomach began to gurgle as he thought about breakfast. 'Oh, how I wish I had a great big sausage to eat.'

No sooner had Hans said those words than a giant link of sausages appeared on the table in front of him. The couple stared, dumbstruck, at the sausages.

'Oh no, Hans, you wished for a sausage, and that's what you've got!' Hilde pointed a trembling finger at the string of sausages.

'Ahh, I didn't mean to wish for that; it just slipped out.' Hans looked upset.

Hilde thought aloud, 'Oh my goodness, this means it's true, and you really do have three wishes!'

Then Hilde began to look annoyed, 'Hans, you just wasted one of our wishes on a sausage. You could have wished for a whole piggery with hundreds of pigs – they would have made millions of sausages. But you wished for just ONE sausage!'

Hans's face turned red. 'At least it's a massive link of sausages. It will give us enough to eat for breakfast, dinner, and supper.'

Hilde was still vexed. 'Now we only have two wishes left. So what can we wish for? I would like a big house with servants and a farm, so we never go hungry again.'

'We could wish for silver and gold and buy all of the farms in the country.' Hans replied enthusiastically.

'I want lots of new clothes and horses, Hans – a stable filled with the finest horses. Also, a cook to make our meals. We could have big parties and feed all of the neighbours. We would invite the Mayor and even royalty to our fine castle and grand parties. But what wishes should we choose? We can't wish for it all because you blew one of our wishes on a sausage. You are the sausage Hans, a stupid, silly sausage. I'm so angry with you for wasting a wish on a link of sausages! I wish that sausage was hanging off the end of your nose. That would teach you not to waste our wishes, you fool!'

No sooner had Hilde said these words than the sausages rose up from the table and landed on the end of Hans's nose.

The couple stared in horror as it dawned on them what had happened. Hans stood up and yelled while Hilde sat down and cried.

'You are an idiot, Hilde! You have wasted another of our special wishes, and I have a large sausage link stuck to the end of my nose.' Hans pulled at the sausages until his nose became bright red.

Hilde grabbed the end of the sausage and tugged and pulled. The more they yanked at it, the more painful it became. Hilde tried cutting it off with a knife, then scissors, but they became blunt and bounced off the sausage. They tried Hans's axe. However, this was a magical sausage, and the axe didn't even make a dent. All day and most of the night, they tried to remove the giant link of sausages from Hans's nose. Eventually, the couple were exhausted. Hilde thought hard: She could have great wealth, but then Hans would still have a link of sausages dangling from his nose. Or she could have her husband's face sausage free and no riches whatsoever! They both knew the only way to get the sausage from his nose was by using the last of their three wishes. Finally, they agreed that a husband with a normal nose was the best choice they could make.

Hilde held Hans's hand, and he made the final wish, 'I wish this sausage would leave my nose.'

The sausage link fell onto the table. Hilde bathed poor Hans's nose in cooled camomile tea. Then together, they cooked and ate a hearty sausage supper. The couple went to bed with full tummies and slept like logs.

Hans decided to quit his job as a forester. He found a new way to make a living – painting pictures of tree sprites onto tree branch cookies. Hilde sold the picture cookies to tourists who visited the Black Forest. They lived together happily for the rest of their lives, sharing their story of trees, tree sprites, and sausages for supper!

4

The Talkative Turtle

Long ago, an olive-brown, spotted turtle lived in a big pond in India. This pond had lots of snails, shrimp, aquatic plants, overhanging trees, and sunny mud banks – everything a turtle loved. Well, not quite everything. One thing was missing – the turtle had no one to talk to. Unfortunately, that was precisely what this turtle liked most – he loved to talk.

When he was young and had first arrived at the pond, there were plenty of other creatures to talk to, like fish – many different types of fish. The turtle was always the first to greet them in the morning, 'Hi fish! What a beautiful day. Oh my, look how the sunshine makes your scales sparkle. See how the ripples catch the light and make you look like you're dancing under the water. And if I stare hard enough at you, I start to feel dizzy…. ha, ha, ha, come on, fishes, let's dance! Who wants to play ring of roses with me? Oh, maybe we should call it a ring, a ring of ripples instead, ha, ha, ha, ha … Come back fishes, what's up, why are you all swimming away so fast? Come back and play!'

The fish had swum off to get on with their fishy business. They didn't have time to dance or play with the talkative turtle. From that day, whenever the fish saw turtle coming toward them, they would swim off quickly in the other direction.

The pond was also full of frogs, but they wouldn't talk to the turtle either. When they first met the turtle, he constantly sang frog songs, like: 'Five Little Speckled Frogs', 'A Frog He Would A Wooing Go', and 'The Frog Chorus' by Paul McCartney – this one was so catchy, they couldn't stop singing it, and that really got on their nerves!

'Oh, come back, frogs, come and sing to me,' The turtle would call out to them. 'I love your croaky voices and how you sing to the moon at night. Please come back and warble your frog chorus to me.'

Bum bum-bum
Bum bum-bum
Bum, bum bum bum bum bummm …

Sang turtle, as he chased after the splashes of kicking frogs' legs. But the frogs were gone; they had no time for the talkative turtle.

Many creatures came to the pond to drink and hunt for food, such as snakes, bats, birds, rats and deer. Every time a different species arrived, the turtle would race out of the water and introduce himself to the stranger.

'Well, hello there, you are a fine-looking … lizard, gazelle, elephant, parrot, tiger! Ahh! Do tigers eat turtles? I'm not staying here long enough to find out! See you later, stripey cat …'

A few polite animals would listen to the turtle's chatter for a minute or two. Turtle liked to complain to them about the full-moon parties.

'Not a single living beast slept at this pond last night!' exclaimed turtle to a passing snake. 'It's those crickets, don't you know, and the frogs. When the moon is full, they start up the band and party all night long. Croaking and chirping, plopping and splashing, the whole pond turns into a water disco. Grasshoppers and pond skaters singing "Frog Fever" and dancing like no one is watching. None of the rest of us can get any sleep. We're exhausted by sunrise; it's just not fair! Look at the bags under my eyes. I don't suppose you could eat a few pesky crickets for breakfast, could you, snake?'

Then visitors, like the snake, would make an excuse, 'Oh, is that the time? Sorry, got to go, got a train to catch!' And off they would slither, scuttle, gallop and fly before their eardrums burst.

Every animal in the area learned to avoid the turtle. This meant that the poor turtle became terribly lonely. The other pond dwellers felt sorry for the turtle, but they thought it was his own fault. He never let them take their turn to speak. Turtle was not a good listener. So they all ignored him. Eventually, he just began to talk to himself. Muttering about how cold or warm the water was. Complaining about the pond parties, the mess moulting ducks made, the smell of rat pee – he complained about everything!

One day, turtle heard a whooshing noise above him. He looked up, and two large geese were landing on the pond. He swam straight over to the geese.

'Hello, strangers. What brings you here, are you on your holidays, or are you planning to stay? Oh my, what fine, long necks you have. And look at your beaks, gosh, they look very sharp; I bet they could give someone a nasty peck. Oh, and would you look at that! You both have pink feet; I didn't know that geese had pink feet – did you stand in paint, or is that normal?'

Turtle didn't stop to take a breath or let the birds reply; he just kept on talking to them. The geese looked at each other and honked – laughing in goose language, because they were both thinking, 'We can't stay here and listen to this turtle chattering on and on. We'll get headaches if we stay here.'

The two birds began stretching their wings, ready to take off and fly away.

Turtle spluttered, 'Nooooo, please don't go. Stay and chat with me for a while. I'm so bored and lonely; I need someone to talk to. Please stay.'

The geese felt sorry for the turtle. They folded their wings back by their sides.

'Okay,' said the kindly female goose, 'We'll stay for a little while. We just wanted to rest our wings before heading off to our favourite winter lake.'

'Oh, tell me where it is? What's it like? Is it big? Are there many other creatures who live in your winter pool?' Turtle asked.

'Indeed there are,' said the geese. 'It's much larger than this pond. Hundreds of different animals, fish, and birds live there.'

For a brief moment, the turtle was silent. Then he yelled in excitement, 'Take me with you! Please, geese, take me to your winter lake. I need a different place to roam and make new friends. I want a better life, far away from this miserable little pool. A place with friendly neighbours. Not a puddle full of stuck-up insect-eaters like this! Take me too…. please …'

The geese were unsure. 'But how can we take a turtle through the air? You couldn't ride on our backs; it wouldn't be safe. You might fall off!'

Once again, the turtle was quiet for a second, but then he yelled, 'A stick, dear geese! Get a big strong stick.'

It didn't take them long to find a good stick.

'Now,' said the turtle, 'each take an end of the stick in your beaks. I will bite hard in the middle of the stick, and hey-ho, away we go. You can fly to the lake carrying me on the stick.'

The geese thought that this was a clever idea. Then the male goose had a worrying thought.

'What if you fell, turtle? The lake is far away. What if your jaws aren't strong enough to hold on for such a distance?'

'My jaws are the strongest in all the land!' yelled turtle. 'I can bite and lock my jaws like a crocodile. Nothing could pull me from this stick.'

The male goose replied, 'Yes, I'm sure you have very strong jaws.' Then he whispered to his mate, 'strong from all the exercise they get talking.' The geese honked.

'But what if you started to speak, turtle, then you would fall? You must be quiet and not talk for a long time,' said the female goose.

Turtle looked offended, 'Are you saying I can't keep quiet? I can be very quiet when I need to be. I'm not stupid, you know!'

The geese did not want to upset the turtle, so they agreed to take him to their winter pool. Turtle bit down hard in the middle of the stick, and the geese beat

their wings and took off, each goose
holding either end of the stick in its beak.
They flew high above the land, trees, and
rivers below. The turtle dangled from the
stick, his powerful mouth clamped tight
shut. As they passed above a village, some
school children looked up.

'Two geese are carrying a turtle on a stick!' exclaimed the astonished children.

'What an amazing thing to see,' said one child.

'How clever the geese are to think of doing that. Well done, geese, you are so smart!' All of the children clapped and cheered.

Turtle heard all this praise for the geese, and he was furious. It had not been the birds' idea to carry him on a stick. It was his idea! The children should be shouting, 'Clever turtle!'

As this thought whizzed through the turtle's mind, he burst into sound and yelled out, 'It was my ideaaaaaaaa ...'

Turtle fell, down, down, and crashed into the ground. He survived the fall, but his shell was cracked all over. And that is why turtles have the patterns on their shells today.

It's also why you never hear a turtle talking to anyone – now, they prefer silence to noisy chatter!

5

The Zombie Cow

The cow in the stable was not his cow. It sounded just like his cow when it mooed. It was the same colour as his cow and had the same markings. But Norman knew that the cow in the stable was definitely not his!

His cow always twitched her ears when he called her. But this cow's ears didn't move at all. Even when he shook a tin of oats, it just stood stock-still. His Eilidh would lick his hand when he rubbed her nose. This cow looked straight ahead and ignored him.

Worst of all, when he began to milk this strange cow, blue, stinking liquid shot out of its udders. The smell was so disgusting that it made Norman feel sick. He backed out of the stable to get away from the stench and the weird animal. This was a changeling. Someone or something must have taken his cow and left this zombie cow in Eilidh's place.

Norman bolted the stable door and went straight down the glen to the house of Maggie McGhee, the wise woman of Skye.

He told Maggie about the ghastly zombie cow in his yard. She listened intently to his tale and questioned him carefully about the blue milk. Then Maggie asked, 'Tell me, Norman, did you curse your cow?'

He jumped up shouting, 'No!' But Norman had to sit down again quickly because of the terrible pain in his legs and hips. You see, Norman had arthritis. He had been fit when he was young, but old age had been cruel, crippling him with arthritic knees, hips and elbows.

'I would never curse my cow, Maggie. Never! That cow means everything to me. Her soft twitchy ears. Her pink tongue. I talk to her every day, and she gives me the creamiest milk. I would never say a bad word about her – she's my best friend.'

Norman was getting quite emotional; he had tears in his eyes. 'I love that cow, Maggie!'

'Oh, I know how much she means to you, Norman, but think, did you maybe curse her by accident?' Maggie asked calmly.

Then a thought dawned on him, 'Oh dear. I'd milked her yesterday, and she had given the frothiest, sweetest milk you've ever seen. I gave her a treat, a sliced carrot, and she pushed my hip against the wall as she took it from me. Oh, it was that sore … I think I said, "Dammit, Eilidh, can you not be more careful when you turn around?"'

Maggie nodded her head sadly, 'That's it, Norman. You cursed your cow, and now the wee folk have taken her. That's the way of it, use a curse word to your cow, and you gift her to the wee people.'

'No!' cried Norman, 'They can't have her. She's my only friend. What can I do to get her back from them?'

'Well, you can give them gifts. If you take them fine clothes, you might get her back. But it can be dangerous going into their world.'

'I'll give them anything they want to get my Eilidh back, anything!' said Norman.

'Go home and put on your very best clothes. Take a silver pin from your mother's sewing basket and a wooden mallet. Go to the changeling cow and hit that pin into the rafter above its head. Hold onto the halter as tight as you can, and don't let go, whatever happens.'

Norman thanked Maggie for her help and hurried home.

He went to his bedroom and looked for his best clothes. He found a pair of top-quality deerskin boots, hardly worn. Norman put them on. Next, he looked in the wardrobe and took the linen shirt his mother had made for him. It was the last thing she had ever given to him. It was dyed golden yellow with tormentil, the little yellow flowers that bloomed all over the island. He put the shirt on. Then he took out his woollen plaid – like a kilt with extra pleats. It was the purest-spun wool, in green and blue tartan. Norman found a leather belt made of bull hide and buckled it around his waist. He looked magnificent in his finest clothes, like a rich toff from a big Highland estate.

Norman took a thick, silver pin from the sewing box. He picked up a wooden mallet from the shed; then went to face the zombie cow.

As he approached the stable where the beast stood, robotically chewing its cud, he felt a shiver of fear run through him.

He looked at the alien animal and thought of his beautiful cow, his beloved Eilidh. Norman took a deep breath, then hit the pin with one swift blow into the wooden beam above the imposter's head. Norman grabbed its halter with both hands and woosh …

Norman was thrown into the air, still holding tight to the head collar. Together, man and zombie cow were flying fast through the air. Norman was face down, holding onto the cow. They flew over moors, hills, lochs, mountains, and sea, then down a dark tunnel. He landed with a thump at the bottom of a deep cave. Norman still had the cow's halter in his hands, but it was empty; the cow was gone. However, he wasn't alone in the cave; hundreds of small people surrounded him.

A miniature man and woman of the elfin race came towards him. They both wore golden bands on their heads – the King and Queen of the Northern Shee – a tribe of elves from the north of Scotland.

The Queen pointed to the empty head collar in Norman's hands and smiled.

'Oh ho,' said the King. 'You are returning our fairy cow to us.'

'Yes, I am,' said Norman, 'and I would like my cow back, please.'

'But you cursed your cow man,' the Queen replied, 'You made a gift of her to us when you cursed your cow, you foolish human.' The King and Queen of the Shee laughed at Norman.

He got down on his sore knees and begged, 'But please, your majesties. I did not mean to curse her. My hips are so sore these days that sometimes I grumble out loud about it. I didnae mean to curse Eilidh. She means everything to me. She's my best friend. Please give her back to me – I love that cow!' Norman felt so emotional that he was sobbing in front of the whole tribe of elfin folk.

'Well, if you can prove how much you love your cow Norman, then we'll consider giving her back to you,' said the King.

'What is she worth to you, Norman?' asked the Queen. 'What could you give us in return for your Elidh?'

Norman wiped the tears from his face and stood up. 'I'm not a rich man, but you can have anything you see on me. I have on my most valuable clothes.'

The fairy folk were coming closer for a better look at Norman's outfit. Their King beckoned to an elder of the elfin folk, who came up to Norman and inspected his boots.

'Aye, those deerskin boots look fit for us. If we were to have them, we could make deerskin boots for all our people!'

Norman took off his boots and handed them to the elfin elder, 'They are yours gladly; please take them.'

Next, an elder of the female elves came up to Norman and poked a finger at his plaid.

'He is wearing a good woollen plaid. If we had that, every elf in this tribe could have their own woollen garment made from his kilt!'

Norman took off the belt and plaid and handed it to the old Shee woman, 'Have it; my plaid is yours.'

A young elf-man stepped forward and took the belt, 'This is excellent bull hide. We could each have a belt of our own from this. When we have finished crafting this leather, our belts will be even better than this!' The young elf said proudly.

Norman handed over the belt. He was now standing barefoot with only his shirt left on him.

A young elfin girl skipped over to Norman and stroked his linen shirt, 'Ah, this is the best cloth from the Isle of Skye and such a rich golden yellow. If we were to have this shirt, every Shee in our land could have a shirt as beautiful as this!'

Norman paused for a second. He remembered how this was the last thing his mother had ever given him.

'Ahh, look at that now,' said the Queen, 'He doesn't love his cow as much as he thinks. He doesn't want to give us the shirt for his cow.'

Norman pulled the shirt up over his head and gave it to the elfin girl, 'You may have it. My mother made that for me with her own hands, but I love my cow! Please take it and let me have my sweetest Eilidh back.'

The girl took the shirt to her elfin sisters, who all admired the quality of the golden-coloured cloth.

Norman had given all of his clothes to the Shee and was completely naked!

'Well, Norman,' said the King, 'you have given us good gifts for your cow. Now we must return the favour and give good gifts to you.' The King waved his tribe forward and the women and girls surrounded Norman. Each held bundles of nettles, witch hazel wands, thistles and other prickly plants. The female Shee beat Norman about his buttocks, knees, hips, and elbows with handfuls of stinging, healing herbs. They thrashed him until he cried in pain. As Norman yelled out, he again found himself flying through the air. Face down, he was hurtling over the sea, over mountains, lochs, hills and moor, until he landed safely on the ground.

He turned to see where he was, and there beside him was his cow, his beloved Eilidh. He spoke to her gently and she twitched her ears. He stroked her nose and she licked his hand fondly with her big, pink tongue. He reached for her collar and started to lead her home.

As they walked through the glen, local folk stopped what they were doing and stared and pointed, 'Look, there's Norman and his cow, and he's … naked!'

Norman looked down and got a surprise. He was naked, but his legs, hips and arms were now as strong and healthy as they had been when he was young.

From that day on, people smiled when they saw him and called him 'Naked Norman'. But he didn't mind one bit because his arthritis was cured, and he had his best friend back; Eilidh, his beloved cow.

6

Monkey Misery

Natacha and her brother Samuel looked after their family's beehives on the Caribbean Island of Haiti. They kept the wooden hive boxes clean and rainproof. When the summer flowers faded, they fed the bees sugar-water from the sugar cane that grew on the island. At harvest time, the pair calmed the bees with a bee smoker – a can of cool, pine-needle smoke. Then they collected the fragrant forest honey in clay pots and jars. The family kept most of the honey to eat and enjoy, but one big pot was always sold at the market. This was the job of Martha, their mother. Martha was a great saleswoman and made plenty of money from the honey.

The market started very early, so Martha had to hurry. It was a long walk through the forest to the marketplace.

She must have been walking too fast because Martha tripped on a tree root and fell. The pot she had been carrying on her head smashed into a tree trunk and shattered into many pieces. Thick honey oozed out over the tree. It trickled slowly onto the ground, covering leaves and twigs in a glistening golden goo.

Martha wailed in despair, 'Oh Nooooo! Oh my Lord, it's gone everywhere!'

She picked herself up, brushed the dirt and leaves from her clothes, and began to cry.

'Papa God, why do you bring me so much misery? It's all gone! Oh Papa God, why you give me all this misery?'

Martha left the spilled honey and went home, still sobbing about her bad luck.

A little monkey sitting in a nearby tree had seen and heard everything that had happened. The creature climbed down from the tree, curious about the broken pot lying on the ground. Monkey sniffed the strange thick sap that covered the pieces of pottery. The young monkey had never smelled anything like this before! Monkey put a finger into the honey, sniffed it, then tasted it.

'Mmm …' What a pleasant surprise – it tasted so sweet. Monkey scooped up more of the golden syrup and devoured it. She could not believe how yummy this stuff tasted. She licked it from the broken pottery, twigs, leaves, and tree bark. She lapped up every little drop she could find until it was all gone. Then, all monkey could think about was getting more of this delicious stuff.

She thought hard, where would she find more? What had the woman said? The woman had wailed and cried and said, 'Papa God, why you bring me so much misery?'

That must be it! Thought monkey, Papa God must have some misery.

Monkey wanted more of this misery right now, so she set off to visit Papa God. She climbed up the golden stairs, across the rainbow bridge, through the pearly gate, and into Papa God's garden. Papa God was sitting on a garden chair, napping in the sunshine. Monkey scampered up to him and asked, 'Papa God, please can you give me some more misery?'

Papa God looked at the monkey in surprise, 'You want me to give you "Misery" young monkey?'

'Yes, Papa God! Oh yes, please, Sir. Misery is sweet and sticky. Misery is delicious. I want more misery!'

'Okay, little one. If misery is what you want, then misery is what you shall have.' said a puzzled Papa God.

He went to his house and came back with a large suitcase on wheels.

'Here you go, monkey. Take this bag and carry it back down to earth. You must take it to a place where no trees grow and open it there.' Papa God chuckled, 'Inside this bag, you will find plenty of misery. All the misery a monkey could ever want. And remember, only open the bag where there are no trees!

Monkey thanked Papa God and ran back down the garden path, over the bridge, and down the stairs to earth. She pulled the suitcase on wheels behind her. It was huge and heavy. It must contain so much misery, thought the monkey.

She pulled it through the forests and hills of Haiti until she reached a large, sandy beach.

Monkey dragged the bag into the middle of the enormous beach. On one side was the sea, and on the other side, sand dunes stretched for many miles. This was a place where no trees grew.

She stopped to open the bag. Her tummy rumbled and she licked her lips with hunger. Monkey was excited at the thought of all that gooey, lovely misery. She unzipped the bag, grabbed the lid, and pulled it open. Then, out of the bag sprang, not one, not two, but three, huge, snarling … Dogs!

The dogs sprang towards the monkey – their jaws open wide, sharp teeth gleaming.

The monkey screamed, 'Arghhhhh …'

Monkey ran along the beach, her tail high. Her paws were moving so fast that it looked like she was flying over the

sand. The three big dogs chased after
the monkey. The dogs sprinted quickly –
getting closer and closer until they were
almost on top of the monkey. Monkey
ran and ran – running for her life.

The monkey screamed, 'Arghhhhh!'

This was the worst misery she had ever known! When she thought it was all over and the dogs were about to eat her, a tree appeared in front of her. Monkey sprang onto the tree, raced up the trunk, and clung to the top branches. The dogs leaped up, baying at the monkey. Fortunately for the monkey, these dogs could not climb trees – they could not reach her.

The monkey hung on to a tree branch all day and most of the night, shivering and shaking. The dogs circled below the tree, growling and snarling at the frightened monkey.

As the moon rose in the night sky, the dogs gave up waiting for their monkey supper. They howled in disappointment and slunk away to hunt for rabbits instead.

The monkey climbed down from the tree and ran back to the forest. When she was safely home with her family, she told them about the misery and the big fierce dogs.

The baby monkeys wanted to know who had put the tree in the sand dunes where no trees grow?

Do you know who put the tree there?

Perhaps it was Papa God who made the tree appear – after all, too much misery is not good for anyone, especially monkeys!

7

How to Flummox a Fairy

The King and Queen of the fairy folk were annoyed that they never got to eat the best cake in Scotland. Why should they and their tribe only ever eat second-rate cakes?

You see, there was never anything left of the best cakes for fairies to steal and eat. This was because the best cakes in Scotland were made by a master baker. When she whipped up a cream cake or a walnut loaf, every last crumb was gobbled up by the lucky person who was eating it. The elfin race do not make cakes or any other type of food. They prefer to steal their food from humans. At night, they sneak into our kitchens, dining halls, cafes, caravans, tents – anywhere humans live – and pinch our tasty leftovers. I'm sure that this has happened to you! You've left half a chocolate bar next to your bed. When you wake up, it's gone, vanished into thin air. Where did it go? You question everyone in your house about the missing treat – they all deny eating your chocolate. Your sweets have been taken by fairies – not your siblings, parents, dog or guinea pig. They've been stolen by elves!

The master baker made such delicious cakes, biscuits, cookies, and muffins that people paid lots of money to buy them. She worked five days a week, making and baking for rich and poor people alike.

She was also very kind. If a neighbour couldn't afford to buy their child a birthday cake, she would bake them one for free.

One day, the fairies thought of a cunning plan to kidnap the master baker. At dusk that evening, the fairies lay in wait for her, hidden behind bushes and trees. As she passed by on her way home from the town, they buzzed out and blew fairy dust around her.

When the magical mixture of pollen landed on her nose, she became drowsy and slumped down upon the grass.

'Oh, how tired I feel … I'll just have a wee nap …' she yawned as her eyes shut and her chin dropped to her chest.

Quick as lightning, fairies swarmed around the sleeping woman. They lifted her up and carried her down to their underground cavern.

Sometime later, she woke up. She looked around at the hundreds of tiny faces gazing expectantly at her.

'Oh my!' she exclaimed, 'What am I doing here? Are you elves?'

The King and Queen stepped forward, 'Yes, you are in our kingdom. We dwell below your human world. We have brought you here to live with us,' said the King.

'We would like you to stay here and make cakes for us,' added the fairy Queen.

The cake maker was so surprised that she wasn't sure what to say.

The Queen said, 'Your cakes are the best in the world. We rarely get even a crumb from one of your delicious bakes. We want you to stay here and bake wonderful cakes for us.'

The master cake baker was an extremely smart woman. She didn't like the idea of living underground for the rest of her life. Definitely not! She wanted to get back home as fast as she could.

She smiled warmly at the fairies, rubbed her hands together and said, 'Absolutely, your majesties and elfin people. I will be your personal cake maker. Let's not waste a second longer, bring me everything I need to make you a cake.'

The fairies buzzed with excitement. Their silver wings lifted them up a few centimetres into the air.

'Thank you!' chorused all of the fairy folk.

'But what exactly do you need to make our first cake?' asked the Queen.

The cake baker replied kindly to the Queen, 'I need a big mixing bowl, a spoon, cake trays, a sieve, grease-proof paper, a spatula …'

As she named each item of kitchen equipment, the King and Queen looked more and more unhappy.

'I'm sorry, but we don't have these things,' the King replied.

'Ahh, but we may have a bowl!' the Queen said, 'We love some of the pretty things humans make. Fairies, find a bowl.'

Each fairy took off and flew around the cavern, looking for a bowl. They searched high and low – in playrooms, under beds, in cupboards, through chinks of the walls, in the tree-root roof … they searched everywhere.

Eventually, a fairy found a tiny china teacup in a toy box – the kind that human children use for teddy bears' picnics. She proudly brought it to the Queen, who handed it to the cake maker.

The cake maker held it up, looked at it, turned to the fairies, and sighed, 'Too small, dear friends. I wouldn't even be able to make a fairy cake in a bowl this size!'

The sad fairies let out a huge sigh of disappointment and sank down to the floor of the cave.

'Oh no! Don't give up that easily,' said the cake maker. 'You can go to where I live and get everything you need from my kitchen.'

The King buzzed brightly in the air and waved his hand towards the secret door, 'To the baker's house, my loyal fairies. Fetch a bowl, a spoon, a sieve, cake trays, and anything else this good woman wants. Go swiftly, for the faster you fetch what she needs, the quicker we get our cake!' The baker listed everything she would need to make a cake.

I am sure that you, dear readers, all know what ingredients you need to make a cake. Flour, eggs, butter, sugar, milk, baking powder, icing sugar, cherries, cream, chocolate drops. Can you think of anything else to add to the list?

The fairies fluttered fast towards the baker's house. They nipped in through the letter box. In the kitchen, they darted around looking for all the things the baker had asked for. When the wee people were loaded up with baking utensils and cake ingredients, they flew back along the road. They buzzed down through the secret entrance of the fairy mound into their underground cavern. The tiny beings presented each item to the baker. Then they fell down on their couches, exhausted after carrying such heavy baking equipment.

Then she cracked the eggs. Next, she added milk and beat the mixture with her spoon. All was going well – she was smiling, humming a tune, and beating …

Suddenly, she stopped beating, held up the spoon, and shook her head. 'Mm, no, no, oh dear, whatever is the matter here?

I can't seem to find my rhythm. I'm sorry, fairy folk, this is not going very well.'

The fairies looked upset.

'You see, when I make a cake at home, my cat curls up on my lap and purrs. Perhaps it's the gentle rhythm of her purring that helps me to beat out the cake batter. I'm sorry, fairies, but I need my pussy cat here, and then I can make you a good cake.'

The King pointed to the door, clapped his tiny hands, and yelled, 'Fetch the woman's cat, and make haste.'

Each little creature stretched out its wings and swarmed out of the fairy cavern once more. They flew to the baker's house and found the cat, who was sleeping on a chair. Many fairy hands lifted the cat and went away out through the cat-flap, carrying the startled moggie. They flew back along the road, past the blacksmith's forge, and down through the secret entrance of the fairy mound. The cat was placed before the baker. She stretched her paws and leaped up onto her human's knees. The puss curled up upon her lap and began to purr. The baker scratched her pet's head and smiled at the fairies, 'That should do the trick, thank you, fairies. Now I can make your cake.'

She began to beat again, adding butter and creaming the mixture with the back of the wooden spoon. Next, the sugar and milk, some baking powder, and then more rhythmic beating …

The baker stopped again, with the spoon in her hand and a frown on her face. The cat was purring softly.

'Oh dear, something is still not right. I can't seem to get into my stride with this cake.'

The fairies looked distraught – little howls of despair filled the cave, 'Wahhhhhh …'

'Ah, dear fairies, I think I know what's wrong,' she smiled sympathetically at the elfin folk; at home, my dog lies in front of the kitchen fire, and bless him, he snores. Perhaps it's the rhythm of his snoring that I need to help me make a great cake …'

The King didn't wait for her to ask; he just raised his hand and told the fairies to 'Fetch her dog'.

Once more, the little folk buzzed in a stream of silver sparkles out of the mound. They sped on the wind to the baker's home. In through the dog flap they went. There on the hearth rug slept the hound. As invisible hands raised him up, he woke, lifting his nose to sniff the air. There was nothing he could do except stare in amazement as he was transported along the road. They carried him: past the blacksmith's forge, through the darkened village streets, and down through the entrance of the fairy mound to their underground cavern. The fairies collapsed onto the ground. Wagging his tail with delight, the dog bounded over to his human. She rubbed his head affectionately and told him he was a good boy. He lay down at her feet, closed his eyes, and began to snore loudly.

'That's perfect,' she said and beat the cake batter again. The cat purred, the dog snored, and the baker beat the cake-mix, beat, beat, beat ... But again, she stopped, put down her spoon, and shook her head, 'No, I'm sorry, something still doesn't seem right. Now, what could it be?'

The fairies groaned, 'Nooooo – what's wrong now?'

'Ah, I know what it is! My baby! It's past her feeding time, and my baby girl will need her feed. If you could just bring her to me. She's only a wee nipper and will be no trouble at all.'

The fairies raised their weary wings, the King pointed to the door, and off they flew. They squeezed in through the keyhole when they reached the baker's cottage. They found the big baby, gurgling and giggling in her high chair. The child squealed with delight as little fairy hands lifted her into the air. They flew out of the door with her. The wind rushed past the baby's face as she was carried along the road, past the blacksmith's forge, through the darkened village streets, over the duck pond and down through the entrance of the fairy mound.

When the toddler saw her mummy, she reached out and burbled a happy baby greeting. Her mother held her high and tickled her tummy. Then set the child down next to her. The cat purred, the dog snored, and the baby chortled. The baker continued to make the cake. Her spoon beat, beat, beat, beat … But the baby's burbles and gurgles soon became cries of hunger. It was long past the child's feeding time, and her clever mother knew this. The baby began to wail loudly, 'Wahhhhh, wahhhh, waaaahhhhh …'

The fairies put their fingers in their ears.

'Oh dear,' said the baker. 'Is she too noisy for you? I'm very sorry.'

The baby began screaming at the top of her voice. 'Wahhhhhhhhhhhhhhhhhh …'

'Oh, what a noise! You see, it's past her dinner time, and she is hungry. At home, my husband picks her up, which calms her down. That's what we need, fairies! We need my husband to look after the baby.'

The Queen of the fairies was beginning to get a headache. She gestured to her fairies and then to the door. The distressed creatures mustered all their strength and streamed up and out of fairyland. They buzzed in through the back door when they got to the cottage. They swarmed around the big man sitting in the living room reading his newspaper. They sprinkled the flower dust around his nose. As soon as he breathed it in, he sneezed and fell asleep, head first into his paper. The fairies used their magical strength to lift the sleeping man above their shoulders. Then they flexed their tired wings and flew him out of his house. They struggled along the road, past the blacksmith's forge, through the darkened village streets, over the duck pond, along the woodland path, and down through the entrance of the fairy mound.

After the sleeping dust had worn off, the husband rubbed his eyes and looked around in amazement. He saw his wife sitting, making a cake. The cat was purring on her lap, the dog snoring at her feet, and their baby was screaming her head off. But what surprised him most was the hundreds of little people with wings.

'Fairies?' he asked his wife.

'Yes, that's right,' she replied, smiling at him. 'These dear wee people have asked me to live here and make cakes for them. The only problem is our child wants her dinner and is making far too much noise for their sensitive ears.'

The woman stretched over and gave her baby the wooden spoon. Immediately the child stuck the spoon in her mouth and sucked happily on the sweet cake mixture.

The baker whispered in her husband's ear, 'Whistle your favourite tune.'

He looked at her, then began to whistle a tune. This woke up the dog. The dog hated whistling and began to howl. That woke the cat, who started yowling because she couldn't stand howling. Once the baby had sucked all the cake mix from the spoon, she banged the spoon on the table and squealed noisily.

All of the fairies flew for cover. Some buried themselves under duvets, others under sofas, and a few flew inside cupboards and up among the tree roots. The ones who couldn't find shelter slithered down the walls in a hysterical frenzy. They covered their ears with their hands, frightened that their heads would explode with the pain in their ears. Finally, the King yelled, 'Stop! Please stop all of this racket! We can't stand the noise!'

The baker signalled to her husband to stop whistling. As soon as he did, the dog stopped howling, and the cat ceased yowling. The baker took the spoon from the baby.

'I'm so sorry, your majesties and fairy folk. Are we making too much noise? Don't worry, my magical friends, because the batter is ready. It's time to put it in the oven, and you shall have your cake within the hour.'

The King and Queen looked at each other in dismay.

'We don't have an oven here! We don't cook anything. We steal our food from humans,' said the Fairy Queen.

The baker looked at the Queen and King and then at all the exhausted fairies. She smiled kindly at them, 'Well, never mind, don't worry, my fraught friends, I have an idea. Why don't I take these trays of cake batter home and I'll bake them in my own oven? When they are ready, I'll bring them back to you. Then I can stay and make your cakes for evermore.'

The King looked pleased with this suggestion. 'Yes, it would be fantastic if you could cook them in your oven. However, you don't need to come back here and live with us. We've changed our minds about that. You, humans, are far too loud and noisy. Our ears are very delicate, too sensitive to be near humans. Please take your husband and baby, your dog and cat, and leave us in peace.'

The door to the underground cave opened. The moon was shining brightly from a clear night sky.

Out trooped the woman, carrying her kitchen utensils and two tins of cake batter. Next came her husband, holding their baby, followed by their dog and cat. They were all relieved that the fairies had let them go. When they reached home, the baby was fed, and her husband made them hot chocolate – the cat and the dog each had a treat. Remembering her promise to the fairies, the baker baked the cakes in her oven. She smothered them in icing, cherries, cream, and chocolate drops.

She wrapped them carefully, and then her husband accompanied her back through the moonlight to the fairy mound. She placed the cake, wrapped in paper, on a smooth stone, by the fairy door. Next to the stone, she noticed a small pouch. As she picked the pouch up, it jingled. She looked inside and was delighted to find coins made of fairy gold – the purest gold in the world!

From then on, the master baker made a weekly cake for the fairy folk. She and her family walked to the secret fairy kingdom and placed the cake upon the stone. The elves always left a purse of purest gold in gratitude for the cakes. The master baker became the richest cake maker in Scotland. Her husband was incredibly happy because he knew how lucky he was to eat the best cakes and be married to the cleverest woman he had ever met.

Hopefully, one day, your talents will make you rich and happy too!

8

Hyena and the Talking Tree

Hyena woke from a bad dream, 'Ugh!' he shuddered. He shook his body from the end of his nose to the tip of his tail. A good morning shake to throw off the horrid dream. He stretched himself forward and backward – down dog and up dog, his favourite doggy yoga. Then Hyena yawned, showing perfect rows of sharp teeth. He ambled down to the watering hole for a drink, still thinking about the dream; 'Huh, of course, other animals like me!' he muttered to himself.

In his dream, every animal he met had ignored him. When he said, 'Hello,' each creature had walked by without even a glance at Hyena. It was as if he had done something wrong, and none of the other animals were talking to him.

While he lapped up cool water from the muddy water hole, he thought hard about anything he might have done to annoy the local animals. 'Nope!' there was nothing he could think of. Ah, except the other day, he'd eaten some wildebeest ribs that a mother lion had hidden for her cubs. Oh, and yesterday, he had chased some young rabbits into their burrow. Oops, he had also laughed at a baby giraffe, who had eaten a prickly pear and was spitting out prickles.

'Mmm, perhaps my dream is trying to tell me something. Maybe I should try and be nicer to everyone I meet today. Yes, I'll be very friendly; it doesn't cost anything to be nice!' Hyena said to himself.

A flock of parakeets flew down to the water hole for a drink. Hyena got ready to practise his new good manners, 'Good day to you feathery friends. Oh, what glorious colours your tails and wings are.' Hyena smiled his pointy-toothed grin at the birds.

The parakeets stepped sideways away from Hyena, chattering to each other. They didn't say a word back to him. They bobbed their beaks up and down while drinking from the pool.

'Oh dear, they don't want to be my friends,' thought Hyena. He trotted off to try being nice to someone else. As he passed a huge rock, he bowed to it and said in his best voice, 'How do you do, big rock? Nice, sunny morning isn't it?' The rock stayed silent. Even if it had heard Hyena, it was not going to reply.

Hyena moved on. He spotted a lizard sunning itself on a smooth tree trunk. He walked over to the tree, 'Hello, Lizard. How are you today? It's warming up, isn't it? I reckon that today is going to be a scorcher!'

The lizard blinked at Hyena and then scuttled away into the bushes, gone in a flurry of dust. Hyena looked at the smooth tree, 'Hello tree, it's a jolly good day. How are you today?'

The tree waved its branches in the breeze and then replied, 'I am very well, thank you, Hyena, and how are you today?'

Hyena couldn't believe his ears! The tree had spoken to him. He was so happy that someone was talking to him that he barked for joy, 'Woof! Oh my, a talking tree!'

As soon as Hyena said these words, the tree reached down with one of its big branches. It grabbed Hyena around his middle, picked him up, and smashed him onto the ground.

Hyena was knocked out for a moment, then he opened his eyes. Seeing stars, he staggered up onto his paws.

'Oh tree, what did you do that for?' Hyena gasped, the wind knocked out of him.

The tree was settling her branch back into a comfortable position. She replied, 'I cannot stand rudeness. I ask politely how you are today, and all I get back is, "Oh my, a talking tree!" What is so exceptional about a talking tree?' The tree was clearly offended.

Hyena apologised to the tree and limped away to lie down in the shade.

Hyena's ribs were badly bruised. It took him a whole week to recover and feel well enough to look for food; his stomach was empty. Then the hungry hyena had an idea about how to get his dinner. He went to the water hole and waited for the first animal to come along. It was an impala, a type of deer. Hyena smiled at the deer and spoke in his most polite voice, 'Dear Impala, I know you and I have had our differences over the years, but I have changed. I've learned to be a kinder creature and have become a vegetarian. I will no longer chase your wife and family ever again! In fact, I would like to make it up to you by letting you into an amazing secret.'

Impala looked at Hyena suspiciously. He didn't believe a word this scruffy dog was saying. Hyena could see that Impala was unconvinced, so he rolled over, waving his paws in the air like a pup.

'It really is a very special secret, Mr Impala. A real treat. You can see for yourself. In this savanna, there is a tree that can speak. This tree can tell you your fortune! Come on, I will show you.'

Now, the impala was interested, 'Okay, Hyena, no harm looking, I suppose.'

Hyena led Impala to the smooth tree. He whispered in Impala's ear, 'All you need to do is go up to the tree and say very politely, "How are you today, tree?" The tree will reply, and you must say, "Oh my, a talking tree!" Then the tree will tell you incredible secrets about your future.'

Impala decided that he might as well give it a go. He approached the tree and said in his most charming voice, 'Hello dear tree, how are you today?'

The tree looked at the deer and replied, 'I'm very well, thank you. And how are you today, Impala?'

Impala was surprised; he had never had a conversation with a tree before. He noticed Hyena waving his paws, gesturing for him to speak back to the tree. Impala remembered what Hyena had told him to say, and in his very clearest voice, he replied, 'Oh my! A talking tree.'

The tree let out a loud creak. She stretched down a smooth branch, gripped Impala firmly, and slammed him into the ground. Impala did not get back up.

Hyena barked for joy. He waited while the tree settled her branch back and grumbled about bad-mannered animals. Then Hyena sneaked forward, grabbed Impala's lifeless body, and pulled it away to the bushes. He feasted on deer till he could eat no more. After a week, Hyena thought it was time to get another tasty meal. He stretched his paws and made straight for the water hole. This time, he met a young elephant. Hyena repeated the trick and told the elephant about the talking tree, a tree that could tell him his fortune. The elephant followed Hyena to the smooth tree. Hyena whispered under the elephant's ear flap, 'And remember, you say, "Oh my, a talking tree." Then all of your dreams will come true.'

So Elephant began, 'Good day to you tree. How are you doing today?'

'Very well, thank you. How are you today Elephant?' said the talking tree.

'Oh my. A talking tee!' replied Elephant, winking at Hyena, who was hiding behind a bush.

Swiftly the grumpy tree stretched out her branch, picked Elephant up, and swung him to the ground. Poor Elephant did not move again.

'That's the last time you upset me, or any other tree!' spluttered the angry tree.

Hyena spent a month sneaking back and forth from Elephant's lifeless body.

Each time he went, he ate a meal of elephant steak until his belly was full. Then he slept for days, with a smile on his blood-stained mouth. Eventually, there was nothing left of Elephant, only bare bones and ivory tusks. Hyena's stomach became empty. It was time to find another meal.

Down at the water hole, he met an old rabbit.

'Mmm, not much meat on this old rabbit,' thought hungry Hyena, 'but better than no meat at all!'

Hyena repeated his story about a talking tree that told fortunes to the rabbit. Then he managed to persuade the bunny to come and see for herself. When they reached the talking tree, Rabbit sniffed the air and looked around. Hyena rolled over, acting like a playful puppy, to win Rabbit's trust. He told Rabbit that the talking tree had given him the secret of free food. 'All you have to do, Rabbit, is be very polite, and when the tree speaks, you say, "Oh my, a talking tree." Then the tree will reward you with everything you could ever want.'

The rabbit blinked, looked at Hyena, and then at the smooth tree. She hopped towards the tree, sat and scratched her fur for a moment, and then said, 'Hello, tree. How are you today?'

The tree looked at the old bunny and replied, 'I'm very well, thank you, Ms Rabbit, and how are you today?'

Rabbit was a little surprised. She had never realised that trees could talk before. She noticed Hyena springing back and forth and round and round in the bushes. He was clearly over-excited, thought Rabbit. Hyena waved at Rabbit and mouthed silently at her, 'Oh my. A talking tree.'

Rabbit mouthed back at Hyena, 'What?'

Hyena sat up and hissed quietly towards the stupid rabbit, 'Oh my, a talking tree!'

Rabbit shook her head and, with a puzzled expression, asked again, 'Say what?'

Hyena crawled closer to Rabbit, 'Say, Oh my, a talking tree!'

Rabbit leaned her head towards Hyena, 'Sorry, I'm a bit deaf. What did you say?'

Hyena whispered loudly, 'Oh My. A Talking Tree! Go on, say it!'

Rabbit's jaw fell open, and she looked confused, 'Speak up, Hyena, I can't quite make out what you are saying, "Oh my a …?" She shrugged her shoulders and shook her head.

Hyena sprang up to Rabbit and yelled at the top of his voice, 'You Say, OH MY A TALKING TREE!'

The tree groaned, reached with her branch, grabbed Hyena, and threw him down onto the ground with an almighty thwack. This time, Hyena did not get up.

Rabbit hopped out of the way. Then she listened to the tree complaining about all of the animals who upset her with their rudeness.

'That will teach that Hyena! He ought to have learned some good manners,' grumbled the tree.

'It certainly will teach him, dear tree. Politeness makes all the difference,' agreed Rabbit.

She waggled her long ears and lolloped away to nibble grass in a quieter part of the savanna.

9

Cow on the Roof

One morning, Sean looked at the sky's dark thunderclouds.

'Oh no! Would you look at that, Sian. It's going to rain, and I'll be soaked while I work in the field today. I must get the hay harvested quickly. If it gets wet, it will grow mould and be no good for the beasts.'

Sian put her hand on Sean's shoulder, 'Well, my love, if you work fast, you can get it in the barn by midday. I'll make a pot of your favourite soup for lunch,' she said soothingly.

Then Sean said something that he probably shouldn't have said, 'Pfhh! It's alright for you, isn't it, my dear? Sat here in a nice warm kitchen all day. Chopping a few vegetables, feeding the chickens, washing a few smelly socks. You have an easy time while I'm outside working hard in all weathers!'

Sian couldn't believe her ears. 'Oh really, Sean!' she replied. 'I'll have you know that I make your breakfast, lunch, dinner, and supper. I keep our home warm and clean. I wash, dry, and iron our clothes. I feed all of the livestock. I milk the cow, churn the butter, collect the eggs, and sell them at the market. My "easy time", as you call it, is as hard a day's work as you've ever done! In fact, it's probably harder …' She was very annoyed by Sean's thoughtless words.

Sean burst out laughing – which made Sian even madder at him.

'Okay then, my dear, let's prove who has the hardest day's work. You go out and harvest the hay, and I'll stay in the house and do your chores. We'll see who is the most tired at the end of the day,' Sean said smugly.

Sian agreed to the work swap. She knew that he wouldn't have that smirk on his face by the end of the day. She took off her apron and threw it at Sean. Then she put on her welly boots and rainproof coat. As she marched out the door, she yelled over her shoulder, 'When the baby wakes, feed her cream and porridge. I'll be in for my lunch at noon. Don't forget to take Rosa to the meadow for her afternoon feed.'

Sian made her way across the yard and disappeared into the barn. She collected the scythe for cutting the hay and went to the field to do her husband's work.

Sean turned to look at the kitchen, 'Ahhh,' he sighed happily, 'What an easy, relaxing time I'm going to have today.'

He put the kettle on for another cup of tea. Then, Sean sat down, put his feet up, and read his paper. He would have plenty of time to feed the chickens, milk Rosa the cow, and make soup for lunch.

He must have dozed off because he woke with a start, spilling what was left of his tea down his shirt. The baby had woken up and was crying. Sean jumped up and took little Daisy-May out of her cot. Sean felt the damp nappy and tried to comfort Daisy-May, but the more he tried, the more she cried.

Now, what had Sian said about the baby? 'Ah, I'm to feed you porridge and cream, my little Sweet Pea,' he said to his child.

He bounced her on one arm, reaching into the cupboard for the porridge oats. He shook oats into the milk pan and was about to add milk when he tripped over the baby's blanket. He held on tightly to Daisy-May, but the pan flew across the room, scattering oats all over the floor.

'Oh dear,' said Sean, 'Well, how about some cream for breakfast, my little angel? That should keep you happy for a while.'

He went to the larder to find some cream for the baby, but the jug was empty.

'Okay, don't cry now, Daisy-May. I'll milk Rosa and get you some fresh cream.' Sean put the baby in her chair. He gave her a teddy bear for comfort and went to milk the cow. Rosa was in her stall, stamping her hooves and bellowing loudly.

'Oh, my, I haven't fed you yet!' said Sean. He was beginning to feel flustered. He put a scoop of chaff into the cow's bucket.

Then he sat on a stool next to Rosa's rear end, ready to milk her. Sean had seen Sian milk the cow hundreds of times, so he felt confident that he knew what to do. He grabbed a teat and squeezed downwards towards the milking pail.

Sean's hands were big and rough, and he squeezed Rosa's udder so hard that she kicked out in fright. With a clatter and bang, Sean and the bucket flew across the stable.

'Oww ...' moaned Sean, rubbing his sore chest. 'Let's try that again, Rosa, only I'll be more gentle this time,' he said, trying to reassure the startled cow.

A little squirt of milk hit the bucket, but Rosa was not a happy cow, and she kept stamping her hooves. He squeezed as carefully and gently as he could. Eventually, he managed to fill one-quarter of the bucket with milk.

This was not as much milk as Sian would get from the cow, but Sean's hands were getting tired. He hoped it would be enough milk to make some cream and butter.

'Oh, dear!' Sean said to the cow, 'Sian said to take you to graze in the meadow, but I need to make the cream, butter, soup, and feed the baby. I haven't got time to walk to the meadow with you. There must be some grass closer to home for you, Rosa? He looked about the yard and vegetable garden. 'No, best not let you eat the carrots and cabbages; Sian would be mad at me if I did that!' Sean noticed how thick and long the turf on the roof of the house was growing. It was filled with dandelions and cow parsley too.

'That's a sure sign,' shouted Sean, 'our turf roof is overgrown and full of cow parsley. Just what a hungry cow needs.

You can have a day up there, old girl. You'll get plenty of fresh herbs, and the roof will get a good trim too.'

Sean was pleased with this idea. He tied a rope to Rosa's head collar and led her to the back of the house, where the roof sloped down to the ground. It was easy for the cow to step up onto the turf. She began to munch happily on the flowery carpet of plants that grew on the roof.

Although the roof at the back of the house was close to the ground, the front was much higher. This worried Sean. If Rosa fell down from here, she might break a leg. Sean didn't want Rosa to be injured, then he would be in big trouble with his wife. So he clambered up on the roof, tied a rock to the end of the cow's rope, and dropped it down the chimney. Now Sean could see if the cow pulled the rope, as the rock would go up and down.

'Good, that's the cow safe and secure,' thought Sean happily. He climbed down to the ground and hurried back to the baby.

What a scene awaited Sean in the house. Daisy-May was screaming at the top of her lungs, and a chicken was sitting on her head. In fact, there were chickens everywhere!

Sean had left the kitchen door open, and the hungry birds had come in to look for their breakfast. They had found porridge oats scattered on the floor, the table, chairs, and a few stuck to the baby!

Sean grabbed a broom and shooed the chickens out into the yard. He threw a scoop of chicken feed across the cobbles, and the hungry hens chased after their late breakfast.

Back in the house, Daisy-May was crying louder than ever – she wanted her feed! Sean went back out to fetch the pail of milk from the barn. He ran back to the kitchen and set up the butter and cream churn.

'There, there, baby dumpling. Daddy will make you some cream.'

He fished a couple of dead flies from the top of the milk and poured the little he had into the wooden churner. Then Sean sat and turned the handle. He turned it, and he turned it, round and round it went. The sloshing of milk and thumping and thudding of the wooden churn wheel made a calming, steady rhythm. But Daisy-May kept right on crying, so Sean sang to her.

He sang: The Grand Old Duke of York, Mary Mary Quite Contrary, Baa Baa, Black Sheep, and Sing a Song of Sixpence.

Suddenly, there was a clatter and bang as the stone to which the cow's tether was attached began to disappear up the chimney. Sean leaped after it and grabbed the rope. He heard Rosa mooing frantically outside. Then he saw the cow as she swung past the window. She had slipped off of the roof and was dangling by the rope! Sean pulled on the rope with all his strength until he pulled the cow back onto the roof.

'Phew!' He said, wiping the sweat from his forehead. He sat for a moment, thinking – how could he stop the cow from falling? 'Ah, I know,' said Sean.

He untied the stone, then tied the end of the rope to his own leg. 'Now, if Rosa starts slipping off the roof, I'll know immediately.'

Sean felt very pleased with his idea and returned to churning cream and singing nursery rhymes to Daisy-May.

Thunder rumbled in the distance. 'Ah,' thought Sean, ' Soon it will rain, and Sian will be soaked, working out in the hay meadow.'

Then he remembered that he was supposed to chop the vegetables and make soup for lunch.

'But this bloomin' cream isn't ready yet!' He grumbled as he took a look inside the churner. It was still thin and milky, not thick and creamy. Sean changed his tired arm and turned the handle round and round.

When he had run out of nursery songs to sing, he sang a lullaby instead, 'Rock a bye baby on the tree top, when the wind blows the cradle will rock …'

Sean was exhausted. His head nodded forward as he drifted off to sleep …

The next thing he knew, he was waking up on the kitchen floor! He was dragged by the rope around his leg towards the fireplace. He tried grabbing a chair as he slid, but it came with him. As the rope flew up the chimney, Sean was whisked along with it, and up he went, feet first. Pulled up by one leg, Sean's body lodged firmly in the blackened chimney shaft. He was still holding on to the kitchen chair, which fell into the hearth and broke into pieces.

Daisy-May clapped her hands for joy and gurgled with laughter, 'Daddy up chi-ma-nee. Daddy funny – ha ha ha!'

All that morning, dark thunderclouds rolled closer and closer to their home. Sian worked steadily, cutting and stacking the meadow hay. She tied a cord around the last bundle. Just in time, before it rains, she thought, satisfied with her morning's work.

Sian heard the church bell chime twelve. She would check that lunch was nearly ready, then bring the hay into the barn. As Sian hurried home, she stopped dead in the yard and stared, open-mouthed, up at the roof.

The cow was hanging from a rope over the edge of the cottage. Rosa was mooing loudly and swinging backward and forwards in front of the kitchen window. Sian ran inside. Daisy-May stood up in her chair, laughing and giggling and pointing at the cow as she swung past. Then Daisy-May pointed at the chimney, where Sean's cries and groans could be heard.

'Help! I can't move. I'm stuck. Help me, I'm trapped up here!' Sean's muffled voice called from the chimney.

Sian pushed her way through the flock of hens, who were back in, eating the carrots and potatoes which had been left out for soup. She stuck her head up the chimney and saw her husband's face, covered in soot, suspended above her.

'Hello dear,' Sean said, 'I'm tied to Rosa. I'm not sure where she is, though.'

Sian went back out to the cow. She grabbed the wood axe and climbed onto the roof. With one blow, the axe cut through the rope, and the cow landed on her feet in the yard. She bellowed loudly and galloped off to the meadow. Sean fell into the cold fire grate. A cloud of thick, black soot filled the air. Coughing and spluttering, he apologised to Sian and told her what had happened.

While Sean cleaned himself up, Sian started her second day's work. She swept the floors, cleaned the table, fixed the chair, finished churning some cream, fed the baby, and made a big pot of vegetable soup. Once everyone's tummies were full, they all began to see the funny side of the eventful morning. Sian and Sean went out to gather in the hay before the rain soaked their harvest. The heavens opened just as they brought the last sheaf of hay into the dry barn. Torrential rain poured down, thunder boomed, and lightning lit up the countryside. Sean grabbed Sian around the waist and gave her the biggest hug. He winced in pain because his arm hurt from milk-churning, his chest hurt from Rosa's kick, and he had cuts and scrapes from being up the chimney. But then he told Sian how much he loved her and apologised.

'I'm sorry Sian. I was wrong about your work in the house and byre. It isn't easy at all!'

They both agreed that from that day on, they should stick to their own jobs. Unless Sean was ill with a cold or flu, then Sian would do everything around the home and farm. After all, she had proved that she was the only one who could do both of their jobs!

10

Outwitting the Trolls

Once upon a time, a hunter trapped a polar bear, leaving her little cub to fend for itself. As the tiny bear looked for food and shelter, a farmer heard the creature's frightened cries. He felt sorry for the orphaned cub and took her into his house. He fed the baby bear and looked after her like she was his child. When the bear was fully grown, he made her a collar and took her everywhere he went. But the bear needed to hunt fish and seals, so the farmer decided to take her to the sea and set her free.

The farmer and the polar bear set off on their journey with a bag of snacks. They walked all day through fields and forests. It was mid-winter, and snow lay deep on the hills and mountains.

As night set in, the farmer knew that they must find shelter or he would freeze.

Crunching through a snowy woodland, they spotted a house, lights twinkling warmly from its windows.

'Come on, bear, there is a homestead. We will ask the people there to give us a place to sleep tonight.'

The farmer knocked on the door, and a tall man answered. 'Who are you, and what do you want?' the tall man asked – he looked very worried.

The farmer explained he was taking his bear to the sea, and they needed somewhere to stay that evening. But the tall man, whose name was Henning, replied, 'No, you cannot stay here. Do you know what night this is? It's Christmas Eve!'

As he peered anxiously at the farmer and bear, his wife and children stood nervously behind the door.

'Oh, please let us come in,' begged the farmer, 'we can sleep on the floor. We won't get in your way, and we'll go as soon as it's light in the morning.'

Henning shook his head sadly, his wife bit her lip, and the children began to cry.

'Don't be frightened of my bear, little ones,' said the farmer to the scared family. 'She is the friendliest bear you will ever meet. She is as gentle as a kitten.'

He clicked his tongue and winked at the bear, who sat down on her bottom and waved both paws. 'There, see, she is very tame, just a big playful pet.'

'Oh dear,' said Anna, Henning's wife, 'we are not mean people. Normally we would be happy to give you shelter, but tonight is Christmas Eve.'

Then the whole family said, 'On Christmas Eve, Trolls Come!'

'You see,' said Henning, 'a whole tribe of trolls come here every Christmas Eve. They smash up our house and ruin our Christmas dinner. We would love to give you and your bear shelter, but we are going out to hide in the barn.'

Henning opened the door wider for the farmer and bear to see inside. The room was sparkling with Christmas decorations, and the tree hung with golden glass balls.

The kitchen table was laid with plates and food for Christmas Eve dinner.

The farmer laughed, 'Ah, but I'm not afraid of trolls, and neither is my bear. They will not bother us.'

The bear opened her mouth and let out a soft growl. Her delicate black lips curled upwards – she looked like she was smiling.

'Okay, come in then,' Henning said, shaking his head solemnly, 'but we have warned you, the trolls will come; they always do.'

The farmer and the bear lumbered into the house, thanking the family for their kindness.

Together the man and bear settled comfortably, on a rug, in the corner of the room. They watched through sleepy eyes as the family finished laying the dinner table with delicious Christmas food. As the clock chimed seven, Henning and the children put on their warm coats, hats, boots, and gloves. Then, they went into the cold night to hide in their barn.

Anna invited the farmer to join them, but he smiled and assured her that he and the bear were not frightened of trolls.

'We have warned you,' said Anna as she shut the door and hurried away from the house.

The fire burned warmly. The bear fell asleep, her head resting on two enormous white paws. The farmer threw another log into the flames and settled down to rest. Then, he heard the thudding of many feet pounding through the snow towards the house. Suddenly, the door burst open, and in crowded a pack of trolls. Some fell down the chimney into the fire. They screamed and jumped onto the table, plunging their burnt feet into the bowl of fruit punch. Steam hissed from the sweet berry juice as the trolls cooled their singed toes. Others sprang up through floorboards, shouting, 'Surprise! We're back!' And, 'Merry Christmas!' at the tops of their voices.

Dozens of trolls cascaded and cartwheeled through the house. They vaulted onto the food-laden table, one swinging from the light, others hanging from curtains. They shook the Christmas tree and played catch with the glass balls. Each troll grabbed a handful of Christmas decorations and adorned themselves: putting tinsel around their necks, stars over their ears, and angels in their spiky hair. The trolls were all shapes and sizes – some big and heavy with long noses and huge hairy feet, others tiny and acrobatic, with upturned snouts. All of them were very, very noisy. They screamed and whooped, shrieked and squealed, and sang Christmas songs – out of tune!

Jingle Bells,
Santa Smells,
Rudolph did a poop,
The girls and boys,
They got no toys,
Cause the elves,
Went loop da loop …

They all laughed, snorting and spluttering, spraying the room with disgusting troll-snotters. A knobbly kneed troll drop-kicked the turkey over the table. An even uglier troll caught the cooked bird in the bread basket. Two tiny ginger trolls grabbed the turkey drumsticks and tried to juggle with them. A greedy troll ate all the Brussels sprouts – then he was terribly sick in the gravy jug. A gangly teenage troll threw jelly at the ceiling to see if it would stick – it didn't. The littlest troll squeaked in a high-pitched voice, 'Look at the pretty pink windows. Look at me; I'm making lovely Christmas pictures,' as she smeared strawberry jam on the windows.

Then, a giant hairy troll noticed the bear sleeping in the corner of the room. The troll pointed and said in a very silly voice, 'Aww, look at the big pussy cat … pussy is sleeping. Aw, nice white pussy.'

The troll grabbed a sausage from the table and waved it under the bear's nose. The bear opened an eye and sniffed. Bears love sausages, and this bear was hungry. She licked her lips and went to eat the sausage, but the troll pulled it away just as her jaws closed.

The troll screamed with delight, 'Aww, the pussy cat wants a sausage!' He dangled the sausage in front of the bear's nose and taunted her. 'Pussy cat like a sausage? Mmm, yum yum, nice juicy sausage …'

Again the bear tried to eat the sausage, and once more, the troll whisked it away from the bear's open mouth. The troll squealed louder than ever, mocking the frustrated bear. 'Stupid pussy cat can't get a sausage. Stoopid cat! Ha ha ha ha ha ha ...'

All the trolls howled with laughter, grabbing sausages from the plate and thrusting them at the bear. They chanted together, 'Want a sausage? Want a sausage? Stupid cat! Stupid cat!'

Finally, the bear had had enough. She stood up on her hind legs, opened her mouth, and roared angrily. Her huge white head reached the ceiling, and her enormous teeth and claws made her look ferocious. The trolls dropped the sausages and screamed in terror. They scattered. Tripping over and banging into each other, trying to get out of the door. Some risked burning their feet and bottoms as they shot back up the chimney. Others dived under the floorboards. The entire pack of trolls ran away into the forest, fleeing from the angry bear.

When they were gone, the farmer stood up from his hiding place and patted the bear, 'Well done, princess, you are the best bear.' He picked up the sausages and fed them all to his big pet. He went to the barn and told the family that the trolls had gone and that it was safe to come in. It didn't take long to tidy up the mess the trolls had made. The bear happily licked jam from the windows and lapped up a pool of jelly from the floor. The family saved what was left of their Christmas Eve dinner. They grilled fresh sausages and steamed some more sprouts. Then everyone sat down with their special guests, the bear, and the farmer, for a merry festive dinner.

In the morning, it was Christmas Day. The farmer thanked the family and left with the bear to continue their journey.

Some say that they met the King of Norway and the bear went to live with the King. Henning, Anna, and the children never saw the farmer or the polar bear again.

However, the following year, on Christmas Eve, Henning was outside, chopping firewood. Suddenly he heard the sound of trolls' feet thundering through the forest.

One troll popped its head around a tree and called to him, 'Hey Henning!'

Henning looked up. 'Yes, I'm Henning; what do you want?'

The troll replied, 'Have you still got that big white cat at your house?'

Henning had to stop and think for a moment, then he replied, 'Ah, yes! Yes, I have got the big white cat. I've still got her, and she has had kittens. Six enormous kittens, all of them bigger than their mother. Would you like to come and see them?'

The trolls shrieked in terror and ran away back into the forest.

From that day on, the trolls never bothered Henning, Anna, and their family ever again.

11

The Badger Teapot

Once upon a time, in Japan, there lived a woman who loved animals. Although she was poor, she always helped injured or hungry creatures. She gave them shelter, cleaned and bandaged their wounds, and gave them food and water.

One time, during a drought, the tanuki (badgers) became so desperate for water that they travelled far from their homes to get a drink. Many died of thirst, and others were killed by wild dogs.

The kindly woman found a dying badger at the side of the road. She carried it to her tiny hut and gave it water and fruit from her cherry tree to eat. Soon, the badger recovered. But this was no ordinary badger. This creature knew the ancient art of shape-shifting. It winked at the kind woman and thanked her for saving his life.

'If you bring me a leaf from your cherry tree, I will do something magical to help you,' said the badger.

The woman fetched a cherry tree leaf. Badger put the leaf upon his head. He shivered and shook and turned himself into a bronze teapot.

The leaf flew up in the air, and the badger sucked it down into the teapot's spout.

'Now, I am a tea kettle,' the badger told the woman. 'I am made of solid bronze and must be worth much of your human money. You may take me to the curiosity shop and sell me to the shopkeeper. Then you will have enough money to live on and eat well for the rest of your life. This is how I wish to repay you for saving my life.'

The poor woman was overjoyed. She thanked the badger tea kettle and took him to the curiosity junk shop.

The shopkeeper was impressed with the beautiful teapot and paid the poor woman an excellent price. The kind woman was now rich. She went home and continued to care for sick and hungry animals for the rest of her life.

The badger tea kettle was looking forward to a new adventure in the shop. At first, he was displayed in the window. But no one could afford the shopkeeper's price for the teapot.

Then he was put on a shelf in the corner of the shop, and no one noticed him any more. As time passed, the teapot became dusty, forgotten, and lonely.

One day, a holy priest from the Temple of Morinji went shopping in the village. This priest loved to go bargain hunting. When he went into the junk shop, he searched every corner for good deals. He couldn't believe his luck when he saw the dusty, antique tea kettle under a pile of old, broken fans. The shopkeeper had forgotten that the teapot was there, so she let the priest have it for just three copper coins. The priest was pleased; he could use this teapot for his evening tea ceremony.

Back at the temple, the priest gave a novice monk the job of cleaning the old tea kettle. It was scrubbed and scoured until all the dirt was removed, and the bronze shone and gleamed. The priest was delighted with his magnificent teapot. He placed it on a wooden lacquer box in the middle of his room. Then he sat and admired the tea kettle – it was exquisite, a fine work of art. He sat and gazed at the bronze pot; its beauty hypnotised him. He stared until his head nodded forward, and he fell fast asleep.

While the holy man slept, the teapot began to shimmy and shake. It blew the cherry tree leaf out of the spout. The leaf flew up and landed on the tea kettle. Then it opened its two bright eyes; they peeped out from inside the spout. A small black, shiny nose popped out and sniffed the air. The lid jumped up as the bronze pot sprouted thick fur over its back. Four hairy paws appeared, and a bushy tail sprang out of the handle. One furry paw picked up the leaf and tucked it inside an ear.

The magic tea kettle looked around the temple room and grinned with delight.

'Ahh, so comfortable a room, like a palace,' he said. 'And a fine lacquer box for my throne!' The badger tea kettle patted the box proudly. Then he jumped down and began to hop and dance around the priest's room. The strange creature leaped and skipped on his black leathery paws. Then he began to sing for joy.

'I am so happy to be out of that shabby junk shop!' he warbled at the top of his voice, 'and even more pleased to be in this beautiful temple.'

As the badger teapot tap-danced and sang in the priest's room, the boys studying in the next room looked up from their books. 'Our teacher is happy tonight,' they whispered together.

The teapot was thumping and clanking about so noisily that the boys began to giggle.

'Whatever can our master be up to?' they asked each other.

However, the banging and crashing sounds grew louder, and the singing more lively. When the boys heard furniture being knocked over, they slid the screen door open and peeked in to see what was happening.

'Aaghh! There is a goblin in here! Our master's new tea kettle has changed into a demon badger!' screamed one boy.

The others stood back in shock and watched.

'To think I cleaned that old pot just a few hours ago. I thought it was an ordinary bronze teapot,' said another young student.

'It's bewitched! Heaven protect us from this devil!' said a boy.

'I want a better look at the hairy hobgoblin,' the first student said. He boldly ran in to try and grab the dancing teapot.

The badger tea kettle leaped out of his reach and ran around the room. It laughed and kicked up its furry heels in the boy's faces. All of the boys chased after the teapot. They yelled and screamed, slipped on the floor mat, and banged into furniture and each other.

The priest awoke from his nap and looked at the boys running wildly about his room.

'What in Buddha's name are you doing in here? Have you lost your minds?' he yelled at his students.

'Your bronze pot, oh holy teacher, it's a demon! It contains a bewitched badger. We are trying to capture the wicked beast!' gasped the students, who were red-faced and panting for breath.

They all turned to look at the teapot, which was back upon the box. Sitting still and silent – no badger in sight! It was just a bronze tea kettle again.

'What nonsense, you silly boys! See, my tea kettle is a fine antique teapot. There is no badger in this room. All of you go back to your studies, waking me rudely from my meditations! You must go and pray to be saved from the dangers of delusion.'

The novices bowed their heads and returned to their books.

That evening the priest filled his new kettle with water from the spring and set it upon his fire to boil. Now, he could make the best tea in his magnificent pot. He would enjoy his special tea ceremony more than ever.

But as soon as the water became hot, the teapot opened its eyes, pushed out his paws, and screamed. 'Ow, Ow, Oww!

I'm on fire. Help me! Someone save me from this roasting!' The badger jumped out of the hot embers. He sprang about the priest's room, blowing cool air on his paws and burnt tail.

The priest shouted in terror, 'A monster is inside my tea kettle! Help! Save me from this shape-shifting devil!'

The holy man grabbed a broom, swiping at the badger as he chased it around the room. The novices heard the hullabaloo and came running to rescue their teacher.

'You were right, boys; the teapot is a badger. It talks and jumps about the room ...' The priest stood, waving the broom in the air.

'Your holiness, pardon us, dear teacher, but your teapot is sitting quietly – there is no badger.'

The boys pointed at the bronze tea kettle, sitting silently and still upon its box!

'We will all go and pray to be saved from the dangers of delusion!' the novices sniggered.

The next day, the priest sold the tea kettle to a passing tinker. The tinker was happy to buy the bronze teapot for ten copper coins. He took it home and admired its quality, turning it this way and that, stroking the round, bronze sides.

'I will be able to sell you for more money than I paid; I'll make an excellent profit,' said the happy tinker. He fell asleep with the teapot next to his bed. At midnight, he woke up. The moon was full and shining brightly onto the tea kettle. The tinker gazed at it in the light of the moon. Then the teapot began to shimmy and shake. A leaf flew out of the spout and landed on the teapot's lid. It opened its two bright eyes, and a black, shiny nose popped out of the spout. The lid jumped up, thick fur sprouted from its back, hairy paws and a bushy tail appeared. The magic tea kettle looked at the tinker, swished its tail, and winked at him.

'Hello,' said the tinker.

'Please don't sell me again,' said the teapot, 'I'm not wicked, and I'm not a demon.'

'Okay, that's good,' replied the tinker.

'I'm a badger tea kettle, and if I am treated well, I will bring you happiness and good fortune,' said the teapot.

'Oh, I like the sound of that,' replied the tinker.

'At the temple, they called me nasty names! They chased me, beat me, and then put me on the fire. It was horrible!' said the badger.

'I'm sorry to hear that. I promise to treat you well. You seem like a charming badger teapot to me,' replied the tinker.

'I think I would like to stay with you,' said the badger with a big smile.

'Shall I get you a lacquer box?' asked the tinker.

'Oh no, nothing fancy, thank you. Let me hang out with you, and we can keep each other company.'

'I should like that very much,' replied the tinker.

'I like to eat sweet things,' said the badger, 'and the occasional cup of green tea.'

'Okay,' said the tinker, 'I like them too; I will share all my meals with you.'

'The night is turning very chilly, dear tinker. May I sleep next to you?'

The tinker lifted his bed cover and the badger teapot snuggled next to him. From then on, the tinker and the badger tea kettle became best friends. The tinker was a gentle and friendly man, and the badger was clever and funny. They had great fun together and enjoyed each other's company.

One day, the badger asked, 'Would you like to be rich?'

'Ah, badger, I have very little money; being rich would be a dream come true,' replied the tinker.

'I know a way to make you a wealthy man. My name is Bumbuku Chagama. I am the only badger tea kettle in the world. I can sing, dance, and make people happy. You and I could put on a theatre show together. I will perform, and you can take the audience's money. What do you think? Shall we make people laugh and earn some money?'

'But my friend, Bumbuku, would that not be hard work for you?' said the tinker.

'No, I love to sing and dance. Come on, let's do it!' The badger clapped his paws and turned a cartwheel.

分福茶釜

茶釜むじな才能世界一

The tinker hired a big room and bought some fancy theatre curtains. He made a poster for 'Bumbuku Chagama – The World's Most Talented Badger Teapot'. Tickets for the first show sold out quickly. Bumbuku sang, told hilarious jokes, and performed incredible magic tricks. He also cartwheeled and back-flipped on a tightrope. People flocked in their thousands to see him. The princess of the land invited Bumbuku to the royal palace. Bumbuku was a smash hit – the royal family laughed and clapped at his jokes and tricks. Everyone loved him!

After many years of performing, Bumbuku and the tinker became wealthy. They had enough money to stop working and enjoy the rest of their lives in comfort. Bumbuku decided he would like to become the bronze tea kettle once again and have a good, long rest. He asked the tinker if he would take him back to the temple at Morinji.

'Tell the monks that I am a magical badger tea kettle. And if they are kind to me, I will bring them happiness and good fortune.'

The tinker felt sad that his friend was leaving, but he knew he could visit Bumbuku at the temple whenever he wanted.

Bumbuku asked the tinker to bring him a cherry tree leaf. The tinker found a leaf and placed it upon Bumbuku's back. The badger's eyes shone brightly, his thick fur bristled, his hairy paws trembled, and his bushy tail waved goodbye. He reached out to the tinker and stroked the man's hand. 'Goodbye, dear friend, and thank you for all the fun and laughter we shared. A best friend like you is the most precious gift a creature can have.'

Then, the badger tea kettle stopped talking and turned back into an antique bronze teapot.

The tinker gifted the precious teapot to the temple. They were delighted; the monks made a shrine to display the tea kettle. People came from everywhere to pray for happiness in front of the bronze teapot.

Bumbuku, the badger tea kettle, is still there, bringing people good fortune, laughter and much happiness.

Sources and Notes

1. Monkey See, Monkey Do

This story makes everyone laugh, no matter what age they are. Contemporary Indian storytellers say it comes from India, while other people think it comes from Africa. But stories like to travel all over the world, so this version of the tale takes place in Ecuador, South America, in a town I once visited called Montecristi, where everyone made hats!

You can find other versions of this story in: Esphyr Slobodinka, *Caps for Sale* (William R. Scott, US, 1940).

I.F. Bulatkin, *Eurasian Folk and Fairy Tales* (Criterion Books, New York, 1965).

It's called an Egyptian tale – 'Fez ,Tarboosh' – in Frances Carpenter's *African Wonder Tales* (Doubleday 1963).

Chris Smith, 'Monkeys and Hats', *World Tales for Family Storytelling. 53 Traditional Stories for Children* (Hawthorn Press, Stroud, 1988).

Or listen to it online: Peter Chand tells *The Cap Seller and the Monkeys* on www.storymuseum.org. uk/1001-stories/the-cap-seller-and-the-monkey

2. Why Dogs Live with People

I first heard the famous storyteller Taffy Thomas MBE telling this story in a cosy yurt tent at a festival in Cumbria, England. Taffy told me that he found it in a book of Russian stories.

Margaret Read MacDonald's *Storyteller's Source Book, 1983–1999* lists several different places that the tale has been told: A Congo tale by Diana Pitcher in *Tokoloshi: African Folktales Retold*: Dog smells food from woman's fire and joins humans; Julius Lester (African American) *Last Tales of Uncle Remus*: Dog comes to Miz Woman for fire and food. Becomes tame. Warns Mr Man of Brer Wolf.

Margaret also cites the folklore classification system by Stith Thompson for Lithuanian and Indian variants of this tale: A2513.1 Origin of dog's service. Dog must obey man for meagre recompense.

A2513.1.1 Dog looks for most powerful master. Stays for good in man's service, since man fears no one. Lithuanian source.

A2513.1.1.1 Caribbean: Sherlock, West, Lapland, Carpenter, *Wonder Tales of Dogs*.

Taffy's version of the story is called 'Why Dog Lives with Man', and is printed by Education Publishing Services, Darwin.

3. Sausages for Supper

This story is from Germany, England, France, Sweden, Hungary, Puerto Rico, Korea – in fact, it's a tale from all over the world! A great story scholar, Joseph Jacobs, thought that it was originally a story from India.

It's been popular with children and grown-ups for a very long time – probably because almost everyone loves sausages, vegetarian or not. ☺

You will find another version called 'The Three Wishes' in Heather Forest's book *Wisdom Tales from Around the World* (August House Publishers Inc., Little Rock, 1996).

And another version also called 'The Three Wishes', by Martha Hamilton and Mitch Weiss, in *More Ready-to-Tell-Tales*, edited by David Holt & Bill Mooney (August House Publishers Inc., 2000).

4. The Talkative Turtle

This story comes from India, from the Jataka Tales. It is sometimes told about a tortoise, but they live on land and not in water like the turtle.

Turtles do not make good pets – they need lots of very special care and it's impossible to recreate their natural homes. They are never happy in captivity.

The turtle Lucinda and I based our turtle on for *Funny Folk Tales*, is called the Spotted Pond Turtle (Geodemys hamiltonii). Sadly, they are one of India's many endangered species. Turtle Survival Alliance (TSA-India) have collaborated with Uttar Pradesh Forest and Wildlife Department to set up conservation breeding programmes for endangered turtles at Kukrail Centre, Lucknow. TSA-India are on Twitter, Facebook, Instagram, YouTube & Linked-In. If you love turtles, then you can find out how to help them through wildlife charities that protect their natural habitats.

There are hundreds of different versions of this story. You will find one in Heather Forest's book *Wisdom Tales From Around The World* (August House Publishers, Inc., Little Rock, 1996). Also, 'Bye-Bye' in *The Magic Orange Tree and Other Haitian Folktales*, by Diane Wolkstein (Schoken Books New York, 1978). Margaret Read MacDonald's source books include: J2357 Tortoise speaks and loses his hold on stick. Versions in: Margaret Green - *Big Book of Animal Fables*; Edward Korel - *Listen and I'll Tell You*; Davis - *Lion's Whiskers*; Isabelle Chang - *Tales from Old China*; Isabelle Chang - *Chinese Fairy Tales*;

Adele Lin - *The Milky Way*; Ruth Tooze - *The Wonderful Wooden Peacock Flying Machine*; Bonnie Carey - *Baba Yaga's Geese*; Genevieve Barlow - *Latin American Tales*; Thornhill - *Crow and Fox*; Patricia Plante - *The Turtle and the Two Ducks* (Animal Fables from La Fontaine).

5. Hyena and the Talking Tree

I first heard this story many years ago from my friend, author and storyteller, Lari Don, who had heard it from another storyteller. I've never found it in a book. I think it comes from an African country, but which one?

My friend Margaret Read MacDonald looked in her story source book and told me that there are lots of similar stories. Margaret wrote, 'My *Storyteller's Sourcebook 1983–1999* cites *Anasi and the Moss Covered Rock* (Erik Kimmel), which is a very well-known picture book in the US. Anansi makes a remark about the rock and is knocked unconscious. He tricks others into doing the same until deer feigns ignorance and causes Anansi to say the words. A version from Jamaica (Richard Young, *African-American Folktales for Young Readers*) has Anansi putting his hand into a hole and being flung a mile. Amabel Wiliams-Ellis, in *Tales from the Enchanted World*, has a witch who makes anyone saying 'five' fall dead. My *Storyteller's Sourcebook 1982* cites two versions from the West Indies (throw-a-mile version); one from North Africa (*Manning-Sanders*

Book of Sorcerers and Spells, probably Kimmel's source); and the same "five" version from Jamaica (in Williams-Ellis, *Round the World Fairy Tales*).

'Though I don't have the hyena version in either index, this is clearly the same motif. There is a strong tradition of hyena tales, so I think you can claim the tale is African with confidence, though which culture area I cannot say.'

6. The Zombie Cow

This story is from the great Scottish storyteller George MacPherson. When George was a boy, he heard many people tell this story while visiting his family on the Ardnamurchan Peninsula, in north-west Scotland. He told me that he put the best bits from all the different versions together (especially his grand uncle John Cameron's version) and came up with this cracking tale.

When one storyteller passes a story on to the next teller, they always make the tale a little different from the one they heard – they put their own imagination into the story. That is what I've done with this story. If you want to read George's story, which is called 'Tormad Crupach' (that's Gaelic for 'Crippled Norman') you can find it in *Tales on the Tongue. Storytelling Voices in Scotland,* edited by Bea Ferguson (Scottish Storytelling Centre, 2006).

This is the only printed version of George's story. I'm very grateful to George for letting me retell his tale. The cow's name, Eilidh, is a Scottish Gaelic name, pronounced 'aylee' in English.

7. Monkey Misery

This story comes from the island of Haiti, in the Caribbean. In 2010 a massive earthquake devastated the capital city, Port-au-Prince, killing hundreds of thousands of people and animals. They are still rebuilding and trying to recover from this catastrophe, even to this day!

There are many beehives and honey enterprises across the island.

You will also find this story in Diane Wolkstein, *The Magic Orange Tree and Other Haitian Folktales* (Schocken Books, New York, 1978).

And a version called 'Monkey and Papa God', in a fab picture book by Hugh Lupton, *Tales of Wisdom and of Wonder* (Barefoot Books, Bath, 2006).

8. How to Flummox a Fairy

This is a very popular Scottish folk tale – fairies that kidnap folk and delicious cakes, what's not to like?

The woman who first collected this tale, Sorche NicLeodhas, said that it came from a *seanachie* (a Gaelic traditional storyteller) in Durris, Aberdeenshire, Scotland. And her grandfather told it to her.

Sorche Nic Leodhas, *Thistle & Thyme, Tales & Legends from Scotland* (The Bodley Head Ltd, London, 1960/1962).

Since Sorche shared the story in 1960, many other people have told it and rewritten it, including: Ellin Greene, *Clever Cooks, a Concoction of Stories, Charms, Recipes and Riddles* (Lothrop, Lee & Shepard Company, New York, 1973) and Heather Forest, *The Woman Who Flummoxed The Fairies* (August House, 2013).

Also Taffy Thomas MBE has a lovely version in his book *A Feast of Folk Tales, The Storyteller's Supper* (The History Press, Cheltenham, Gloucestershire, 2021).

9. The Cow on the Roof

People say that this story originally comes from Ireland, or Wales, or Norway. So I called the woman in my version Sian (a Welsh name, pronounced, 'Sharn') and her husband, Sean (an Irish name) and the cow is called Rosa (a popular name for a pet cow in Norway!) You can read other versions by Eric Maddern, *The Cow on the Roof* (Frances Lincoln Children's Books, 2006).

Also, 'The Cow on the Roof' by Kevin Crossley-Holland (ed.) in *Folk Tales of the British Isles* (Pantheon Books, New York, 1985).

A Norwegian version of the story is called 'The Husband Who was to Mind the House' in Peter

Christian Asbjornsen and Jorgen Moe, *Norwegian Folktales* (Dreyers Forlag, Oslo, 1960).

You can listen to Daniel Morden tell this tale on the Story Museum website: www.storymuseum.org.uk/1001-stories/the-cow-on-the-roof

10. Outwitting the Trolls

This story comes from Norway, Scandinavia, where everyone believes in trolls – supernatural creatures that live deep in the forests.

If you ever visit Norway, on misty mornings and moonlit nights, you will see how the birch and pine trees look like giant woodland creatures – trolls! It's a magical land, full of folklore and stories.

You will find a version of this tale, called 'A Very Big Cat', by Nora Clarke, in Ian Whybrow (ed.), *The Kingfisher Book of Classic Christmas Stories* (Kingfisher, London, 2006).

And from Norway, 'The Cat on the Dovrefjell', by Peter Christian Asbjornsen and Jorgen Moe, *Norwegian Folktales* (Dreyers Forlag, Oslo, 1960).

11. The Badger Teapot

While storytelling for the Scottish Badger Trust in 2022, I discovered this delightful story from Japan. In Japan, a badger, or raccoon-dog, is called Tanuki. There are many different Japanese Tanuki stories where the badger is either a cheeky rascal, a trickster or a shape-shifter. Lucinda drew the Bumbuku Chagama show poster in Japanese, after consulting with her friend who speaks Japanese.

Other versions of this story can be found online: https://www.curiousordinary.com/2021/09/bunbuku-chagama.html; 'The Wonderful Tea Kettle', by Mrs T.H. James, Japanese fairy tale series No. 16 (archive.org) (19/08/2022).

The Magic Tea Kettle; A Japanese Legend, T. Ching, https://www.tching.com (19 August 2022).

Jo Byrne, *The Badger Book* (Graffeg: www.graffeg.com, 2021).

Society *for*
Storytelling

Since 1993, The Society for Storytelling has championed the ancient art of oral storytelling and its long and honourable history – not just as entertainment, but also in education, health, and inspiring and changing lives. Storytellers, enthusiasts and academics support and are supported by this registered charity to ensure the art is nurtured and developed throughout the UK.

Many activities of the Society are available to all, such as locating storytellers on the Society website, taking part in our annual National Storytelling Week at the start of every February, purchasing our quarterly magazine Storylines, or attending our Annual Gathering – a chance to revel in engaging performances, inspiring workshops, and the company of like-minded people.

You can also become a member of the Society to support the work we do. In return, you receive free access to Storylines, discounted tickets to the Annual Gathering and other storytelling events, the opportunity to join our mentorship scheme for new storytellers, and more. Among our great deals for members is a 30% discount off titles from The History Press.

For more information, including how to join, please visit

www.sfs.org.uk

UNIVERSITY OPTICS

90 0750777 7

Charles Seale-Hayne Library
University of Plymouth
(01752) 588 588
LibraryandITenquiries@plymouth.ac.uk

UNIVERSITY OPTICS

Volume 2

D. W. TENQUIST, M.SC.

R. M. WHITTLE, B.SC., PH.D.

J. YARWOOD, M.SC., F.INST.P.

LONDON   ILIFFE BOOKS

THE BUTTERWORTH GROUP

Butterworth & Co (Publishers) Ltd
London: 88 Kingsway WC2B 6AB

AUSTRALIA

Butterworth & Co (Australia) Ltd
Sydney: 20 Loftus Street
Melbourne: 343 Little Collins Street
Brisbane: 240 Queen Street

CANADA

Butterworth & Co (Canada) Ltd
Toronto: 14 Curity Avenue, 374

NEW ZEALAND

Butterworth & Co (New Zealand) Ltd
Wellington: 49/51 Ballance Street
Auckland: 35 High Street

SOUTH AFRICA

Butterworth & Co (South Africa) Ltd
Durban: 33/35 Beach Grove

First published in 1970 by
Iliffe Books an imprint of
the Butterworth Group

© D. W. Tenquist, R. M. Whittle and J. Yarwood, 1970

ISBN 0 592 05055 6

Printed in Hungary

PLYMOUTH POLYTECHNIC
LEARNING RESOURCES CENTRE

ACCN. NO.   95610

CLASS NO.   535 TEN

Contents

Contents

Preface

In conjunction with its companion, Volume 1, this text is intended to cover the requirements in the subject of optics for the student preparing for Part 1 of an Honours Degree in Physics, a General Degree in Science, or Ancillary Physics to an Honours Degree in Chemistry or other main discipline. It is also suitable for students reading for the Higher National Certificate or Diploma in Physics, or the Graduateship Examination of The Institute of Physics and The Physical Society.

In general, this second volume is intended for the second year of a two-year course in optics at undergraduate level. It is assumed that the reader is familiar with introductory vector calculus, although much of the text can be understood without such knowledge.

The text departs to some extent from the conventional treatment of optics in undergraduate books in that a considerable emphasis is placed on quantum theory in order to provide a theoretical background to the subsequent study of spectra and the optical maser.

Grateful thanks are due for their assistance in the preparation of this book to Dr Peter Morse of the Physics staff at The Polytechnic, Regent Street, to those University authorities who have kindly permitted the inclusion of exercises from their examination papers, and to Mrs Elizabeth Bangham who typed most of the text.

LONDON   D.W.T.

1970   R.M.W.

                                                J. Y.

7

CHAPTER 1

Electromagnetic Theory of Radiation

1.1 The Electromagnetic Field and Radiation

The complete electromagnetic spectrum from wavelengths in free space of 10^{-11} cm or less up to those of several metres comprises γ-radiation, X-radiation, ultra-violet radiation, visible light, infrared radiation and radio waves. All these radiations essentially originate from the movement of electric charge. For example, the emission of visible light results from the change of energy of an atom or molecule when electrons in the atoms or molecules of a substance undergo a transition from a higher to a lower energy state consequent upon the substance being excited, as in a discharge, or molecules being set in vibration when the substance is heated. Again, radio waves are produced by the repeated accelerations and decelerations of electrons in a conductor (for example, the transmitter aerial) when a varying current is passed through the conductor, whilst X-rays result from the rapid deceleration of electrons in motion when they impinge on a solid.

An electric field accompanies electric charge: a free electron in space is the seat of electrostatic field lines; charged conductors contain in the region between and around them an electrostatic field. If the electric charge is in motion relative to the observer or his measuring instruments, the electrostatic field in motion results in the detection of a magnetic field by the observer. For example, electrons travelling in a wire constitute an electric current which is inevitably attended by a magnetic field in the surrounding medium.

Thus, electric charge, electrostatic field and magnetic field, as

1

phenomena, are interdependent: the presence of one implies that of the other two. Electrostatic and magnetic fields are inevitably both present: whether or not the electrostatic or magnetic field effect predominates, as it clearly does in many observations, is a question of the magnitude of the relative speed and acceleration between the electric charge and the observer.

The theory of this interdependence, leading to the electromagnetic theory of radiation, was first given in about 1865 by Clerk Maxwell and forms one of the outstandingly original contributions in theoretical physics.

1.2 The Electromagnetic Field: Maxwell's Equations

The two concepts with which Maxwell was chiefly concerned and which were well established before his electromagnetic theory were both associated with magnetic fields in the vicinity of conductors. The first of these is Ampère's circuital law; the second is Neumann's equation which followed Faraday's laws of electromagnetic induction (about 1831). Using consistent rationalised units, Ampère's circuital law may be expressed mathematically as

$$\oint H \cos \theta \, dl = i \qquad (1.1)$$

or, in vector notation,

$$\oint \boldsymbol{H} . d\boldsymbol{l} = i \qquad (1.2)$$

where $\boldsymbol{H}$ is the magnetic field vector of magnitude H, the field strength, at a point on a closed path around the current i of magnitude i, at which point there exists an element of path of length dl, vector $d\boldsymbol{l}$, at an angle θ to the direction of $\boldsymbol{H}$ (Fig. 1.1).

Maxwell's generalisation of this result was that the concept still applied *even if no actual conduction current i existed*, and that a time variation of an electrostatic field $\boldsymbol{E}$ in free space or a dielectric was also attended by a magnetic field. He introduced the concept of *displacement current* and showed that, if consistent rationalised units are employed,

$$\boldsymbol{j}_D = \frac{\partial \boldsymbol{D}}{\partial t} \qquad (1.3)$$

where the vector $\boldsymbol{j}_D$ of magnitude j_D is the displacement current density at a time t due to the time variation of the electric displacement $\boldsymbol{D}$ of magnitude D; as is well known,

$$\boldsymbol{D} = \varepsilon \boldsymbol{E} \qquad (1.4)$$

E being the electric field strength, and ε the permittivity of the medium.

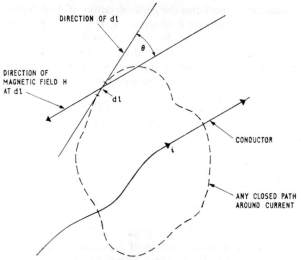

DIRECTION OF dt

θ

DIRECTION OF
MAGNETIC FIELD H
AT dt

dt

CONDUCTOR

i

ANY CLOSED PATH
AROUND CURRENT

Fig. 1.1. Ampere's circuital law

In his generalisation of Neumann's equation

$$e = -\frac{\partial \Phi}{\partial t} \qquad (1.5)$$

where e is the e.m.f. around a circuit through which the magnetic flux is Φ at time t, Maxwell again argued that an e.m.f. would be set up even if no actual conductor were present; this is tantamount to the concept that a time variation of magnetic flux in free space or a dielectric is accompanied by an electrostatic field, the e.m.f. over any element of path in this field being the electrostatic field strength multiplied by the path length.

The consequences of these two generalisations, when expressed in the form of the appropriate differential equations, led to the famous Maxwell equations for the electromagnetic field.* Relative to a right-handed set of Cartesian axes, these equations are:

$$\frac{\partial H_z}{\partial y} - \frac{\partial H_y}{\partial z} = j_x + \frac{\partial D_x}{\partial t} \qquad (1.6a)$$

$$\frac{\partial H_x}{\partial z} - \frac{\partial H_z}{\partial x} = j_y + \frac{\partial D_y}{\partial t} \qquad (1.6b)$$

$$\frac{\partial H_y}{\partial x} - \frac{\partial H_x}{\partial y} = j_z + \frac{\partial D_z}{\partial t} \qquad (1.6c)$$

* For proofs of these equations see, for example, J. H. FEWKES and J. YARWOOD, *Electricity and Magnetism*, University Tutorial Press, Cambridge, Vol. 1, 1965.

There equations arise from the generalisation of Ampère's circuital law, where H is magnetic field strength, D is electric displacement and j is conduction current density; the suffices x, y and z denote components along the x, y and z directions respectively, and it is assumed that both conduction currents and displacement currents exist at the point (x,y,z) in the region concerned. The equations

$$\frac{\partial E_z}{\partial y} - \frac{\partial E_y}{\partial z} = -\frac{\partial B_x}{\partial t} \tag{1.7a}$$

$$\frac{\partial E_x}{\partial z} - \frac{\partial E_z}{\partial x} = -\frac{\partial B_y}{\partial t} \tag{1.7b}$$

$$\frac{\partial E_y}{\partial x} - \frac{\partial E_x}{\partial y} = -\frac{\partial B_z}{\partial t} \tag{1.7c}$$

where E denotes electric field strength and B magnetic flux density, also arise from the generalisation of Neumann's equation.

In vector calculus form, these Equations 1.6 and 1.7 become, respectively,

$$\text{curl } \boldsymbol{H} = \boldsymbol{j} + \frac{\partial \boldsymbol{D}}{\partial t} \tag{1.8}$$

and

$$\text{curl } \boldsymbol{E} = -\frac{\partial \boldsymbol{B}}{\partial t} \tag{1.9}$$

These, of course, apply in any system of coordinates.

To these equations must be added the conditions arising from Poisson's analytical form of Gauss's theorem in electrostatics and in magnetism, which may be expressed as

$$\frac{\partial D_x}{\partial x} + \frac{\partial D_y}{\partial y} + \frac{\partial D_z}{\partial z} = \varrho$$

or, in vector form,

$$\text{div } \boldsymbol{D} = \varrho \tag{1.10}$$

where ϱ is the charge per unit volume present in the region; also

$$\frac{\partial B_x}{\partial x} + \frac{\partial B_y}{\partial y} + \frac{\partial B_z}{\partial z} = 0$$

or

$$\text{div } \boldsymbol{B} = 0 \tag{1.11}$$

In the majority of cases of interest in optics, the medium is not electrically conducting, so conduction current does not exist; the medium is also isotropic and uniform, so the electric displacement D is always in the same direction at any point as the electric field strength vector E, and the magnetic flux density vector B is always in the same direction as the magnetic field strength vector H. Furthermore, the permittivity ε and the magnetic permeability μ are constant. Maxwell's equations (Equations 1.8 and 1.9) then become, respectively,

$$\text{curl } H = \varepsilon \frac{\partial E}{\partial t} \qquad (1.12)$$

and

$$\text{curl } E = -\mu \frac{\partial H}{\partial t} \qquad (1.13)$$

1.3 Electromagnetic Waves in a Uniform Isotropic Dieletric

Taking the curl of curl E in Equation 1.13 gives

$$\text{curl curl } E = -\mu \text{ curl } \frac{\partial H}{\partial t} = -\mu \frac{\partial}{\partial t} (\text{curl } H) \qquad (1.14)$$

A standard result from vector calculus for any vector such as E is

$$\text{curl curl } E = \text{grad div } E - \bigtriangledown^2 E \qquad (1.15)$$

Equation 1.10 shows that div $D = \text{div } (\varepsilon E) = 0$ if no space charge is present, so div $E = 0$ and

$$\text{curl curl } E = -\bigtriangledown^2 E$$

Equation 1.14 therefore becomes

$$\bigtriangledown^2 E = \mu \frac{\partial}{\partial t} (\text{curl } H) \qquad (1.16)$$

Differentiation with respect to time of Equation 1.12 gives

$$\frac{\partial}{\partial t} (\text{curl } H) = \varepsilon \frac{\partial^2 E}{\partial t^2}$$

Substituting this result in Equation 1.16, it follows that

$$\bigtriangledown^2 E = \mu \varepsilon \frac{\partial^2 E}{\partial t^2} \qquad (1.17)$$

where, in Cartesian coordinates,

$$\nabla^2 E = \frac{\partial^2 E}{\partial x^2} + \frac{\partial^2 E}{\partial y^2} + \frac{\partial^2 E}{\partial z^2}$$

On precisely similar lines, it is established that

$$\nabla^2 H = \mu\varepsilon \frac{\partial^2 H}{\partial t^2} \tag{1.18}$$

Equations 1.17 and 1.18 are the general differential equations of wave motion in three dimensions. They show that the variations of the electric vector E and of the magnetic vector H are propagated with a wave velocity of v, where

$$\nabla^2 E = \frac{1}{v^2} \frac{\partial^2 E}{\partial t^2} \tag{1.19}$$

and likewise for $\nabla^2 H$; the speed of propagation is given by

$$v = \frac{1}{\sqrt{(\mu\varepsilon)}} \tag{1.20}$$

Where the medium is free space, $\mu = \mu_0$ and $\varepsilon = \varepsilon_0$. Using rationalised m.k.s. units,

$$\mu_0 = 4\pi \times 10^{-7} \text{ H m}^{-1}$$

and

$$\varepsilon_0 = \frac{1}{4\pi} \times 1 \cdot 11 \times 10^{-10} \text{ F m}^{-1}$$

The speed of light in free space is therefore predicted by electromagnetic theory to be

$$c = \frac{1}{\sqrt{(1 \cdot 11 \times 10^{-17})}} \text{ m s}^{-1}$$

$$= \frac{10^9}{\sqrt{11 \cdot 1}} \text{ m s}^{-1}$$

$$= 3 \times 10^8 \text{ m s}^{-1}$$

This value agrees with experimental observation (see Chapter 5 of Volume 1), and thus represents triumphant verification of the electromagnetic theory of radiation.

Note that this calculation is correct dimensionally. Thus, the dimensions of inductance (unit, the henry) in the m.k.s. system of units are $[I^{-2}ML^2T^{-2}]$ and of capacitance (unit, the farad) are $[I^2M^{-1}L^{-2}T^4]$. Consequently, the dimensions of inductance times capacitance are $[T^2]$. So $1/\sqrt{(\mu_0\varepsilon_0)}$ is in the units metre per second.

For almost all the transparent dielectrics encountered as optical media for use in the visible spectrum, the magnetic permeability is very nearly equal to μ_0, that for free space. It follows from Equation 1.20, therefore, that the speed of light v in a medium of permittivity ε should be related to the speed c in free space by

$$\frac{v}{c} = \sqrt{\frac{\varepsilon_0}{\varepsilon}} = \frac{1}{\sqrt{\varepsilon_r}} \tag{1.21}$$

where ε_r is the relative permittivity of the medium, i.e. $\varepsilon = \varepsilon_r\varepsilon_0$.

1.4 Plane Electromagnetic Waves

Referring to a right-handed set of Cartesian axes (Fig. 1.2) suppose the wavefront at any instant of time is in a plane parallel to the plane yOz. The electric vector E and the magnetic vector H will have components in such a wavefront which do not vary with y and z because they are constant at the given instant of time. Therefore $\partial E_y/\partial y$, $\partial E_z/\partial z$, $\partial H_y/\partial y$ and $\partial H_z/\partial z$ are all zero. It follows from Equations 1.10 and 1.11, when no space charge is present, that

$$\frac{\partial D_x}{\partial x} = \frac{\partial E_x}{\partial x} = 0 \tag{1.22}$$

and

$$\frac{\partial B_x}{\partial x} = \frac{\partial H_x}{\partial x} = 0 \tag{1.23}$$

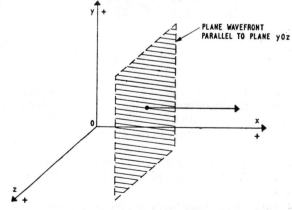

Fig. 1.2. Plane wavefront referred to right-handed Cartesian axes

Thus, E_x and H_x do not vary with x, so there are no spatial varia-tions of the components of these fields in the direction of x.

From Equation 1.6a, when no conduction current is present, $j_x = 0$ and it follows that

$$\frac{\partial D_x}{\partial t} = \varepsilon \frac{\partial E_x}{\partial t} = 0$$

and, from Equation 1.7a, it follows that

$$\frac{\partial B_x}{\partial t} = \mu \frac{\partial H_x}{\partial t} = 0$$

Consequently, time variations of the x-components of $\boldsymbol{E}$ and $\boldsymbol{H}$ are also zero. Admittedly, constant electric and magnetic fields may exist with components in the x-direction but only field variations are of any significance in wave propagation.

The wave equation for the electric field (Equation 1.17) is

$$\triangledown^2 \boldsymbol{E} = \frac{\partial^2 \boldsymbol{E}}{\partial x^2} + \frac{\partial^2 \boldsymbol{E}}{\partial y^2} + \frac{\partial^2 \boldsymbol{E}}{\partial z^2} = \mu\varepsilon \frac{\partial^2 \boldsymbol{E}}{\partial t^2}$$

Since E_y and E_z do not vary with y and z respectively, and E_x does not vary with x, y or z, this expression for $\triangledown^2 \boldsymbol{E}$ reduces to

$$\frac{\partial^2 E_y}{\partial x^2} + \frac{\partial^2 E_z}{\partial x^2} = \mu\varepsilon \frac{\partial^2 \boldsymbol{E}}{\partial t^2}$$

As $\partial E_x / \partial t = 0$, it follows that

$$\frac{\partial^2 E_y}{\partial x^2} = \mu\varepsilon \frac{\partial^2 E_y}{\partial t^2} \qquad (1.24)$$

and

$$\frac{\partial^2 E_z}{\partial x^2} = \mu\varepsilon \frac{\partial^2 E_z}{\partial t^2} \qquad (1.25)$$

From Equations 1.24 and 1.25 it is clear that the wave motion is propagated along the direction of the x-axis. Combined with the fact already established that no time variation of E_x occurs, it follows that the electric vector in the wavefront is perpendicular to the direction of propagation. The same analysis applies to the mag-netic vector. Thus, the wave motion is transverse, with the electric and magnetic vectors both in a plane perpendicular to the direction of propagation.

If the wave be propagated in the positive direction of x with a wave velocity $v = 1/\sqrt{(\mu\varepsilon)}$, the y and z components of the electric and magnetic fields respectively may be expressed by the following equations:

$$E_y = f_1(x - vt) \tag{1.26}$$

$$E_z = f_2(x - vt) \tag{1.27}$$

$$H_y = g_1(x - vt) \tag{1.28}$$

$$H_z = g_2(x - vt) \tag{1.29}$$

where f_1, f_2, g_1 and g_2 are periodic functions. Now from Equation 1.6b,

$$\frac{\partial H_z}{\partial x} = -\varepsilon \frac{\partial E_y}{\partial t}$$

Substituting for H_z from Equation 1.29 and for E_y from Equation 1.26 gives

$$\frac{\partial}{\partial x}[g_2(x - vt)] = -\varepsilon \frac{\partial}{\partial t}[f_1(x - vt)]$$

$$= \varepsilon v f_1'(x - vt)$$

where f_1' is the first derivative of $f_1(x - vt)$. But, from Equation 1.20, $v = 1/\sqrt{(\mu\varepsilon)}$. Therefore

$$\frac{\partial}{\partial x}[g_2(x - vt)] = \sqrt{\frac{\varepsilon}{\mu}} f_1'(x - vt)$$

Integrating,

$$g_2(x - vt) = \sqrt{\frac{\varepsilon}{\mu}} f_1(x - vt) \tag{1.30}$$

where a constant of integration is not involved because constant fields are not of concern. Likewise, employing Equation 1.6c,

$$g_1(x - vt) = -\sqrt{\frac{\varepsilon}{\mu}} f_2(x - vt) \tag{1.31}$$

Hence, Equations 1.26, 1.27, 1.28 and 1.29 can be written:

$$E_y = f_1(x - vt)$$

$$E_z = f_2(x - vt)$$

$$H_y = -\sqrt{\frac{\varepsilon}{\mu}} f_2(x - vt)$$

$$H_z = \sqrt{\frac{\varepsilon}{\mu}} f_1(x - vt)$$

The resultant electric and magnetic fields are E and H respectively, of magnitudes

$$E = \sqrt{(E_y^2 + E_z^2)} = \sqrt{\{[f_1(x-vt)]^2 + [f_2(x-vt)]^2\}}$$

and

$$H = \sqrt{(H_y^2 + H_z^2)} = \sqrt{\frac{\varepsilon}{\mu}} \sqrt{\{[f_2(x-vt)]^2 + [f_1(x-vt)]^2\}}$$

Therefore

$$H = \sqrt{\frac{\varepsilon}{\mu}} E \qquad (1.32)$$

Furthermore, the electric field vector E is at an angle θ_1 to the y-axis given by

$$\tan \theta_1 = \frac{E_z}{E_y}$$

and the magnetic field is at an angle θ_2 to the y-axis given by

$$\tan \theta_2 = \frac{H_z}{H_y}$$

But

$$\frac{E_z}{E_y} = \frac{f_2(x-vt)}{f_1(x-vt)}$$

and

$$\frac{H_z}{H_y} = -\frac{f_1(x-vt)}{f_2(x-vt)}$$

Therefore

$$\tan \theta_1 = -\cot \theta_2$$

and

$$\theta_1 + \theta_2 = 90°$$

It follows that the electric field vector E is always at right angles to the magnetic vector H in a plane wavefront propagated in a dielectric.

To summarise, therefore, an electromagnetic vibration propagated with a plane wavefront is such that the electric and magnetic vectors are perpendicular to one another in this plane wavefront and this plane is perpendicular to the direction of propagation.

1.5 Velocity of Electromagnetic Radiation and Refractive Index

Equation 1.21 relates the wave velocity in a medium of relative permittivity ε_r to the velocity in free space:

$$\frac{c}{v} = \sqrt{\varepsilon_r}$$

The refractive index n of a medium is defined by the following relationship;

$$n = \frac{\text{velocity of electromagnetic radiation in free space}}{\text{velocity of radiation in the medium}}$$

Thus

$$n = \frac{c}{v}$$

or

$$n = \sqrt{\varepsilon_r} \qquad (1.33)$$

i.e. the refractive index should equal the square root of the relative permittivity for a dielectric for which the relative permeability is unity.

This relationship is obeyed satisfactorily for gases, but does not at first appear to be correct for liquids and solids. For example, for distilled water $n = 1\cdot33$ whereas $\varepsilon_r = 81$ and $\sqrt{\varepsilon_r} = 9$. However, this large discrepancy is because $\varepsilon_r = 81$ if the measurement of relative permittivity is carried out under d.c. or low-frequency a.c. conditions. The high value obtained is due to orientation of the dipole water molecules in the electric field. At very high frequencies, this orientation is not effective. Presuming, therefore, that the refractive index n and the relative permittivity ε_r were both carried out at optical frequencies, Equation 1.33 would be correct for water and other liquids and solids.

1.6 The Reflection and Refraction of Linearly Polarised Monochromatic Light at the Boundary between Two Transparent Isotropic Dielectric Media

At any boundary between two media 1 and 2, it can be readily shown by electrical theory that the vector E denoting the electric field strength is such that its components tangential to the boundary are continuous. This means that the component of E tangential to the boundary in medium 1 is equal to that in medium 2. If the boundary is the xOz plane in Cartesian coordinates,

$$E'_x = E''_x \qquad (1.34)$$

and

$$E'_z = E''_z \qquad (1.35)$$

where E'_x is the resultant component of the electric vector E in the x-direction in medium 1, E''_x is the resultant component of E in the x-direction in medium 2, and the z suffices are for the z-direction.

Furthermore, the boundary conditions are such that the same result applies for the magnetic vector H, so

$$H'_x = H''_x \qquad (1.36)$$

and

$$H'_z = H''_z \qquad (1.37)$$

However, for the electric displacement vector D and the magnetic flux vector B, it is the components *normal* to the boundary that are continuous. Hence, with similar notation,

$$D'_y = D''_y \qquad (1.38)$$

and

$$B'_y = B''_y \qquad (1.39)$$

For optical media where the magnetic permeability is equal to that of free space (μ_0) and where the permittivity ε is constant throughout for a given isotropic dielectric material, $B = \mu_0 H$ and $D = \varepsilon E$; thus Equations 1.38 and 1.39 become

$$\varepsilon_1 E'_y = \varepsilon_2 E''_y \qquad (1.40)$$

where ε_1 is the permittivity of medium 1 and ε_2 that of medium 2; also

$$H'_y = H''_y \qquad (1.41)$$

Consider a simple harmonic wave of electromagnetic radiation in a collimated beam along AO in medium 1 of permittivity ε_1 and incident at an angle I on the boundary in the xOz plane at which $y = 0$; this beam will give rise to a reflected beam along OB at an angle I' to the normal (specular reflection will occur if the boundary is smooth, as when light in air impinges upon polished glass) and a refracted beam along OC at an angle R to the normal in the medium 2 of permittivity ε_2 (Fig. 1.3).

It is assumed that the incident monochromatic radiation travelling along AO is in the plane xOy and is linearly polarised in a plane of which the direction is not specified. Conventionally, the direction

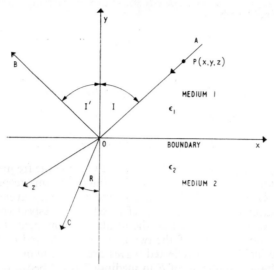

Fig. 1.3. *Reflection and refraction of light at the boundary between two transparent isotropic dielectric media*

of linear polarisation is the direction of the electric displacement vector in the wave. The equation for this propagated wave is

$$E = E_0 \cos 2\pi\left(\frac{t}{T_1} - \frac{d}{\lambda_1}\right)$$

where E is the electric field vector at time t at a point P distant d from the origin at O, E_0 is the peak value of E, λ_1 is the wavelength of the radiation in medium 1, and T_1 is the corresponding period. If (x,y,z) are the coordinates of P,

$$d = l_1 x + m_1 y + n_1 z$$

where l_1, m_1 and n_1 are the direction-cosines of OA with respect to the x, y and z axes respectively. Therefore

$$E = \text{Re}\ \{E_0 \exp \text{j}\ [\omega_1 t - \alpha_1(l_1 x + m_1 y + n_1 z)]\} \qquad (1.42)$$

where $\omega_1 = 2\pi/T_1 = 2\pi\nu_1$, ν_1 being the frequency, and $\alpha_1 = 2\pi/\lambda_1$.

For the reflected beam, let the electric field vector be E' and the direction-cosines be l_2, m_2 and n_2, whilst for the refracted beam the corresponding symbols are E'', l_3, m_3 and n_3. Denoting the z-components of E and E_0 by E_z and E_{0z}, and correspondingly for E', E_0', E'' and E_0'', the following equations arise from Equation 1.42.

For the incident beam,

$$E_z = E_{0z} \exp j\left[\omega_1 t - \alpha_1(l_1 x + m_1 y + n_1 z)\right] \qquad (1.43)$$

For the reflected beam,

$$E_z' = E_{0z}' \exp j\left[\omega_2 t - \alpha_2(l_2 x + m_2 y + n_2 z)\right] \qquad (1.44)$$

For the refracted beam,

$$E_z'' = E_{0z}'' \exp j\left[\omega_3 t - \alpha_3(l_3 x + m_3 y + n_3 z)\right] \qquad (1.45)$$

where $\omega_2 = 2\pi\nu_2$ and $\omega_3 = 2\pi\nu_3$, ν_2 and ν_3 being the frequencies of the vibrations in the reflected and refracted beams respectively; $\alpha_2 = 2\pi/\lambda_2$ and $\alpha_3 = 2\pi/\lambda_3$, where λ_2 and λ_3 are the wavelengths of the radiation in the reflected and refracted beams respectively.

It is clear from Fig. 1.3 that the resultant component of E in medium 1 is now the sum of the two components E_z and E_z' (because both the incident and reflected waves are in medium 1), whereas the resultant component of E in medium 2 is E_z'' because only the refracted wave exists in medium 2. Therefore

$$E_z + E_z' = E_z'' \qquad (1.46)$$

at the boundary plane xOz where $y = 0$. This can only be true if Equation 1.46 is satisfied at the boundary for all values of x, z and t (i.e. if the coefficients of x in Equations 1.43, 1.44 and 1.45 are equal) and similarly for the coefficients of z and t. Equating the coefficients of t,

$$\omega_1 = \omega_2 = \omega_3$$

or

$$\nu_1 = \nu_2 = \nu_3 = \nu \text{ (say)}$$

The vibrations in the incident, reflected and refracted waves are therefore all of the same frequency; reflection and refraction does not cause any change of the frequency of the incident radiation.

Because the incident and reflected beams are in the same medium, they must have the same velocity (Equation 1.20). As their frequencies are the same, they therefore have the same wavelength. Hence $\alpha_1 = \alpha_2$. Equating coefficients of z in Equations 1.43, 1.44 and 1.45 and putting $\alpha_1 = \alpha_2 = \alpha$,

$$\alpha n_1 = \alpha n_2 = \alpha_3 n_3$$

But $n_1 = 0$ because the incident beam is perpendicular to the z-axis. Therefore

$$n_1 = n_2 = n_3 = 0$$

It follows that all three beams, incident, reflected and refracted, must be in the same plane, the plane of incidence xOy, which contains the normal. This is the *first law of reflection and also of refraction* in optics.

Equating coefficients of x,

$$\alpha l_1 = \alpha l_2 = \alpha_3 l_3$$

As $l_1 = \sin I$ and $l_2 = \sin I'$,

$$I = I'$$

which is the *second law of reflection*: the angle of incidence equals the angle of reflection.

Further, $l_3 = \sin R$. Therefore

$$\alpha \sin I = \alpha_3 \sin R$$

or

$$\frac{\sin I}{\sin R} = \frac{\alpha_3}{\alpha} = \frac{2\pi}{\lambda_3} \div \frac{2\pi}{\lambda_1} = \frac{\lambda_1}{\lambda_3}$$

Now $\lambda_1 = v_1/v$ and $\lambda_3 = v_2/v$, where v_1 and v_2 are the wave velocities in media 1 and 2 respectively, the frequencies being the same. Therefore

$$\frac{\sin I}{\sin R} = \frac{v_1}{v_2}$$

Thus, from Equations 1.20 and 1.33,

$$\frac{\sin I}{\sin R} = \sqrt{\frac{\varepsilon_2}{\varepsilon_1}} = n$$

where n is the refractive index of medium 2 relative to that of medium 1. This is the *second law of refraction*, known as Snell's law.

1.7 The Reflection and Refraction of Light at a Boundary: Fresnel's Equations

Now that it has been shown that the electromagnetic theory is consistent with the well-known laws of reflection and refraction, a more important development from the concepts of Section 1.6 is to consider the state of polarisation of the reflected and refracted light in relation to that of the incident light.

The direction of the electric vector E in the light waves can be anywhere at a particular time t. Whatever this direction, it can be resolved into E_l parallel to the plane of incidence, which also contains the reflected and refracted rays, as shown, and E_r perpendicular to this plane. The r-direction is the same as the z-direction in Fig. 1.3. Therefore E_r is considered positive if it lies in the positive direction of z and negative if in the opposite direction. To specify the positive direction of E_l, let it be such that the vector E_l in the plane of incidence is to the right-hand side of the direction of propagation; negative E_l then corresponds to the left-hand side (Fig. 1.4).

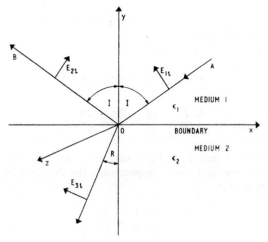

Fig. 1.4. *Reflection and refraction at a boundary with the positive directions of the components E_l shown*

Equations 1.43, 1.44 and 1.45 can be written for the incident beam with electric vector components E_{1l} and E_{1r}, for the reflected beam with components E_{2l} and E_{2r}, and for the refracted beam with components E_{3l} and E_{3r}. These equations can be simplified because it has been shown that $\omega_1 = \omega_2 = \omega_3 = \omega, \alpha_1 = \alpha_2 = \alpha, n_1 = n_2 = n_3 = 0$ and $l_1 = l_2$. Hence, for the incident beam:

$$E_{1l} = E_{10l}\ \exp j\,[\omega t - \alpha(l_1 x + m_1 y)] \qquad (1.47a)$$

$$E_{1r} = E_{10r}\ \exp j\,[\omega t - \alpha(l_1 x + m_1 y)] \qquad (1.47b)$$

For the reflected beam:

$$E_{2l} = E_{20l}\ \exp j\,[\omega t - \alpha(l_1 x + m_2 y)] \qquad (1.48a)$$

$$E_{2r} = E_{20r}\ \exp j\,[\omega t - \alpha(l_1 x + m_2 y)] \qquad (1.48b)$$

For the refracted beam:

$$E_{3l} = E_{30l} \exp j \left[\omega t - \alpha_3 (l_3 x + m_3 y) \right] \quad (1.49\text{a})$$

$$E_{3r} = E_{30r} \exp j \left[\omega t - \alpha_3 (l_3 x + m_3 y) \right] \quad (1.49\text{b})$$

From the boundary condition represented by Equations 1.35 and 1.46 at $y = 0$,

$$E_{1r} + E_{2r} = E_{3r} \quad (1.50)$$

Applying the boundary condition of Equation 1.36 and referring to Fig. 1.4 (in which H can be considered to replace E) it is seen that

$$H'_x = H_{1l} \cos I - H_{2l} \cos I = H''_x = H_{3l} \cos R \quad (1.51)$$

Equation 1.32 shows that

$$H_{1l} = \sqrt{\frac{\varepsilon_1}{\mu_0}} E_{1r}$$

$$H_{2l} = \sqrt{\frac{\varepsilon_1}{\mu_0}} E_{2r}$$

and

$$H_{3l} = \sqrt{\frac{\varepsilon_2}{\mu_0}} E_{3r}$$

Therefore, substituting in Equation 1.51,

$$(E_{1r} - E_{2r}) \cos I = (E_{3r} \cos R) \sqrt{\frac{\varepsilon_2}{\varepsilon_1}} = n E_{3r} \cos R \quad (1.52)$$

where n is the refractive index of medium 2 relative to that of medium 1. The boundary condition of Equation 1.34 gives

$$E'_x = (E_{1l} - E_{2l}) \cos I = E''_x = E_{3l} \cos R \quad (1.53)$$

whilst boundary condition of Equation 1.37 gives

$$H_{1r} + H_{2r} = H_{3r} \quad (1.54)$$

Substituting $H_{1r} = \sqrt{(\varepsilon_1/\mu_0)} E_{1l}$, $H_{2r} = \sqrt{(\varepsilon_1/\mu_0)} E_{2l}$ and $H_{3r} = \sqrt{(\varepsilon_2/\mu_0)} E_{3l}$ derived from Equation 1.32, it follows that

$$E_{1l} + E_{2l} = \sqrt{\frac{\varepsilon_2}{\varepsilon_1}} E_{3l} = n E_{3l} \quad (1.55)$$

The results following from the application of the boundary conditions are thus:

$$E_{1r}+E_{2r} = E_{3r}$$

$$(E_{1r}-E_{2r}) \cos I = nE_{3r} \cos R$$

$$(E_{1l}-E_{2l}) \cos I = E_{3l} \cos R$$

$$E_{1l}+E_{2l} = nE_{3l}$$

If the expressions for electric field components given by Equations 1.47, 1.48 and 1.49 are substituted in these four equations, a simplification results from the fact that at the boundary $y = 0$; the exponential factors in Equations 1.47, 1.48 and 1.49 are then all equal because $\alpha_3 l_3 = \alpha l_1$, as shown in Section 1.6. For convenience, the amplitudes $E_{10l}, E_{10r}, E_{20l}, \ldots$ of $E_{1l}, E_{1r}, E_{2l}, \ldots$ are replaced by $A_{1l}, A_{1r}, A_{2l}, \ldots$ Then the amplitude values for Equations 1.50, 1.52, 1.53 and 1.55 become, respectively:

$$A_{1r}+A_{2r} = A_{3r} \tag{1.56}$$

$$(A_{1r}-A_{2r}) \cos I = nA_{3r} \cos R \tag{1.57}$$

$$(A_{1l}-A_{2l}) \cos I = A_{3l} \cos R \tag{1.58}$$

$$A_{1l}+A_{2l} = nA_{3l} \tag{1.59}$$

Equation 1.57 divided by Equation 1.56 gives

$$(A_{1r}-A_{2r}) \cos I = n(A_{1r}+A_{2r}) \cos R$$

Therefore

$$A_{2r} = A_{1r} \frac{\cos I - n \cos R}{n \cos R + \cos I}$$

Substituting $n = (\sin I)/(\sin R)$ from Snell's law,

$$A_{2r} = A_{1r} \frac{\cos I \sin R - \sin I \cos R}{\sin I \cos R + \cos I \sin R}$$

Thus

$$A_{2r} = -A_{1r} \frac{\sin (I-R)}{\sin (I+R)} \tag{1.60}$$

which relates the amplitude of the perpendicular component of the electric vector in the reflected beam to that in the incident beam.

Equation 1.58 divided by Equation 1.59 gives

$$n(A_{1l}-A_{2l}) \cos I = (A_{1l}+A_{2l}) \cos R$$

Substituting $n = (\sin I)/(\sin R)$,

$$A_{2l} = A_{1l} \frac{\sin I \cos I - \sin R \cos R}{\sin R \cos R + \sin I \cos I}$$

Therefore

$$A_{2l} = A_{1l} \frac{\sin 2I - \sin 2R}{\sin 2I + \sin 2R}$$

i. e.

$$A_{2l} = A_{1l} \frac{\tan (I - R)}{\tan (I + R)} \tag{1.61}$$

which relates the amplitude of the parallel component of the electric vector in the reflected beam to that in the incident beam.

To relate the amplitude A_{3r} of the perpendicular component of the refracted beam to that in the incident beam, substitution of A_{2r} from Equation 1.60 in Equation 1.56 gives

$$A_{3r} = A_{1r} \left[1 - \frac{\sin (I - R)}{\sin (I + R)} \right]$$

$$= A_{1r} \frac{\sin (I + R) - \sin (I - R)}{\sin (I + R)}$$

Thus

$$A_{3r} = A_{1r} \frac{2 \sin R \cos I}{\sin (I + R)} \tag{1.62}$$

Finally, to relate the amplitude A_{3l} of the parallel component of the refracted beam to that in the incident beam, substitution of A_{2l} from Equation 1.61 in Equation 1.58 gives

$$A_{3l} = A_{1l} \frac{\cos I}{\cos R} \left(1 - \frac{\sin 2I - \sin 2R}{\sin 2I + \sin 2R} \right)$$

$$= A_{1l} \frac{2 \sin 2R \cos I}{\cos R (\sin 2I + \sin 2R)}$$

Thus

$$A_{3l} = 4 A_{1l} \frac{\sin R \cos I}{\sin 2I + \sin 2R} \tag{1.63}$$

Equations 1.60, 1.61, 1.62 and 1.63 are the *Fresnel equations*.

The situation where the light is at normal incidence is of special interest, since then $I = R = 0°$. Fresnel's equations, as derived in the general case above, are thus indeterminate. For example, Equation 1.60 immediately leads to

$$A_{2r} = - A_{1r} \frac{0}{0}$$

To explore normal incidence, it is therefore necessary to return to the initial Equations 1.56, 1.57, 1.58 and 1.59. With $I = R = 0°$ (i.e. $\cos I = \cos R = 1$), these equations become respectively:

$$A_{1r} + A_{2r} = A_{3r} \tag{1.64}$$

$$A_{1r} - A_{2r} = nA_{3r} \tag{1.65}$$

$$A_{1l} - A_{2l} = A_{3l} \tag{1.66}$$

$$A_{1l} + A_{2l} = nA_{3l} \tag{1.67}$$

From Equations 1.64 and 1.65, eliminating A_{3r},

$$n(A_{1r} + A_{2r}) = A_{1r} - A_{2r}$$

Thus

$$A_{2r} = -A_{1r}\frac{n-1}{n+1} \tag{1.68}$$

where n is the refractive index of medium 2 with respect to that of medium 1, as before. Similarly, eliminating A_{3l} from Equations 1.66 and 1.67,

$$n(A_{1l} - A_{2l}) = A_{1l} + A_{2l}$$

Therefore

$$A_{2l} = A_{1l}\frac{n-1}{n+1} \tag{1.69}$$

Inserting A_{2r} from Equation 1.68 in Equation 1.64,

$$A_{3r} = A_{1r}\left(1 - \frac{n-1}{n+1}\right) = A_{1r}\frac{2}{n+1} \tag{1.70}$$

and inserting A_{2l} from Equation 1.69 in Equation 1.66,

$$A_{3l} = A_{1l}\left(1 - \frac{n-1}{n+1}\right) = A_{1l}\frac{2}{n+1} \tag{1.71}$$

Equations 1.68, 1.69, 1.70 and 1.71 are Fresnel's equations for normal incidence.

With normal incidence, the reflection coefficient (defined as the ratio of the incident intensity to the intensity of the reflected beam) is easily worked out. Recalling that intensity is proportional to the square of the amplitude, it is clear that the intensity of the incident beam is proportional to $A_{1r}^2 + A_{1l}^2$, whereas the intensity of the reflected beam is proportional to $A_{2r}^2 + A_{2l}^2$. Therefore

$$\text{reflection coefficient} = \frac{A_{2r}^2 + A_{2l}^2}{A_{1r}^2 + A_{1l}^2}$$

Substitution from Equations 1.68 and 1.69 gives

$$\text{reflection coefficient} = \frac{A_{1r}^2[(n-1)/(n+1)]^2 + A_{1l}^2[(n-1)/(n+1)]^2}{A_{1r}^2 + A_{1l}^2}$$

Therefore

$$\text{reflection coefficient} = \left(\frac{n-1}{n+1}\right)^2 \qquad (1.72)$$

With light incident normally in air on glass of refractive index 1·5, the reflection is therefore $(0{\cdot}5/2{\cdot}5)^2 \times 100 = 4\%$.

1.8 The Reflection and Refraction of Light at a Boundary: Practical Results

Fresnel's equations, deduced in Section 1.7, give the amplitudes of the parallel components of the electric field vectors in the reflected and refracted light in terms of the amplitude of the parallel component in the incident light, and similarly for the perpendicular components. In practice, the incident light may be unpolarised, partly polarised or fully polarised. Whatever the state of polarisation, the electric vector can be resolved into parallel and perpendicular components. If the electric vector amplitudes of these components are known, those in the reflected and refracted light can be calculated by means of Fresnel's equations.

As an example, let the amplitudes A_{1l} and A_{1r} of the perpendicular components in the incident beam of light both be unity, and suppose incidence is in air on a polished glass surface of refractive index $n = 1{\cdot}5$. It is required to plot the amplitudes A_{2l} and A_{2r} in the reflected beam, and A_{3l} and A_{3r} in the refracted beam against the angle of incidence I.

It should be noted that the case where A_{1l} and A_{1r} are equal is of interest when the incident light is unpolarised, because unpolarised light can be resolved into components of equal amplitude.

Curve 1 of Fig. 1.5 shows A_{2l} against I. For $I = 0°$, it is seen from Equation 1.69 that $A_{2l} = 0{\cdot}2$. As I increases, A_{2l} decreases (as is shown by Equation 1.61) to reach zero when the denominator of Equation 1.61 is infinite; i.e. $I+R = 90°$ when $\tan 90° = \infty$. At this particular angle of incidence, the electric vector vibration in the plane of incidence vanishes and only the perpendicular component A_{2r} remains. Therefore, when the reflected and refracted rays are at right angles to one another, the reflected beam is plane-polarised with its electric vector vibrating perpendicular to the plane of incidence. This occurs for a particular angle of incidence I_B. As $(\sin I_B)/(\sin R) = n$ (Snell's law) and $R = 90° - I_B$,

$$\frac{\sin I_B}{\cos I_B} = \tan I_B = n \tag{1.73}$$

where I_B is the Brewster angle of incidence (Section 3.2). With $n = 1.5$, this Brewster angle is $\tan^{-1} 1.5 = 56.3°$.

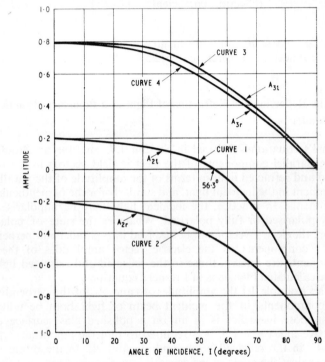

Fig. 1.5. Variation with angle of incidence of amplitudes of parallel and perpendicular components of reflected and refracted beams ($n = 1.5$ and the amplitudes of components in the incident beam are both unity)

For angles of incidence I greater than I_B, $I + R$ exceeds $90°$ and $\tan(I + R)$ is negative. Equation 1.61 shows that A_{2l}/A_{1l} is then negative: the direction of the electric vector is reversed and the vibrations in the reflected light are $180°$ out of phase with those of the incident light. As I increases to $90°$, corresponding to grazing incidence, A_{2l} becomes equal to -1.0.

The plot of A_{2r} against I is shown in curve 2 of Fig. 1.5. Equation 1.60 shows that A_{2r}/A_{1r} is always negative, so the phase is reversed. At $I = 0°$, $A_{2r} = -0.2$ (Equation 1.68); and as I increases, A_{2r} increases to become -1.0 at $I = 90°$.

Curve 3 of Fig. 1.5 shows A_{3l} against I. Equation 1.63 is involved. At $I = 0°$, $A_{3l} = 0·8$ (Equation 1.71); A_{3l}/A_{1l} is always positive, and A_{3l} decreases to zero at $I = 90°$.

The plot of A_{3r} against I is shown in curve 4 of Fig. 1.5. As is seen from Equation 1.62, the variation of A_{3r} departs only slightly from the similar curve for A_{3l}.

From these results, the reflection coefficients for various angles of incidence may be obtained, since intensity is proportional to the square of the amplitude. Thus, from Fig. 1.5, where the components of A_{1l} and A_{1r} are both unity, the reflected intensities are given by plotting A_{2l}^2 and A_{2r}^2 against I.

The statement is often made that there is a phase change of 180° when light is reflected at the surface of an optically denser medium, i.e. the light is incident in a medium of refractive index n_1 and encounters the surface of a medium of refractive index n_2, where $n_2 > n_1$. Study of one of Fresnel's equations (Equation 1.60) shows that this is always true for the electric vector components perpendicular to the plane of incidence (see also curve 2 of Fig. 1.5), but is only true for the components parallel to the plane of incidence if the angle of incidence exceeds the Brewster polarising angle, as is shown by Equation 1.61 for $I+R > 90°$. Thus, for angles of incidence I less than the Brewster angle, A_{2l}/A_{1l} is positive and apparently the electric vector in the reflected beam is in phase with that in the incident beam.

However, in Fig. 1.6 let AO be a beam of light at angle of incidence I_1, less than the Brewster angle, the incidence being near normal. Suppose the arrow perpendicular to AO represents E_{1l}, the electric vector in the incident beam. This is assumed to be in the positive direction, so is drawn to the right-hand side of the direction

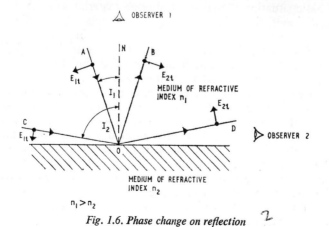

Fig. 1.6. Phase change on reflection

of the incident light. In the reflected beam OB, E_{2l} is again positive (no phase change) and is again drawn to the right-hand side of the direction OB. But the light direction is *reversed* on reflection. Hence, to an observer 1 receiving light in the direction roughly along the normal ON, the vibrations in the incident and reflected beams *would* appear to be in anti-phase.

Furthermore, when the incident beam CO is at an angle of incidence I_2 which exceeds the Brewster angle, I_2 being nearly 90°, E_{1l} is drawn to the right of CO if it is positive; on the other hand, E_{2l} in the reflected beam OD would be drawn to the left of OD, as it will be negative because E_{2l}/E_{1l} is negative when $I+R > 90°$ (Equation 1.61). To an observer 2 receiving light resulting from reflection with grazing incidence, the electric vector vibrations will appear to be in anti-phase.

The initial statement about the phase change of 180° is therefore true for the parallel components as well as the perpendicular ones if the viewing conditions are appropriate and, indeed, are those which usually prevail in interference experiments between coherent incident and reflected beams of light.

1.9 Electromagnetic Theory of the Scattering of Light

The electromagnetic theory cannot give a detailed explanation of the effects of the scattering of light by molecules of a material; instead, quantum theory is required. In quantum theory, the light is considered to be propagated in the form of photons, where the energy of a photon at frequency v is hv, h being Planck's constant.

Certain important aspects of the scattering of light can, however, be satisfactorily discussed by the use of electromagnetic theory. The basic situation is that the scattering material concerned is a dielectric consisting of an assembly of molecular electric dipoles; the electric vector alternating in magnitude in the impinging electromagnetic wave will be able to set the bound charges in the dipoles in motion. To gain an insight into the ideas involved, consider the dielectric to be water. The hydrogen atoms have positive nuclei each of charge $+e$, where e is the electronic charge. The oxygen atom has a nucleus of charge $+8e$. These three nuclei will have an equivalent 'seat' of positive charge $+10e$ somewhere within the molecule. The electron in orbit around each hydrogen atom will be intermingled in its motion with the outermost electrons of the oxygen atom. The molecule is electrically uncharged as a whole, because the $+10e$ charge on the nuclei is balanced by the $-10e$ charge on the electrons. The equivalent 'seat' of negative charge due to the electrons does not coincide with the 'seat' of positive charge: there is a small distance between them. Hence the water molecule is, electrically, a dipole, and has a dipole moment. Many molecules such as water are permanent dipoles; many others have a zero or very small dipole moment which is increased on subjection to an electric field, i.e. these molecules become induced dipoles.

The nuclei have much larger masses than the electrons, because the proton mass is 1,836 m_e and the neutron mass is 1,838 m_e, where m_e is the rest mass of the electron. When an electromagnetic wave impinges on a molecule, it is consequently only the electrons which undergo any significant motion in the alternating electric field. In a dipole, such electrons are bound charges, not free as in a conductor. Therefore, any tendency for the electric field in the electromagnetic wave to set these electrons in motion is retarded by the attraction of the electron to the positive nuclei and also by forces between molecules. The intermolecular forces will be much stronger in solids and liquids, where the separations between molecules are of the order of 10^{-8} cm, than in gases where, at atmospheric pressure, the separation is a few hundred times greater.

When the electromagnetic wave impinges on the dielectric material, the bound electrons in the dipoles are set into motion and they will oscillate under oscillatory forces in the direction of the alternating electric vector in the wave. It is fundamental to the production of electromagnetic radiation that it is a result of accelerated electric charge. The forced oscillations of the bound electrons will consequently result in electromagnetic radiation; this will be the scattered light.

The bound electrons in the material will themselves have a natural frequency or, in general, a series of natural frequencies of vibration. If the frequency of the impinging electromagnetic wave is not equal to the frequency of vibration of the bound electrons, the forced oscillations will be of small amplitude and subject to damping. The scattered radiation will therefore be weak and of the same frequency as that of the incident wave, but containing also harmonics. In certain circumstances, scattered radiation of lower frequency (longer wavelength) can also be produced, as in the *Raman effect* (Section 2.22) and in *fluorescence*, but these effects cannot be adequately explained without recourse to quantum theory.

The electromagnetic theory can also explain aspects of the distribution of intensity with direction of the scattered light. Let a plane-polarised electromagnetic wave with the electric vector E vibrating along the y-axis and the magnetic vector H in the perpendicular z-direction be travelling along the x-axis to encounter a bound electron at point O (Fig. 1.7). The electron will execute forced vibrations along the y-axis under the action of the oscillating E and H. This vibration of the electron along the y-axis cannot produce a transverse electromagnetic wave along the y-axis, so the intensity of the scattered light along OA and OB will be zero. The most intense scattered light will be along the radii from O terminating on the equatorial circle $CEFG$. This scattered light will be plane-polarised with its electric vector vibrations in a direction parallel to the vector E in the incident radiation. Let its amplitude be A at any point on the circle $CEFG$. At any other point P on the sphere around O, the component of the vibration of the electron projected perpendicular to OP will be effective. If angle

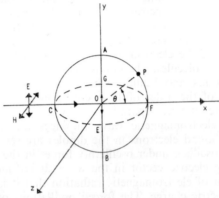

Fig. 1.7. *Distribution of scattered light around a bound charge at O due to plane-polarised light incident along the x-axis (circle CEFG is in the plane xOz)*

POF is θ, the amplitude of the wave in the direction θ to the plane $CEFQ$ is $A \cos \theta$. Hence, the intensity varies as $\cos^2 \theta$.

If the light incident along x on the electron at O is unpolarised, in a finite time the vector E will be equally likely to occupy any direction in a plane perpendicular to the direction of propagation along the x-axis. The light scattered along the x-axis is likewise unpolarised, whereas that scattered in any direction in the plane yOz will clearly be plane-polarised.

These predictions assume that the axis of the induced dipole is in the direction of the electric vector in the incident radiation. This is not necessarily so; if it is not, the scattered light will be partially polarised.

1.10 The Electromagnetic Theory of the Absorption of Light

As in scattering, a full account on the basis of electromagnetic theory is inadequate and the quantum theory has to be applied. Again, important ideas can nevertheless be put forward by utilising electromagnetic theory.

The situation is as in Section 1.9 in that the forced vibrations induced in the bound charge in a dielectric are concerned, but free electrons in a conductor must now also be considered. The strongest absorption will occur when the frequency of vibrations in the incident electromagnetic wave is equal to a natural frequency of vibration of a bound charge in the dielectric. Resonance will then occur, the essential origin of absorption spectra being concerned here. For a conductor, the free electrons available will be vibrated in the direction of the oscillatory electric vector, and this will occur largely irrespective of the frequency of the incident radiation. The induced electric currents resulting will cause energy dissipation, and strong absorption of the incident light energy will occur.

1.11 The Theory of Dispersion

Electromagnetic theory leads to Equation 1.33

$$n = \sqrt{\varepsilon_r}$$

for the refractive index n of a transparent dielectric medium of relative permittivity ε_r and a relative permeability of unity. There is no immediate indication of a variation of refractive index with the frequency f of the radiation, i.e. no indication of dispersion.

Lorenz in 1880 and Lorentz in 1909 developed the electromagnetic theory of dielectrics to show that dispersion came about because of the molecular dipole structure of materials, i.e. because of the presence of bound electrons. In the 'macroscopic' electromagnetic theory, the setting in motion of bound charges on the passage of an electromagnetic wave is not taken into account. The interaction of light with matter on the molecular scale requires explanation in terms of quantum theory, but the Lorenz–Lorentz development of classical electromagnetic theory leads to valuable results.

To give a simplified account of this Lorenz–Lorentz theory, suppose an electric field E causes electric polarisation P of a medium of relative permittivity ε_r. In rationalised units, a well-known result from electrostatics is

$$D = \varepsilon_0 E + P = \varepsilon_0 \varepsilon_r E \qquad (1.74$$

where D is the electric displacement, ε_0 is the permittivity of free space, and P (the polarisation) is the electric moment per unit volume of the dielectric. Therefore

$$\varepsilon_r = 1 + \frac{P}{\varepsilon_0 E}$$

and Equation 1.33 gives

$$n^2 = 1 + \frac{P}{\varepsilon_0 E} \qquad (1.75)$$

Suppose the polarising electric field E at time t is caused by a plane electromagnetic wave passing through the dielectric medium where

$$E = E_0 \exp j\omega t$$

E_0 being the peak value of the electric vector in the wave, and $\omega = 2\pi\nu$ where ν is the frequency of the wave. This alternating electric field E sets the bound electrons in the molecular dipoles in motion. The electron is subject to an elastic restoring force assumed to be proportional to its displacement x from its equilibrium position. This restoring force will be given by $m_e\omega_0^2 x$ where $\omega_0/2\pi = \nu_0$ is the natural frequency of vibration of the electron in the material. In addition, the electron will be subject to a resisting or damping force assumed to be r per unit mass per unit velocity. The equation of motion of the electrons, each of charge e and mass m_e, will therefore be

$$m_e(\ddot{x} + r\dot{x} + \omega_0^2 x) = Ee$$

If r is assumed to be negligibly small for simplicity, then

$$\ddot{x} + \omega_0^2 x = \frac{Ee}{m_e} = \frac{E_0 e \exp j\omega t}{m_e} \qquad (1.76)$$

Putting $x = x_0 \exp j\omega t$, where x_0 is the peak displacement which is assumed to have the same frequency as and to be in phase with E,

$$\ddot{x} = -\omega^2 x_0 \exp j\omega t = -\omega^2 x$$

and Equation 1.76 becomes

$$x(\omega_0^2 - \omega^2) = \frac{Ee}{m_e} \qquad (1.77)$$

The dipole moment due to the displacement of one electron through a distance x is ex. If there are N electrons per unit volume, the total electric moment per unit volume $= P = N ex$. Substituting for x from Equation 1.77,

$$P = \frac{Ne^2 E}{m_e(\omega_0^2 - \omega^2)}$$

Substituting this expression for P in Equation 1.75,

$$n^2 = 1 + \frac{Ne^2}{m_e \varepsilon_0 (\omega_0^2 - \omega^2)}$$

or, putting $\omega_0 = 2\pi\nu_0$ and $\omega = 2\pi\nu$,

$$n^2 = 1 + \frac{Ne^2}{4\pi^2 m_e \varepsilon_0 (\nu_0^2 - \nu^2)} \qquad (1.78)$$

If it is assumed that Ne^2 is small, i.e. that $\boldsymbol{P}$ is small compared with $\varepsilon_0 E$ in Equation 1.75,

$$n = 1 + \frac{Ne^2}{8\pi^2 m_e \varepsilon_0 (\nu_0^2 - \nu^2)} \qquad (1.79)$$

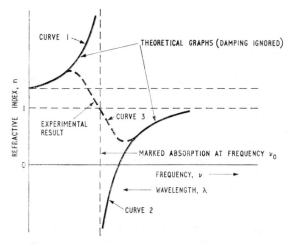

Fig. 1.8. Variation of refractive index with frequency

This equation gives the variation of refractive index n with frequency ν of the radiation. At $\nu = \nu_0$, n becomes infinite. This is because of strong absorption of the radiation at the frequency ν_0, corresponding to a line in the absorption spectrum of the material. A more complex theory including, in particular, a damping term represented by a finite value of r, the resisting force per unit mass per unit velocity, would show the discontinuity in the plot of n against ν at $\nu = \nu_0$ but without n becoming infinite. The full line in Fig. 1.8 shows a typical plot from Equation 1.79. The abrupt discontinuity at the absorption line is not experienced in practice; the dashed curve shows the experimental result obtained in the region of the absorption.

Equation 1.78 and Fig. 1.8 apply to a gas in which the electric polarisation $\boldsymbol{P}$ would be weak; this would be the case except at high pressure. It is also assumed that only one absorption band is present. Nevertheless, Fig. 1.8 illustrates well the marked change in refractive index on either side of the absorption line.

The variation of refractive index n with wavelength λ is often represented by the empirical equation of Cauchy

$$n = A + \frac{B}{\lambda^2} \qquad (1.80)$$

where A and B are constants for a given material. The dispersion $dn/d\lambda$ is given by

$$\frac{dn}{d\lambda} = -\frac{2B}{\lambda^3}$$

This equation represents fairly satisfactorily *normal dispersion*, for which n decreases with increase of wavelength and so decrease of frequency. In Fig. 1.8, n decreases with decrease of frequency for curves 1 and 2, but at frequencies ν in the neighbourhood of ν_0, the resonant absorption frequency, the dashed curve 3 shows that the refractive index n decreases with *increase* of frequency. This effect is known as *anomalous dispersion* and is exhibited by materials in the neighbourhood of frequencies at which absorption is marked.

Many common optical media (for example, glasses and water) do not have electron resonance frequencies in the visible region, so for practical optical purposes they exhibit normal dispersion. They will show anomalous dispersion in the ultra-violet and infra-red regions where absorption is marked at particular frequencies. Sodium vapour, on the other hand, shows marked absorption electron resonance frequencies at corresponding wavelengths of 5,890 Å and 5,896 Å. Sodium vapour will therefore exhibit anomalous dispersion in the visible spectrum in the region around 5,893 Å.

Replacing ν_0 by c/λ_0 and ν by c/λ in Equation 1.78, where c is the velocity of light in free space whilst λ_0 and λ are wavelengths (in free space) corresponding to ν_0 and ν respectively, gives

$$n^2 = 1 + \frac{Ne^2}{4\pi^2 m_e \varepsilon_0 [(c^2/\lambda_0^2) - (c^2/\lambda^2)]} = 1 + \frac{Ne^2 \lambda^2 \lambda_0^2}{4\pi^2 m_e \varepsilon_0 c^2 (\lambda^2 - \lambda_0^2)}$$

This assumes that the material has only one absorption band at the wavelength λ_0, which is a constant for a given dielectric. Therefore

$$n^2 = 1 + \frac{A'\lambda^2}{\lambda^2 - \lambda_0^2} \qquad (1.81)$$

where A' is a constant for a given material. Equation 1.81 is Sellmeier's formula.

If the wavelength λ_0 is far removed on the short wavelength side from the region where the dispersion is required, $\lambda^2 \gg \lambda_0^2$; so

$$n^2 = 1 + A'\left(1 - \frac{\lambda_0^2}{\lambda^2}\right)^{-1} = 1 + A' + \frac{A'\lambda_0^2}{\lambda^2}$$

Therefore

$$n = 1 + A' + \frac{A'\lambda_0^2}{2\lambda^2}$$

which is of the same form as Cauchy's equation where, in Equation 1.80, $A = 1 + A'$ and $B = A'\lambda_0^2/2$.

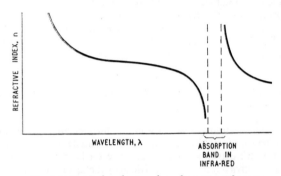

REFRACTIVE INDEX, n

WAVELENGTH, λ

ABSORPTION
BAND IN
INFRA-RED

Fig. 1.9. Normal and anomalous dispersion of quartz

In general, there will be a number of absorption bands in the spectrum at wavelengths λ_1, λ_2, λ_3, ... Equations 1.78, 1.79 and 1.81 then have to be modified. In particular, Sellmeier's equation will be of the form

$$n^2 = 1 + \sum_j \frac{A_j\lambda^2}{\lambda^2 - \lambda_j^2} \qquad (1.82)$$

where A_j is proportional to the number of electrons of which the natural vibration frequency corresponds to a wavelength in free space of λ_j.

Equation 1.78 is of interest in connection with X-rays. The frequencies involved in X-radiation are much larger than electron resonance frequencies, so $\nu \gg \nu_0$. Therefore, the term

$$\frac{Ne^2}{4\pi^2 m_e \varepsilon_0 (\nu_0^2 - \nu^2)} = \frac{-Ne^2}{4\pi^2 m_e \varepsilon_0 \nu^2}$$

is negative and the refractive index n is less than unity.

Finally, a typical experimental result in which the refractive index n is plotted against wavelength λ for a transparent optical medium having a marked absorption band in the infra-red is exhibited by quartz (Fig. 1.9).

Exercise 1

Note.   In the exercises at the end of each chapter, the abbreviations in brackets at the end of a question denote the university or institution concerned. These abbreviations are as follows.

L.G.   B.Sc. General Degree of the University of London
L.P.   B.Sc. (Special) Physics Degree of the University of London
L.Anc. Ancillary examination in Physics to the B.Sc. (Special) Chemistry Degree of the University of London
City   B.Sc. Degree in Applied Physics of the City University
M.P.   B.Sc. Honours Degree in Physics of the University of Manchester
Poly   B.Sc. Honours Degree in Physics (C.N.A.A.) of The Polytechnic, Regent Street, London, W. 1

The values of physical constants needed in numerical examples are given on page 367.

1. For a plane electromagnetic wave in a non-conducting medium, establish that in the wavefront at a given time the magnitude of the magnetic vector divided by the magnitude of the electric vector is equal to the square root of the permittivity of the medium divided by the square root of the permeability, and establish also that these two vectors are perpendicular to one another.

2. Derive from the appropriate equations in electromagnetic theory for a dielectric medium of which the relative magnetic permeability is unity, that the refractive index is numerically equal to the square root of the relative permittivity. Comment on this result in relation to experimentally determined values of the refractive indices and relative permittivities for gaseous, liquid and solid dielectrics.

3. Give a theoretical treatment which establishes that the conditions which apply at a plane boundary between two different transparent dielectric media in relation to the continuity of the components of the electric field lead to the laws of reflection and of refraction in optics.

4. Derive Fresnel's equations relating the amplitudes of the reflected to those of the incident beam for reflection at a plane interface between two transparent dielectric media.
A beam, which is plane polarised at 45° with the plane of incidence, falls on the interface. Describe how the state of polarisation of the reflected beam varies with the angle of reflection.   (L.P.)

5. Plane polarised light is incident on a plane surface separating two homogeneous isotropic dielectrics, the light being incident from the medium of lower refractive index. Draw diagrams which show qualitatively the way in

which the amplitude, phase and intensity of the reflected disturbance vary with the angle of incidence when the electric vector of the incident light lies (a) in the plane of incidence and (b) perpendicular to the plane of incidence. Derive an expression for the reflection coefficient at normal incidence in terms of refractive indices. (L.P.)

6. Write an essay on the evidence supporting the idea that light consists of electromagnetic waves. (L.P.)

7. Obtain an expression for the ratio of the amplitudes of the electric and magnetic vectors in a plane polarised light wave in a dielectric.
   Find the reflected intensity when the light is incident normally at a plane surface of separation between air and diamond of refractive index 2·42. (L.P.)

8. What is meant by a *displacement current* and why is the concept adopted? A plane electromagnetic wave in free space is incident normally on the plane boundary of a homogeneous loss-free medium of magnetic permeability $\mu = 2$ and dielectric constant $\varepsilon = 0.5$. Find the reflection coefficient after deriving the necessary formula. (L.P.)

9. Explain the terms *normal dispersion* and *anomalous dispersion*. Draw a rough graph to illustrate the dispersion of a dielectric throughout a spectral region containing absorption bands.
   Discuss briefly the classical electromagnetic theory of dispersion. (L.P.)

10. Discuss the effects of *resonance* and *relaxation* processes on the passage of electromagnetic radiation through matter. (L.P.)

11. The rate of flow of energy per second through unit area drawn within a plane wavefront of electromagnetic radiation in which the electric intensity is E V m^{-1} and the magnetic intensity is H A m^{-1} is given by

$$N = EH \text{ J m}^{-2}\text{s}^{-1}$$

Calculate the root-mean-square electric field strength in air at a distance of 5 m from a 10 kW lamp (assumed to be a point source) which is radiating uniformly in all directions.

12. Describe the chief characteristics of the dispersive behaviour of insulating materials with respect to electromagnetic waves.
    Discuss the principal processes involved and explain in qualitative terms how refraction and dispersion are related to scattering. (I.P.)

CHAPTER 2

Quantum Theory of Radiation

2.1 Origins of the Quantum Theory

The quantum theory began in 1900 with the famous theoretical work of Max Planck concerned with the distribution of energy in the spectrum of the radiation from a black-body at a temperature $T°K$. This theory is normally studied within the subject of statistical thermodynamics and so will not be developed fully here. Previous work by Lord Rayleigh and Sir James Jeans attempted an explanation in which the radiation energy per unit volume $Q(v)$ at a frequency v was considered to be in dynamic equilibrium with that possessed by the vibrating molecules in the walls of the black-body cavity. These vibrating molecules are dipoles and as such their electric charges in motion radiate electromagnetic energy. The term 'harmonic oscillators' was used to describe them. In accordance with classical concepts, these harmonic oscillators were allowed to have any arbitrary energy which was a continuous function of the temperature T. This approach, based on statistical thermodynamics in which the energy per degree of freedom is $\frac{1}{2}kT$, where k is Boltzmann's constant, led to an equation

$$Q(v)\,\mathrm{d}v = \frac{8\pi v^2}{c^3}\,kT\,\mathrm{d}v$$

where $Q(v)$ is the energy per unit volume in the frequency range $\mathrm{d}v$. The prediction is consequently that the energy density of the radiation increases progressively with increase of the frequency v of the radiation.

The experimental results disagree profoundly with this theoretical prediction. As shown in Fig. 6.4 of Volume 1, there is a maximum in the curve of $Q(v)$ plotted against v. The energy density attains a peak value at a particular frequency, depending on the temperature of the black-body. At frequencies greater than this value, the energy density *decreases* with increase of frequency.

This magnificent failure of classical physics led Max Planck to postulate that the vibrating molecules (harmonic oscillators) cannot have any arbitrary energy, but only energy values restricted to integral multiples of a finite amount of energy ε, where

$$\varepsilon = hv$$

h being Planck's constant $= 6 \cdot 625 \times 10^{-34}$ J s. This concept that energy can only occur in integral multiples of little packets or quanta enabled Planck to deduce the equation

$$Q(v)\,dv = \frac{8\pi hv^3}{c^3}\,\frac{1}{\exp\left[(hv/kT)-1\right]}\,dv \qquad (2.1)$$

A plot of $Q(v)$ against v based on Equation 2.1 gives a curve which agrees with that obtained experimentally. This triumph of the concept of the quantisation of energy inaugurated a revolution in the fundamentals of physics of phenomena on the atomic and molecular scale of dimensions.

The expression for $Q(\lambda)$, where λ is the wavelength corresponding to the frequency v, is obtained on substituting $v = c/\lambda$ in Equation 2.1; where the wavelength interval $d\lambda$ is related to the frequency interval dv by differentiation of the equation

$$v = \frac{c}{\lambda}$$

to give

$$dv = -\frac{c}{\lambda^2}\,d\lambda$$

So Equation 2.1 can be expressed in the form

$$Q(\lambda)\,d\lambda = \frac{8\pi hc}{\lambda^5}\,\frac{1}{\exp\left[(hc/k\lambda T)-1\right]}\,d\lambda \qquad (2.2)$$

This great pioneer work of Planck led subsequently to two further results which form substantial foundation stones of the quantum theory: the first was the theoretical work of Einstein in 1905 on the photoelectric effect; the second, in 1913, was the theory of Niels Bohr of the spectrum of the hydrogen atom.

2.2 Einstein's Equation for the Photoelectric Effect

In his theory of the emission of radiation by a heated body, Planck postulated that any change in the energy of a vibrating molecule within the body must take place in integral multiples of $h\nu$ when radiation of frequency ν is emitted; however, he did not assume that the energy in the radiation itself was quantised. Possibly he was reluctant to do this because of the powerful hold of the electromagnetic theory of radiation.

It was Einstein who, in 1905, put forward the idea that the radiation itself was in the form of quanta, later called *photons*. He used this hypothesis to explain the emission of electrons from the surface of a conducting material when illuminated by monochromatic radiation of frequency ν. The energy $h\nu$ of a photon in this radiation must exceed ϕe, the work function energy of the material, to cause electrons to be ejected. The excess of $h\nu$ over ϕe will give the ejected electrons their maximum kinectic energy $\frac{1}{2}m_e v_m^2$, where v_m is their maximum velocity and m_e is the mass of an electron.

The appropriate equation for the photoelectric emissive effect is therefore

$$h\nu - \phi e = \tfrac{1}{2} m_e v_m^2 \qquad (2.3)$$

This result was amply verified by the experiments of Millikan and others on the photoelectric effect. Equation 2.3, deduced by the use of a quantum theory of radiation, gives correct results which cannot be explained by the electromagnetic theory of radiation. Two main considerations in this connection are:

1. The maximum energy with which electrons are emitted from a given material depends only on the frequency ν of the incident radiation; it does not depend on the illumination of the surface. This is in accordance with quantum theory.

   On a wave theory basis, on the other hand, it would certainly be expected that the amount of energy concentrated on one electron in the surface would be dependent on the illumination. For example, for a lamp which approximates to a point source, halving the lamp-to-surface separation would increase this energy calculated on a wave basis by four times. But this change of illumination has no influence on the energy of the ejected electrons. The *number* of electrons emitted per second will, however, increase in direct proportion to the illumination.

2. As an example, suppose a collimated beam of light of wavelength $\lambda = 5,000\text{Å}$ falls normally on a photocathode surface of work function energy 1 eV and that the beam conveys to this surface an energy of $10^{-9}\,\text{J m}^{-2}\,\text{s}^{-1}$. Experiment shows

that electrons are emitted as soon as the photocathode receives the light, the time lag being less than a few nanoseconds. This is explicable on the basis that the light is in the form of photons; as soon as any one photon of energy

$$hv = \frac{hc}{\lambda} = \frac{6 \cdot 625 \times 10^{-34} \times 3 \times 10^{18}}{5,000} = 4 \times 10^{-19} \text{ J}$$

reaches the surface, it makes available energy of $4 \times 10^{-11}/(1 \cdot 6 \times 10^{-19}) = 2 \cdot 5$ eV. Since this exceeds the work function energy of 1 eV, electrons with a maximum energy of $1 \cdot 5$ eV are emitted. Considering the light as electromagnetic waves, the area of the photocathode which is effectively illuminated by any one wave is $\lambda^2 = (5 \times 10^{-7})^2$ m^2. The rate at which energy is expended over this area by the beam of light is $10^{-9} \times 25 \times 10^{-14}$ J s^{-1}. To provide the necessary work function energy of 1 eV $= 1 \cdot 6 \times 10^{-9}$ J would consequently require a time given by

$$\frac{1 \cdot 6 \times 10^{-19}}{25 \times 10^{-23}} = 6 \cdot 4 \times 10^2 \text{ s}$$

This implies that an electron could not be emitted unless there were a time lag of $10\frac{2}{3}$ min, which is completely out of accordance with the experimental facts.

2.3 The Bohr Theory of the Spectrum of the Hydrogen Atom

Atomic spectra are in the form of lines, molecular spectra have a band appearance, the spectrum of radiation from a heated solid body is a continuum.

The simplest atom is that of hydrogen: the nucleus is a proton, and outside the nucleus is a single electron. Hydrogen gas is normally in the molecular state, the hydrogen molecule H_2 consisting of two hydrogen atoms bonded together. If an electrical discharge is maintained in hydrogen, the molecular bonds will be split up. The emission spectrum from a hydrogen discharge is thus due primarily to the atoms: a line spectrum is observed.

The work of Balmer in 1885 and subsequent investigations by Rydberg in 1890, Lyman in 1906 and Paschen in 1908 established the empirical equation

$$\bar{v} = R \left(\frac{1}{m^2} - \frac{1}{n^2} \right) \tag{2.4}$$

where $\bar{v}$ is the wave number (the reciprocal of the wavelength), m and n are integers with $m < n$, and R is a constant. This equation gave the wave numbers of the lines seen in the emission spectrum of hydrogen. In the ultra-violet region, studied by Lyman, $m = 1$ and $n = 2$, 3, 4,...; in the visible region, $m = 2$ and $n = 3$, 4, 5,...; in the infra-red region, studied by Paschen, $m = 3$ and $n = 4$, 5, 6,....

There was no fundamental explanation of this equation until the work of Bohr in 1913. In particular, no clear idea had been presented as to why the radiation should be at discrete wavelengths and the occurrence of an equation involving a difference term of the form $(1/m^2) - (1/n^2)$ was a mystery.

In 1911, Rutherford and his co-workers had established the nuclear model of the atom by their work on the large-angle scattering of alpha particles transmitted through a thin foil. This model, with a central positive nucleus of charge Ze, where Z is the atomic number and e the electronic charge, surrounded by electrons in elliptical orbits decided by the electrostatic attraction between the nucleus and the electrons in accordance with the Coulomb inverse square law, was established for atoms in the thin metallic foils of the metals used in the scattering experiments. Assuming that this model also held for the hydrogen atom and for the simplest case where the elliptical orbit of the electron is a circle with the nucleus at the centre, Bohr extended the quantum ideas of Planck and Einstein to obtain a fundamental explanation of the Balmer equation.

The electron is considered to rotate in a circular orbit around the nucleus; in doing so, it is subject to an electrostatic force of attraction towards the central nucleus which is balanced against its mass times its radial acceleration away from the nucleus. The appropriate equation is therefore

$$\frac{Ze \times e}{4\pi\varepsilon_0 r^2} = \frac{m_e v^2}{r} \tag{2.5}$$

where m_e is the mass of the electron, v is its linear velocity along the tangent of the orbit of radius r, and ε_0 is the permittivity of free space.

The electron is subject to radial acceleration. In accordance with electromagnetic theory, accelerated charge radiates energy. The rotating electron should therefore radiate energy continuously and spiral into the nucleus in so doing. The concept of the planetary model becomes untenable. Faced with this dilemma, Bohr asserted that the electron did *not* always radiate energy continuously, so the electromagnetic theory was inadequate in this context. It remained to formulate a quantum approach to this problem. To do this, Bohr introduced the postulate that 'stationary states' exist in the atom. In a stationary state, electrons in the atom can only rotate around the nucleus in certain allowed orbits obeying specified quantum conditions. An electron can rotate indefinitely in such an orbit without radiating energy.

The quantum condition demanded in such a stationary state was shown to be that the action (linear momentum multiplied by distance) of the electron in traversing once a circular orbit is an integral multiple of Planck's constant h. This condition is therefore expressed mathematically as

$$m_e v \times 2\pi r = nh \tag{2.6}$$

The integer n became known subsequently as the *principal quantum number*.

It remained to explain how the atom *could* radiate energy. Bohr alleged that such radiation was the consequence of a transition of an electron from one allowed orbit to another. For energy to be emitted, this demands that the energy of the atom in the initial stationary state exceeds that in the final stationary state. The postulate needed can be worded in the following form: if an electron is rotating in an allowed orbit for which the energy of the corresponding stationary state of the atom is E_n, it can make a quantum jump to another allowed orbit for which the energy of the stationary state of the atom is E_m. If $E_n > E_m$, this transition will result in the emission of a photon of energy $h\nu$, where ν is the frequency of the radiation. Thus

$$E_n - E_m = h\nu \tag{2.7}$$

Considering the mechanism further, the hydrogen atom is initially in an unexcited ground state with its electron in an orbit at the minimum allowed distance from the nucleus. Let the energy of the atom in this ground state be E_0. Within a gaseous discharge or consequent upon other means of excitation, the electrons can be raised to allowed orbits of larger radii, for which the energies of the stationary states of the atom are E_n. The atom can only normally remain in such an excited state for a time less than 10^{-8} s. Under the electrostatic attraction of the nucleus, the electron makes a transition to another allowed orbit, whereby the energy of the atom is reduced from E_n to E_m where $E_n > E_m$. The frequencies ν of the emitted radiations are consequently decided by the relationship

$$\nu = \frac{E_n - E_m}{h} \tag{2.8}$$

where a range of values of E_n corresponding to $n = 2, 3, 4 \ldots$ exist, and also of E_m corresponding to $m = 1, 2, 3, \ldots$, where E_0 is the value of E_m for $m = 1$.

The normal unexcited atom in the energy state E_0 can only absorb radiation at frequencies decided by the relationship

$$\nu = \frac{E_n - E_0}{h} \tag{2.9}$$

The absorption spectrum is immediately seen to contain fewer lines than the emission spectrum, because there is only one value of E_0 in Equation 2.9 but a series of values of E_m in Equation 2.8; this is in accordance with experimental observation.

The energy of a hydrogen atom due to its electron is equal to the sum of the potential energy E_p and the kinetic energy E_k. The latter is $\frac{1}{2}m_e v^2$, assuming that the electron does not move with relativistic speeds. To specify the potential energy E_p, it is assumed that this is zero when the electron is removed to outside the influence of the nucleus, i.e. the atom is ionised, tantamount to the radius r becoming infinite. Therefore the potential energy when the electron is at a distance r from the nucleus is decided by the work done on the electron in bringing it from infinity to the distance r. This will be negative, because the electron is attracted to the nucleus. Therefore

$$E_p = \int_{\infty}^{r} \frac{Ze^2}{4\pi\varepsilon_0 r^2}\, \mathrm{d}r = \frac{-Ze^2}{4\pi\varepsilon_0 r}$$

The energy E_n of a hydrogen atom with its electron at distance r is therefore given by

$$E_n = E_k + E_p = \frac{1}{2}m_e v^2 - \frac{Ze^2}{4\pi\varepsilon_0 r}$$

As

$$\frac{m_e v^2}{r} = \frac{Ze^2}{4\pi\varepsilon_0 r^2}$$

so

$$\frac{1}{2}m_e v^2 = \frac{Ze^2}{8\pi\varepsilon_0 r}$$

Therefore

$$E_n = -\frac{1}{2}m_e v^2 = -\frac{Ze^2}{8\pi\varepsilon_0 r} \tag{2.10}$$

Collecting together the equations relevant to the Bohr theory of the hydrogen atom:

$$\frac{Ze^2}{4\pi\varepsilon_0 r^2} = \frac{m_e v^2}{r} \tag{2.5}$$

$$2\pi r m_e v = nh \tag{2.6}$$

$$E_n - E_m = h\nu \tag{2.7}$$

$$E_n = -\frac{1}{2}m_e v^2 = -\frac{Ze^2}{8\pi\varepsilon_0 r} \tag{2.10}$$

If Equation 2.5 is divided by Equation 2.6,

$$v = \frac{Ze^2}{2\varepsilon_0 nh}$$

Substituting this expression for v in Equation 2.10,

$$E_n = -\frac{1}{2}\, m_e\, \frac{Z^2 e^4}{4\varepsilon_0^2 n^2 h^2} = \frac{-Z^2 e^4 m_e}{8\varepsilon_0^2 n^2 h^2} \tag{2.11}$$

Hence, Equation 2.7 becomes

$$hv = -\frac{Z^2 e^4 m_e}{8\varepsilon_0^2 h^2} \left(\frac{1}{n^2} - \frac{1}{m^2} \right)$$

Therefore

$$\bar{v} = \frac{v}{c} = \frac{Z^2 e^4 m_e}{8\varepsilon_0^2 ch^3} \left(\frac{1}{m^2} - \frac{1}{n^2} \right) \tag{2.12}$$

This equation compares with the empirical Balmer equation (Equation 2.4) where the constant R, known as the Rydberg constant, is given by

$$R = \frac{e^4 m_e}{8\varepsilon_0^2 ch^3} \tag{2.13}$$

for hydrogen, the atomic number Z being unity.

Substituting $e = 1 \cdot 6 \times 10^{-19}$ C, $m_e = 9 \cdot 11 \times 10^{-31}$ kg, $\varepsilon_0 = 8 \cdot 854 \times 10^{-12}$ F m^{-1}, $c = 3 \times 10^8$ m s^{-1} and $h = 6 \cdot 625 \times 10^{-34}$ J s,

$$R = \frac{(1 \cdot 6)^4 \times 10^{-76} \times 9 \cdot 11 \times 10^{-31}}{8 \times (8 \cdot 854 \times 10^{-12})^2 \times 3 \times 10^8 \times 6 \cdot 625^3 \times 10^{-102}} \quad \text{m}^{-1}$$

$$= 1 \cdot 098 \times 10^7 \text{ m}^{-1}$$

This value agrees to within 1 part in 1,000 with that found experimentally by spectroscopy. This major triumph firmly established the validity of the Bohr theory of the spectrum of the hydrogen atom and inaugurated a new quantum approach to the consideration of the radiation in the line spectra from excited atoms.

An energy-level diagram for the hydrogen atom shows the transitions between energy levels which give rise to the lines in the spectrum (Fig. 2.1). In this diagram, fine structure of the lines is neglected. It is drawn on the basis that the energy E_n is related to the principal quantum number n by Equation 2.11, which can be written in the form

$$E_n = -\frac{Rch}{n^2}$$

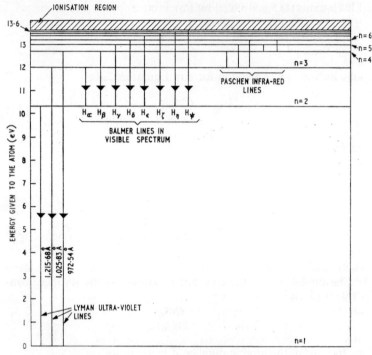

Fig. 2.1. Energy-level diagram for the hydrogen atom

To excite the atom from the ground state, in which $E_n = E_0$ and $n = 1$, to a stationary state, for which n is an integer exceeding one, requires an excitation energy E_e to be given *to* the atom decided by

$$E_e = Rch \left(\frac{1}{1^2} - \frac{1}{n^2} \right)$$

Therefore

$$E_e = 1{\cdot}098 \times 10^7 \times 3 \times 10^8 \times 6{\cdot}625 \times 10^{-34} \left(\frac{1}{1^2} - \frac{1}{n^2} \right) \text{ J}$$

$$= \frac{2{\cdot}182 \times 10^{-18}}{1{\cdot}6 \times 10^{-19}} \left(\frac{1}{1^2} - \frac{1}{n^2} \right) \text{ eV}$$

$$= 13{\cdot}67 \left(\frac{1}{1^2} - \frac{1}{n^2} \right) \text{ eV} \tag{2.14}$$

The energy required to excite the atom from the ground state to the state where $n = 2$ is therefore

$$E_e = 13{\cdot}67(1 - \tfrac{1}{4}) = 10{\cdot}25 \text{ eV}$$

This is the first excitation potential of the hydrogen atom. It is easily seen that the second excitation potential ($n = 3$) is $13 \cdot 67 \times \frac{8}{9} = 12 \cdot 15$ eV, and so on for $n = 4, 5, 6, \ldots$. Substitution of $n = \infty$ in Equation 2.14 corresponds to the removal of the electron to outside the atom (i.e. the ionisation of atom); thus the ionisation energy is $13 \cdot 67$ eV, which agrees reasonably well with the experimentally determined value of $13 \cdot 584$ eV.

The wave number of the radiation in the line spectrum corresponding to any transition is also readily calculated. For example, from $n = 3$ to $n = 2$ will result in radiation of wave number $\bar{v}$ given by Equation 2.12 as

$$\bar{v} = R \left(\frac{1}{2^2} - \frac{1}{3^2} \right)$$
$$= 1 \cdot 098 \times 10^7 \times 0 \cdot 139 \text{ m}^{-1}$$
$$= 1 \cdot 525 \times 10^6 \text{ m}^{-1}$$

The corresponding wavelength $= 1/\bar{v} = 6 \cdot 563 \times 10^{-7}$ m $= 6,563$ Å in the visible spectrum.

The energy-level diagram (Fig. 2.1) shows that the Balmer series of lines in the visible spectrum, known as the $H_\alpha, H_\beta, H_\gamma, \ldots$ lines, are brought about by electron transitions terminating at $n = 2$, the Lyman series in the ultra-violet are due to transitions terminating at $n = 1$, whilst lines in the infra-red part of the spectrum are caused by transitions terminating at $n = 3$ (Paschen series), $n = 4$ (Brackett series) and $n = 5$ (Pfund series).

The less convenient orbital picture of the hydrogen atom, with some of the electron transitions concerned, is shown in Fig. 2.2.

2.4 The Further Development of the Theory of Spectra

Bohr's theory of the spectrum of the hydrogen atom inaugurated a revolution in theoretical concepts in that it related the structure of the atom to the radiation it emits when excited and also to the radiation it absorbs. This theory forms, however, only the beginning of a study which has become very complex. This complexity is due to the necessity of accounting for the spectra of the atoms with several extra-nuclear electrons, and also to the advent of quantum mechanics which has demanded an extensive re-appraisal of fundamental ideas, even to the extent of rejecting the concept of electrons circuiting specific orbits.

Today, the theoretical treatment is quantum-mechanical; the notions about electrons confined to orbits about the nucleus need to be substantially modified and indeed are, strictly speaking, obsolete. But it is very demanding on mathematical knowledge

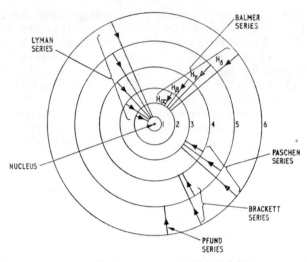

Fig. 2.2. Circular orbits for the hydrogen atom in the ground state (n = 1) and in excited states for which n = 2, 3, 4, 5 and 6

to study the subject from the purely quantum-mechanical stand-point; moreover, many of the ideas and much of the terminology still extant are based on the orbital approach; finally, the strict mathematical treatment tends to obscure insight into the physical processes involved.

The approach here is therefore to deal with the theory of spectra from the orbital standpoint and to show the modifications needed in the light of the quantum-mechanical treatment.

The topics arising in developing the theory, most of which are the concern of subsequent sections of this book, may be listed as follows:

1. In the theory of the spectrum of the hydrogen atom given in Section 2.3, the motion of the nucleus has been ignored. Moreover, the element may consist of a mixture of isotopes, so that nuclei with the same charge but different masses are involved.

2. An electron revolving about a nucleus under the action of an inverse square law of attraction will, in general, describe an elliptical orbit of which the circle is only a special case.

3. The electron will itself spin about its own axis as it revolves in an elliptical orbit about a nucleus.

4. The hydrogen atom has only one extra-nuclear electron. More complex atoms, ranging from helium (atomic number $Z = 2$) up to uranium ($Z = 92$) will have between two and

92 orbiting electrons. At first sight, this problem seems impossibly formidable. For example, iron ($Z = 26$) has 26 extra-nuclear electrons. Fortunately, a 26-body problem is not needed to explain its spectrum! For the energies involved in the production of spectra in the ultra-violet, infra-red and visible regions, only the outermost electrons and their motions are concerned. The problem is reducible to the consideration of spectra involving one, two or three electrons in the majority of cases.

5. A single line in an emission spectrum is split into a small number of lines when the emitting atoms are within a strong magnetic field: a phenomenon known as the *Zeeman effect*. There is a corresponding phenomenon in an intense electric field known as the *Stark effect*. The Zeeman effect is of fundamental importance in considering inter-relationships between the structure of atoms, radiation and magnetic phenomena.

6. Light scattered on its passage through a transparent medium exhibits components having frequencies different from those in the incident light. This phenomenon—which is inexplicable on the basis of the electromagnetic theory, but is rational in terms of the quantum theory—is known as the *Raman effect*.

7. The emission and absorption spectra of molecules will be considerably different from atomic spectra because of the bonds between atoms in the molecule. Band spectra and not line spectra are concerned.

8. The structure of the energy-levels for isolated atoms (in the gaseous or vapour state) will be substantially different from that involved for atoms in the solid state.

9. The nucleus of an atom has spin, which will result in a hyper-fine structure of the spectral lines emitted.

2.5 Influence of the Finite Mass of the Nucleus in the Bohr Theory of the Spectrum of the Hydrogen Atom

The nucleus of the hydrogen atom is a proton of mass $M_p = 1{,}836\,m_e$, where m_e is the rest mass of the electron. The theory given in Section 2.3 assumes that this nucleus is stationary, which is tantamount to considering it to be infinitely massive compared with the electron. In fact, the electron will not rotate about the nucleus but about the common centre of mass of the nucleus and the electron.

The centre of mass will be on the line joining the proton and the electron. If r is the separation between the proton and the electron,

r' is the distance from the proton to the centre of mass and r'' the distance from the centre of mass to the electron, clearly $r = r' + r''$ and

$$m_e r'' = M_p r' = M_p(r - r'')$$

Therefore

$$r'' = \frac{M_p r}{m_e + M_p}$$

and

$$r' = \frac{mr}{m_e + M_p}$$

The total moment of momentum of the electron and proton about the centre of mass is

$$m_e(r'')^2\omega + M_p(r')^2\omega$$

where ω is the angular velocity of the electron (or proton) about the centre of mass. Substituting for r'' and r' from the previous equations, the total moment of momentum is

$$\frac{\omega r^2}{(m_e + M_p)^2}(m_e M_p^2 + M_p m_e^2) = \frac{m_e M_p}{m_e + M_p}\,\omega r^2$$

This agrees with $m_e vr = m_e \omega r^2$ of Equation 2.6, provided that m_e is replaced by m_e', where

$$m_e' = \frac{m_e M_p}{m_e + M_p} \tag{2.15}$$

so that Equation 2.12 becomes

$$\bar{\nu} = \frac{Z^2 e^4 m_e'}{8\varepsilon_0^2 ch^3}\left(\frac{1}{m^2} - \frac{1}{n^2}\right) \tag{2.16}$$

The term m_e' is known as the 'reduced' mass of the electron.

Equation 2.12 would be correct if the mass of the nucleus were infinitely large. Thus, R in Equation 2.13 is best written as R_∞, the Rydberg constant for infinite mass. It is easily seen that the relationship between R_H and R_∞ is then

$$R_H = \frac{R_\infty M_p Z^2}{m_e + M_p} \tag{2.17}$$

where R_H is the Rydberg constant for hydrogen.

2.6 The Spectra of Deuterium and of Ionised Atoms having a Single Orbital Electron

Deuterium ($^2_1$H or $^2_1$D), singly ionised helium ($^4_2$He$^+$), doubly ionised lithium ($^7_3$Li^{++}), triply ionised beryllium ($^9_4$Be^{+++}), and so on, will all have nuclei surrounded by a single electron. For example, the $^7_3$Li atom has three orbital electrons and two of these are removed on doubly ionising positively. Deuterium and these ions would therefore be expected to have 'hydrogen-like' spectra. They will have, but the wave numbers of the lines concerned will be decided by an equation of the form

$$\bar{v} = RZ^2\left(\frac{1}{m^2} - \frac{1}{n^2}\right) = \frac{R_\infty M}{m_e + M}\left(\frac{1}{m^2} - \frac{1}{n^2}\right) \qquad (2.18)$$

where, for the atom or ion concerned, R is the Rydberg constant, M is the mass of its nucleus and Z the atomic number. For example, for singly ionised helium

$$\bar{v} = R_{\text{He}^+}Z^2\left(\frac{1}{m^2} - \frac{1}{n^2}\right) = \frac{R_\infty M_{\text{He}}}{m_e + M_{\text{He}}}Z^2\left(\frac{1}{m^2} - \frac{1}{n^2}\right) \qquad (2.19)$$

where R_{He^+} is the Rydberg constant for singly ionised helium, M_{He} is the mass of the helium nucleus, and $Z = 2$. The wave numbers of the lines in the spectrum of singly ionised helium will be therefore slightly different from four times the wave numbers of the lines in the hydrogen spectrum, the difference being due to the factor $M_{\text{He}}/(m_e + M_{\text{He}})$ where M_{He} is approximately equal to $7,300m_e$.

The example of deuterium is of interest: its spectrum will differ slightly from that of hydrogen because M is two atomic mass units instead of approximately one. This difference led to the original discovery of deuterium (heavy hydrogen) by Urey, Brickwedde and Murphy in 1932, who detected the difference in wave numbers by the use of a 21 ft concave grating spectrometer.

Spectrum lines are thus seen to exhibit fine structure (i.e. the fact that a single line as observed in a spectrometer of limited resolving power will be shown to have a multiplet structure on examination at higher resolution); this is brought about by the occurrence of isotopes whereby two or more kinds of atoms, having substantially the same electron configurations but nuclei of slightly different masses, are present in the emitter. It is stressed that there are several other causes of fine structure, some of more significance than the occurrence of isotopes. Nevertheless, spectroscopic study of fine structure is important in methods of determining isotopic constitution.

2.7 Electrons in Elliptical Orbits

Wilson in England and Sommerfeld in Germany, working independently in 1915 to 1916, developed Bohr's original quantum theory of the hydrogen atomic spectrum to take into account the fact that an electron rotating under a central attractive force to the nucleus, which varies inversely as the square of the electron-nucleus separation (ignoring the small correction due to motion of the nucleus), will follow an elliptical path which, in special circumstances only, is a circle.

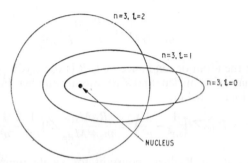

Fig. 2.3. Elliptical orbits for n = 3

They argued that each degree of freedom in the elliptical motion is separately quantised. From this premise it follows that only those specific elliptical orbits are allowable which satisfy the criterion

$$\frac{b}{a} = \frac{l+1}{n} \tag{2.20}$$

where b is the semi-minor axis and a the semi-major axis of the ellipse concerned, n is the principal quantum number and l the *orbital quantum number*, also an integer, such that the angular momentum of the electron about the nucleus is $lh/2\pi$.

The orbital quantum number l is a vector because it denotes angular momentum, and is considered to be in the direction perpendicular to the plane of the elliptical orbit. The possible values of l are $n-1, n-2, n-3, \ldots, 0$. If $n = 3$, for example, l can be 2, 1 or 0. Three orbits are therefore possible: they are shown in Fig. 2.3.

An empirical selection rule is found to hold whereby, in transitions of electrons from one orbit to another, l can only change by unity; thus $\Delta l = \pm 1$.

For a given value of a, the semi-major axis, a well-known result in non-relativistic dynamics is that, for a particle travelling in an elliptical orbit under an inverse square law of attraction to a fixed focus, the total energy is independent of the eccentricity of the ellipse. New energy levels of electrons in an atom due to their following elliptical orbits instead of only a circular one are thus apparently not introduced. Why, therefore, should there be any difference between transitions from or to any one of the three orbits illustrated in Fig. 2.3, for example? The answer is that a relativity correction is required. In its path in the ellipse, the electron will move faster in the immediate vicinity of the nucleus than it does further away. The mass changes in accordance with the equation of the special theory of relativity:

$$m = m_0(1-\beta^2)^{-1/2} \qquad (2.21)$$

where $\beta = v/c$, c being the velocity of light in free space, m_0 the mass of the particle at rest and m its mass when travelling with a velocity v.

The full, rather complicated, study of this relativistic correction leads to a picture of a precessing elliptical orbit whereby there *are* small energy changes with eccentricity. Consequently, fine structure of the spectrum lines results from the fact that n elliptical orbits are possible for a principal quantum number n, and these orbits have somewhat different energies.

The mechanics of elliptical orbits, elegantly developed by Sommerfeld, Wilson and others, has tended to be thrown into the limbo of theoretical physics because of the advent of quantum mechanics. Nevertheless, the spectral notation, still in current use, has come from these ideas. The system of notation is given in Table 2.1. Placing the principal quantum number n before the appropriate letter, gives, for example, a $4p$ electron as one for which $n = 4$ and $l = 1$. A simple picture of its elliptical motion via Equation 2.20 is then immediately visualised.

Table 2.1.

THE SPECTRAL NOTATION OF ORBITING ELECTRONS IN ATOMS

Orbital angular momentum of the electron = $lh/2\pi$, where l is	0	1	2	3	4	5	6	7
State of the electron denoted by	s	p	d	f	g	h	i	j
Corresponding state of the atom denoted by	S	P	D	F	G	H	I	J

Note from Equation 2.20 that, when $b = a$, the ellipse is a circle. Circular orbits thus correspond to $l+1 = n$. It follows that $1s$, $2p$, $3d$, $4f$, $5g$, ... electrons are all in circular orbits.

2.8 Electron Spin

In several cases of the fine structure of spectra, the hypothesis of elliptical orbits has proved not to furnish an adequate explanation. In particular, the spectra of the alkali metals (for which the optical spectra involve transitions of only the single-valence electron) have lines which exhibit a doublet structure (the well-known example being the sodium D lines at wavelengths of 5,890 Å and 5,896 Å) which could not be explained.

In 1925, Goudsmit and Uhlenbeck postulated that the electron rotated about its own axis at the same time as it was rotating in an elliptical orbit about the nucleus. The obvious analogy is with the spin of the Earth and the other planets about their axes as they revolve around the Sun, though it is not satisfactory to read too much into such an analogy or even the concept of physical spin of the electron itself. They further assumed that this spin had an angular momentum of $\frac{1}{2}(h/2\pi)$ and was represented by a spin quantum number $s = \frac{1}{2}$.

This spin quantum number s was shown to be associated with the orbital quantum number l in such a way that

$$j = l \pm s$$

where j is an additional quantum number, called the *inner quantum number*, and s is either parallel or anti-parallel to l. An electron in a $2p$ state, for example, having $l = 1$, would therefore have $j = 1\frac{1}{2}$ or $\frac{1}{2}$. The full designation of this electron state is therefore $2p_{1/2}$ and $2p_{3/2}$, abbreviated to $2^2p_{1/2}$.

Again, an empirical selection rule applies to allowed transitions between orbits whereby j can only change by 0 or ± 1, so $\Delta j = 0$ or ± 1.

2.9 The Magnetic Quantum Numbers; Space Quantisation

The Zeeman effect has already been mentioned (Section 2.4) concerning the effect of a magnetic field on the spectra emitted by excited atoms. It is to be expected that the interactions between a magnetic field and an atom should also be quantised in some fashion.

As an electron in motion inevitably produces a magnetic effect, an electron in an elliptical orbit about a nucleus would be expected to have a magnetic moment. The analogy is with the closed-current loop and its equivalence to a magnetic dipole. The electric current I equivalent to the charge e of an electron rotating f times per second around the nucleus in an elliptical orbit (Fig. 2.4) is given by $I = ef$, where I is in amperes if e is in coulombs. If the area of this elliptical orbit is A, the magnetic moment M due to this current is directed perpendicularly to the plane of the orbit and given by

$$M = \mu_0 I A \qquad (2.22)$$

where μ_0 is the magnetic permeability of free space.

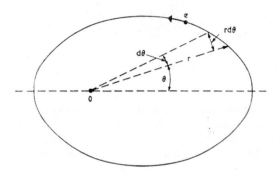

Fig. 2.4. *Magnetic moment of an electron in an elliptical orbit*

The area A is easily seen from Fig. 2.4 to be given by

$$A = \tfrac{1}{2} \int_0^{2\pi} r^2 \, d\theta \qquad (2.23)$$

The angular momentum p of the electron of mass m_e moving in an elliptical orbit is constant (a fact which follows from Kepler's laws in dynamics in the non-relativistic case, assumed here for simplicity). Therefore,

$$p = m_e r^2 \frac{d\theta}{dt} = \text{constant} \qquad (2.24)$$

Equation 2.23 can therefore be written as

$$A = \frac{1}{2} \int_0^T \frac{p}{m_e} \, dt = \frac{pT}{2m_e}$$

where $T = 1/f$ is the time taken by the electron to complete one circuit in the orbit.

Equation 2.22 therefore becomes

$$M = \frac{\mu_0 e}{T} \times \frac{pT}{2m_e} = \frac{\mu_0 pe}{2m_e} \qquad (2.25)$$

But the angular momentum $p = lh/2\pi$, so

$$M = l\frac{\mu_0 he}{4\pi m_e} \qquad (2.26)$$

The factor $\mu_0 he/4\pi m_e$ depends only on fundamental constants: it is regarded as a fundamental unit of magnetic moment β, known as the *Bohr magneton*. The value of β is found by putting $\mu_0 = 4\pi \times 10^{-7} \text{ H m}^{-1}$, $h = 6 \cdot 62 \times 10^{-34} \text{ J s}$, and $e/m_e = 1 \cdot 759 \times 10^{11} \text{ C kg}^{-1}$. Therefore

$$\beta = \frac{4\pi \times 10^{-7} \times 6 \cdot 62 \times 10^{-34} \times 1 \cdot 759 \times 10^{11}}{4\pi} = 1 \cdot 165 \times 10^{-29} \text{ Wb m}$$

When an atom containing an electron rotating in such an elliptical orbit is placed in an external magnetic field of flux density B, it would be expected that the plane of the orbit—and so the magnetic dipole of moment $l\beta$—would be oriented with respect to the direction of the magnetic field lines. This indeed occurs but, as shown by the Zeeman effect and by the experiments of Gerlach and Stern on the passage of beams of atoms through magnetic fields, it is found that the orientation of the vector l with respect to the field is subject to a remarkable phenomenon known as *space quantisation*.

According to the principle of space quantisation, the directions that the vector l (perpendicular to the plane of the orbit and in the direction of the magnetic moment due to the orbit) can take up are only such that the projections of l in the directions of the flux density B are integers. In Fig. 2.5, therefore, where $l = 3$, the directions of l with respect to the flux direction along B must be such that the projections of l on the line B have the integral values $0, 1, 2, 3, -1, -2, -3$.

The projections of l on the direction of the magnetic flux are designated by m_l, called the *orbital magnetic quantum number*. There are clearly $2l+1$ values of m_l, all of which are integers, of possible values $\pm l$, $\pm(l-1)$, $\pm(l-2)$, ..., 0.

There is also a *spin magnetic quantum number* m_s, which is associated with the magnetic moment due to the spin of the electron about its own axis. A simple analytical treatment of this concept is not possible. It must suffice to assert that the spin magnetic moment is found to have a value of β, the Bohr magneton, and that a wide variety of magnetic phenomena can be explained on this basis.

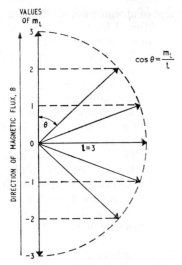

Fig. 2.5. Space quantisation and the orbital magnetic quantum numbers

The corresponding spin magnetic quantum number m_s can have only two values, $+\frac{1}{2}$ or $-\frac{1}{2}$, depending on whether it is parallel or anti-parallel to the external magnetic flux.

2.10 The Pauli Exclusion Principle and the Basis of the Periodic Table of the Elements

The quantum numbers so far introduced are n, l, s, j, m_l and m_s, and the vector combination of m_l and m_s gives rise to a seventh one, m_j. It is not necessary, however, to give all these seven quantum numbers to specify precisely the state of an electron in an atom. The principal quantum number n and the orbital quantum number l are necessary, but only two of the remaining five are needed. Of these five, those usually selected are m_l and m_s, because, then, the values of s, j and m_j are predetermined.

The four quantum numbers n, l, m_l and m_s are regarded as basic. They form a necessary and sufficient set to specify fully the quantum state of an electron in an atom.

In 1925, Pauli put forward his famous *exclusion principle* which may be stated in the form that *each and every electron in an atom has a quantum state which corresponds to the specification of the four basic quantum numbers, that all of the electrons which make up the structure of a given atom are different in this respect, and that no two electrons can exist in the atom in the same quantum state* (i.e. no two electrons can have the same set of quantum numbers n, l, m_l and m_s).

For a given element of atomic number Z, there are Z electrons in the extra-nuclear structure. Electrons in a given atom having the same principal quantum number n are said to be in the same *shell*. For the K shell, $n = 1$; for the L shell, $n = 2$; for the M shell, $n = 3$; for the N shell, $n = 4$, and so on.

Electrons within a given shell in an atom which have the same orbital quantum number l are said to be in the same *sub-shell*. There are consequently sub-shells corresponding to $l = 0$ (designated by letter s for the electron), $l = 1$ (letter p), $l = 2$ (letter d), $l = 3$ (letter f) and so on (see Table 2.1).

Within a given sub-shell for which the principal quantum number is l, there are $2l+1$ possible values of the orbital magnetic quantum number m_l (Section 2.9), and each of these may have two different values of the spin magnetic quantum number m_s, which is either $\frac{1}{2}$ or $-\frac{1}{2}$. In accordance with the exclusion principle, it therefore follows that the maximum possible number of electrons in a given sub-shell is $2(2l+1)$.

It further follows that the maximum possible number of electrons in a shell for which the principal quantum number is n is decided by the summation of all possible values of $2(2l+1)$, where $l = 0, 1, 2, \ldots, n-1$. This maximum number is consequently given by

$$\sum_{l=0}^{l=n-1} 2(2l+1) = 2\{1+3+5+ \ldots +[2(n-1)+1]\}$$
$$= 2n^2$$

In addition to the principle whereby electrons go into different quantum states with $2n^2$ in a shell for which the principal quantum number is n and $2(2l+1)$ in a sub-shell for which the orbital quantum number is l, the electrons, in taking up 'positions' around a nucleus, go into the most tightly bound state possible, so entering the lowest possible energy levels. This means that the shell with $n = 1$ will become filled first, then that with $n = 2$, and so on. The maximum possible number of electrons in successive shells with $n = 1, 2, 3, 4$ and 5 are therefore $2, 8, 18, 32$ and 50. The first thirteen elements from hydrogen ($Z = 1$) to aluminium ($Z = 13$) in the periodic table are considered in Table 2.2.

In Table 2.2 in relation to atomic spectra, it is noteworthy that lithium and sodium each has a single electron outside a closed shell structure. They are consequently monovalent and exhibit one-electron type optical spectra; only this outermost electron is concerned in transitions which give rise to spectra in the optical region. On the other hand, beryllium and magnesium are seen to be divalent and will give two-electron optical spectra, whilst boron and aluminium are trivalent and have three-electron spectra.

Table 2.2.

ELECTRONS IN THE K, L AND M SHELLS OF THE FIRST THIRTEEN ELEMENTS

Element	Z	K shell ($n = 1$) $l = 0$ $1s$	L shell ($n = 2$) $l = 0$ $2s$	$l = 1$ $2p$	M shell ($n = 3$) $l = 0$ $3s$	$l = 1$ $3p$	$l = 2$ $3d$
Hydrogen	1	1					
Helium	2	2*					
Lithium	3	2	1				
Beryllium	4	2	2‡				
Boron	5	2	2	1			
Carbon	6	2	2	2			
Nitrogen	7	2	2	3			
Oxygen	8	2	2	4			
Fluorine	9	2	2	5			
Neon	10	2	2	6†			
Sodium	11	2	2	6	1		
Magnesium	12	2	2	6	2		
Aluminium	13	2	2	6	2‡	1	

* Shell filled: an inert gas.

† Maximum number in sub-shell with $l = 1$, shell filled: an inert gas.

‡ Maximum number in sub-shell with $l = 0$.

2.11 Spectra of the Alkali Metals

Table 2.2 shows that the alkali metals lithium and sodium each has a single electron in the outermost sub-shell which surrounds a closed shell structure. These elements are in group 1A of the periodic table; they exhibit one-electron spectra and are monovalent. The further alkali metals in group 1A are potassium ($Z = 19$), rubidium ($Z = 37$) and caesium ($Z = 55$). The potassium atom has filled K and L shells, having together 10 electrons, and the remaining nine electrons are in the M shell, for which $n = 3$ and which can therefore contain a total of 18 electrons. Of these nine electrons, two are in the sub-shell $3s$ (for which $l = 0$) and six in the sub-shell $3p$ (for which $l = 1$). The final valence or optical electron would hence be expected to be in the unfilled sub-shell $3d$ (for which $l = 2$). In fact, it is not but is in the fourth or N shell in the $4s$ state. This is because the principle of least energy operates, rather than the quantum considerations, in deciding the state of the atom. Similarly, it can be shown that the other alkali metals, rubidium and caesium, have a single optical electron in the outermost shell: the O shell ($n = 5$) for rubidium, and the P shell ($n = 6$) for caesium.

The alkali metals are consequently monovalent with a single electron responsible for the transitions which give rise to the spectra in the visible or near-visible regions. In considering such spectra, the chief features are explicable on the basis that this single electron undergoes energy level changes outside a structure consisting of the nucleus (positive charge Ze) surrounded by a closed shell structure containing the other $Z - 1$ electrons.

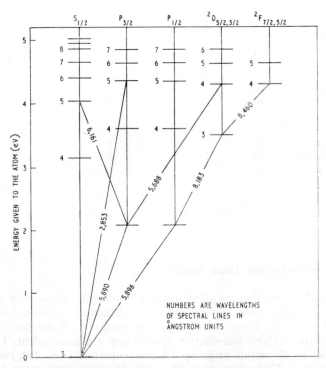

Fig. 2.6. Energy-level diagram for the sodium atom, showing some of the transitions in accordance with $\Delta j = 0$ or ± 1

The energy-level diagram and some of the transitions involved in the sodium atom are shown in Fig. 2.6. The well-known sodium doublet at wavelengths of 5,890 Å and 5,896 Å is explained as due to transitions of the atomic state represented by:

$3P_{3/2} \rightarrow 3S_{1/2}$, for which $\Delta j = 1$, to give the 5,890 Å line;

$3P_{1/2} \rightarrow 3S_{1/2}$, for which $\Delta j = 0$, to give the 5,896 Å line.

2.12 Spectra of Atoms Due to the Transitions of Two or Three Electrons

The elements beryllium and magnesium each has two electrons in the outermost sub-shell (Table 2.2). These are group IIA elements in the periodic table, of which the further members are calcium, strontium, barium and radium; in the companion group IIB occur zinc, cadmium and mercury. In all of these elements, two electrons are active in producing the emission spectra of the excited atoms.

Let one of these electrons be in an orbit for which the orbital quantum number is l_1 and the spin quantum number s_1, and the other have corresponding quantum numbers l_2 and s_2. In these group II elements, the spins combine vectorially to give a resultant spin S decided by

$$S = s_1 + s_2$$

and the orbital quantum numbers also combine vectorially but separately to give a resultant orbital quantum number L decided by the vector addition

$$L = l_1 + l_2$$

The spins s_1 and s_2 are both $\frac{1}{2}$, corresponding to spins of $\frac{1}{2}(h/2\pi)$, but the spins may be either parallel or anti-parallel to each other. Therefore the value of S is either 0 or 1.

The total inner quantum number J is decided by the vector addition

$$J = L + S$$

In the unexcited state, the two optical electrons are in an s state for which l is zero. However, when excited, these electrons can be raised to the p state, for example, for which l is a finite number. Suppose $l_1 = 1$ and $l_2 = 0$, then $L = 1$. Therefore, by vector addition, since $J = L + S$, $J = 1$ when $L = 1$ and $S = 0$. Following the system of notation in Table 2.1, $L = 1$ corresponds to a P state of the atom. A singlet level designated by $^1P_1$ is therefore involved.

The vector addition of $L = 1$ and $S = 1$, however, can take place in three different ways (Fig. 2.7) to give $J = 2$, 1 or 0, so there are three different levels because of slightly different energies of the magnetic interactions between orbital and spin motions, depending on their orientations. The three levels are now designated by $^3P_1$, $^3P_2$ and $^3P_0$, the superscript 3 denoting the triplet, and the subscript 1, 2 or 0 denoting the J value.

As a second example, suppose the values of l_1 and l_2 are both 1. The total orbital quantum number L is now the result of the vector addition

$$L = l_1 + l_2$$

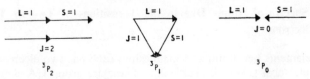

Fig. 2.7. The vector addition of **L** and **S**, where $L = 1$ and $S = 1$, to give $J = 2, 1$ or 0

which gives the results 0, 1 or 2 [Fig. 2.8(a)]. The corresponding atomic states are S, P or D respectively. As before, $S = 0$ or 1. Therefore for $L = 2$ and $S = 0$

$$J = L + S = 2$$

giving a singlet $^1D_2$. For $L = 2$ and $S = 1$, the value of J is found by the vector addition of $L + S$. From Fig. 2.8(b) this can be seen to give the value of J as 1, 2 or 3, i.e. there is a triplet $^3D_1$, $^3D_2$ and $^3D_3$. Transitions between such levels obey the selection rule $\Delta J = 0$ or ± 1. The complex pattern of spectral lines obtained can be interpreted in this way.

Typical elements in group III of the periodic table are boron and aluminium (Table 2.2). Now three electrons will be active in producing the spectrum of the excited atoms. For these light elements and several of the heavier ones, simplification of the mechanism of the energy levels involved arises because of *Russell–Saunders* or *LS coupling*. This type of coupling is such that the resultant spin quantum number S is the vector sum of the individual electron spin

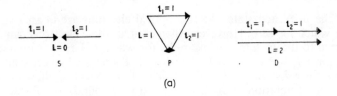

(a)

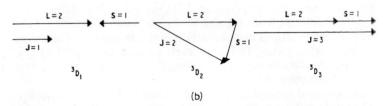

(b)

Fig. 2.8. (a) The vector addition of l_1 and l_2, where $l_1 = l_2 = 1$, to give $L = 0, 1$ or 2; (b) the vector addition of **L** and **S**, where $L = 2$ and $S = 1$, to give $J = 1, 2$ or 3

quantum numbers s_1, s_2 and s_3, each $\frac{1}{2}$, which are either all parallel so $S = \frac{3}{2}$, or with one anti-parallel so $S = \frac{1}{2}$. Furthermore, the resultant orbital quantum number L is separately the vector sum of the individual quantum numbers l_1, l_2 and l_3, i.e.

$$L = l_1 + l_2 + l_3$$

Also

$$J = L + S$$

is such that the resultant vector J is half-integral when S is half-integral.

For example, for $L = 2$ (a D term) the values of J are decided by either the vector addition of $L = 2$ and $S = \frac{3}{2}$ (which must give a result in the form of a half-integral, $\frac{7}{2}, \frac{5}{2}, \frac{3}{2}$ or $\frac{1}{2}$, corresponding to quadruplet energy levels designated by $^4D_{7/2}$, $^4D_{5/2}$, $^4D_{3/2}$ and $^4D_{1/2}$) or the vector addition of $L = 2$ and $S = \frac{1}{2}$ (giving half-integrals in the form of doublet energy levels denoted by $^2D_{3/2}$ and $^2D_{5/2}$).

Another mode of coupling in three-electron spectra, known as jj coupling, occurs but it is rare. The orbital quantum numbers l_1, l_2 and l_3 for the three electrons each combine vectorially with their individual quantum numbers s_1, s_2 and s_3 to give three inner quantum numbers j_1, j_2 and j_3. The resultant inner quantum number J is then decided by the vector addition

$$J = j_1 + j_2 + j_3$$

The explanation of the mechanisms involved in the interpretation of the spectra of the heavier trivalent elements is difficult; a type of coupling intermediate between Russell–Saunders (LS) and jj is involved.

2.13 The Wave Nature of 'Particles'

In 1924, Louis de Broglie extended quantum concepts to include aspects of the motion of particles. Before 1924, quantum theory had been concerned only with electromagnetic radiation, but de Broglie attributed to a particle of mass m travelling with a velocity v relative to the observer a wavelength λ given by

$$\lambda = \frac{h}{mv} = \frac{h}{p} \tag{2.27}$$

where $p = mv$ is the momentum of the particle, and h is Planck's constant.

This theoretical study by de Broglie was verified experimentally for electrons in 1927 with the work on the diffraction of electrons by crystals by Davisson and Germer and, soon afterwards, by G. P. Thomson. Subsequent experimental studies by other investigators established that this 'de Broglie' wavelength is also true for protons, atoms, molecules, neutrons and other particles.

In the years immediately following 1924, the subject of wave mechanics (quantum mechanics) was developed by Heisenberg, Schrödinger, Born and others who established the basic concepts and equations concerned in describing particle motions from the wave standpoint. These ideas revolutionised the original treatment of atomic spectra as initially given by Bohr and, in particular, enabled the intensities of spectral lines to be accounted for in relation to the probabilities of electron transitions, a topic about which the 'classical' quantum theory was relatively silent.

The electron has a mass of $m_e = 9 \times 10^{-31}$ kg. If it is accelerated through a potential difference of V V, it acquires a velocity of v m s^{-1} given by

$$\tfrac{1}{2}m_e v^2 = Ve$$

where e is the electronic charge $= 1 \cdot 6 \times 10^{-19}$ C. (The relativistic correction is ignored here.) Therefore

$$v = \sqrt{\frac{2Ve}{m_e}}$$

and the de Broglie wavelength of the electron in motion is given by substituting $h = 6 \cdot 625 \times 10^{-34}$ J s into Equation 2.27 as

$$\lambda = \frac{h}{m_e v} = \frac{h}{\sqrt{(2Vem_e)}}$$

or

$$\lambda = \frac{6 \cdot 625 \times 10^{-34}}{\sqrt{(2V \times 1 \cdot 6 \times 10^{-19} \times 9 \times 10^{-31})}} \text{ m}$$

Therefore

$$\lambda = \frac{12 \cdot 26}{\sqrt{V}} \times 10^{-10} \text{ m} = \frac{12 \cdot 26}{\sqrt{V}} \text{ Å} \qquad (2.28)$$

An electron accelerated from rest through $V = 100$ V, so acquiring an energy of 100 eV, therefore has a wavelength of $1 \cdot 226$ Å. This is of no account if it passes through, say, a spacing of $0 \cdot 1$ mm between grid wires in a thermionic vacuum tube but it is clearly of fundamental importance in describing interactions between electrons and lattice spacings in a crystal of the order of a few Ångstrom units and the motion of electrons in atoms of dimensions 1–5 Å.

The concept of the de Broglie wavelength gives immediately fundamental significance to the postulate of Bohr that, in the stationary state, an atom does not radiate energy and that this state corresponds to an electron in a circular orbit for which, from Equation 2.6,

$$2\pi r m_e v = nh$$

The assumption implicit in Equation 2.6 is satisfactory in that it led to the triumph of the Bohr theory of the hydrogen atom, but unsatisfactory in that there was no fundamental justification for it. Using the de Broglie hypothesis, however, $\lambda = h/m_e v$ inserted in Equation 2.6 gives

$$2\pi r = n\lambda$$

where n is an integer. The allowed orbits are consequently those which will exactly accommodate the de Broglie waves associated with electrons. An allowed orbit is thus one in which a stationary (or normal mode of) vibration takes place. The analogy is with the vibrations possible in a stretched string fixed at both ends.

2.14 Schrödinger's Equation for a Single Particle

In 1926, Schrödinger formulated the fundamental differential equation for the wave motion associated with a particle. In order to simplify the theory involved, consider a plane wave propagated in one direction along an x-axis with a wave velocity u, where the displacement is ψ at a time t. The differential equation representing wave motion is then

$$\frac{\partial^2 \psi}{\partial x^2} = \frac{1}{u^2} \frac{\partial^2 \psi}{\partial t^2} \tag{2.29}$$

The steady-state solution of this equation in the form of a simple harmonic function of time is

$$\psi = \Psi \exp j\omega t \tag{2.30}$$

where $\omega = 2\pi v$, v is the frequency and Ψ is the amplitude of the wave motion. If Equation 2.30 is differentiated twice, it gives

$$\frac{\partial^2 \psi}{\partial t^2} = -\omega^2 \Psi \exp j\omega t = -\omega^2 \psi$$

so Equation 2.29 becomes

$$\frac{\partial^2 \psi}{\partial x^2} = -\frac{\omega^2 \psi}{u^2} = -\frac{4\pi^2 v^2 \psi}{u^2} = -\frac{4\pi^2}{\lambda^2} \psi \tag{2.31}$$

because $u = v\lambda$. As these waves are associated with particles, Equation 2.27 must apply, so h/mv can be substituted for λ, where

m is the mass of the particle and v is the velocity of the particle along the x-axis (not the same as the wave velocity u). Equation 2.31 therefore becomes

$$\frac{\partial^2 \psi}{\partial x^2} = \frac{-4\pi^2}{(h/mv)^2}\,\psi \tag{2.32}$$

It is convenient to express this differential equation in terms of the total energy E and the potential energy V of the particle, where V is a function of x. Now

$$E = E_K + V$$

where E_K is the kinetic energy of the particle, given in the non-relativistic case by $E_K = \frac{1}{2}mv^2$. Therefore

$$mv = \sqrt{[2(E-V)m]} \tag{2.33}$$

Substituting for mv in Equation 2.32 from Equation 2.33 gives

$$\frac{\partial^2 \psi}{\partial x^2} = \frac{-8\pi^2(E-V)m}{h^2}\,\psi$$

Therefore

$$\frac{\partial^2 \psi}{\partial x^2} + \frac{8\pi^2 m}{h^2}(E-V)\psi = 0$$

Recalling the assumption that $\psi = \Psi \exp \mathrm{j}\omega t$, division throughout by $\exp \mathrm{j}\omega t$ gives

$$\frac{\partial^2 \Psi}{\partial x^2} + \frac{8\pi^2 m}{h^2}(E-V)\Psi = 0 \tag{2.34}$$

which is the steady-state form of Schrödinger's wave equation in one dimension for a single particle; it is independent of time.

This simple proof of Schrödinger's equation gives some insight into the elements of wave mechanics. It should be stressed, however, that the assumption implicit in Equation 2.30 is not strictly justifiable. In fact, taking into account that $E = h\nu$, it can be shown that ψ must be described by a complex expression of the form

$$\psi = C \exp\left[\pm \mathrm{j}(2\pi\nu t - kx)\right]$$

where it is customary to use the negative exponent. From this it can be shown that the amplitude Ψ is a complex quantity of the form $a + \mathrm{j}b$.

2.15 The Heisenberg Uncertainty Principle; The Probability Concept

A consequence of the de Broglie assertion as to the wave nature of a particle is that the position of a particle in space cannot be exactly specified. The electron cannot therefore be considered as having a position which is precisely defined by, for example, spherical polar coordinates (r,θ,ϕ) within an atom, because it is not possible to consider the electron as a point but only as a small group or packet of waves. Within the hydrogen atom, for example, the wavelength of the electron in the state where the principal quantum number is unity (i.e. the ground state) is shown in Section 2.13 to be equal to the circumference of the postulated circular orbit.

In 1927, Heisenberg enunciated his famous uncertainty principle. This may be expressed by the equation

$$\Delta x \, \Delta p_x \geqslant h \qquad (2.35)$$

when referring to a particle travelling along an x-axis with a momentum p_x at the position coordinate x. The term Δx is the uncertainty in the specification of x, Δp_x the uncertainty in determining p_x, and h is Planck's constant. It follows that the distance x of an electron from an origin can only be specified as being between x and $x + \Delta x$, and that Δx can only be reduced at the expense of increased lack of certainty in giving the linear momentum.

This principle sets a fundamental limit to the possibility of determining, by any conceivable experiment or theoretical method, the position of a particle in space. There is consequently no certainty in specifying the position of an electron in an atom: the picture of elliptical electron orbits is useful but fundamentally without precise meaning. What model of the atom exists therefore in quantum mechanics?

In dealing with wave motion, consider first the electromagnetic theory of light. Suppose the amplitude of the electric field strength in a uniform collimated beam of light at a point in space is E_0. The intensity of the light is proportional to E_0^2. If this beam of light were described from the particle point of view, the intensity at the point in question would be given by the number N of photons that passed per second through unit area drawn around the point in the plane perpendicular to the beam. As these two methods of specifying the intensity must be equivalent, it follows that

$$E_0^2 = \text{constant} \times N^2 \qquad (2.36)$$

where the constant of proportionality depends simply on the units chosen.

In describing the motions of electrons and other particles by quantum mechanical procedures, Schrödinger's equation is used. Solution of this equation gives Ψ, the amplitude of the wave motion associated with the particle at the coordinate x. In atomic structure, only one or a few electrons are involved and not a large number of them as with photons in a beam of light. The procedure, therefore, is to extend the idea implicit in Equation 2.36 by introducing the *probability concept*. For a small volume δv around a point with given coordinates, the probability P of the particle existing within δv is taken to be the product of δv and the square of the wave amplitude Ψ. Thus,

$$P = \text{constant} \times |\Psi|^2 \, \delta v \qquad (2.37)$$

where $|\Psi|$ is the modulus of the complex amplitude Ψ of the wave function.

2.16 The Quantum Mechanical Theory of the Hydrogen Atom

To use the Schrödinger time-independent equation in dealing with the probable locations of electrons in the theory of atomic structure, Equation 2.34 must be extended to three-dimensions. It becomes

$$\nabla^2 \Psi + \frac{8\pi^2 m_e}{h^2} (E - V)\Psi = 0 \qquad (2.38)$$

where m_e is the mass of the electron and ∇^2 is a differential operator which is given in Cartesian coordinates by

$$\nabla^2 = \frac{\partial^2}{\partial x^2} + \frac{\partial^2}{\partial y^2} + \frac{\partial^2}{\partial z^2}$$

and in spherical polar coordinates, which are obviously more appropriate in relating probable electron positions to a point nucleus (assumed to be stationary), by

$$\nabla^2 \Psi = \frac{\partial^2 \Psi}{\partial r^2} + \frac{2}{r} \frac{\partial \Psi}{\partial r} + \frac{1}{r^2} \frac{\partial^2 \Psi}{\partial \theta^2} + \frac{1}{r^2} \cot \theta \frac{\partial \Psi}{\partial \theta} + \frac{1}{r^2 \sin^2 \theta} \frac{\partial^2 \Psi}{\partial \phi^2}$$

$$(2.39)$$

where the spherical polar coordinates of the electron are (r, θ, ϕ) relative to the nucleus at the origin.

The potential energy V of the electron when at a distance r from the nucleus is $-Ze^2/4\pi\varepsilon_0 r$, as shown in Section 2.3. The equation to be solved for Ψ is therefore given by substituting this expression for V and Equation 2.39 for $\nabla^2 \Psi$ into Equation 2.38. It is convenient to put $\hbar = h/2\pi$. Thus,

$$\frac{\partial^2 \Psi}{\partial r^2} + \frac{2}{r}\frac{\partial \Psi}{\partial r} + \frac{1}{r^2}\frac{\partial^2 \Psi}{\partial \theta^2} + \frac{1}{r^2}\cot \theta \frac{\partial \Psi}{\partial \theta} + \frac{1}{r^2 \sin^2 \theta}\frac{\partial^2 \Psi}{\partial \phi^2} +$$

$$\frac{2m_e}{\hbar^2}\left(E + \frac{Ze^2}{4\pi\varepsilon_0 r}\right)\Psi = 0 \qquad (2.40)$$

Solutions of this wave equation are sought subject to the conditions that Ψ must be everywhere finite, single-valued, a continuous function of the coordinates (r, θ, ϕ) and have continuous first derivatives. These stipulations replace, in effect, the Bohr postulate of stationary states in the older theory.

The full solution of Equation 2.40 is complicated. It must suffice here to state that it can be conveniently expressed in the form of three equations:

$$\frac{d^2 f(r)}{dr^2} + \frac{2}{r}\frac{df(r)}{dr} + \frac{2m_e}{\hbar^2}\left(E + \frac{Ze^2}{4\pi\varepsilon_0 r}\right)f(r) = 0 \qquad (2.41)$$

where $f(r)$ is a function of r only,

$$\frac{d^2 f_1(\theta)}{d\theta^2} + \cot \theta \frac{df_1(\theta)}{d\theta} + l(l+1)f_1(\theta) - \frac{m_l^2 f_1(\theta)}{\sin^2 \theta} = 0 \qquad (2.42)$$

where $f_1(\theta)$ is a function of θ only, and m_l and l are constants, and

$$\frac{d^2 f_2(\theta)}{d\phi^2} + m_l^2 f_2(\phi) = 0 \qquad (2.43)$$

where $f_2(\phi)$ is a function of ϕ only. Moreover,

$$\Psi = f(r) f_1(\theta) f_2(\phi)$$

The conditions stipulated further demand that l and m_l are integers and that m_l has the $2l+1$ values $l, l-1, l-2, \ldots, 0, 1, 2, \ldots, l$. Solution of Equation 2.41 with these provisos results in an expression for the allowed energy values of the hydrogen atom which is the same as that given by Bohr (Equation 2.11).

It can further be shown that $\sqrt{[l(l+1)]}$ is the magnitude of the orbital quantum number l introduced in the elliptical orbit theory (Section 2.7) and that m_l is the magnitude of the orbital magnetic quantum number m_l introduced in Section 2.9.

A result of quantum mechanics which demands modification of previously expressed ideas is that the magnitudes of the quantum number vectors l and s are not simply l and s but $\sqrt{[l(l+1)]}$ and

$\sqrt{[s(s+1)]}$. This requires reappraisal of the ideas of vector addition of l and s to give the inner quantum number j. This vector addition must be such that the magnitude of j is not simply j but such that

$$\sqrt{[j(j+1)]} = \sqrt{[l(l+1)]} + \sqrt{[s(s+1)]}$$

(see Section 2.19).

It is an instructive simplification to consider only the spherically symmetrical example of the hydrogen atom, and so assume that Ψ varies only with the radius vector r. Equation 2.41 alone is then required because variations with θ and ϕ are ignored. Equation 2.41 can then be written as

$$\frac{d^2\Psi}{dr^2} + \frac{2}{r}\frac{d\Psi}{dr} + \frac{2m_e}{\hbar^2}\left(E + \frac{Ze^2}{4\pi\varepsilon_0 r}\right)\Psi = 0 \qquad (2.44)$$

The simplest solution of this equation is

$$\Psi = \exp\left(-ra\right) \qquad (2.45)$$

where a is a constant, a solution which satisfies the requirement that Ψ tends to zero at large distances r of the electron from the nucleus. Substituting in Equation 2.44 from Equation 2.45 gives

$$a^2 \exp\left(-ra\right) - \frac{2a}{r}\exp\left(-ra\right) + \frac{2m_e}{\hbar^2}\left(E + \frac{Ze^2}{4\pi\varepsilon_0 r}\right)\exp\left(-ra\right) = 0$$

Dividing through by $\exp\left(-ra\right)$,

$$a^2 - \frac{2a}{r} + \frac{2m_e}{\hbar^2}\left(E + \frac{Ze^2}{4\pi\varepsilon_0 r}\right) = 0 \qquad (2.46)$$

As Equation 2.46 must be true for all values of r, it follows that the sum of the terms which are independent of r must be zero. Therefore

$$a^2 + \frac{2m_e E}{\hbar^2} = 0 \qquad (2.47)$$

The coefficient of $1/r$ must also be zero. Therefore

$$-2a + \frac{2m_e}{\hbar^2} \times \frac{Ze^2}{4\pi\varepsilon_0} = 0$$

or

$$a = \frac{m_e Ze^2}{4\pi\hbar^2\varepsilon_0} \qquad (2.48)$$

Substituting this value for a in Equation 2.47 gives

$$E = -\frac{\hbar^2 a^2}{2m_e} = -\frac{\hbar^2}{2m_e} \times \frac{m_e^2 Z^2 e^4}{16\pi^2 \hbar^4 \varepsilon_0^2} = -\frac{m_e Z^2 e^4}{32\pi^2 \hbar^2 \varepsilon_0^2}$$

or, as $h = 2\pi\hbar$,

$$E = -\frac{Z^2 e^4 m_e}{8\varepsilon_0^2 h^2} \qquad (2.49)$$

which is the same as for the expression for the energy E given by the Bohr theory for the case where the principal quantum number $n = 1$ (Equation 2.11).

Applying the probability concept, as expressed by Equation 2.37, to the hydrogen atom, it is seen that the probability of finding the electron within the spherical shell having inner and outer radii of r and $r + \delta r$ is decided by $|\Psi|^2 \, 4\pi r^2 \delta r$ because $\delta v = 4\pi r^2 \delta r$. Presuming that $|\Psi|^2$ has been evaluated for the hydrogen atom, the probability P_r of the electron being at a distance r from the nucleus is therefore given by

$$P_r = \text{constant} \times |\Psi|^2 \, r^2$$

Plots of P_r against r are given for the hydrogen atom in Fig. 2.9, for the principal quantum numbers $n = 1$, 2 and 3.

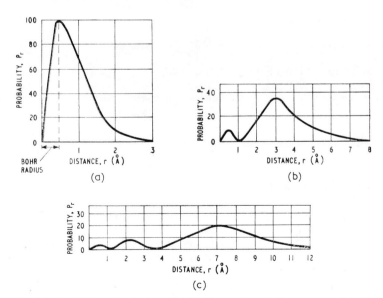

Fig. 2.9. Probability distributions for the electron in a hydrogen atom: (a) for $n = 1$; (b) for $n = 2$; (c) for $n = 3$

The quantum-mechanical picture of the hydrogen atom (with extensions to more complicated atoms) is different from the Bohr or older quantum theory model. The electron is now considered to have a probability of existing at any distance from the nucleus, though its exact position cannot be specified because of the uncertainty principle. Indeed, as shown by the graphs of Fig. 2.9, the electron has a very small probability not only of existing very close to the nucleus but also at distances significantly greater than the Bohr orbital dimensions. This model is more satisfying than the curious Bohr one in which electrons can only exist in certain specific orbits with 'nothing' between these orbits.

The most probable position of the electron within the electron 'cloud' about the nucleus is where P_r is a maximum. Where $n = 1$ and the hydrogen atom is spherically symmetrical, putting $\Psi = \exp(-ra)$ from Equation 2.45 gives

$$P_r = \text{constant} \times r^2 \, |\Psi|^2 = \text{constant} \times r^2 \exp(-2ra)$$

The maximum value of P_r occurs at $r = r_1$, where

$$\frac{\mathrm{d}}{\mathrm{d}r}[r^2 \exp(-2ra)] = 0$$

i.e. where

$$-2a \exp(-2r_1a)r_1^2 + 2r_1 \exp(-2r_1a) = 0$$

Thus

$$r_1 = \frac{1}{a}$$

Substituting for a from Equation 2.48,

$$r_1 = \frac{4\pi\hbar^2\varepsilon_0}{m_eZe^2} = \frac{\varepsilon_0h^2}{\pi m_eZe^2}$$

which is the same as the Bohr radius for $n = 1$.

2.17 The Zeeman Effect

This effect is that spectral lines are split up into components when the emitting atoms are placed in a magnetic field.

The effect may be observed in a college experiment by the use of a neon-filled Geissler tube placed in a strong magnetic field provided by an electromagnet. The *longitudinal effect* is observed in the light emanating from the discharge tube in the direction of the magnetic field lines. This requires that a hole be bored in one of the magnet pole-pieces [Fig. 2.10(a)]. The *transverse effect* is observed in the light passing perpendicularly to the magnetic field lines; this is more convenient in practice as it does not require a bored pole-piece.

If the frequency of one of the lines in the spectrum is v (zero magnetic field) it will be split into components of frequencies v_1 and v_2 when the magnetic field is applied. Observation of the longitudinal effect is represented in Fig. 2.10(b): the lines of frequency v_1 and v_2 (assuming there are only two) appear on either side of the position of the initial line of frequency v, which is absent. The light in

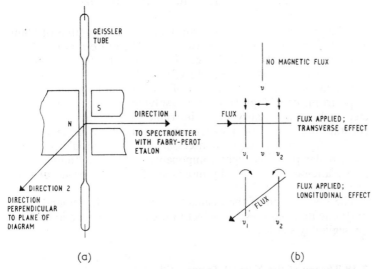

(a)   (b)

Fig. 2.10. Observation of the Zeeman effect: (a) experimental arrangement (direction 1 is longitudinal, and direction 2 is transverse); (b) appearance of spectrum lines (the light direction is perpendicular to the plane of the diagram)

these components is circularly polarised, one being in the clockwise direction and the other anticlockwise. In the transverse effect, the components again appear at v_1 and v_2 but their electric vectors are linearly polarised in the direction perpendicular to both the field direction and the light direction; furthermore, the original line of frequency v is now present.

It can be shown (Section 2.18) that

$$v_1 = v + \frac{Be}{4\pi m_e} \tag{2.50}$$

and

$$v_2 = v - \frac{Be}{4\pi m_e} \tag{2.51}$$

where B is the magnetic flux density in webers per square meter, e is the electronic charge in coulombs and m_e the mass of the electron in kilograms. If B is measured and the change of frequency $\Delta v = v_1 - v = v_2 - v$ is determined, the specific charge e/m_e of the electron can be found.

Given that $e/m_e = 1 \cdot 759 \times 10^{11}$ C kg^{-1}, suppose that a magnetic flux density of $0 \cdot 2$ Wb m^{-2} (2,000 gauss) is used. The change of frequency Δv is then

$$\Delta v = \frac{0 \cdot 2}{4\pi} \times 1 \cdot 759 \times 10^{11} = 2 \cdot 8 \times 10^9 \text{ Hz}$$

The frequency v will be at a corresponding wavelength λ of about 6,000 Å in the red of the spectrum, say. Therefore $v = (3 \times 10^{18})/ 6,000 = 5 \times 10^{14}$ Hz. The change of frequency brought about by a flux density of $0 \cdot 2$ Wb m^{-2} is therefore only $2 \cdot 8 \times 10^9$ in 5×10^{14}, or 1 part in $1 \cdot 78 \times 10^5$. Observation of such a small change requires a spectrometer of high chromatic resolving power; an interferometer such as the Fabry–Perot instrument in conjunction with a constant-deviation prism spectrometer is therefore demanded. As an interference technique is necessary, it is essential to change the circular-polarised light components in the longitudinal effect into plane-polarised light by insertion of an appropriate quarter-wave plate (Section 3.10).

The observation of the Zeeman effect obviously demands large magnetic flux densities; the effect in the Earth's magnetic field will be negligibly small.

2.18 Theory of the Normal Zeeman Effect

The Zeeman effect is often referred to in two connotations as the normal Zeeman effect and the anomalous Zeeman effect. This division is artificial, however: the distinction is that in the normal effect (which can be explained by classical electron theory) the spin of the electron is absent and only the electron orbital motion need be considered, whereas in the anomalous effect (which cannot be explained without quantum theory) both spin and orbital motions play a part.

The sophisticated theory of the Zeeman effect is a quantum-mechanical one. This is demanding mathematically and will not be attempted here. The theory given is based on the older quantum theory of electron orbits, but modifications are introduced as required in the light of quantum mechanics. Despite the artificiality of the distinction between the normal and anomalous effects, it is convenient to consider the normal effect first because it does not involve the introduction of electron spin.

The orbital angular momentum of an electron making an ellipti-cal circuit about a nucleus in an atom is given by $l\hbar$, where l is the orbital quantum number and $\hbar = h/2\pi$ (Section 2.7). Associated with this orbit is a magnetic moment of $l\beta$, where β is the Bohr magneton $= \mu_0 \, he/4\pi m_e$ (Section 2.9).

Suppose the elliptical orbit for the optical electron concerned is in a plane such that the perpendicular vector l of length $l\hbar$ (the angular momentum) is OA at an angle θ to the lines of force of a magnetic field of flux density B (Fig. 2.11). The vector OC of length $l\beta$ representing the magnetic dipole moment of the orbiting electron will also be perpendicular to the plane of the orbit.

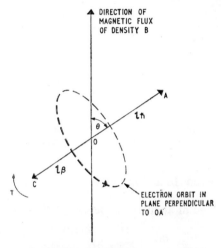

Fig. 2.11. Elliptical orbit of electron within a magnetic field (OA is not in general in the plane of the diagram; OC is anti-parallel to OA)

By convention, the vector representing the angular momentum of a body is drawn in the direction of forward travel of a right-handed corkscrew turned in the direction of the rotation of the body. The direction of OA in Fig. 2.11 is thereby decided. The con-ventional direction of the electric current in a circuit is that of a positive charge; the electron in the orbit is negatively charged. The equivalent conventional current direction is therefore opposite to that of the electron. The vector OC of length $l\beta$ representing the magnetic moment of the dipole equivalent to the circulating elec-tron is therefore anti-parallel to OA.

If a dipole of magnetic moment M is placed in a magnetic field of strength H at an angle θ to the field lines, it experiences a couple of magnitude $MH \sin \theta$. Hence the magnetic dipole of moment $l\beta$ will experience a couple T of magnitude $l\beta H \sin \theta$. The effect of this couple is to make the elliptical orbit precess about the magnetic field direction, so the vector OA of length $l\hbar$ will do likewise. Owing to this couple, acting perpendicular to OA, the angular momentum will change in direction but not in magnitude.

In Fig. 2.12(a), the vector $l\hbar$ is along OA at a time t, where OA is at an angle θ to OX, the direction of the magnetic flux of density B. Suppose OA moves to OD, still at the angle θ, in time δt, where the

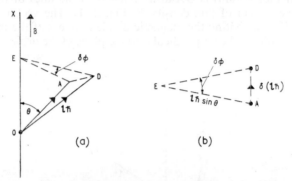

Fig. 2.12. *Precession of angular momentum vector* $l\hbar$ *about the direction of the magnetic flux (AE and DE are perpendicular to OX; OD is behind OA and* $\angle DOE = \theta$)

small angle between AE and DE (both drawn perpendicular to OX) is $\delta\phi$, and $AE = DE = l\hbar \sin \theta$. In Fig. 2.12(b), therefore, AD represents the change of angular momentum $\delta(l\hbar)$ in the time δt and

$$\delta\phi = \frac{AD}{EA} = \frac{\delta(l\hbar)}{l\hbar \sin \theta} \qquad (2.52)$$

Now $\delta(l\hbar)$ is due to the couple T acting for the time δt. Therefore

$$\delta(l\hbar) = T \, \delta t = l\beta H \sin \theta \, \delta t$$

so Equation 2.52 becomes

$$\frac{\delta\phi}{\delta t} = \frac{l\beta H \sin \theta}{l\hbar \sin \theta}$$

Hence, the angular velocity of precession of the elliptical orbit is ω, where

$$\omega = \frac{d\phi}{dt} = \frac{l\beta H \sin \theta}{l\hbar \sin \theta} = \frac{\beta H}{\hbar}$$

As $\beta = \mu_0 he/4\pi m_e$ and $\hbar = h/2\pi$,

$$\omega = \frac{\mu_0 Hhe/4\pi m_e}{h/2\pi} = \frac{\mu_0 He}{2m_e} = \frac{Be}{2m_e} \qquad (2.53)$$

The change of angular velocity due to this precession of the orbit is much smaller than the angular velocity ω_0 of the electron in the elliptical orbit around the direction of the magnetic flux lines. If I_B is the moment of inertia of the orbiting electron about the direction of the magnetic flux of density B, the change in the kinetic energy ΔE on applying the magnetic flux is given by

$$\Delta E = \tfrac{1}{2} I_B (\omega_0 + \omega)^2 - \tfrac{1}{2} I_B \omega_0^2$$

As ω is much less than ω_0,

$$\Delta E = I_B \omega_0 \omega = I_B \omega_0 \frac{Be}{2m_e} \qquad (2.54)$$

To consider the effect of this additional kinetic energy ΔE it must be taken into account that the angle θ between the vector $l\hslash$ and the magnetic flux direction can only assume certain values in accordance with the principle of space quantisation (Section 2.9). From Fig. 2.5, it is easily seen that the permitted values of the angle θ are such that

$$\cos \theta = \frac{m_l}{l} \qquad (2.55)$$

where m_l is the orbital magnetic quantum number.

The orbital angular momentum is $l\hslash$, so its component parallel to the magnetic flux lines is $l\hslash \cos \theta$, which is seen to be $m_l\hslash$ from Equation 2.55. This component of the orbital angular momentum is also given by $I_B \omega_0$; therefore

$$I_B \omega_0 = m_l \hslash$$

Substituting these values for $I_B \omega_0$ into Equation 2.54 gives

$$\Delta E = m_l \hslash \frac{Be}{2m_e} = \frac{m_l h}{2\pi} \times \frac{Be}{2m} \qquad (2.56)$$

where m_l has the range of values $l, l-1, l-2, \ldots, 0, 1, 2, \ldots, l$.

Equation 2.56 will apply only to an atom within a magnetic field of which a particular line in the spectrum is not affected by electron spin. An example is the red line of cadmium at 6,438 Å, for which the two optical electrons have spins which are anti-parallel to one another so the resultant spin is zero. Consider, then, a transition from a state where $L = 2$ to $L = 1$, where the corresponding energy levels are E_2 and E_1, and $E_2 > E_1$. In the usual spectrum with no external magnetic flux applied, a single line of frequency ν is emitted by the excited cadmium where

$$\nu = \frac{E_2 - E_1}{h}$$

h being Planck's constant. On application of the magnetic flux, the energy level E_2 corresponding to $L = 2$ will be split into five different levels corresponding to $2L+1$ different values of m_l. These energies E_{2B} will be decided by Equation 2.56, so are given by the equation

$$E_{2B} = E_2 + m_l \frac{he}{4\pi m_e} B$$

where $m_l = 2, 1, 0, -1, -2$, represented by the upper set of energy levels in Fig. 2.13.

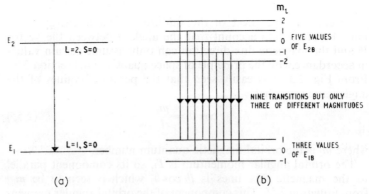

Fig. 2.13. *Allowed transitions in the normal Zeeman effect: (a) no applied magnetic flux; (b) magnetic flux of density B applied*

In the magnetic flux, the energy level E_1, corresponding to $L = 1$, will split into three different levels corresponding to $2L + 1$ values of m_l. Now E_{1B} will be decided by the equation

$$E_{1B} = E_1 + m_l \frac{he}{4\pi m_e} B$$

where $m_l = 1, 0, -1$, represented by the lower set of energy levels in Fig. 2.13.

Transitions in the emission spectrum with the magnetic field applied take place from the upper set of five levels to the lower set of three, in accordance with the selection principles that m_l must change by 0 or ± 1, whereas L must change by ± 1. These emission spectrum lines of frequencies ν_B are therefore decided by

$$h\nu_B = E_{2B} - E_{1B} = E_2 - E_1 + \Delta m_l \frac{he}{4\pi m_e} B$$

where Δm_l, the allowed changes of m_l, are ± 1 or 0. For $\Delta m_l = 0$,

$$v'_B = \frac{E_2 - E_1}{h} = v$$

the original frequency with $B = 0$. For $\Delta m_l = +1$,

$$v''_B = \frac{E_2 - E_1}{h} + \frac{Be}{4\pi m_e}$$

For $\Delta m_l = -1$,

$$v'''_B = \frac{E_2 - E_1}{h} - \frac{Be}{4\pi m}$$

The change of frequency Δv from the original frequency v is consequently given by

$$\Delta v = v''_B - v = v - v'''_B = \frac{Be}{4\pi m} \tag{2.57}$$

In the energy-level diagram of Fig. 2.13, there are nine possible transitions for $\Delta m_l = 0$ or ± 1, but clearly only three components of different frequencies are emitted.

2.19 The Theory of the Anomalous Zeeman Effect

In the anomalous Zeeman effect, the electron spin now contributes to the spectrum, so the inner quantum number j is involved instead of l alone, where

$$j = l + s$$

According to the older quantum theory, the magnitudes of the vectors l and s are integers and $\pm\frac{1}{2}$ respectively, and the vector addition concerned is simply a parallel or anti-parallel addition, so $j = l \pm \frac{1}{2}$. Subsequent developments in quantum mechanics have shown that this is incorrect. Without entering into the complexities of the quantum-mechanical theory it suffices to state that the older quantum theory based on orbital considerations gives substantially satisfactory results provided that the magnitude of l is taken to be $\sqrt{[l(l+1)]}$ and that of s to be $\sqrt{[s(s+1)]}$ (Section 2.16). If, for example, $l = 2$ where $s = \frac{1}{2}$, then the vectors l and s must be added in such a way that the length of vector l is taken to be $\sqrt{[2(2+1)]} = \sqrt{6}$; the length of the vector s is taken to be $\sqrt{[\frac{1}{2}(\frac{1}{2}+1)]} = \frac{1}{2}\sqrt{3}$; and the resultant vector has a length $\sqrt{[j(j+1)]}$ where $j = 2\frac{1}{2}$, so is of length $\sqrt{[\frac{5}{2}(\frac{5}{2}+1)]} = \frac{1}{2}\sqrt{35}$. This means that

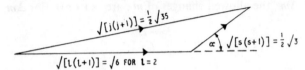

Fig. 2.14. *The quantised vector addition of* **l** *and* **s**, *in accordance with quantum mechanics, for* **l** = 2 *and* **s** = $\frac{1}{2}$

the angle α between the vector **l** and **s** is predetermined and is seen from Fig. 2.14 to be given by

$$j(j+1) = l(l+1)+s(s+1)+2\sqrt{[l(l+1)\,s(s+1)]}\cos\alpha$$

Therefore

$$\cos\alpha = \frac{j(j+1)-l(l+1)-s(s+1)}{2\sqrt{[l(l+1)\,s(s+1)]}} \qquad (2.58)$$

The magnetic moment M_l due to the orbital motion of the electron is given by $l\beta$, where β is the Bohr magneton, and the magnetic moment M_s due to the electron spin is β (Section 2.9). The resultant magnetic moment M will be given by the vector addition

$$M = M_l + M_s$$

Consider an atom where $l = 1$ and $s = \frac{1}{2}$, and only one electron is involved in producing the spectrum. In Fig. 2.15, vector OA is of length $\sqrt{[1(1+1)]} = \sqrt{2}$ to represent **l**, whilst OB is of length $\sqrt{[\frac{1}{2}(\frac{1}{2}+1)]} = \frac{1}{2}\sqrt{3}$ to represent **s**, giving a resultant **j** along OF,

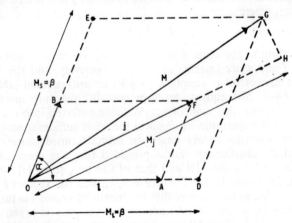

Fig. 2.15. *The vectors representing orbital and spin angular momentum and magnetic moment for an atom with a single optical electron*

where $\angle BOA = \alpha$ is decided by Equation 2.58 to be

$$\cos^{-1} \frac{\frac{3}{2}(\frac{3}{2}+1)-1(1+1)-\frac{1}{2}(\frac{1}{2}+1)}{2\sqrt{[1(1+1)\frac{1}{2}(\frac{1}{2}+1)]}} = \cos^{-1} 0 \cdot 408 = 65°54'$$

The orbital magnetic moment M_l will be β and so will the spin magnetic moment. These will be represented by vectors OD and OE respectively; these vectors are in the directions OA and OB respectively, but have a resultant M which is along OG and clearly not along the direction of OF, which represents j.

Fig. 2.15 represents the vectors l and s in a particular plane. In a finite time, the electron orbit (and therefore these vectors) will occupy all possible planes so, in effect, will rotate about the vector j; they will rotate much more rapidly than the precession about the magnetic flux direction. The average effect of the components M_l and M_s in a direction perpendicular to j is therefore zero. So the average effect over a finite time of M will be M_j, the projection of M on vector j, which is OH in Fig. 2.15. Within a magnetic flux of density B, the energy associated with a magnetic dipole M_j at an angle θ to the direction of the magnetic flux is given by $M_j B \cos \theta$. The values of θ permitted in accordance with the principles of space quantisation are decided by the equation

$$\cos \theta = \frac{m_j}{j}$$

where m_j is a magnetic quantum number having $2j+1$ possible values. The possible energy values E associated with the effect of the magnetic flux on the orbiting electron are hence decided by $m_j M_j B / j$.

The magnetic moment M_j is equal to the sum of the projections of M_l and M_s resolved along the direction of the vector j. Therefore

$$M_j = M_l \cos (l, j) + M_s \cos (s, j)$$

where (l, j) is the angle between vectors l and j, and (s, j) that between s and j. Therefore

$$M_j = \beta [l \cos (l, j) + 2s \cos (s, j)] \qquad (2.59)$$

because $M_l = l\beta$ and $M_s = \beta = 2s\beta$ where $s = \frac{1}{2}$. From Fig. 2.14, it is seen that

$$s(s+1) = j(j+1) + l(l+1) - 2\sqrt{[j(j+1)\,l(l+1)]} \cos (l, j)$$

Therefore

$$\cos (l, j) = \frac{j(j+1) + l(l+1) - s(s+1)}{2\sqrt{[j(j+1)\,l(l+1)]}}$$

and, likewise,

$$\cos(s, j) = \frac{j(j+1) + s(s+1) - l(l+1)}{2\sqrt{[j(j+1)\,s(s+1)]}}$$

Substituting these values for cos (l, j) and cos (s, j) in Equation 2.59, together with $\sqrt{[l(l+1)]}$ and $\sqrt{[s(s+1)]}$ for the magnitudes of l and s respectively,

$$M_j = \beta\frac{j(j+1) + l(l+1) - s(s+1) + 2[j(j+1) + s(s+1) - l(l+1)]}{2\sqrt{[j(j+1)]}}$$

$$= \beta\,\frac{3j(j+1) + s(s+1) - l(l+1)}{2\sqrt{[j(j+1)]}}$$

As the possible energies E due to the magnetic flux are $m_j M_j B/j$, putting the magnitude of j as $\sqrt{[j(j+1)]}$ gives

$$E = \frac{m_j}{\sqrt{[j(j+1)]}}\,\beta\,\frac{3j(j+1) + s(s+1) - l(l+1)}{2\sqrt{[j(j+1)]}}\,B$$

Thus

$$E = m_j g\beta B \tag{2.60}$$

where

$$g = \frac{3j(j+1) + s(s+1) - l(l+1)}{2j(j+1)}$$

i.e. where

$$g = 1 + \frac{j(j+1) + s(s+1) - l(l+1)}{2j(j+1)} \tag{2.61}$$

The factor g is called the *Landé splitting factor*.

There are $2j+1$ possible values of m_j, seen from Equation 2.60 to correspond to energy levels separated by intervals of $g\beta B$. For example, the spectrum of sodium contains a line of wavelength 5,896 Å owing to the transition $3P_{1/2} \rightarrow 3S_{1/2}$ (Section 2.11). In the $3P_{1/2}$ state of the atom, corresponding to $3p_{1/2}$ for the single optical electron involved, $l = 1$, $s = -\frac{1}{2}$ (of magnitude $\frac{1}{2}$) and $j = \frac{1}{2}$, so

$$g = 1 + \frac{\frac{1}{2}(\frac{1}{2}+1) + \frac{1}{2}(\frac{1}{2}+1) - 1(1+1)}{2 \times \frac{1}{2}(\frac{1}{2}+1)} = \frac{2}{3}$$

In the $3S_{1/2}$ state, which is $3s_{1/2}$ for the electron, $l = 0$, $s = \frac{1}{2}$ and $j = \frac{1}{2}$, hence

$$g = 1 + \frac{\frac{1}{2}(\frac{1}{2}+1) + \frac{1}{2}(\frac{1}{2}+1) - 0}{2 \times \frac{1}{2}(\frac{1}{2}+1)} = 2$$

In each instance, $m_j = \pm\frac{1}{2}$; so gm_j is $\pm\frac{1}{3}$ for the $3P_{1/2}$ term and

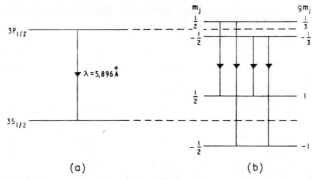

Fig. 2.16. Transitions in the anomalous Zeeman effect resulting from the splitting of energy levels $3P_{1/2}$ and $3S_{1/2}$ for the sodium atom: (a) zero magnetic flux (single line); (b) magnetic flux applied (four lines for $\Delta m_j = \pm 1$ or 0)

± 1 for the $3S_{1/2}$ term. As the change of m_j permitted is ± 1 or 0, the four transitions possible between energy levels give a quadruplet in place of the original single line (Fig. 2.16).

2.20 The Stark Effect

Zeeman discovered the effect named after him in 1896. In 1913, Stark observed that the lines in the visible spectrum of hydrogen atoms were all split symmetrically into components when the emitting source was subject to an electric field of about 10^5 V cm^{-1}.

The explanation of this phenomenon again demands the quantum theory of radiation, but is too complex to consider here. It can be established that changes $\Delta\bar{\nu}$ which occur in wave number $\bar{\nu}$ of an emitted line as a result of an electric field of strength E V cm^{-1} are given by

$$\Delta\bar{\nu} = 6 \cdot 45 \times 10^{-5}(n_1 - n_2) + ak_lk_s$$

where a is a constant, k_l and k_s are the projections of orbital and spin angular momentum in the direction of the electric field (so they compare with the magnetic quantum numbers m_l and m_s), n is the principal quantum number and n_1 and n_2 are modified values of n which can be deduced from quantum theory.

2.21 Molecular Spectra

In an introductory explanation of the mechanisms involved in the productions of band spectra by molecules, it is convenient to consider a molecule containing only two atoms, bearing in mind that the concepts enunciated below for diatomic molecules also apply to polyatomic molecules.

When energy E is imparted to a diatomic molecule, the magnitude of E may be such that it can excite quantised molecular energy levels as a result of three main phenomena: rotation of the molecule about an axis between the constituent atoms with which are associated *rotational energies* E_{rot}; vibration of the atoms within the molecule about their mean positions along the line connecting their nuclei, with which is associated *vibrational energies* E_{vib}; transitions between orbits of the outermost electrons within the structure of the constituent atoms, with which are associated *electronic energies* E_{elec}. In general, $E_{elec} > E_{vib} > E_{rot}$.

If $E_{vib} > E > E_{rot}$, molecular rotational energies only will be stimulated, giving pure *rotational spectral bands*. If $E_{elec} > E > E_{vib}$, both vibrational and rotational energies will be excited, giving *rotational–vibrational spectral bands*. If $E > E_{elec}$, all three kinds of energy levels are excited and the complete molecular spectrum is produced.

Where $E_{vib} > E > E_{rot}$ (so rotational spectra only are produced), the energy imparted to the molecule alters its angular velocity of rotation. If I is the moment of inertia of the molecule about its axis of rotation, the condition representing quantisation of the angular momentum is

$$I\omega = \frac{kh}{2\pi}$$

where k is an integer, h is Planck's constant and ω is the angular velocity of the rotation. The kinetic energy of rotation is therefore given by the equation

$$E_{rot} = \tfrac{1}{2}I\omega^2 = \frac{k^2 h^2}{8\pi^2 I}$$

In order to introduce the generally applicable correction resulting from quantum mechanics, k^2 is replaced by $k(k+1)$ (see Section 2.9), so

$$E_{rot} = \frac{k(k+1)h^2}{8\pi^2 I}$$

In absorption spectra (the study of molecular spectra is usually by absorption rather than emission), if it is assumed that the energy of the photon of radiation absorbed increases k by unity,

$$h\nu = \frac{h^2}{8\pi^2 I}\left[(k+1)(k+2) - k(k+1)\right]$$

where ν is the frequency of the radiation, so

$$\nu = \frac{h}{4\pi^2 I}(k+1) \qquad (2.62)$$

a series of lines in the rotational band spectra being obtained for $k = 0, 1, 2, \ldots$. The frequencies involved in rotational spectra are in the far infra-red, where the corresponding wavelengths are about 10^{-2} cm or 10^6 Å. The moment of inertia I of the molecule can be obtained from a study of these far infra-red spectra.

Where $E_{\text{elec}} > E > E_{\text{vib}} > E_{\text{rot}}$, both the vibrational energies and the rotational energies of the molecules are excited but not the electronic.

The vibrational energies of a diatomic molecule are due to the oscillatory motion of the constituent atoms along the line joining their nuclei. These oscillatory motions are not simple harmonic ones and are consequently not easily analysed. The values of E_{vib} are found to be quantised in accordance with an expression of the form

$$E_{\text{vib}} = \left(v+\tfrac{1}{2}\right)h\nu - \left(v+\tfrac{1}{2}\right)^2 hx\nu + \left(v+\tfrac{1}{2}\right)^3 hy\nu$$

where v is the *vibrational quantum number*, h is Planck's constant, ν is the frequency of the photon of radiation in the vibrational spectrum, and x and y are empirically determined *anharmonicity constants*.

For a particular frequency ν_1 in this vibrational region, there will be an associated fundamental band of frequencies because of excitation of the molecular rotational energies (unless the material is near to the absolute zero of temperature); Equation 2.62 is therefore also involved to give

$$\nu = \nu_1 \pm \frac{h^2}{4\pi^2 I}(k+1) \qquad (2.63)$$

where ν is a frequency in the rotational–vibrational band and has a series of values for $k = 0, 1, 2, \ldots$. The rotational–vibrational band spectra are in the near infra-red region.

Where the energy E imparted to the molecule exceeds the electronic energy E_{elec}, all three types of molecular energies are excited. Most of the characteristics of the spectra of molecules may then be explained on the assumption (not strictly true) that the total energy of excitation E_e is equal to the sum of the electronic, vibrational and rotational contributions, so

$$E_e = E_{\text{elec}} + E_{\text{vib}} + E_{\text{rot}}$$

The transitions between the electronic energy levels E_{elec} are generally considerably more energetic than those between vibrational levels and are correspondingly associated with the absorption or emission of the most energetic photons of frequencies within the ultra-violet and visible spectral regions, known as *electronic spectra.*

Interpretation of the electronic spectra is in the light of the quantum numbers and allowed transitions for the constituent atoms. Suppose that a diatomic molecule comprises one atom having a resultant orbital quantum number L_1 and a resultant spin quantum number S_1 (usually resulting from Russell–Saunders coupling) and a second atom for which these quantum numbers are L_2 and S_2. For the molecule, the resultant orbital quantum number L is given in magnitude by

$$L = L_1 + L_2 - N$$

where $N = 0, 1, 2, \ldots, 2L$, so that a series of $2L+1$ values of L are obtained. The resultant spin quantum number S is given in magnitude by

$$S = S_1 + S_2 - M$$

where $M = 0, 1, 2, \ldots, 2S$, so there are also $2S+1$ values of S.

Between the nuclei of the two atoms in the molecule there exists a strong internuclear electric field. A consequence of this field is that the resultant orbital and spin angular momentum vectors of magnitudes $Lh/2\pi$ and $Sh/2\pi$ respectively are caused to precess about the internuclear axis. The principle of space quantisation holds in a manner analogous to that in the magnetic case (Section 2.9), in that a quantum number Λ prevails which is the projection of the resultant orbital quantum number L on the internuclear axis, where the possible magnitudes of Λ are given by

$$\Lambda = L, \; L-1, \; L-2, \; \ldots, \quad 0, \; -1, \; -2, \; \ldots, \; -L$$

so there are $2L+1$ values in all.

To designate the electronic states of molecules, letters are used in a manner similar to that for atoms (Table 2.1) except that the Greek capital letters Σ, Π, Δ, and Φ are used instead of the equivalent capitals S, P, D and F. Thus, the electronic state for which $\Lambda = 0$ is characterised by Σ; for $\Lambda = 1$, the letter Π is used; $\Lambda = 2$ is represented by Δ; and $\Lambda = 3$ by Φ. Symbols of the type $^3\Delta$, for example, arise where the superscript denotes the multiplicity $2S+1$ of resultant spin quantum numbers S.

2.22 The Raman Effect

When light is incident upon a transparent medium and is scattered on its passage through the medium two types of scattering may be identified: *Rayleigh scattering*, in which the frequencies present in the scattered light are the same as those in the incident light, no frequency changes being experienced; and *Raman scattering*, in which the frequencies present in the scattered light are different from those in the incident light, and frequency changes do take place.

In general, Rayleigh scattering predominates greatly in intensity. For particles in suspension in a liquid or gas, the Rayleigh

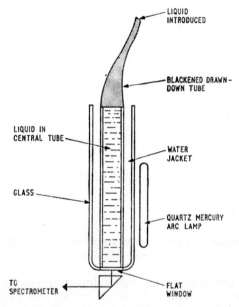

Fig. 2.17. Observation of the Raman effect in a liquid

scattering intensity is proportional to the square of the volume of the particle and proportional to the fourth power of the frequency (i.e. proportional to $1/\lambda^4$, where λ is the wavelength). In the Rayleigh effect, the photons in the incident light are elastically scattered by the molecules in the medium.

The Raman effect, discovered experimentally by Raman and Krishnan in 1928 in India, and independently by Landsberg and Mandelstamm in Russia, is a consequence of inelastic scattering of the incident light photons by the molecules of a medium. For a given medium, the Raman scattering per unit volume is usually about 0·001 of the intensity of the Rayleigh scattering. There is usually no phase relationship between the scattered light and the incident light in Raman scattering.

Observation of the Raman effect demands intense incident light because the scattering intensity is low. Developments from a simple arrangement due to R. W. Wood are often employed. The scattering liquid is in a cylindrical glass tube, about 1 cm in diameter and 10 cm in length, which is strongly illuminated along its length by light from a quartz mercury arc lamp (Fig. 2.17); filters are interposed if it is required to isolate particular wavelengths. The light

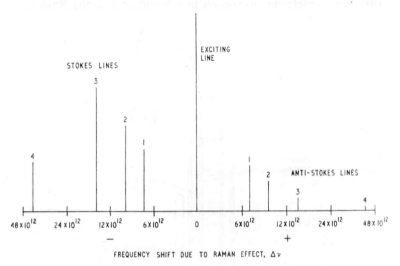

Fig. 2.18. A Raman spectrum for carbon tetrachloride (heights of lines are proportional to intensities)

scattered in the liquid which passes down the axis of the tube is observed through a plane end-window by means of a spectrometer. The other end of the tube is blackened to provide a dark background to the scattered light observed.

Whereas the Rayleigh scattering can be largely explained in terms of electromagnetic theory, the Raman effect demands the quantum theory. If the incident light photon of energy hv impinges upon a molecule of the scattering medium and the energy state of this molecule changes from E_1 to E_2, the energy of the Raman scattered photon is given by $hv-(E_2-E_1)$. Thus $hv' = hv-(E_2-E_1)$, where v' is the frequency of the scattered light, provided that the incident photon excites a molecule of the scattering medium from a lower energy level E_1 to the higher one E_2, so the energy of the scattered photon is less than that of the incident photon. This gives a Raman line of which the frequency is Δv less than v by the amount $v-v' = (E_2-E_1)/h$; such lines of lower frequency in the Raman spectrum are called *Stokes lines*.

Alternatively, but usually with much less probability, the molecule in an excited state E_2 moves to a lower state E_1 by giving energy to the incident photon to form a more energetic scattered photon. Now,

$$hv' = hv + (E_2 - E_1)$$

where v' is the frequency of the higher frequency scattered radiation in the *anti-Stokes lines*. The frequency change is again $\Delta v = v' - v = (E_2 - E_1)/h$.

The Stokes and anti-Stokes lines thus appear in pairs which are symmetrical about the initial exciting line in the Raman spectrum. The anti-Stokes lines are weaker in intensity than the Stokes lines, because the excited states of the molecules at energies such as E_2 are more sparse than the ground states at energies such as E_1. A Raman spectrum for carbon tetrachloride is represented in Fig. 2.18.

In the visible region, the Raman frequency changes Δv owing to the excitation of vibrational energy changes in molecules have been useful in supplementing data about molecular vibrational energies obtained from near infra-red spectra (Section 2.21).

2.23 The Stimulated Emission of Radiation

So far, frequent use has been made of the quantised energy states in which atoms and molecules may exist, in particular in relation to their emission and absorption of radiation, but no reference has been made to the relative numbers of atoms or molecules in a given material which are in the various states. For a given mass of material in thermal equilibrium with its surroundings at an absolute temperature T, the appropriate equation is

$$N_e = g_e N_0 \exp\left(-\frac{E_e - E_0}{kT}\right) \tag{2.64}$$

where N_e is the number of atoms (or molecules) in the excited state E_e (so N_e is said to be the *population* of the state E_e), E_0 is the ground state energy for which the population is N_0, k is Boltzmann's constant, and g_e is the *degeneracy* of the energy level E_e (a factor required to take into account the fact that several states may have the same energy associated with them and are indistinguishable unless, say, a magnetic field is applied).

From Equation 2.64 it is apparent that the population of the excited states is very much less than that of the ground state unless the temperature T is very high. Thus, since Boltzmann's constant $k = (1/11,600) \, \text{eV deg}^{-1} \, \text{K}$, the value of kT is $(T/11,600) \, \text{eV}$.

Suppose $E_e - E_0 = 2$ eV, then $(E_e - E_0)/kT = 23{,}200/T$. Assuming for simplicity that g_e is unity,

$$\frac{N_e}{N_0} = \exp\left(-\frac{23{,}200}{T}\right) = 10^{-23{,}200/2 \cdot 3T} = 10^{-10{,}000/T} \text{ approx.}$$

At $T = 300°$K $(27°$C$)$, therefore, $N_e/N_0 = \exp(-33)$; so an exceedingly minute fraction of atoms or molecules will exist in a state of excitation at an energy 2 eV above the ground state at room temperature. Even at a temperature of 2,000°K, when $N_e/N_0 = 10^{-5}$ approx., only one in 100,000 atoms or molecules are in excited states at 2 eV.

Therefore, in order to create in a material a significant number of excitation energies, it is necessary to elevate the temperature excessively, or provide excitation by the impact of electrons or other particles, as in a gaseous discharge, or indulge in the absorption of a photon of the appropriate energy. The last of these methods of excitation is our present concern.

When a photon is absorbed by an atom or molecule, if its energy equals or exceeds $E_e - E_0$ for the material, the excited state E_e will be produced. The photon of frequency v will provide an amount of energy hv, where h is Planck's constant $= 6 \cdot 63 \times 10^{-34}$ J s $= 4{,}15 \times 10^{-15}$ eV s. An excitation energy E_e of 2 eV will thus be created by the absorption of radiation of frequency given by

$$4 \cdot 15 \times 10^{-15}v = 2$$

Therefore

$$v = \frac{2 \times 10^{15}}{4 \cdot 15} = 4 \cdot 8 \times 10^{14} \text{ Hz}$$

which corresponds to a wavelength of 6,250 Å in the red part of the visible spectrum. The atom or molecule will remain in the excited state of energy E_e for a *spontaneous emission time* before it decays to the ground state (or to some intermediate quantised energy level between E_0 and E_e in which it remains for a second spontaneous emission time) by the emission of another photon of energy $E_e - E_0$.

It is of interest to determine the rate at which energy levels are excited by the absorption of photons, the rate at which spontaneous emission occurs, and also to consider whether it is possible to stimulate emission of photons from the excited state to the ground state in such a way that more photons are emitted than are absorbed, so that a form of amplification of radiation is obtained.

The rate of excitation of an energy level E_e or, more specifically, the time rate of increase of the population N_e brought about by the absorption of photons of energy $E_e - E_0$ and frequency

$v = (E_e - E_0)/h$, is taken to be proportional to the population N_0 of the ground state and also proportional to the energy per unit volume $U(v)$ in the radiation due to these photons. Therefore,

$$\frac{dN_e}{dt} = BU(v)N_0 \qquad (2.65)$$

where B is the *Einstein coefficient for absorption*, named after Einstein who introduced the concepts outlined in this section.

If the material is in thermal equilibrium with its surroundings at an absolute temperature T (with no radiation from an external source incident upon it, so that the photons available for the excitation are simply due to the radiation from the material), Planck's equation for the distribution of energy in the spectrum (Equation 2.1) applies:

$$U_T(v) = \frac{8\pi h v^3}{c^3[\exp (hv/kT) - 1]} \qquad (2.66)$$

in which $U_T(v)\, dv$ is the energy density at temperature T in the small frequency interval v to $v + dv$, and c is the velocity of light in free space.

The spontaneous emission of photons by the excited atoms or molecules is proportional only to the population N_e of the excited state, so the rate of decay of excitation, or rate of decay of population of the excited state, is decided by

$$\frac{dN_e}{dt} = -AN_e \qquad (2.67)$$

where A is a *second Einstein coefficient for spontaneous emission*.

To cause *stimulated emission of radiation*, the material is irradiated from an external source with photons of the same energy as those which are spontaneously emitted. The object is to trigger the excited states by the incident photons in such a manner that the number of photons emitted on de-excitation *exceeds* the number absorbed. Stimulated emission can take place on such irradiation, but whether it results in amplification or not is an additional matter requiring investigation.

In such stimulated emission, the time rate of decay of population of the excited state (dN_e/dt) is proportional to the energy density in the incident radiation as well as to the population, so

$$\left(\frac{dN_e}{dt}\right)_s = -CU(v)N_e \qquad ($$

where C is a constant and the suffix s denotes stimulated ϵ

During stimulated emission, all three processes represented by Equations 2.65, 2.67 and 2.68 occur, so

$$\frac{dN_e}{dt} = BU(v)N_0 - AN_e - CU(v)N_e \qquad (2.69)$$

Whilst it is clear from Equation 2.66 that the possibility of stimulated emission occurring is exceedingly remote and that amplification is impossible in a material in thermal equilibrium with its surroundings at a temperature T and not subject to external radiation, it nevertheless leads to useful results to consider the situation where $U(v)$ is simply $U_T(v)$ as decided by Equation 2.66. When the gas or solid material is in such thermal equilibrium, the *principle of detailed balance* requires that all transitions occur at equal rates in both directions. Therefore,

$$\frac{dN_e}{dt} = 0 \qquad (2.70)$$

From Equations 2.69 and 2.70, where $U(v) = U_T(v)$,

$$U_T(v) = \frac{A}{B(N_0/N_e) - C} \qquad (2.71)$$

The factor N_0/N_e is given by Equation 2.64, where $E_e - E_0 = hv$ and assuming $g_e = 1$, to be

$$\frac{N_0}{N_e} = \exp\frac{hv}{kT}$$

Substitution in Equation 2.71 gives

$$U_T(v) = \frac{A}{B \exp(hv/kT) - C} \qquad (2.72)$$

As Equations 2.66 and 2.72 must be equivalent, it follows that $B = C$, which is generally true, and that for thermal equilibrium

$$\frac{A}{B} = \frac{8\pi hv^3}{c^3} \qquad (2.73)$$

The ratio p/p_s, where p is the probability of spontaneous emission and p_s is the probability of stimulated emission, is given by Equations 2.67 and 2.68 as

$$\frac{p}{p_s} = \frac{dN_e/dt}{(dN_e/dt)_s} = \frac{A}{BU(v)} \qquad (2.74)$$

because $B = C$. For thermal equilibrium where no radiation is present except that due to the temperature of the gas or solid material itself, $U(v)$ becomes $U_T(v)$, so Equations 2.66, 2,73 and 2.74 can be combined to give

$$\frac{p}{p_s} = \frac{A}{BU_T(v)} = \frac{8\pi h v^3}{c^3} \times \frac{c^3[\exp (hv/kT) - 1]}{8\pi h v^3}$$

Therefore

$$\frac{p}{p_s} = \exp \left(\frac{hv}{kT}\right) - 1 \qquad (2.75)$$

At a temperature T of $300°K$ ($27°C$), $kT = 300/11,600 = 0.026$ eV. For radiation in the visible spectrum at a frequency of, say, 6×10^{14} Hz ($\lambda = 5,000$ Å), $hv = 4.15 \times 10^{-15} \times 6 \times 10^{14} = 2.49$ eV. Hence

$$\frac{hv}{kT} = \frac{2.49}{0.026} = 96$$

so

$$p = [\exp (96) - 1] p_s = 10^{41.6} p_s$$

Thus stimulated emission is exceedingly unlikely, except at high temperatures. Stimulated emission of any significance at optical frequencies consequently demands the use of external radiation so that Equation 2.74 applies. Even so, $U(v)$ has to be substantially monochromatic radiation. To arrange that such stimulated emission results in a larger number of photons emitted than are absorbed (i.e. light amplification), the population N_e of the excited state must be made to exceed the population N_0 of the ground state (or at least of a lower energy state) a process known as *population inversion*. Population inversion leading to light amplification is practised in a technique known as *optical pumping* utilised in the *optical maser* or *laser* (Chapter 9).

On the other hand, in the microwave region at a wavelength of, say, 1 mm corresponding to a frequency of 3×10^{11} Hz, the energy hv of the photon is only $4.15 \times 10^{-15} \times 3 \times 10^{11} = 1.245 \times 10^{-3}$ eV. Now at $300°K$,

$$\frac{hv}{kT} = \frac{1.245 \times 10^{-3}}{2.6 \times 10^{-2}} = 0.048$$

so

$$\frac{p}{p_s} = \exp (0.048) - 1 = 0.05$$

and stimulated emission predominates.

In the microwave region, again a method of obtaining population inversion is required to lead to amplification; it is practised in the *maser*, an essentially electronic device not to be described further in this text.

Exercise 2

1. Write an essay on the introduction of quantum theory into theoretical physics, dealing particularly with the main concepts needed to explain the distribution of energy in the spectrum from a heated black-body, the emission of electrons from a conducting surface exposed to radiation, and the Bohr theory of the spectrum of the hydrogen atom.

2. The work function energy of molybdenum is 4·15 eV. Calculate: (a) the threshold wavelength of the radiation which is just able to release electrons from this metal; and (b) the maximum speed of the electrons emitted when the molybdenum is exposed to ultra-violet radiation of wavelength 2,000 Å.

3. Given that the wavelengths λ of the lines in the spectrum of the hydrogen atom may be calculated from the equation

$$\frac{1}{\lambda} = \frac{e^4 m_e}{8\varepsilon_0^2 ch^3} \left(\frac{1}{m^2} - \frac{1}{n^2} \right)$$

where e and m_e are the charge and mass respectively of the electron, ε_0 is the permittivity of free space, c is the velocity of light in free space, and h is Planck's constant, calculate: (a) the wavelengths of the radiation emitted in the visible spectrum for transitions from the energy level for which $m = 2$ to levels for which $n = 3, 4$ and 5; and (b) the ionisation potential of atomic hydrogen.

4. Calculate from first principles the radius of the Bohr orbit for the hydrogen atom in the ground state for which the principal quantum number $n = 1$.

5. Write down the Schrödinger equation for the motion of a particle in one dimension under the influence of a force which may be derived from a potential energy $V(x)$, explaining the physical significance of the various terms. A spherically symmetrical state in three dimensions can be described by a wave function $r^{-1} u(r)$ where $u(r)$ obeys an equation exactly similar to the one-dimensional Schrödinger equation. Hence or otherwise, derive formulae and numerical values for the ionisation potential and Bohr radius of the ground state of the hydrogen atom. **(M. P.)**

6. Write an account of the Zeeman effect, in which a distinction is made between the normal and anomalous effects, and an experimental set-up is described suitable for determining by means of the Zeeman effect the specific charge e/m_e for the electron.

7. Account for the simple Zeeman effect which is observed with certain spectrum lines when the source is maintained in a magnetic field.
   A source, normally emitting a singlet line, is subjected to a magnetic field of 12 kilogauss (1·2 weber m^{-2}) and is observed from a direction perpendicular to the lines of force through a sheet of Polaroid and a Fabry–Perot etalon of separation 1 cm. The Polaroid is rotated until the interference

pattern consists of two overlapping ring systems. If the difference in order of interference between the two systems is 2·24 at the centre of the pattern, calculate the ratio of the charge of the electron to its mass and indicate the orientation of the transmission direction of the Polaroid. (Take $c = 3 \times 10^{10}$ cm sec^{-1}.) [Note: see also Section 4.2.]   (L.P.)

8. The D_2 line in the spectrum of the sodium atom is split into six components when the sodium source is placed in a magnetic field of flux density 3 Wb m^{-2}. The separations (in wave numbers) of these lines from the original D_2 line in zero magnetic field are $\pm 0·47$ cm^{-1}, $\pm 1·41$ cm^{-1} and $\pm 2·35$ cm^{-1}. With reference to the appropriate energy-level diagram, give an outline explanation of this phenomenon.

9. Give a simple explanation of the Zeeman effect and draw diagrams to show the polarisations to be expected in the various components. How may the observed effect differ from your simple theory?
   Use your theory of the Zeeman effect to calculate the separations in the pattern to be expected for a singlet line of wavelength 5000·0 Å in a field of 185 kilogauss (or 18·5 weber m^{-2}). (Take the electronic charge to be $1·60 \times 10^{-20}$ e.m.u. $= 1·60 \times 10^{-19}$ coulomb, mass of electron $= 9·1 \times 10^{-28}$ gm, $c = 3 \times 10^{10}$ cm sec^{-1}.)   (L.P.)

10. Write an essay on the band spectra of molecules.

11. Explain the meaning of the terms *spontaneous emission of radiation*, and *stimulated emission of radiation*.
    Give a theoretical argument which establishes that stimulated emission of radiation at optical frequencies is not normally possible for a system in thermal equilibrium with its surroundings.

CHAPTER 3

Polarisation of Light

In electromagnetic theory it is shown that visible light consists of trains of electromagnetic waves having wavelengths between 4×10^{-5} cm and 7×10^{-5} cm approximately. When travelling through an isotropic medium, the electric and magnetic field variations in this radiation are both in directions perpendicular to the direction of propagation. As the electric field vector is generally perpendicular to that of the magnetic field and the magnitudes of the two are related in a manner depending upon the medium, it is usually only necessary to specify one of them. The one chosen is the electric field vector. At a particular instant of time at a specified point, this electric field vector in a beam of light will be in a certain direction.

If the light is unpolarised, over a finite period of time this direction of the electric field will vary from one instant to the next to occupy all positions around the direction of propagation, where the likelihood of any one perpendicular direction being occupied is equal to that of any other.

If by some means the electric field is confined to one perpendicular direction about the propagation direction, the light is said to be linearly polarised in a given plane.

An example of polarised waves is provided by long-wavelength radio waves travelling over the Earth's surface. At a distance of a few wavelengths from the transmitter aerial, only the vertical component of the electric field vector can exist; any horizontal component will have been eliminated because it will set up, in the conducting earth, eddy currents which will dissipate quickly the energy in the horizontal field. Such radio waves, having no horizontal component of the electric field, are said to be linearly polarised in the vertical plane.

3.1 Polarisation by Selective Absorption

Polarisation by selective absorption occurs in some crystalline substances because they are not isotropic: for example, the permittivity and thermal expansion coefficients are not constants but depend on direction relative to the crystal axes. Crystals of quinine iodosulphate absorb energy from electric field variations in a particular direction. Microcrystals of this material within a cellulose film

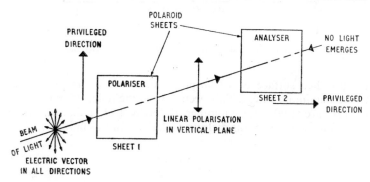

Fig. 3.1. Polarisation of light by sheets of Polaroid (sheet 1 is oriented so as to transmit vertical electric field vibrations and absorb horizontal ones; sheet 2 transmits horizontal electric field vibrations and absorbs vertical ones)

have their normally random orientations changed to one direction in the manufacturing process, which involves stretching the film. The resulting product—Polaroid—is a greenish material produced in large thin sheets costing about two shillings per square inch. The large area obtainable is convenient, and the angle of incidence of the light is relatively unimportant, but minor disadvantages are coloration and the transmission of not quite 100% polarised light (Fig. 3.1).

3.2 Polarisation by Reflection

The phenomenon of polarisation by reflection was discovered by Malus in 1808. It may be demonstrated experimentally by observing light from an extended source both directly and after reflection from, for example, a glass sheet, or the surface of water or even of polished wood (Fig. 3.2). The reflected light will appear to be appreciably plane-polarised. Rotation of the polaroid analyser will cause variation in the light intensity seen by the observer.

As shown theoretically in Section 1.8, there is an optimum angle of incidence, the Brewster angle I_B, at which the light reflected from

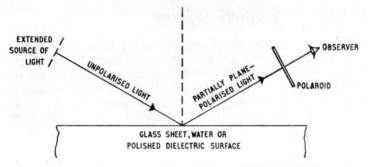

Fib. 3.2. Demonstration of the polarisation of light by reflection

the polished surface of a transparent dielectric is plane-polarised
to the maximum extent. This occurs when the reflected and refracted rays are at 90° to one another. Referring to Fig. 3.3, where n is
the refractive index of the dielectric relative to air as unity,

$$n = \frac{\sin I_B}{\sin R}$$

and

$$R = 90° - I_B$$

Therefore

$$n = \frac{\sin I_B}{\sin (90° - I_B)} = \tan I_B$$

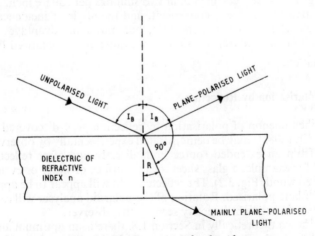

Fig. 3.3. The Brewster angle of incidence

The reflected light is seldom completely plane-polarised, because scattering of light owing to the presence of dust on the surface forbids perfection.

At the Brewster angle of incidence, the direction of the linearly polarised electric field vibration in the reflected light is perpendicular to the plane of incidence (Section 1.8). Electric field variations parallel to the plane of incidence are eliminated from the reflected beam, but they appear in the refracted and transmitted beam. The transmitted light is never completely plane-polarised, because some of the incident vibrations perpendicular to the plane of incidence are transmitted. The unwanted component in the transmitted light can be reduced by passing the light through another plate, parallel to the first, or, better, through a pile of parallel plates.

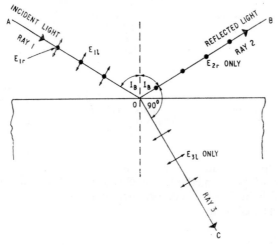

Fig. 3.4. Production of plane-polarised light on reflection at the Brewster angle

The electric vector E_1 in the incident light (ray 1) along AO in Fig. 3.4 is resolved into two components: E_{1l} in the plane of incidence, and E_{1r} perpendicular to this plane (see Section 1.7). The reflected and refracted rays (rays 2 and 3 respectively) may be considered as arising from a point source O in the dielectric medium just below the surface. When the reflected and refracted rays are separated by an angle of 90°, it is seen from Fig. 3.4 that the component E_{3l} in the plane of incidence is only possible in the refracted beam, and that such a component cannot exist in the reflected beam because E_{3l} is parallel to OB and an electric vector in the direction of propagation is untenable.

The use of reflecting glass surfaces as polariser and analyser is shown in Fig. 3.5(a) and Fig. 3.5(b), and the use of the more

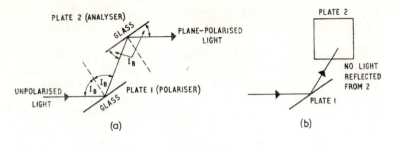

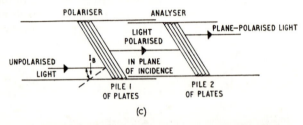

Fig. 3.5. Use of plates of glass at the Brewster angle of incidence as polariser and analyser: (a) single plates, plate 1 parallel to plate 2; (b) single plates, plate 2 rotated through 90° relative to its position in (a); (c) pile of plates (the intensity of the plane-polarised light is reduced as pile 2 is rotated, and reaches zero when pile 2 is at 90° to pile 1)

effective 'pile of plates' for these purposes is shown in Fig. 3.5(c). The pile of plates method is a cheap way of obtaining plane-polarised light, but it is cumbersome and seldom produces 100% plane-polarised light.

3.3 Polarisation of Light by Scattering

The production of polarised light by scattering has no advantages over other methods in laboratory practice, but it is important as a natural phenomenon. The electromagnetic theory involved is outlined in Section 1.9. Light from the sky, which is scattered by dust particles and gas molecules, and from a rainbow is partially polarised, and therefore variations in intensity will be observed on viewing it through a Polaroid sheet which is rotated. Although it is a simple matter to produce polarised light by scattering in a laboratory demonstration, it is not possible to make an analyser based upon the principle of scattering.

Light is passed through a tank containing a cloud of fine particles in the form of smoke or a colloidal suspension in a liquid (Fig. 3.6). If the incident light is unpolarised, the scattered light in two directions mutually at right angles is plane-polarised, as may be observed by the use of a Polaroid sheet. If the incident light is plane-polarised (by the insertion of a Polaroid sheet at D), then the transmitted light emerging at E is plane-polarised. As the plane of polarisation of the incident light is rotated by rotation of the sheet at D, the intensities at A and B in Fig. 3.6 vary so that when a maximum occurs at A there is a minimum at B, and vice versa.

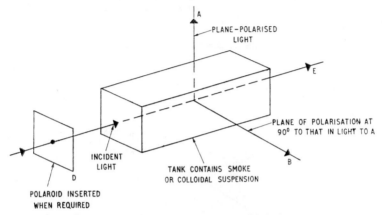

Fig. 3.6. Demonstration of the polarisation of light by scattering

The explanation given in Section 1.9 may be expressed simply by stating that an incident transverse wave will excite the scattering particles and, in the arrangement of Fig. 3.6, no horizontal vibration can be propagated to B and no vertical vibration to A, so the two scattered components of the light when viewed at 90° to the direction of propagation are plane-polarised.

3.4 Polarisation of Light by Passage through Wire Grids

In 1963, Bird and Parrish made a polariser in the form of a set of parallel conductors. They used a transmission diffraction grating ruled with 20,000 lines to the centimetre; each ruling of the form shown in Fig. 3.7(a) was therefore of width approximately equal to the wavelength of blue-green light. Gold was then evaporated in a vacuum to deposit on the vertical left-hand side edges of the grating, so producing 20,000 gold conducting wires per centimetre. The sloping bases of the grooves were free of gold. Such gold deposits were made several hundred atoms thick, but much less than the wavelength of the light.

Unpolarised light normally incident on such a wire grid [Fig.

3.7(b)] was shown on transmission to be plane-polarised, with the electric field variations in the electromagnetic waves confined to the direction *perpendicular* to the grid wires. The component parallel to the wires was absorbed. This is as would be expected, because any electric field component in the direction of the conductor would set up alternating potential differences which would

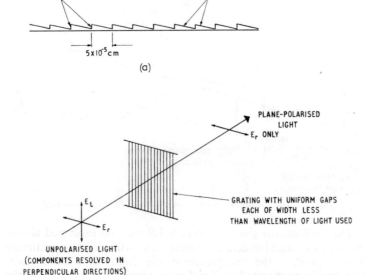

Fig. 3.7. Polarisation of light by a specially constructed wire grid: (a) transmission diffraction grating; (b) polarisation of the light (l signifies component parallel to wires; r signifies component perpendicular to wires)

cause alternating currents to flow. These currents would dissipate rapidly the energy in the parallel field components. Excessive thickness of the gold deposit was avoided, as otherwise electric field variations across the thickness would be absorbed.

It is interesting to note that this experiment shows that the simple analogy often quoted of the vibration of a rope in a slot is false in discussing the polarisation of light.

A demonstration experiment similar to that of Bird and Parrish with much more easily constructed wire grids having spacings of the order of millimetres can be used when the incident radiation is in the form of microwaves which are of only a few centimetres in length.

3.5 Double Refraction and Polarisation of Light by Crystals

There are several crystals which exhibit double refraction (also known as *birefrigence*): a beam of light incident upon such a crystal will give rise to two distinct refracted beams within the crystal. The two beams of light are plane-polarised in directions at 90° to each other. This double refraction was first observed by Bartholinus, in 1669, on studying calcite crystals.

Unpolarised light incident on a calcite crystal will give rise to two rays within the crystal: the *ordinary ray* in the same plane as the incident ray, and the *extraordinary ray* which is not in the same plane as the incident ray. The crystal will also have two different refractive indices: n_o for the ordinary ray and n_e for the extraordinary ray. Beyond the calcite crystal, two images of a single source of light are seen. If these images are viewed through a plate of tourmaline, which is optically active, rotation of the tourmaline changes the brightness of the two images and one of them attains maximum brightness when the other one becomes invisible.

Calcite (or Iceland Spar), which is crystalline calcium carbonate, shows marked double refraction. If a calcite crystal is placed over a pinhole in a horizontal screen which is illuminated from below, and the crystal is oriented so that viewing is along the optic axis of the crystal, only one image of the pinhole is seen. When the crystal is in any other orientation, two images are visible. If the crystal is rotated about a vertical axis, a line through the two images will be parallel to the projection of the optic axis on the crystal face.

The separation of the two plane-polarised beams in the calcite crystal is shown in Fig. 3.8. The calcite crystal is a rhomb, the six faces being parallelograms of which the angles are 101°55′ and 78°5′. At point X [Fig. 3.8(a)] and at the opposite corner, three obtuse angles each of 101°55′ meet. The *optic axis* of the crystal is a direction making equal angles with the three faces at X. Along the optic axis, birefrigence does not occur. Calcite and quartz crystals are uniaxial—they have only one optic axis. A *principal section* of the calcite rhomb is a plane which contains the optic axis and is normal to a face of the rhomb: there are clearly three principal sections for every point in the rhomb. Fig. 3.8(b) illustrates a principal section $ABCD$ of the rhomb. The angle at A is approximately 71° and at B is approximately 109°. A beam of unpolarised light incident normally on the face AB at P gives rise to an ordinary ray, which is not deviated, and to an extraordinary ray, which is deviated (even though incidence is normal) and thus constitutes a laterally displaced emergent beam. In Fig. 3.8(c) is shown the exit face of the rhomb: the electric vector

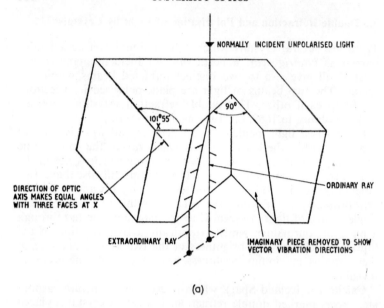

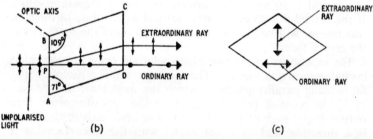

Fig. 3.8. Double refraction in calcite crystal

vibrations in the ordinary ray are parallel to the longer diagonal of this section, the vibrations in the extraordinary ray are parallel to the shorter diagonal.

3.6 Prism Polarisers

The *Wollaston polariser* [Fig. 3.9(a)] is made from two right-angled quartz prisms *A* and *B* with their hypotenuse faces in contact; this device is particularly useful in the ultra-violet. In

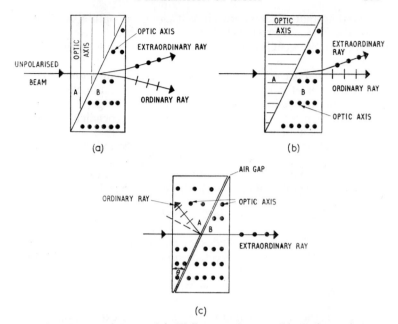

(a)

(b)

(c)

Fig. 3.9. Prism polarisers: (a) Wollaston polariser; (b) Rochon polariser; (c) Glan–Foucault polariser

prism *A*, the direction of the optic axis is perpendicular to the direction of the normally incident light, in prism *B*, the optic axis is perpendicular both to the incident light and to the optic axis in *A*. The incident unpolarised light is divided into two components which diverge in prism *B*. In prism *B*, the extraordinary ray in prism *A* becomes the ordinary ray, and vice versa. Divergence occurs in such a way that two plane-polarised beams emerge in different directions from the exit side of *B*. These two beams have equal intensities, and this is a convenience in comparing images of the two beams, which are side by side with vibrations perpendicular to one another.

The *Rochon polariser* [Fig. 3.9(b)], also of quartz and used in the ultraviolet, is similar to the Wollaston arrangement except that the first prism *A* now has its optic axis parallel to the normally incident light. The unpolarised incident beam of light is split into two plane-polarised components, but both travel with the same speed in the direction of the optic axis in *A*. The division of the two rays takes place at the boundary. The divergence is only about half that produced by a Wollaston prism of the same size. The advantage of the Rochon polariser is that the ordinary ray is transmitted without deviation for all wavelengths. It should always be used so that the light travels first along the optic axis. If it is used the other way round, light rays of different wavelengths will emerge in different directions because rotation will depend on wavelength.

The *Glan–Foucault polariser* [Fig. 3.9(c)] is cut from a large crystal, often of calcite, and consists of two right-angled prisms with their hypotenuse faces separated by an air-gap. The optic axes of both prisms are in the same direction, perpendicular to that of the incident light. The angle θ is chosen so that the ordinary ray in the first prism A is totally internally reflected at the hypotenuse boundary. The thickness of the prism does not matter but the incident beam divergence must not exceed 7°. With $\theta = 38 \cdot 5°$, $\sin \theta = 0 \cdot 6225$ and, since $n_o = 1 \cdot 6584$ at $\lambda = 5,893$ Å,

$$n_o \sin \theta = 1 \cdot 033$$

where n_o is the refractive index of calcite for the ordinary ray, which is totally internally reflected; similarly, since $n_e = 1 \cdot 4864$ at $\lambda = 5,893$ Å,

$$n_e \sin \theta = 0 \cdot 93$$

where n_e is the refractive index of calcite for the extraordinary ray, which is transmitted. As compared with the Nicol prism (Section 3.7) the Glan–Foucault arrangement is useful in that it can be used in the ultra-violet, and it is shorter but has a more limited angular field. Canada balsam used in the Nicol and other prisms absorbs ultra-violet radiation.

3.7 The Nicol Prism

First introduced in 1828 by Nicol, this prism is able to produce a 100% plane-polarised beam of light without coloration. A calcite crystal is cut across a diagonal, and the two halves cemented together with Canada balsam or other optical cement. The ordinary ray is eliminated by total internal reflection at the Canada balsam layer. A polariser for visible light of excellent quality is thus available, but the difficulty of finding large crystals of calcite makes it an expensive device for producing plane-polarised light.

A calcite crystal is chosen of which the ratio of the long edge to the short edge is between 3·0 and 3·7. The principal section $ABCD$ of the rhomb has angles of 71° at A and C. The end faces AB and CD are first ground and polished to reduce these angles to 68°. The prism is then cut diagonally along BD [Fig. 3.10(a)], the plane of this cut being normal to the end faces AB and CD and normal to the principal section [Fig. 3.10(b)]. The cut surfaces

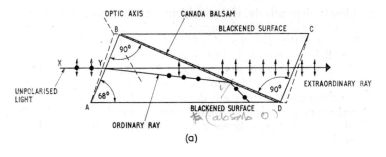

(a)

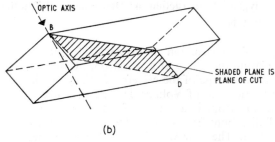

(b)

Fig. 3.10. The Nicol prism

are then optically polished and cemented together again with Canada balsam.

The principal refractive indices at the wavelength of sodium light ($\lambda = 5,893$ Å) for calcite are $n_o = 1\cdot66$ for the ordinary ray and $n_e = 1\cdot49$ for the extraordinary ray; the refractive index n of Canada balsam is $1\cdot55$. A ray XY parallel to the long edges of the prism incident on the end face AB is divided into two components: the ordinary ray is totally internally reflected at the balsam layer provided that the angle of incidence exceeds 69° (which is the critical angle I, where $\sin I = 1\cdot55/1\cdot66$, so $I = 69°$); the extraordinary ray, for which n_e is less than n, is transmitted. The sides BC and AD of the Nicol prism are blackened so that light in the ordinary ray is absorbed. The transmitted extraordinary ray is completely plane-polarised, with its electric field vibrations parallel to the shorter diagonal of the end face of the rhomb.

With the end faces of the Nicol prism ground to the angle of 68° specified and with Canada balsam as the cement, the angle at the apex of the cone of rays in air about the central ray XY parallel to the long edges of the prism can be about 24°. An incident ray will be at too great an angle to one side of XY if the angle at which the extraordinary ray meets the balsam surface exceeds the critical angle (when both the ordinary and extraordinary rays will be reflected and lost); alternatively, if the incident ray is at too great an angle to the other side of XY, the angle of incidence of the ordinary ray will be below the critical angle of incidence at the surface and both rays will be transmitted. The field of view can be increased by cutting the Nicol prism so that its end faces are normal to the long sides of the rhomb. This also gives the advantages that reflection at the entrance end surface is decreased and the image is not displaced when the prism is rotated about a longitudinal axis. The disadvantage is that a larger calcite crystal is required, which is expensive.

3.8 Huygens' Construction for Determining Refraction in Uniaxial Crystals

Huygens' construction or principle is a geometrical method of calculating the shape of a wavefront at any instant of time from the known shape of the wavefront at any previous instant of time (see Section 7.6 of Volume 1). The principle is that every point on a wavefront is a source of secondary wavelets which radiate in all directions from their centres with the speed of propagation of the wave. The new wavefront is the envelope of the secondary wavelets. In a homogeneous isotropic medium, the wavefronts from a point source of light in the medium are spherical, but many crystals are anisotropic in that they have different optical properties in different directions. In uniaxial birefrigent crystals,

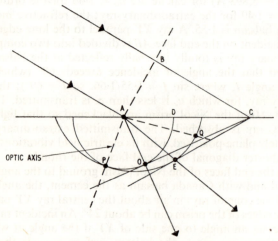

Fig. 3.11. Huygens' construction for representing propagation within a uniaxial birefringent crystal for incident collimated light

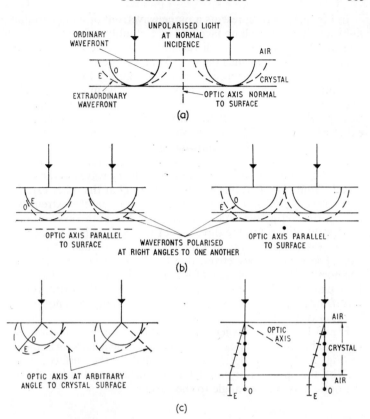

Fig. 3.12. Huygens' construction for propagation in a uniaxial birefringent crystal with normally incident unpolarised light: (a) optic axis normal to surface; (b) optic axis parallel to surface; (c) optic axis at angle to surface

two wavefronts having different speeds depending on direction are produced except along the direction of the optic axis, where the wavefronts have the same speed.

To apply Huygens' construction to light propagation in a uniaxial crystal, imagine a point a source within the crystal. The speed of propagation of each wavefront emanating from this point source depends on the refractive index. The wavefront at any time corresponding to the ordinary rays is a sphere about the point as centre; the wavefront corresponding to the extraordinary rays is a spheroid generated by the revolution of an ellipse about an axis parallel to the optic axis. This agrees with the fact that the refractive index for the extraordinary ray has an extreme value in the direction of the optic axis and a lower extreme value in all directions perpendicular to the optic axis.

In Fig. 3.11, *AB* represents a plane wavefront of monochromatic light incident on a plane face *AC* of a doubly refracting uniaxial crystal. At point *A*, two disturbances originate in the crystal: the ordinary one, of which the wavefront is represented by a sphere; the extraordinary one represented by a spheroid. For convenience, the optic axis in the direction *AP* is taken to be in the plane of the diagram and so of *ABC*. In this plane, the ordinary wavefront through *P* has a section *POD*—it is a circle about *A* as centre; the extraordinary wavefront is an ellipse, part of which is *PEQ*. The axes of this ellipse are *AP* and *AQ*. Whilst light travels in air from *B* to *C*, light in the ordinary waves in the crystal travels from *A* to *O*; in the same time, light in the extraordinary waves in the crystal travels from *A* to *P* at one extreme and to *Q* at the other extreme. The ratios *AP/BC* and *AQ/BC* therefore represent the extreme values of the refractive index, the former for both rays (ordinary and extraordinary) in the direction of the optic axis, and the latter for the extraordinary ray in a direction perpendicular to the optic axis. The resultant wavefront due to all points between *A* and *C* becomes the tangent plane *CO* for the ordinary rays and the tangent plane *CE* for the extraordinary rays. For the extraordinary wavefront, which is elliptical, the ray direction *AE* is not normal to the wavefront.

Fig. 3.12 shows Huygens' constructions for propagation in a uniaxial birefrigent crystal for normally incident unpolarised light. In Fig. 3.12(a), the optic axis is normal to the surface; in Fig 3.12(b), the optic axis is parallel to the surface; and in Fig. 3.12(c), the optic axis is at an angle to the surface.

3.9 The Production of Elliptically Polarised Light by Means of a Uniaxial Crystal Plate

A light vibration incident upon a uniaxial birefrigent crystal is divided into two vibrations polarised at 90° to one another. These vibrations travel through the crystal with the same speed in the direction of the optic axis but with different speeds in directions other than the optic axis, the difference being related to the direction of incidence relative to the optic axis.

If the incident beam direction is at 90° to the optic axis, which is in the surface of the crystal, the maximum difference in speed will be obtained. Suppose this incident beam is plane-polarised in any direction and is of monochromatic light of frequency $v = \omega/2\pi$, where ω is the pulsatance. This incident beam may be resolved into two vibrations at right angles to one another, represented at time t by

$$x = a \sin \omega t$$

and
$$y = b \sin \omega t$$

On emerging from the crystal plate, the vibrations are represented by the two equations
$$x = a \sin (\omega t + \delta_1)$$
and
$$y = b \sin (\omega t + \delta_2)$$

because the two components travel in the crystal with different speeds so a phase difference is introduced. It is convenient to put $\delta_2 - \delta_1 = \delta$, the phase difference between one emergent beam and the other, and write

$$x = a \sin \omega t \tag{3.1}$$

and

$$y = b \sin (\omega t - \delta) \tag{3.2}$$

The manner in which y varies with x can be found by eliminating t. To do this, Equation 3.2 is expanded to give

$$y = b \sin \omega t \cos \delta - b \cos \omega t \sin \delta \tag{3.3}$$

From Equation 3.1

$$\sin \omega t = \frac{x}{a}$$

and

$$\cos \omega t = \sqrt{(1 - \sin^2 \omega t)} = \sqrt{\left(1 - \frac{x^2}{a^2}\right)}$$

Substitution in Equation 3.3 gives

$$y = \frac{bx \cos \delta}{a} - b \sqrt{\left(1 - \frac{x^2}{a^2}\right)} \sin \delta$$

Therefore

$$\left(y - \frac{bx \cos \delta}{a}\right)^2 = b^2 \left(1 - \frac{x^2}{a^2}\right) \sin^2 \delta$$

Thus

$$y^2 - \frac{2bxy \cos \delta}{a} + \frac{b^2 x^2 \cos^2 \delta}{a^2} = b^2 \sin^2 \delta - \frac{b^2 x^2}{a^2} \sin^2 \delta$$

or

$$\frac{y^2}{b^2} + \frac{x^2}{a^2} - \frac{2xy \cos \delta}{ab} = \sin^2 \delta \qquad (3.4)$$

Equation 3.4 is, in general, the equation of an ellipse, but special cases arise.

If $\delta = 0$ or $n\pi$, where n is an integer, Equation 3.4 reduces to $y = bx/a$, which is a straight line representing linearly polarised light in a plane.

If $\delta = \pi/2$, or an odd integral multiple of $\pi/2$, Equation 3.4 becomes

$$\frac{x^2}{a^2} + \frac{y^2}{b^2} = 1$$

which is the equation of an ellipse and represents a particular case of elliptically polarised light.

If $\delta = \pi/2$ or an odd integral multiple of $\pi/2$ and $a = b$,

$$x^2 + y^2 = a^2$$

which is the equation of a circle: the light is circularly polarised.

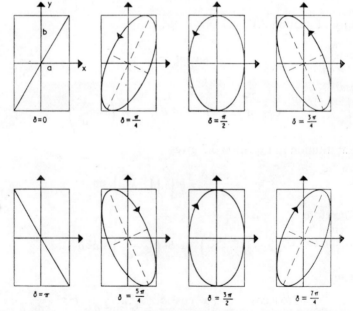

Fig. 3.13. The combination of two sinusoidal variations of the same frequency acting at right angles to one another and differing in phase angle by δ

It is seen that elliptically polarised light is produced on passing a plane-polarised beam of light in a direction through a uniaxial birefrigent crystal so that the phase difference between the two emergent light beams differs by an angle δ.

At a given point in a beam of monochromatic plane-polarised light, the electric vector is confined to a straight line perpendicular to the direction of propagation and the magnitude of its time rate of variation is sinusoidal. For elliptical polarisation, the electric vector rotates about the direction of propagation and varies in magnitude with time in such a way that its end point describes an ellipse.

The form of the ellipse depends on the value of δ. Various values of δ in Equation 3.4 give the traces shown in Fig. 3.13. Note that where $\delta = \pi/2$ (or an odd integral multiple of $\pi/2$) the axes of the ellipse are aligned with the privileged direction in the crystal. The angle θ between the coordinate axes and the axes of the ellipse is given by

$$\tan 2\theta = \frac{2ab \cos \delta}{a^2 - b^2} \tag{3.5}$$

3.10 The Quarter-wave Plate

A uniaxial birefrigent crystal plate of thickness such that the two emergent waves differ in phase by 90° is termed a quarter-wave plate, because such a phase difference clearly corresponds to a path difference of $\lambda/4$, where λ is the wavelength of the incident monochromatic light. A quarter-wave plate need not be extremely thin as there may be n waves in the direction of transmission in one privileged direction and $n+\frac{1}{4}$ in the other, where n can be a large integer.

For monochromatic light of wavelength λ, the minimum thickness x of a quarter-wave plate made from a crystal for which the extreme refractive indices are n_e for the extraordinary ray and n_o for the ordinary ray, is given by

$$x(n_e - n_o) = 0.25\lambda \tag{3.6}$$

Quarter-wave plates are usually made of quartz or of mica (sandwiched between glass plates) cut so that the optic axis is in the plane of the surface [see Fig. 3.12(b)]. For quartz, $n_e - n_o = 9 \times 10^{-3}$ at $\lambda = 5{,}893$ Å, so

$$x = \frac{5{,}893 \times 10^{-8}}{4 \times 9 \times 10^{-3}} = 1.64 \times 10^{-3} \text{ cm}$$

Incident plane-polarised light with electric field vibrations in the direction OZ (Fig. 3.14) has perpendicular components of this field

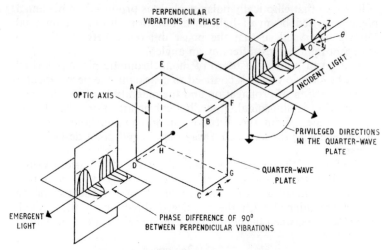

Fig. 3.14. Action of the quarter-wave plate

which vary sinusoidally with time in directions parallel to, and at
right angles to, the crystal optic axis. In the crystal, one component
vibration travels faster than the other; on emergence from the face
ABCD of the crystal, the faster component vibration leads by
a path difference of $\lambda/4$ on the slower. The emergent light is in
general elliptically polarised, though the special cases of emergent
plane-polarised light occur when $\theta = 0°$ or $90°$ and circularly polarised light when $\theta = 45°$, where $90° - \theta$ is the angle between OZ
and the optic axis.

By reversing the direction of the light, the effect of the quarter-
wave plate in changing elliptically polarised light to plane-polarised
light is demonstrated.

3.11 The Half-wave Plate

The half-wave plate is similar to the quarter-wave plate, except that
it is twice the thickness. Thus the equation for minimum thickness
x is seen by comparison with Equation 3.6 to be

$$x(n_e - n_o) = 0·5\lambda$$

so for quartz at $\lambda = 5,893$ Å, the minimum thickness will be $3·28 \times 10^{-3}$ cm.

A diagram similar to that of Fig. 3.14 could be drawn to represent the action of the half-wave plate; the difference between the
emergent light from a half-wave plate and that from a quarter-wave
plate is represented by Fig. 3.15.

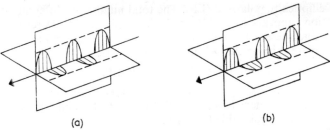

Fig. 3.15. Comparison of vibrations of the electric vector in light emerging from a quarter-wave plate and in that emerging from a half-wave plate: (a) quarter-wave plate (phase difference of 90° between perpendicular components); (b) half-wave plate (phase difference of 180°)

The electric vector OZ in the incident plane-polarised light may be resolved into the perpendicular components Oy and Ox, where $\angle ZOx = \theta$ [Fig. 3.16(a)]. On traversing a half-wave plate, the Ox component gains half a wavelength on the Oy component, corresponding to a phase change of 180°. The direction of Ox is therefore reversed to become Ox' in Fig. 3.16(b). The resultant electric vector

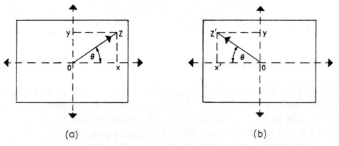

Fig. 3.16. Rotation of the plane of polarisation through a specific angle by means of a half-wave plate: (a) incident light; (b) emergent light

in the emergent light is now represented by OZ'. The half-wave plate simply rotates the plane of polarisation through $(180 - 2\theta)°$. The emergent light is still plane and not elliptically polarised.

Whereas the quarter-wave plate is useful in the analysis of polarised light (Section 3.12), the half-wave plate is not; its main function is as a half-shade device in a polarimeter (Section 3.22) permitting rotations of the plane of polarisation to be determined accurately.

3.12 The Analysis of Polarised Light

The four types of light concerned here are unpolarised (abbreviated to UP), linearly polarised in a plane (PP), circularly polarised (CP) and elliptically polarised (EP). The total number of different combinations appears to be fifteen. In fact only seven different types exist, and these may be identified by a Nicol prism and a quarter-wave plate. Listing the possible combinations:

Alone (four possibilities): UP, PP, CP, EP.

Two types (six possibilities): UP+PP, UP+CP and UP+EP are separately identifiable, but PP+CP, PP+EP and CP+EP are all indistinguishable from EP.

Three types (four possibilities): UP+PP+EP, UP+PP+CP, UP+CP+EP and PP+CP+EP exist, but the last pair of components in each of these combinations is indistinguishable from EP; also, as the first component is either UP, (which will have no effect) or PP (which alters the EP), all these three types are indistinguishable from EP.

Four types (one possibility): UP+PP+CP+EP is the one possibility, but PP+CP components are indistinguishable from EP and UP does not alter the character of EP, so the result is indistinguishable from EP.

The seven distinguishable types of polarised light are thus seen to be UP, PP, CP, EP, UP+PP, UP+CP and UP+EP.

3.12.1 USE OF A NICOL PRISM

The Nicol prism (a sheet of Polaroid can be used as an alternative) transmits light which has its electric vector or a component of this vector in the privileged direction of the Nicol prism. Owing to this selective transmission, when linearly (plane) polarised light (PP) is analysed, there is one orientation of the Nicol prism in which the emergent light intensity is zero.

Let the electric vector in the incident linearly polarised light be resolved into two 'vibrations'

$$x = a \sin \omega t$$

and

$$y = b \sin \omega t$$

where the x-axis is at an angle θ to the privileged direction in the Nicol prism (this direction being parallel to the shorter diagonal of the end face of the Nicol rhomb, Section 3.7). The resultant amplitude of the transmitted electric vector in the privileged direction (Fig. 3.17) is therefore

$$R = a \sin \omega t \cos \theta + b \sin \omega t \sin \theta = \sin \omega t(a \cos \theta + b \sin \theta)$$

whilst at 90° to the privileged direction, the amplitude is

$$R' = b \sin \omega t \cos \theta - a \sin \omega t \sin \theta = \sin \omega t (b \cos \theta - a \sin \theta)$$

The amplitude R' is zero when

$$\tan \theta = \frac{b}{a}$$

Only with linearly polarised light in a plane (PP) is complete extinction observed.

With incident unpolarised light (UP), the electric vector can occupy over a finite period of time any direction perpendicular to the direction of propagation. Rotation of the Nicol prism will merely

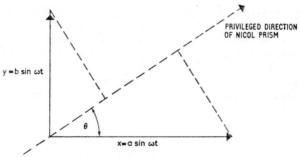

Fig. 3.17. *Resolution of the electric vector in incident plane-polarised light into x and y components, where the x component is at an angle θ to the privileged direction in a Nicol prism*

sample components of electric vectors in its privileged direction, which will be the same regardless of its orientation. Thus unpolarised light is not identifiable by a Nicol prism.

The same effect occurs with incident circularly polarised light (CP). Representing CP by two 'vibrations'

$$x = a \sin \omega t$$

and

$$y = a \cos \omega t$$

reference to Fig. 3.18 shows that the resultant amplitude of the transmitted electric vector in the privileged direction of the Nicol prism is

$$R = a \sin \omega t \cos \theta + a \cos \omega t \sin \theta = a \sin (\omega t + \theta)$$

The value of R does not depend on θ: it is a sinusoidal variation of

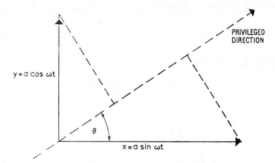

Fig. 3.18. Resolution of the electric vectors in incident circularly polarised light into x and y components, where the x component is at an angle θ to the privileged direction in the Nicol prism

the electric vector of the same frequency and amplitude (assuming there is no absorption of light in the Nicol prism) as the incident electric vector but differs in phase. Thus in examining UP, CP or a mixture of UP and CP, no change is observed in intensity on rotating an analysing Nicol or Polaroid.

If the light incident on a Nicol prism is elliptically polarised (EP), the two x and y 'vibrations' relevant (Fig. 3.19) are

$$x = a \sin \omega t$$

and

$$y = b \cos \omega t$$

The resultant amplitude R of the electric vector in the transmitted light in the privileged direction is given by

$$R = a \sin \omega t \cos \theta + b \cos \omega t \sin \theta$$

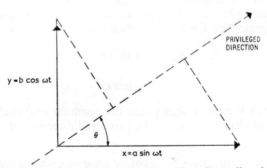

Fig. 3.19. Resolution of the electric vectors in incident elliptically polarised light into x and y components, where the x component is at an angle θ to the privileged direction in a Nicol prism

Thus

$$R = a \sin \omega t \cos \theta + a \cos \omega t \sin \theta - (a-b) \cos \omega t \sin \theta$$

or

$$R = a \sin(\omega t + \theta) - (a-b) \cos \omega t \sin \theta$$

The term $a \sin(\omega t + \theta)$ is independent of θ, as in CP; the term $(a-b)$ $\cos \omega t \sin \theta$ represents a plane-polarised component which can be extinguished by rotation of the Nicol prism. Therefore, rotating a Nicol prism while observing EP will give maxima and minima. Consequently, EP+UP and PP+UP will be indistinguishable from EP by the use of a Nicol prism alone.

So far, the use of only a Nicol prism allows only one (PP) of the seven types of polarised light to be identified.

3.12.2 USE OF A NICOL PRISM AND A QUARTER-WAVE PLATE

If the incident light is passed first through a quarter-wave plate and then examined with a Nicol prism, UP, CP, UP+CP, EP, EP+UP and PP+UP may be further investigated because the quarter-wave plate, by retarding one component relative to the other by a quarter period, converts PP to EP, or CP to PP, for example.

The quarter-wave plate transmits light with the electric vectors vibrating in two planes mutually at right angles, one in the direction of the optic axis and the other at 90° to the optic axis. Hence the effect of the plate will depend on the direction of the electric vectors in the incident light.

The effect of the quarter-wave plate is more complicated than that of the Nicol prism because the two components of the incident light each affect the intensity of the light transmitted in the two privileged directions in the quarter-wave plate.

Consider plane-polarised light (PP) represented by

$$x = a \sin \omega t$$

and

$$y = b \sin \omega t$$

to be incident on the quarter-wave plate, the axes of which are X and Y (Fig. 3.20) and where ϕ is the angle between the x-direction and the X-axis. The electric vectors of the incident light resolved in the X and Y directions are

$$X = a \sin \omega t \cos \phi + b \sin \omega t \sin \phi$$

and

$$Y = b \sin \omega t \cos \phi - a \sin \omega t \sin \phi$$

Let the function of the quarter-wave plate be to advance the Y component by $\pi/2$. Assuming no loss of light by absorption in the plate, the electric vectors in the emergent light will be represented by

$$X = a \sin \omega t \cos \phi + b \sin \omega t \sin \phi$$

which is unchanged, and

$$Y = b \cos \omega t \cos \phi - a \cos \omega t \sin \phi$$

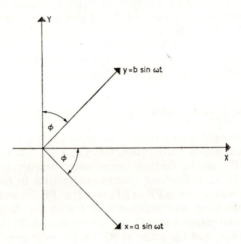

Fig. 3.20. *The x and y components of incident plane-polarised light relative to the privileged X and Y directions of a quarter-wave plate*

in which $\cos \omega t$ replaces $\sin \omega t$ because of the phase change by $\pi/2$. Therefore

$$\frac{X}{a \cos \phi + b \sin \phi} = \sin \omega t$$

and

$$\frac{Y}{b \cos \phi - a \sin \phi} = \cos \omega t$$

Therefore

$$\frac{X^2}{(a \cos \phi + b \sin \phi)^2} + \frac{Y^2}{(b \cos \phi - a \sin \phi)^2} = 1$$

which is the equation of an ellipse as ϕ is a constant for a particular setting of the quarter-wave plate relative to the incident PP light. The emergent light is therefore elliptically polarised (EP). Thus PP light which is incident on a quarter-wave plate is converted, in general, into EP.

In the analysis of polarised light, this fact is only needed for the analysis of mixtures because PP alone is identified by the Nicol prism only, without the use of a quarter-wave plate. Viewing light from the quarter-wave plate with a Nicol prism will now give a partial minimum except in one position producing circularly polarised light, when no change in intensity occurs on rotating the Nicol.

Unpolarised light (UP), represented by electric vectors equal in all directions around the direction of propagation, will be unaffected by rotation of a quarter-wave plate.

Consider elliptically polarised light (EP), and, as a special case, circularly polarised light (CP) incident on a quarter-wave plate. Let this EP be represented by

$$x = a \sin \omega t$$

and

$$y = b \cos \omega t$$

where for CP, $a = b$. The electric vectors in the incident light in the X and Y directions are

$$X = a \sin \omega t \cos \phi + b \cos \omega t \sin \phi$$

and

$$Y = b \cos \omega t \cos \phi - a \sin \omega t \sin \phi$$

In the emergent light, X will remain unchanged whereas

$$Y = -b \sin \omega t \cos \phi - a \cos \omega t \sin \phi$$

The similarity with the incident light vectors shows that the emergent light is also EP.

Thus, a quarter-wave plate converts EP to EP except when $\phi = 90°$, i.e. when

$$X = b \cos \omega t$$

and

$$Y = -a \cos \omega t$$

or

$$Y = \frac{-aX}{b}$$

which represents PP. Similarly, $\phi = 0°$ when

$$X = a \sin \omega t$$

and

$$Y = -b \sin \omega t$$

i.e. when

$$Y = \frac{-bX}{a}$$

which represents PP. It follows that, with incident EP on a quarter-wave plate followed by a Nicol prism, rotation of the Nicol will give complete extinction in a certain direction.

In the special case of CP, $a = b$ so the incident light is represented in the X and Y directions by $X = a \sin(\omega t + \phi)$ and $Y = a \cos(\omega t + \phi)$, and the emergent light by $X = a \sin(\omega t + \phi)$ and $Y = -a \sin(\omega t + \phi)$; this gives $Y = -X$, which represents linearly polarised light at 45° to the axes of the quarter-wave plate. Orientation of the quarter-wave plate has no effect.

Further consideration of the use of a quarter-wave plate and a Nicol prism to analyse polarised light will now be given.

Incident light is elliptically polarised (EP)

Referring to Fig. 3.21, with the Nicol prism alone, maxima and minima will be observed in direction θ. If the quarter-wave plate is inserted between the incident light and the Nicol prism, it can be rotated to give a minimum. The quarter-wave plate converts the incident EP to emergent EP, except when the axes of this plate correspond to the axes of the ellipse representing the incident light; when this happens,

$$x = a \sin \omega t$$

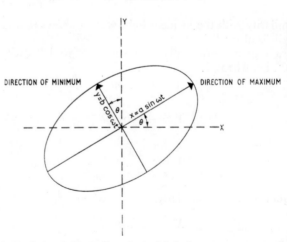

Fig. 3.21. *Analysis of elliptically polarised light by a quarter-wave plate and a Nicol prism (X is an arbitrary direction taken to be horizontal for convenience)*

and
$$y = b \cos \omega t$$

become either
$$X = b \cos \omega t$$

and
$$Y = -a \cos \omega t$$

or
$$X = a \sin \omega t$$

and
$$Y = -b \sin \omega t$$

which represent PP light. Thus rotation of the Nicol prism will give zero intensity in the directions at an angle $\phi = \tan^{-1}(a/b)$ or $\tan^{-1}(b/a)$ from the axes of the ellipse.

With the Nicol prism and the quarter-wave plate, the zero is in a different direction from that with the Nicol prism alone.

Incident light is a mixture of elliptically polarised and unpolarised (EP + UP)

As there is no intensity variation with θ for UP, with the Nicol prism alone the presence of UP will merely modify the shape of the ellipse but not the angle θ giving the directions of maximum and minimum intensities.

Insertion of the quarter-wave plate will convert the EP into PP in four orientations, as described in the section above, but no zero light intensity is observed because UP is unaffected by the quarter-wave plate. The direction ϕ of the minimum will give the ratio of the axes of the ellipse where $\phi = \tan^{-1}(a/b)$ or $\tan^{-1}(b/a)$.

The minimum is in a different direction with both Nicol prism and quarter-wave plate from that with the Nicol prism alone.

Incident light is plane-polarised mixed with unpolarised (PP + UP)

With a Nicol prism alone, a minimum (but not of zero intensity) will be observed in a certain direction depending on the PP.

Insertion of the quarter-wave plate will produce a 'best' minimum. The angle of setting of the Nicol prism will not change. Alternatively, the quarter-wave plate will convert the PP to EP. Thus the emerging light in the X and Y directions of the quarter-wave plate is represented by

$$X = (b \sin \phi + a \cos \phi) \sin \omega t$$

Table 3.1.

THE ANALYSIS OF POLARISED LIGHT

Any of seven different types of polarised light is examined by Nicol prism alone which can be rotated.

Light is extinguished at one orientation of Nicol.
→ PP

No intensity variation is observed.
→ UP, CP, UP+CP

Minimum intensity at one orientation of Nicol and maximum at 90° to minimum. Note orientation θ_1.
→ EP, EP+UP, PP+UP

Insert a quarter-wave plate of which optic axis is in any direction before the Nicol. Rotating this plate has no effect. Now rotate the Nicol.

No intensity variation is observed.
→ UP

Minimum intensity at one orientation of the Nicol.
→ UP+CP

Light is extinguished at one orientation of the Nicol.
→ CP

Insert a quarter-wave plate before the Nicol. Rotate it independently of the Nicol. When ellipse axes correspond to axes of quarter-wave plate, EP→PP, UP is unaffected, PP→EP (in general).

Light cannot be extinguished.
→ EP+UP, PP+UP

Light is extinguished at four orientations of the Nicol; θ_2 different from θ_1. Ellipse axes will be in directions of quarter-wave plate axes. If Nicol privileged direction is at ϕ to axes of quarter wave-plate, $\tan \phi = (b/a)$, where b and a are semi-axes of ellipse.
→ EP

Minimum intensity observed; θ_2 different from θ_1. Then as for EP.
→ EP+UP

Minimum intensity observed; $\theta_2 = \theta_1$. Alternatively, one position of quarter-wave plate gives no intensity variation.
→ PP+UP

and
$$Y = (b \cos \phi - a \sin \phi) \cos \omega t$$

In one orientation of the quarter-wave plate at which PP becomes CP, no variation of light intensity occurs on rotating the Nicol prism. Then
$$b \cos \phi - a \sin \phi = b \sin \phi + a \cos \phi$$

Therefore
$$\frac{\sin \phi}{\cos \phi} = \tan \phi = \frac{b-a}{b+a}$$

The procedure in the analysis of any of the seven different types of polarised light is summarised in Table 3.1.

3.13 The Babinet Compensator

This is constructed from two quartz (or sometimes calcite) prisms of wedge form mounted in a holder with their hypotenuse faces adjacent and so that their optic axes are mutually perpendicular

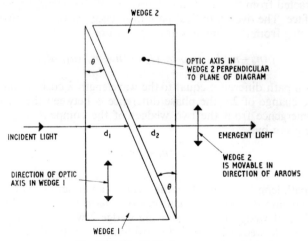

Fig. 3.22. The Babinet compensator

and both are perpendicular to the incident light (Fig. 3.22). The faces of the wedges are cut parallel to the respective optic axes. The wedge angles are each θ, where θ is so small (about $2\frac{1}{2}°$) that the separation of the ordinary and extraordinary rays is negligible. One wedge is fixed in the holder and the other one can be moved by a micrometer screw so that its hypotenuse face slides over that of the adjacent fixed wedge.

Quartz is a positive crystal, so light entering will produce an ordinary ray which travels faster than the extraordinary ray in the wedge 1. On traversing the hypotenuse interface between the wedges, the ordinary ray in wedge 1 becomes the extraordinary ray in wedge 2, and vice versa, because the optic axis of wedge 2 is perpendicular to that of wedge 1. The speeds of travel of these two rays are consequently exchanged at the interface between the two wedges.

Let the thickness of wedge 1 traversed by the transmitted light be d_1, and let n_o be the refractive index of quartz for the ordinary ray and n_e the refractive index for the extraordinary ray at a given wavelength λ. For quartz, $n_o < n_e$. The optical path length in wedge 1 is therefore $n_o d_1$ for the ordinary ray, and $n_e d_1$ for the extraordinary ray. The difference between these optical lengths is $(n_e - n_o)d_1$.

The light then enters wedge 2 to traverse a thickness d_2. On passing the hypotenuse interface between wedges 1 and 2, that light which constituted the ordinary ray in wedge 1 becomes the extraordinary ray in wedge 2, and vice versa. The optical path difference introduced in wedge 2 is $(n_e - n_o)d_2$, but this has to be subtracted from that in wedge 1 because of the interchange at the interface. The overall optical path difference between the two rays emerging from the compensator is therefore

$$(n_e - n_o)d_1 - (n_e - n_o)d_2 = (n_e - n_o)(d_1 - d_2)$$

As a path difference equal to the wavelength λ corresponds to a phase change of 2π, the phase difference ϕ between the two rays on emergence from the two wedges of the compensator is seen to be given by

$$\phi = \frac{2\pi}{\lambda}(n_e - n_o)(d_1 - d_2) \qquad (3.7)$$

The path lengths d_1 and d_2 in the wedges can either both be altered by changing the point of incidence of a narrow beam of light on the face of wedge 1 or, by moving wedge 2 with the micrometer screw while wedge 1 is fixed in position, d_2 can be altered and d_1 kept fixed for a given point of incidence. The phase difference ϕ is zero when $d_1 = d_2$, as is seen from Equation 3.7.

A disadvantage of the Babinet compensator is that a specified value of ϕ is confined to a narrow region of the compensator parallel to the refracting edges of the wedge-shaped prisms. This drawback is overcome in the Soleil compensator which is a modification of the Babinet compensator (Section 3.16).

3.14 The Babinet Compensator Between Crossed Polarisers

Suppose the whole surface of the Babinet compensator is illuminated with collimated plane-polarised monochromatic light obtained by the use of a Nicol prism or by a sheet of Polaroid placed between a collimator and the compensator. It is convenient to adjust the plane of polarisation of this incident light to be at 45°

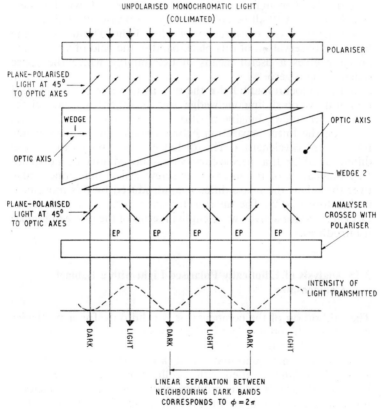

Fig. 3.23. The action of the compensator between 'crossed' polarisers (EP denotes elliptically polarised light)

to the optic axes of the wedges. The ordinary and extraordinary rays in the compensator will then have equal amplitudes.

The transmitted light is viewed with a Nicol prism or Polaroid adjusted to cut out the incident light if the compensator were absent. Thus the polariser 1 in the incident light is 'crossed' with respect to the polariser (analyser) 2 in the emergent light.

Wherever in the field of illumination of the compensator the two wedges are of such thicknesses d_1 and d_2 as to give $\phi = 0$ or 2π, dark bands will appear in the field observed through the analyser. In between these dark bands, where $\phi \neq 0$ or 2π, the light will not be eliminated. At halfway points between the dark bands, where $\phi = \pi$, the light will be plane-polarised. At all other positions, the light will be elliptically polarised. These observations are illustrated by Fig. 3.23.

If the incident light is white, the band at $\phi = 0$ will be black but the others will all be coloured because ϕ now depends on the wavelengths of the constituents of white light. The use of white light and observation of this black band in the field of view of the analyser gives a useful means of determining where the phase difference ϕ is zero.

With monochromatic light, the rays as represented in Fig. 3.23 do not move on sliding one wedge over the other (by means of the micrometer screw), but the positions of the dark bands *do* move. Let s be the linear separation between neighbouring dark bands for a given wavelength λ. This distance s corresponds to a phase difference of 2π. If a specific dark band is moved through a distance l by movement of the micrometer screw which slides one wedge over the other, the phase difference introduced by this movement is therefore $(l/s)2\pi$. The micrometer screw rotation can therefore be calibrated for a given wavelength in terms of the phase difference it introduces.

3.15 Analysis of Elliptically Polarised Light with a Babinet Compensator

The calibration of the compensator is valid only for a particular wavelength. If sodium light is used, for example, the compensator must be calibrated for that light.

A source of monochromatic light (a mercury lamp with a filter, or a sodium lamp) is used with a collimator and polariser (Nicol prism or Polaroid) set to produce plane-polarised light incident upon the Babinet compensator, the direction of linear polarisation being at 45° to the optic axes of the compensator. A second polariser—usually a Nicol prism mounted on the compensator—is used to analyse the emergent light. This second Nicol will produce the dark bands corresponding to $\phi = 2\pi$ when set in a particular orientation, which is the 'crossed' position relative to the first Nicol prism.

On substituting white light for the monochromatic light, the 'zero' position when $d_1 = d_2$ and $\phi = 0$ (Equation 3.7) is recognisable as a black band flanked on each side by coloured bands.

The cross-wires of an eyepiece used to observe the light from the second analyser Nicol prism are set on this zero position black band.

The source of elliptically polarised light (monochromatic of the same wavelength as the original plane-polarised light) is now substituted for the plane-polarised source. The elliptically polarised light comprises two electric vectors at right angles to one another, with a phase difference δ between them. This phase difference is added to that produced by the Babinet compensator. The zero position black band will therefore move in the field of the eyepiece from that which it occupied when white light was used.

If the total phase difference (δ plus that due to the compensator) is adjusted by movement of the compensator micrometer to be zero or π, the light emerging from the compensator will be plane-polarised (see Fig. 3.13). However, it will not in general be at 45° to the optic axes of the quartz wedges of the compensator, so the analyser Nicol and the Babinet compensator will both have to be rotated to produce the darkest band possible.

The distance is noted through which the micrometer screw is moved to go from the zero position band with white light to the dark band (after rotation of the analyser and the compensator) with the elliptically polarised light. As shown in Section 3.14, this recorded traverse of the calibrated micrometer screw gives the phase angle δ or $\pi - \delta$.

If the privileged direction (i.e. along the shorter diagonal of the end face of a Nicol prism) and the setting of the axes of the Babinet compensator at which the dark band is observed with incident elliptically polarised light (rendered plane-polarised by appropriate adjustment of the Babinet compensator) are both recorded, and if θ is the angle between the privileged direction of the Nicol and the direction of the optic axis of the first compensator wedge, then

$$\tan \theta = \frac{b}{a}$$

where b and a are the axes of the elliptical vibration.

3.16 The Soleil Compensator

This is a modification of the Babinet compensator with the advantage that the same phase change occurs over the whole area of overlap of the prisms. The two wedge-shaped prisms 1 and 2 of quartz have their optic axes in the *same* direction, both perpendicular to the incident light, and their hypotenuse faces are adjacent so that wedge 1 can be moved by a micrometer screw to vary the

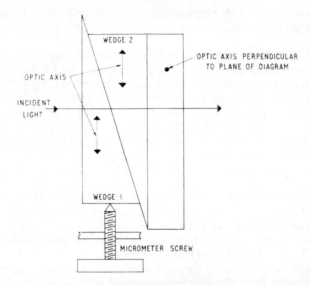

Fig. 3.24. The Soleil compensator

thickness d_1 through *both* prisms (Fig. 3.24). Behind the wedge 2 is a plane-parallel plate of quartz of thickness d_2, the optic axis of which is perpendicular both to the parallel optic axes of wedges 1 and 2 and also to the incident light. In this way is provided a compensator of which the thickness can be varied, but this thickness is the same for all points on its surface at which the light may be incident.

3.17 Optical Activity: Rotation of the Plane of Polarisation

In Section 3.9, the behaviour of birefringent crystals in producing two plane-polarised beams of light from an unpolarised incident beam was stated to be unique in the direction of the optic axis of the crystal in that both these beams supposedly travel at the same speed in this direction and no double refraction occurs. One might expect that light travelling along the optic axis would be completely unchanged. In fact, if plane-polarised light is incident, the plane of polarisation is rotated on traversing the crystal by an amount depending on the material and on the length of the optical path in the crystal.

Many substances exhibit this effect and, strangely, many are liquids or solutions where random orientations of the molecules might be expected to lead to cancellation of this effect. Substances, solid and liquid, which rotate the plane of polarisation are said to be optically active. They are divided into two groups: *dextrorotatory* and *laevorotatory*. The former rotate the plane of polarisation to the right, i.e. clockwise when the observer looks in the direction of the oncoming light; the latter cause rotation to the left, i.e. anticlockwise.

Optically active organic liquids usually contain a carbon atom in the molecule, which is asymmetrically arranged, or have a structure like that of turpentine. The amount of rotation depends on the wavelength of the light—a phenomenon known as *rotatory dispersion*—and, in solutions, on the concentration, though the solvent may cause small variations.

3.18 Fresnel's Theory of Natural Rotation

This optical activity intrinsic to the material, referred to as natural rotation, is explained by Fresnel on the assumption that a plane-polarised beam of light incident on an optically active medium is decomposed into two circularly polarised beams having slightly different speeds in the substance. At any point in the medium at a linear distance z from the incident face, these two components can be combined to form a plane-polarised wave of which the plane of polarisation is turned through an angle which increases with z. This entails a different refractive index for the two circularly polarised components.

A circularly polarised wave can be represented by two equations giving the vibrations of the same amplitude in two privileged directions. These are

$$x_1 = a \cos \frac{2\pi}{T} \left(t - \frac{z}{v_1} \right)$$

and

$$y_1 = a \sin \frac{2\pi}{T} \left(t - \frac{z}{v_1} \right)$$

representing a right-handed circularly polarised wave travelling with speed v_1 in the z-direction, where T is the period, whilst x_1 and y_1 are the displacements at time t.

The other wave (the left-handed circularly polarised one) is represented by

$$x_2 = -a \cos \frac{2\pi}{T} \left(t - \frac{z}{v_2} \right)$$

and

$$y_2 = a \sin \frac{2\pi}{T} \left(t - \frac{z}{v_2} \right)$$

which has a speed v_2.

On emerging from the optically active medium, the two circularly polarised waves are superimposed to form a plane-polarised wave. The resultant amplitudes x and v are seen to be given by

$$x = x_1 + x_2$$

$$= a\left[\cos\frac{2\pi}{T}\left(t-\frac{z}{v_1}\right) - \cos\frac{2\pi}{T}\left(t-\frac{z}{v_2}\right)\right]$$

$$= -2a\sin\frac{2\pi}{T}\left[t-\frac{z}{2}\left(\frac{1}{v_1}+\frac{1}{v_2}\right)\right]\sin\frac{\pi z}{T}\left(\frac{1}{v_2}-\frac{1}{v_1}\right)$$

and

$$y = y_1 + y_2$$

$$= a\left[\sin\frac{2\pi}{T}\left(t-\frac{z}{v_1}\right) + \sin\frac{2\pi}{T}\left(t-\frac{z}{v_2}\right)\right]$$

$$= 2a\sin\frac{2\pi}{T}\left[t-\frac{z}{2}\left(\frac{1}{v_1}+\frac{1}{v_2}\right)\right]\cos\frac{\pi z}{T}\left(\frac{1}{v_2}-\frac{1}{v_1}\right)$$

Therefore

$$\frac{y}{x} = -\cot\frac{\pi z}{T}\left(\frac{1}{v_2}-\frac{1}{v_1}\right)$$

As z increases from zero, y/x will vary between $+\infty$, 0 and $-\infty$ and then back to $+\infty$. A complete rotation will occur when

$$-\cot\frac{\pi z}{T}\left(\frac{1}{v_2}-\frac{1}{v_1}\right) = -\cot 2\pi$$

giving the value of z for one complete rotation to be when

$$\frac{\pi z}{T}\left(\frac{1}{v_2}-\frac{1}{v_1}\right) = 2\pi$$

i.e. when

$$z = \frac{2T}{(1/v_2)-(1/v_1)}$$

Hence, in a distance of z cm the plane of polarisation rotates through 2π rad, and in a distance of 1 cm it rotates through $2\pi/z$ rad. Thus, the rotation per centimetre is given by

$$\text{rotation per centimetre} = \frac{\pi}{T}\left(\frac{1}{v_2}-\frac{1}{v_1}\right)\text{ rad} = \frac{180°}{T}\left(\frac{1}{v_2}-\frac{1}{v_1}\right)$$

$$(\ 3.8)$$

If λ is the wavelength of the light in free space, $T = c/\lambda$ where c is the speed of light in free space. Equation 3.8 then becomes

$$\text{rotation per centimetre} = \frac{180°}{\lambda}\left(\frac{c}{v_2} - \frac{c}{v_1}\right)$$

Now, $c/v_2 = n_2$ and $c/v_1 = n_1$, where n_2 and n_1 are the refractive indices of the material for left-hand and right-hand circularly polarised light respectively. Therefore,

$$\text{rotation per centimetre} = \frac{180°}{\lambda}(n_2 - n_1) \qquad (3.9)$$

If the two refractive indices are the same, the rotation of the plane of polarisation is zero: the material is not optically active.

For solids, the rotation produced by a plate of 1 mm thickness is known as the *specific rotation;* it is seen to be $(18°/\lambda)(n_2 - n_1)$ from Equation 3.9. Throughout most of the visible spectrum, the specific rotation α varies with wavelength λ according to the equation

$$\alpha = A + \frac{B}{\lambda^2} \qquad (3.10)$$

where A and B are constants for a given material. Thus *rotatory dispersion* is present.

3.19 Experimental Support for Fresnel's Theory of Natural Rotation

As stated in Section 3.18, Fresnel's theory presumes that plane-polarised light travelling in the direction of the optic axis in an optically active material such as quartz is divided into two circularly polarised beams travelling with slightly different speeds. The refractive index n_l for left-handed quartz at a wavelength of 4,000 Å is 1·55821, and for right-handed quartz it is $n_r = 1·55810$. Fresnel verified his theory by constructing a combination of three quartz prisms to form a parallelipiped (Fig. 3.25) which produced a divergence of the two components so that each could be separately investigated and shown to be circularly polarised by the use of a quarter-wave plate and a Nicol prism.

Thus, in Fig. 3.25, at the face AC the incident light is divided into two components by the prism ABC made from right-handed (denoted by R in the diagram) quartz, and the right-handed circularly polarised beam travels faster than the left-handed one. This faster beam in ABC becomes the slower beam in the left-handed (denoted by L) quartz prism CBD, and vice versa, and

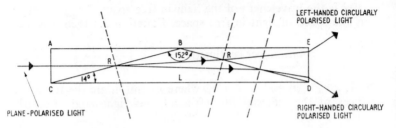

Fig. 3.25. Fresnel's parallelepiped constructed from three quartz prisms to separate the incident polarised light into two circularly polarised beams (at λ = 5,893 Å: in R, $n_l = n_r + 71 \times 10^{-6}$; in L, $n_l = n_r - 71 \times 10^{-6}$)

again there is an interchange on traversing the boundary *BD* into the third right-handed quartz prism *BDE*. At each refraction, the separation of the rays is increased.

3.20 Magnetic Rotation: The Faraday Effect

In 1845, Faraday discovered that the plane of polarisation of light is rotated on passing through transparent isotropic materials in a magnetic field. Later, in 1854, Verdet found that the angle of rotation θ is proportional to the length l of the path in the material and the magnetic flux density B. Hence

$$\theta = wlB$$

where w is *Verdet's constant*, which varies with the wavelength of the light concerned but is almost independent of temperature.

In an experiment to determine Verdet's constant (Fig. 3.26), a cylinder of the transparent material is placed along the axis of a long solenoid which produces a magnetic flux density B (about 0.06 Wb m^{-2} or 600 gauss is suitable) known in terms of the measured current I through the solenoid and its number of turns per unit length. The incident monochromatic collimated beam of light (for example, from a sodium lamp with collimator) is plane-polarised by Polaroid 1, and the emergent light is analysed by Polaroid 2. Polaroid 2 is first adjusted to be crossed with respect to Polaroid 1 when the magnetic flux is absent. The known magnetic flux density is then established by switching on the solenoid current, and the angle through which the plane of polarisation is rotated is determined by rotation of Polaroid 2 to restore a minimum in the emergent light. A magnetic flux density of 0.6 Wb m^{-2} will produce a rotation of the plane of polarisation of about 20°. For a cylinder of a heavy flint glass, $w = \theta/lB$ will be $0.0647''$ cm^{-1} G.

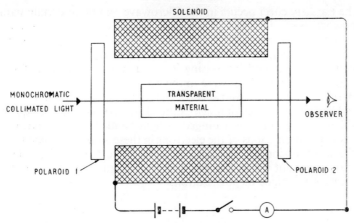

Fig. 3.26. Experiment to determine Verdet's constant for glass or perspex in the form of a cylinder

The magnetic flux density B is related to the current I (in amperes) and the number of turns n per metre of the solenoid by

$$B = \mu_0 nI$$

where μ_0 is the permeability of free space $= 4\pi \times 10^{-7}$ H m^{-1}.

The Faraday effect in solutions is not proportional to the concentration, and the magnitude of the effect at a temperature $t°$C is shown by the value of w for carbon disulphide (CS_2) for which

$$w = 0·04347(1 - 1·69 \times 10^{-3}t)]$$

A *molar magnetic rotation* $[M_B]$ may be defined as $M\alpha\varrho_1/M_1\alpha_1\varrho$, where M_1, α_1 and ϱ_1 are the molecular weight, the rotation for a known magnetic flux density, and the density of water respectively; M, α and ϱ are these values for another liquid.

In a homologous series, the addition of a CH_2 group increases $[M_B]$ by 1·023, i.e.

$$[M_B] = 1·023N + s$$

where N is the number of CH_2 groups and s is a constant for a given series.

3.21 Rotation of the Plane of Polarisation of Microwaves

Materials such as sugar solutions, turpentine and quartz do not measurably rotate the plane of polarisation of microwaves, i.e. radio waves of lengths of the order of a few centimetres. However, the Faraday effect occurs in the microwave region for certain para-magnetic salts, ferrites and plasma in electric discharges in gases.

A twisted waveguide rotates the plane of polarisation of the microwaves that it transmits. Similarly, the plane of polarisation of light can be rotated by passing it through a twisted stack of mica plates whose optic axes were in the same direction before twisting. A succession of polaroid sheets behaves in the same manner.

The X-ray investigation of an optically active solid such as quartz shows that atoms are arranged in right-handed or left-handed he-lices. The oscillations of the electrons in these atoms associated with the transmission of an electromagnetic wave have a direction of easy constraint which changes uniformly from atom to atom, thus rotating the plane of polarisation.

3.22 Polarimeters and Saccharimetry

The property of many substances of rotating the plane of polarisa-tion of light permits quick analysis and is also valuable in that, if a product is dextrorotatory whereas the reactants are laevorotatory, then the speed of a chemical reaction and its endpoint may be readily determined. Many organic materials exhibit this optical activity, but more especially sugar solutions may be quickly identi-fied and analysed; hence the name saccharimetry.

The basis of all saccharimeters is a Nicol prism to convert ordi-nary monochromatic unpolarised light into plane-polarised light, and a coaxial analysing Nicol so orientated initially that no light is transmitted. The optically active material or solution is interposed between the two Nicol prisms; this rotates the plane of polarisation so that further rotation of the analysing Nicol is needed to restore darkness. Usually, cylindrical tubes of the material or of glass con-taining the liquid of two different lengths are used to avoid confusion in measurements of the angle of rotation between θ and $2\pi+\theta$. Other refinements in the instruments are introduced to make the measurement of θ highly accurate. Monochromatic light must be used because θ depends on the wavelength; for quartz at 20°C, this rotation varies between 48° per millimetre at 4,000 Å approx. to about 16° per millimetre at 6,800 Å.

The rotation in a liquid depends on the concentration. If θ is the rotation measured for a length of path in the solution of l decimetre and ϱ is the density of the solution, then the specific rotation or specific rotatory power $[\alpha]$ is given by

$$[\alpha] = \frac{\theta}{l\varrho}$$

If c is the mass of solute in 100 cm^3 of a solution (note: not 100 cm^3 of the solvent),

$$[\alpha] = \frac{100\theta}{lc}$$

The molar rotation $[M]$ is the product of the molecular weight and the specific rotation; i.e.

$$[M] = M[\alpha]$$

The rotatory dispersion is given by Biot's law (1817):

$$[\alpha] = A + \frac{B}{\lambda^2}$$

where A and B are constants for a given material and λ is the wavelength.

In a simple polarimeter, the extinction position of the analyser is seldom precise; thus the early Mitscherlich polarimeter (1844), which uses only a simple polariser and analyser, is not sufficiently accurate for most purposes.

The *Lippich polarimeter* (Fig. 3.27) is similar to the Mitscherlich instrument, but it incorporates a subsidiary Nicol prism N between the polariser and the tube of optically active material. This Nicol N covers one-half of the field of view. If the polariser and analyser are crossed initially, the inclusion of N will cause one-half of the field to become light; the intensity of the light seen through the three Nicol prisms will depend on the degree of rotation of N relative to the analyser. This light intensity can be adjusted to be within the range at which the eye is most sensitive. If, now, the analyser is rotated, the part of the field which was dark becomes light and the part which was light becomes darker, until a position is reached at which both halves of the field of view are equally illuminated. The optically active material is then introduced, and restoration of equally illuminated halves is restored by suitable rotation of the analyser.

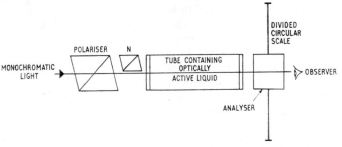

Fig. 3.27. Outline of the Lippich polarimeter (N is replaced by a half-shade device in the Laurent polarimeter)

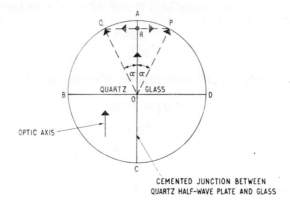

Fig. 3.28. The Laurent half-shade plate

The condition of equal illuminations of the two halves of a field of view can be judged with considerably greater precision than the position of zero illumination which would have to be obtained if the Nicol prism N were absent.

In the *Laurent polarimeter*, the Laurent half-shade plate is used in place of the Nicol prism N. This consists of a semicircular plate of quartz ABC (Fig. 3.28) cut so that the optic axis is parallel to the diameter AOC. This quartz plate is half a wavelength thick for a given wavelength λ. It is cemented along the diametrical edge AOC to a similar semicircular plate of glass ADC. The thickness of this glass is such as to transmit the same amount of light as is transmitted by the quartz plate ABC. The quartz plate introduces a phase change of π, corresponding to a path difference of $\lambda/2$, between the ordinary and extraordinary rays for light of a particular wavelength.

Suppose that the direction of linear polarisation of the light transmitted by the polariser is along OP (Fig. 3.28), at an angle α to the optic axis of the quartz plate. In traversing the quartz, two perpendicular components of amplitudes OR and RP are produced; on emergence from the quartz, the component of amplitude RP is changed in phase by π with respect to component OR; it therefore becomes directed along RQ. In traversing the glass, no such phase change is introduced. Consequently, the direction of linear polarisation of the light emerging from the quartz is along OQ at an angle 2α to that emerging from the glass, which is still along OP.

Rotation of the analyser cannot extinguish the plane-polarised light from the quartz half at the same time as it extinguishes that from the glass, because of the angle 2α between them. Suitable rotation of the analyser can, however, render both halves of the field of view equally illuminated.

The effect of slight rotation of the half-shade plate is easily detected; furthermore, when its orientation is set conveniently, rotation of the plane of polarisation in the instrument brought about by the inserted optically active material can be measured with high precision.

An alternative to the Laurent half-shade plate is a *biquartz plate*. This comprises two equal semicircular pieces of quartz joined along their mutual diameter, one of which rotates the plane of polarisation clockwise and the other anticlockwise. When the analysing Nicol is not correctly oriented, the two halves of the field of view appear unequally illuminated with monochromatic light or unequally coloured with white light. The plates are cut to such a thickness that slight rotation of the analyser turns one half red and the other half blue if white light is used.

Another type of half-shade device is the *Cornu–Jellet prism*, introduced by Jellet in 1860 and modified by Cornu in 1870. This is a Nicol prism from which a wedge of angle about $2\frac{1}{2}°$ has been removed and the prism recemented as shown in Fig. 3.29(a). Such a prism can be used as a polariser or an analyser.

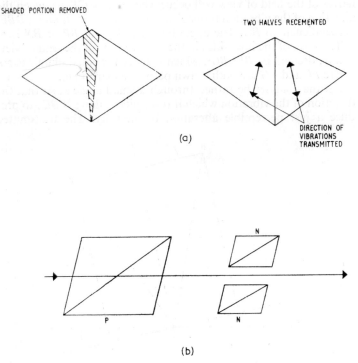

SHADED PORTION REMOVED

TWO HALVES RECEMENTED

DIRECTION OF VIBRATIONS TRANSMITTED

(a)

N

P

N

(b)

Fig. 3.29. (a) The Cornu–Jellet prism; (b) the Lippich triple-field polariser

The Lippich triple-field polariser uses two subsidiary Nicol prisms *N* to provide a more convenient method of dividing the field of view into three parts [Fig. 3.29(b)]. The plane of polarisation transmitted by each Nicol *N* is slightly different from that transmitted by the polariser Nicol *P*. When this arrangement is viewed through a telescope with a short focal length objective, the field of view appears divided into three sections. When balanced, the two outer portions are made to have the same intensity of illumination as the middle portion. In this condition, the incident light must vibrate along a direction bisecting the angle between the directions of linear polarisation transmitted by *P* and *N*.

3.22.1 THE SENSITIVITY OF A POLARIMETER

Suppose *BP* is the direction of the linearly polarised light transmitted by the polariser *P* (Fig. 3.30), and *BN*, at angle 2θ to *BP*, is the direction of that transmitted by *N* (where *N* is a subsidiary Nicol or the quartz of a half-shade device). Equal illumination in the two halves of the field of view will occur when $CN = CP$, i.e. when the direction of the vibration transmitted by the analyser is along *DBE*, perpendicular to *BC*. The angle between *BC* and *BP* or *BN* is θ.

The ratio of the intensities in the two sections of the field of view will be decided by BF^2/BG^2, which is unity for equal illumination, where *PF* and *NG* are both drawn perpendicular to *DE*.

Let the analyser be turned through a small angle α, so that the direction of the vibration which it transmits is along *D'BE'*, to produce a just perceptible alteration in intensity. The transmitted

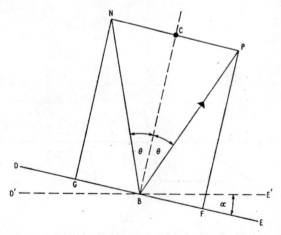

Fig. 3.30. *The sensitivity of a polarimeter*

components are now $BP \cos \angle PBE'$ and $BN \cos \angle NBD'$, which are $BP \sin (\theta - \alpha)$ and $BN \sin (\theta + \alpha)$ respectively. As $BP = BN$ the ratio of the intensities is $\sin^2 (\theta - \alpha)/\sin^2 (\theta + \alpha)$.

The eye can detect 1% difference in intensity. For a given value of θ, for this 1% difference,

$$\sin^2 (\theta - \alpha) = 0.99 \sin^2 (\theta + \alpha)$$

Therefore

$$\sin (\theta - \alpha) = 0.995 \sin (\theta + \alpha)$$

Thus

$$\sin \theta \cos \alpha - \cos \theta \sin \alpha = 0.995(\sin \theta \cos \alpha + \cos \theta \sin \alpha)$$

Therefore

$$0.005 \sin \theta \cos \alpha = 1.995 \cos \theta \sin \alpha$$

i.e.

$$0.0025 \tan \theta = \sin \alpha = \alpha$$

because α is a small angle. Suppose $\theta = 2°$, i.e. 0.035 rad, then the angle α is given by

$$\alpha = 0.0025 \times 0.035 = 0.001 \text{ rad approx.}$$

Therefore $\alpha = 3'$.

With the data specified, a change of rotation of the analyser by $3'$ can be detected as a 1% difference in illumination between the sections of the field of view in the analyser.

3.22.2 THE CONCENTRATION OF A SUGAR SOLUTION

The concentration of a sugar solution is measured with a saccharimeter, which is a polarimeter having a scale calibrated to read sugar concentration directly.

Modern saccharimeters do not depend on the rotation of a Nicol analyser to obtain equal illumination. Instead, a compensator introduced between the crossed Nicol prisms immediately in front of the analyser is used to restore equality of illumination in the field of view. This compensator (Fig. 3.31) consists of two wedge-shaped pieces of quartz, one dextrorotatory and the other laevorotatory. These wedges can be moved across the field of view by micrometer screws, so that altering the thickness of the quartz introduced counterbalances the rotation produced by the sugar solution. The sugar concentration is read directly on the linear micrometer scale.

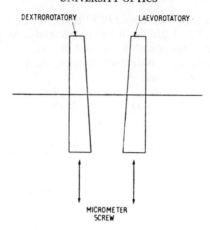

Fig. 3.31. Compensator used as a saccharimeter

3.23 Interference Effects in Uniaxial Crystals

3.23.1 OPTIC AXIS OF CRYSTAL PARALLEL TO FACE AT WHICH LIGHT IS INCIDENT ALONG NORMAL

A plane-parallel plate of the uniaxial crystal is mounted between crossed Nicol prisms [Fig. 3.32(a)]. If the incident light is white, the transmitted light is seen to have certain wavelengths missing. The values of these wavelengths can be calculated if the thickness of the plate and the difference between the two refractive indices at various wavelengths are known.

The incident beam of plane-polarised light on the crystal plate is divided into two components plane-polarised at 90° to each other. These components travel through the crystal with different speeds. When they combine on emergence from the crystal plate, plane-polarised light will be reformed only if the two perpendicular components are in phase, and a complete cut-out of illumination at some wavelengths will occur only if both components are of equal amplitude. It is therefore usual to arrange for the plane of polarisation of the incident light to be at 45° to the optic axis of the crystal plate.

The ray of light *AB* [Fig. 3.32(b)] incident on the crystal plate is divided into two components having speeds v_o and v_e; as the plate is thin and the incidence is normal, the rays do not diverge appreciably, so C is close to D at emergence. The time of transit of the light of speed v_o in the plate is d/v_o, and for speed v_e it is d/v_e, where d is

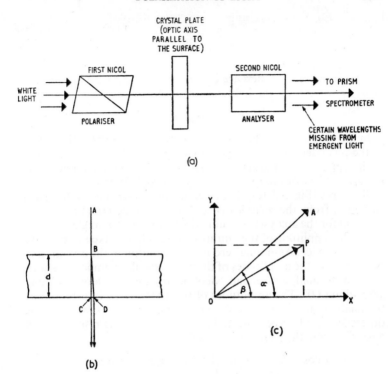

Fig. 3.32. *Study of interference effects in a unixial crystal between crossed polarisers with normally incident collimated white light*

the plate thickness. The time difference t is therefore

$$t = d\left(\frac{1}{v_o} - \frac{1}{v_e}\right) = \frac{d}{c}(n_o - n_e) \qquad (3.11)$$

where c is the speed of light in free space, n_o is the refractive index of the crystal for the light of speed v_o (the ordinary ray), and n_e is the refractive index for light of speed v_e (the extraordinary ray).

The period of the incident wave motion for a constituent of wavelength λ is T where

$$T = \frac{\lambda}{c}$$

The phase difference δ corresponding to the time difference t is hence $2\pi t/T = 2\pi ct/\lambda$ rad. Substituting for t from Equation 3.11, the phase difference is thus

$$\delta = \frac{2\pi c}{\lambda} \times \frac{d}{c}(n_o - n_e)$$

i.e.

$$\delta = \frac{2\pi d}{\lambda}(n_o - n_e) \qquad (3.12)$$

Wherever the phase difference equals $2\pi p$, where p is an integer, the analyser will cut off the light, so this occurs when

$$p\lambda = d(n_o - n_e) \qquad (3.13)$$

In the general case where the analyser is not crossed with respect to the polariser and the incident plane-polarised light is not at 45° to the optic axis of the crystal plate, let OX be the direction of the vibration of the ordinary ray in the crystal and OY that of the extraordinary ray [Fig. 3.32(c)]. The direction of vibration in plane-polarised light from the polariser (first Nicol) is along OP at angle α to OX, and for the analyser (second Nicol) along OA at angle β to OX.

Let the amplitude of the vibration along OP be taken to be unity for convenience. Assuming zero light absorption in the crystals and Nicol prisms, the amplitudes of the perpendicular components incident on the analyser (second Nicol prism) are $\cos \alpha$ along OX and $\sin \alpha$ along OY. The amplitudes of these vibrations transmitted by the analyser are therefore $\cos \alpha \cos \beta$ and $\sin \alpha \sin \beta$, with a phase difference of δ between them. The intensity I of the resultant light emerging from the analyser is therefore given by

$$I = \cos^2 \alpha \cos^2 \beta + \sin^2 \alpha \sin^2 \beta + 2 \cos \alpha \cos \beta \sin \alpha \sin \beta \cos \delta$$

$$= (\cos \alpha \cos \beta + \sin \alpha \sin \beta)^2 - 2 \cos \alpha \cos \beta \sin \alpha \sin \beta (1 - \cos \delta)$$

Thus

$$I = \cos^2 (\alpha - \beta) - \sin 2\alpha \sin 2\beta \sin^2 (\delta/2) \qquad (3.14)$$

If the Nicol prisms are parallel, $\alpha = \beta$ and (from Equation 3.14)

$$I = 1 - \sin^2 2\alpha \sin^2 (\delta/2) \qquad (3.15)$$

If the Nicol prisms are crossed, $\alpha = \beta \pm \pi/2$ and, from Equation 3.14,

$$I = \sin^2 2\alpha \sin^2 (\delta/2) \qquad (3.16)$$

To obtain maximum light intensity with crossed Nicols, Equation 3.16 shows that α must be 45°; i.e.

$$I = \sin^2 (\delta/2) \qquad (3.17)$$

Then I will be zero when

$$\sin (\delta/2) = 0$$

Thus I will be zero when $\delta = 0, 2\pi, 4\pi, \ldots$.

As for a plate of thickness d, from Equation 3.12,

$$\delta = \frac{2\pi d}{\lambda} (n_o - n_e)$$

Therefore

$$2p\pi = \frac{2\pi d}{\lambda} (n_o - n_e)$$

or

$$\lambda = \frac{d}{p} (n_o - n_e) \tag{3.18}$$

where p is an integer for dark bands; this is the same as Equation 3.13.

As an example, the use of a crystal plate of calcite is now considered. The following data are available for calcite:

Wavelength λ (Å)	4,047	4,861	5,893	6,563
$n_0 - n_e$	0·184	0·177	0·172	0·169

If this calcite plate has a thickness of 0·0025 cm, the wavelengths missing from the transmitted light when the plate is between crossed Nicol prisms and the incident plane-polarised light is at 45° to the optic axis are, from Equation 3.18, where

$$p = \frac{0 \cdot 0025 (n_o - n_e)}{\lambda}$$

From the data given, the values of p calculated are:

$$\frac{0 \cdot 0025 \times 0 \cdot 184}{4 \cdot 047 \times 10^{-5}} \qquad \frac{0 \cdot 0025 \times 0 \cdot 177}{4 \cdot 861 \times 10^{-5}}$$

$$\frac{0 \cdot 0025 \times 0 \cdot 172}{5 \cdot 893 \times 10^{-5}} \qquad \frac{0 \cdot 0025 \times 0 \cdot 169}{6 \cdot 563 \times 10^{-5}}$$

These values of p will not, in general, be integers. To find the integral values at which component wavelengths will be absent, a graph of λ against p is drawn for the four values of each, and the integral values of p determined from it; they will be found to lie between 12 and 5.

3.23.2 INCIDENT DIVERGENT LIGHT

Crystal plates viewed in plane-polarised collimated light in the direction normal to the optic axis show phenomena resembling interference, as explained in Section 3.23.1. When the crystal is cut so that the optic axis is in the direction of the chief ray of the incident plane-polarised white light but this light is not collimated, a

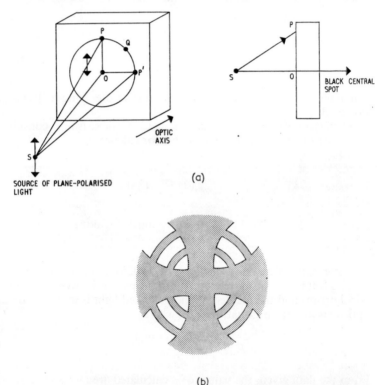

(a)

(b)

Fig. 3.33. Crystal plate between crossed polarisers when the incident light is divergent: (a) arrangement of source and crystal plate (at P, there is an extraordinary ray but no ordinary ray); (b) appearance of central region of field of view beyond the analyser with incident monochromatic light

beautiful series of coloured fringes of various forms appear crossed by dark crosses and brushes.

The crystal plate is between crossed analyser and polariser, where the incident plane-polarised light from the polariser diverges in a cone from a point source S (Fig. 3.33). The axis of this cone is SO, parallel to the optic axis of the crystal. An oblique ray such as SQ will produce both ordinary and extraordinary components in the crystal plate, these components being perpendicular to one another; the phase difference between these components will depend on the thickness of the crystal traversed, and hence on the obliquity of the ray. When this phase difference is an integral number of waves, the light will be extinguished by the analyser. With monochromatic incident light, a series of concentric dark rings will be seen in the field of view beyond the analyser. On these rings will be superimposed a dark pattern along the directions OP and OP', where OP is parallel to the direction of vibration in the incident plane-polarised light and OP' is perpendicular to OP in the plane of the crystal face. The dark cross appears because, for any incident ray such as SQ, the extraordinary component in the crystal is along the radius OQ and the ordinary one is tangential to OQ. Along OP, the light travels in the crystal as an extraordinary ray without an ordinary component because the component tangential to the radius is zero in the incident light. Along OP', only the ordinary ray will appear in the crystal.

For a particular fringe, the phase difference δ between the two components depends on the wavelength λ. If the incident light is white, colours will appear in the field of view beyond the analyser. The locus of a fringe of constant phase difference δ is termed an *isochromatic line*, and there will be a corresponding *isochromatic surface*.

If the incident light is convergent instead of divergent, similar arguments prevail in interpreting the fringe patterns observed in the field of view.

3.24 Measurement of Strain by Polarisation Methods

Some transparent materials, such as Xylonite, produce when stressed an optical effect proportional to the stress. The stress produced in such a material may be made a correct representation of the stress produced in another material not transparent to light (for example, a metal).

The transparent material becomes doubly refracting under stress. If, therefore, it is required to study the stress distribution in some mechanical member when subject to a load (for example, the steel hook attached to a crane), a scale model of this member is made in the transparent plastic and subjected to stress by loading. Circularly polarised light is transmitted through this model, and the emergent light is viewed through a polariser. Wherever the path retardation of one component ray (the extraordinary ray, say) is $\lambda/4$ compared with the other (the ordinary ray), a dark band will be seen provided that the incident circularly polarised light is monochromatic of wavelength λ. The movement of a dark band may be observed (by eye or photography) as the load is altered. Areas of high stress are shown by closely spaced dark bands. Modifications made to the structure, loading and support, simulated in the transparent model, will reveal when the stress and the corresponding strain are distributed more uniformly.

3.24.1 PHOTOELASTIC ANALYSIS

Photoelastic analysis, which is the further development of the polarisation techniques for measuring strain, is one of the most effective methods available for solving problems of stress distribution. It can be used either alone or as a check on mathematical calculations. The transparent material of which the model is made must be homogeneous. Monochromatic light is preferred as the stress lines are sharp enough even in the fifteenth order and considerable optical magnification is possible. White light produces the more picturesque coloured fringes, but these become indistinct above the sixth order. Path retardations brought about by stress can also be measured by the use of such devices as the Babinet and Soleil compensators in more sophisticated photoelastic procedures.

3.25 The Kerr Electro-optical Effect

Many transparent materials which do not normally exhibit double refraction will become doubly refracting and behave like a uni-axial crystal when they are subjected to an electrostatic field. This is because the field produces induced dipoles in a dielectric and increases the dipole moment of any existing polar molecules in the dielectric. These dipoles tend to be oriented in the direction of the electrostatic lines of force, and this renders the material anisotropic.

This effect was discovered by Kerr, in 1895, using glass. The transparent dielectric is placed between the plates of a parallel-plate capacitor across which a potential difference is established. Light incident on the dielectric in the direction normal to the electrostatic field lines gives rise to an ordinary and an extraordinary ray in the dielectric. If n_1 and n_2 are the refractive indices for monochromatic light of which the directions of the electric vector vibrations are respectively parallel and perpendicular to the field lines,

$$n_1 - n_2 = k\lambda E^2 \qquad (3.19)$$

where k is called the *Kerr constant* for the material, λ is the wavelength and E the electric field strength.

The Kerr constant k is particularly large for the liquid nitro-benzene. A Kerr cell consists of a container of nitrobenzene between parallel electrodes and furnished with entrance and exit windows. When such a Kerr cell is set coaxially between crossed Nicol prisms, no light will be transmitted when the p.d. across the cell is zero. When a p.d. is established, light will be transmitted as the plane of polarisation of the light from the polariser is rotated within the Kerr cell to an extent depending on the electric field strength. Though for some solid dielectrics there is a delay of some seconds between the application of the field and the maximum rotation produced, this delay is only 10^{-11} s or less for non-polar liquids. If, therefore, an alternating p.d. of frequency f is set up across a Kerr cell containing nitrobenzene, the light output from the analyser Nicol will be modulated at the same frequency f, which can be as high as 20 MHz.

Detailed investigation of the light transmitted by the Kerr cell when plane-polarised light is incident upon it shows that the emergent light is elliptically polarised. Hence in no position of the analysing Nicol prism will the transmitted light be of zero intensity. The two components of the transmitted elliptically polarised light have an optical path difference between them of x, given by

$$x = klE^2\lambda \qquad (3.20)$$

where l is the optical path length in the cell.

In Equation 3.19, if E is in volts per metre, then at a wavelength λ of 5,893 Å $= 5 \cdot 893 \times 10^{-7}$ m (sodium light), the Kerr constant k is $5 \cdot 2 \times 10^{-14}$ for water, $2 \cdot 5 \times 10^{-12}$ for nitrobenzene and between $3 \cdot 2 \times 10^{-16}$ and $1 \cdot 7 \times 10^{-15}$ for various glasses.

3.26 Experimental Verification of Fresnel's Equations for Light Reflected at an Air–Glass Interface

Fresnel's equations (Section 1.7) based on the electromagnetic theory of light give for light reflected at the interface between two different dielectric media the ratios A_{2l}/A_{1l} and A_{2r}/A_{1r}, where A_{2l} and A_{1l} are the amplitudes in the plane of incidence of the reflected and incident light beams respectively, whilst A_{2r} and A_{1r} are the amplitudes perpendicular to the plane of incidence of the reflected and incident light beams respectively. Thus, Equation 1.61 is

$$\frac{A_{2l}}{A_{1l}} = \frac{\tan (I - R)}{\tan (I + R)}$$

where I is the angle of incidence and R is the angle of refraction;
Equation 1.60 is

$$\frac{A_{2r}}{A_{1r}} = -\frac{\sin (I-R)}{\sin (I+R)}$$

From these two equations it follows that

$$\frac{A_{2r}}{A_{2l}} = -A_{1r}\frac{\sin (I-R)}{\sin (I+R)} \times \frac{\tan(I+R)}{A_{1l}\tan (I-R)}$$

Therefore

$$\frac{A_{2r}}{A_{2l}} = -\frac{A_{1r}}{A_{1l}}\frac{\cos (I-R)}{\cos (I+R)} \tag{3.21}$$

The ratio A_{1r}/A_{1l} is the tangent of the angle α which the direction of the electric vector in the incident linearly polarised light makes with the plane of incidence; similarly A_{ar}/A_{2l} is the tangent of the angle θ which the direction of the electric vector in the reflected light makes with the angle of incidence.

In the experiment a prism is set up on a spectrometer adjusted for parallel light. The spectrometer telescope is furnished with an analyser Polaroid mounted in a divided circle immediately in front of its objective, and a similar polariser Polaroid is mounted immediately in front of the collimator lens.

The procedure is first to determine the refractive index n of the glass of the prism by the well-known method of minimum deviation (the Polaroids being removed) using sodium light. The Brewster or polarising angle I_B is given by $\tan^{-1} n$ (Section 3.2). The analyser Polaroid only is then placed in position before the telescope objective. The telescope is rotated: (a) to receive light reflected from the prism face when the incident light is at the angle I_B, and (b) to receive light refracted through the prism. In each instance, the Polaroid is turned until darkness is obtained in the field of view of the telescope eyepiece. In case (a), the direction of light vibration transmitted by the Polaroid is perpendicular to the electric vector A_{2l}. As the plane of incidence in which A_{2l} lies is horizontal in the experiment, the preferred vibration direction through the crossed Polaroid will be vertical. In case (b), the Polaroid vibration direction will be horizontal, crossed with respect to the vertical electric vector through the prism.

The prism is then removed and the telescope set in line with the collimator. The second Polaroid (the polariser) is mounted in front of the collimator lens and rotated to give darkness in the telescope eyepiece, the polariser and analyser then being crossed. The reading on the divided circle mount of the polariser is noted, and this polariser is then turned through 45°. As the analyser Polaroid has not been rotated meanwhile, it follows that the polariser is trans-mitting light in which the electric vector is at 45° to the plane of incidence, so tan $\alpha = 1$. At such a setting, A_{1l} and A_{1r} are equal, and Equation 3.21 therefore becomes

$$\frac{A_{2r}}{A_{2l}} = -\frac{\cos(I-R)}{\cos(I+R)} \tag{3.22}$$

where tan $\theta = A_{2r}/A_{2l}$.

The telescope is now rotated to receive light reflected from the prism face (Fig. 3.34). As tan θ can be determined from the angle of setting of the analyser Polaroid, A_{2r}/A_{2l} can be found experi-mentally for various values of the angle of incidence I, enabling Equation 3.22 to be verified, which effectively verifies the Fresnel equations.

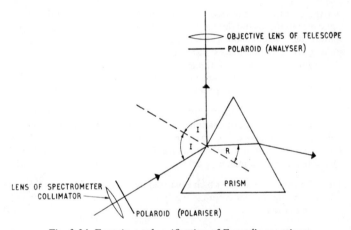

Fig. 3.34. Experimental verification of Fresnel's equations

Exercise 3

1. Describe and explain two methods of producing a beam of plane polarised light. Describe in detail how you would proceed in order to determine the refractive index of an opaque solid dielectric which has a plane polished surface.   (L.G.)

2. Explain how plane polarised light in the visible region may be produced by (a) a Nicol prism, (b) a dichroic polariser, for example Polaroid, (c) reflection at glass surfaces. Consider carefully the advantages and disadvantages of each method.   (L.G.)

3. Describe two methds of producing plane polarised light in the laboratory, and explain how the state of polarisation of light may be determined experi-mentally. A beam of plane polarised light is incident on the polished surface

of a piece of black stone. When the angle of incidence is 60° no reflection takes place for a certain orientation of the beam. Discuss this statement. Estimate the refractive index of the material of the stone. (L. Anc.)

4. What is meant by (a) the optic axis of a uniaxial crystal, (b) a quarter wave plate? Describe and explain how you would distinguish between natural light, plane polarised light, and circularly polarised light of a given wavelength. (L. Anc.)

5. Explain what is meant by linearly, circularly and elliptically polarised light respectively. Describe how these may be distinguished experimentally. The refractive indices of crystalline quartz for a wavelength of 5893 Å are 1·544 for the ordinary ray and 1·553 for the extraordinary ray. Indicate on a diagram how a quarter wave quartz plate should be cut with respect to the optic axis, and calculate the least thickness of the plate. (L.G.)

6. Explain how the state of polarisation of light from a given source may be investigated.
A parallel-sided plate of thickness 0·050 cm is cut from a crystal so that the optic axis of the crystal lies on the plane surface of the plate. Plane polarised light of wavelength 5000 Å is normally incident upon the plate so that the plane of polarisation makes an angle of 45° with the optic axis. Given that the ordinary and the extraordinary refractive indices of the material of the plate are 1·553 and 1·544 respectively, determine the state of polarisation of the light after transmission through the plate. (L. Anc.)

7. Write an account of optical rotation (optical activity) including in this (a) a discussion of its explanation in terms of oppositely circularly polarised light, (b) a comparison of the effects observed in solids and liquids, and (c) a comparison of 'natural' optical activity with the rotation caused in glass by the presence of a magnetic field. (L.P.)

8. Describe two methods by which polarised light can be obtained. How does unpolarised light differ from circularly polarised light? Discuss the use of polarising devices. (M.P.)

9. Explain how you would determine the state of polarisation of a beam of monochromatic light.
In the study of a horizontal beam of elliptically polarised light it is found that on inserting a quarter wave plate in a certain orientation, the emergent light is linearly polarised, the direction of vibration being vertical. When the quarter wave plate is rotated through 90°, the light is linearly polarised with the direction of vibration at 60° to the vertical. Determine the ratio of the axes of the ellipse and the angle that the major axis makes with the vertical. (L.P.)

10. Explain the terms *uniaxial* and *optically active* as applied to a transparent crystal, indicating the structural features with which these properties are associated.
The plane of vibration of a beam of plane polarised monochromatic light is rotated 90° (a) by passing it through an optically active uniaxial crystal in a direction parallel to the optic axis, (b) by passing it through a non-active uniaxial crystal perpendicular to the axis. In each case the crystal has the minimum thickness suitable for the purpose. What is the state of

polarisation of the light half-way through each crystal plate? Explain how you arrived at your conclusions. (L.P.)

11. Explain the terms 'optical activity' and 'rotary dispersion'. The rotation per millimetre for quartz is given by

$$\varrho = -2 \cdot 10 \times \frac{8 \cdot 14}{\lambda^2}$$

where ϱ is in degrees and λ in microns.

If a plate of quartz is placed between polariser and analyser what is the minimum thickness of plate which will give a maximum transmission through the system at 5460 Å?

Calculate the thickness of quartz plate which will cause one quarter of the previous intensity to be transmitted at the same wavelength. (City)

12. Describe and explain the action of some form of precision polarimeter. A thick plate of quartz with its faces cut parallel to the optic axis is placed between crossed Nicols with the faces perpendicular to a beam of white light which is passed through the system and into a spectrometer. A banded spectrum is observed having dark bands with centres at wave numbers k 2266, 2152, 2032, 1904, 1767, 1618 mm^{-1}. Show that this is consistent with a rotation of the plane of polarisation of the quartz proportional to $A + Bk^2$ where A and B are constants. (L.G.)

13. A doubly refracting crystal plate with its optic axis parallel to the surface is placed between two crossed Nicol prisms. The optic axis of the plate makes an angle θ with the plane of transmission of the first Nicol prism. The system is illuminated with a parallel beam of white light, the transmitted light being analysed by a prism spectrometer. Sketch the optical arrangement. Explain what is observed, and how this depends on the plate thickness b. If $b = 0 \cdot 025$ mm, $\theta = 45°$ and the refractive index difference of the plate ($\mu_o - \mu_e$) varies with λ in the manner shown in the table, what wavelengths are absent from the transmitted light in the range 4000–7000 Å?

λ in Å	4047	4861	5893	6563	
$(\mu_o - \mu_e)$	0·184	0·177	0·172	0·169	(L. G.)

14. Describe some form of polarimeter and its use for the accurate measurement of the rotation of the plane of polarisation by an optically active substance. Explain the action of a half shadow device in this connection. Discuss precautions necessary in the experiment. (L. Anc.)

15. What is a quarter wave plate and how is it used?
In a Laurent polarimeter where a half wave plate is used to divide the field, the plane of vibration of the incident plane polarised light makes an angle of 5° with the optic axis of the half wave plate and the analysing Nicol is set in turn in the two positions giving equal brightness in the two parts of the field of view. What is the ratio of the intensities observed in these two positions? (L.G.)

16. Describe some form of compensator such as that of Babinet or Soleil, stating how it could be used for the analysis of a beam of elliptically polarised light. On analysis a horizontal beam of right-handed elliptically polarised light is found to have a ratio of major to minor axis of $\sqrt{3}/1$, the former being at an

angle of 45° to the vertical. What angular measurements were made in obtaining this result? (L.P.)

17. Explain what is meant by optical activity, and give Fresnel's explanation of the phenomenon.
Describe in detail how you would measure to $\pm 0 \cdot 02°$ the optical rotation produced on a beam of plane polarised monochromatic light by a thick quartz plate cut perpendicular to the optic axis. (City)

18. Give Fresnel's theory of the rotation of the plane of polarisation when light travels through an optically active medium. In what way does natural optical activity differ from that produced by a magnetic field acting parallel to the direction of propagation?
What is the rotation experienced by a beam of plane polarised light of wavelength 5000 Å on passing through 10 cm of flint glass cylinder contained in a solenoid energised to give an axial field of 250 oersted, if the Verdet constant of the material for this wavelength is $0 \cdot 032$ minute of arc oersted^{-1} cm^{-1}? What is the difference in refractive index of the relevant circularly polarised components of the beam?
(Alternative values of 200 amp-turn cm^{-1} and $0 \cdot 04$ minutes of arc per amp-turn may be used for the field and Verdet's constant respectively). (L.P.)

19. 'Optical activity is associated with asymmetry.' Discuss this statement when applied to the case of (a) crystalline solids, (b) liquids. Would you expect to observe such an effect in a gaseous medium? Describe how the Fresnel theory accounts for the effect in terms of circularly polarised light.
In an experiment to determine the specific rotatory power of sugar, a solution of a certain concentration was placed in a tube between previously crossed nicols, using monochromatic light. Extinction was regained by rotating the analyser through 72° in a *right-handed* direction. In a second similar experiment using a solution of one-third the previous concentration a *left-handed* rotation through 36° was required. Deduce what you can concerning the actual rotation of the plane of polarisation in each case. What measurements should have been made in order to leave no ambiguities? (L. P.)

20. Give an account of the theory of reflection and refraction of electromagnetic waves at the surface separating air from another medium such as glass, assumed to be a perfect dielectric. It will be sufficient to consider the case of waves polarised in the plane of incidence, i.e. with the electric intensity vector perpendicular to this plane. Establish the formulae for the intensities of the reflected and transmitted waves, viz:

$$\frac{\text{Intensity of reflected wave}}{\text{Intensity of incident wave}} = \left[\frac{\sin (r-i)}{\sin (r+i)} \right]^{2}$$

$$\frac{\text{Intensity of transmitted wave}}{\text{Intensity of incident wave}} = \left[\frac{2 \sin r \cos i}{\sin (r+i)} \right]^{2}$$

where i and r are the angles of incidence and refraction respectively.
Explain, with an account of the apparatus used, how you would proceed to verify these results experimentally. (L.P.)

CHAPTER 4

Multiple-beam Interferometry

4.1 Multiple-beam Interference in a Plane Parallel-sided Plate

The interference of light involving division of amplitude in a parallel-sided transparent plate was considered in Chapter 9 of Volume 1. It was assumed in this account that the surfaces of the plate had low reflection coefficients, so only two beams of light took part effectively in the interference phenomenon. If these surfaces have significant reflection coefficients, multiple beams will be involved in the interference; moreover, the fringes obtained will be sharper not only in the reflected light but also greatly so in the transmitted light. This has led, in particular, to the Fabry–Perot interferometer or etalon which has become of great value, especially in very high resolution spectroscopy, and also the Lummer–Gehrcke interferometer or plate, which has a similar function though is less frequently encountered in practice.

Suppose a parallel-sided slab of uniform material of thickness d has its parallel surfaces silvered or aluminised to have a reflection coefficient r. In general, this material has a refractive index n; in important practical cases, the 'slab' is of air for which $n = 1$, to a high degree of accuracy. The air is enclosed between two plates of glass or silica by a spacer, and the inner surfaces of these plates are silvered or aluminised.

Let an incident ray of monochromatic light of wavelength λ and amplitude unity be incident at P on one surface at an angle θ, and where the corresponding angle of refraction is R in the material of the plate or slab [Fig. 4.1(a)]. As multiple reflections occur, a series of parallel reflected and transmitted beams will arise. The transmitted beams can be brought to a focus by a suitable lens; the reflected beams could be likewise focused.

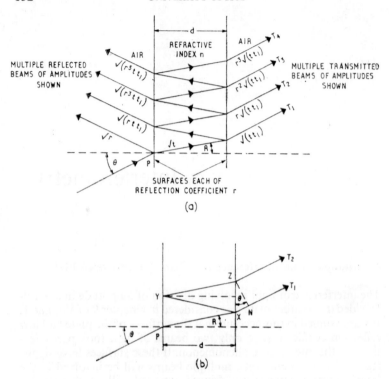

Fig. 4.1. Multiple-beam interference in a plane parallel-sided slab

The reflection coefficients r at each surface are the same. The transmission coefficient is t into the slab and t_1 out of it, where t and t_1 may be, but are not necessarily, equal. As the reflection coefficient is the intensity of the reflected light from a surface divided by the intensity of the incident light (and intensity is proportional to the square of the amplitude), it is easily seen that the amplitude of the successive parallel transmitted beams $T_1, T_2, T_3, \ldots$ are $\sqrt{(tt_1)}$, $\sqrt{(r^2 tt_1)}$, $\sqrt{(r^4 tt_1)}, \ldots$ or $\sqrt{(tt_1)}$, $r\sqrt{(tt_1)}$, $r^2\sqrt{(tt_1)}, \ldots$ The amplitudes of successive reflected beams are also easily seen to be $\sqrt{r}$, $\sqrt{(rtt_1)}$, $\sqrt{(r^3 tt_1)}, \ldots$ The reflected beams are not considered here.

The optical path difference l_0 between successive transmitted beams such as T_1 and T_2 is seen from Fig. 4.1(b) to be $n(XY + YZ) - XN$, where N is the foot of the perpendicular from Z on to XT_1. As $XY = YZ = d \sec R$, $XN = XZ \sin \theta = 2d \tan R \sin \theta$ and $(\sin \theta)/(\sin R) = n$,

$$l_0 = 2nd \sec R - 2nd \sin^2 R \sec R = 2nd \sec R\,(1 - \sin^2 R)$$

Therefore

$$l_0 = 2nd \cos R \qquad (4.1)$$

The corresponding phase difference is

$$\delta = \frac{2\pi}{\lambda} 2nd \cos R = \frac{4\pi nd}{\lambda} \cos R \qquad (4.2)$$

If the first transmitted beam is taken to have zero phase, since its amplitude is $\sqrt{(tt_1)}$, it may be represented by the real part of $\sqrt{(tt_1)} \exp j\omega t$, where $v = \omega/2\pi$ is the frequency of the monochromatic light. The successive beams T_2, T_3, T_4, ... will therefore be represented by the real parts of $r \sqrt{(tt_1)} \exp j(\omega t - \delta)$, $r^2 \sqrt{(tt_1)} \exp j(\omega t - 2\delta)$, $r^3 \sqrt{(tt_1)} \exp j(\omega t - 3\delta)$, ...

When these parallel beams are brought together at a focus by a suitable lens, the resultant amplitude A at the focus will be decided by the sum of the complex series

$$A = \text{Re} \{\sqrt{(tt_1)} [1 + r \exp(-j\delta) + r^2 \exp(-2j\delta) + \dots]\}$$

Clearly, the summation of the infinite series of terms of ratio $r \exp(-j\delta)$ is involved. Therefore

$$A = \text{Re} \left[\frac{\sqrt{(tt_1)}}{1 - r \exp(-j\delta)} \right]$$

The intensity is proportional to the square of the amplitude. The square of the modulus of a complex quantity is found by multiplying by the conjugate, which here is $\sqrt{(tt_1)}/(1 - r \exp j\delta)$. Therefore the intensity I is proportional to

$$\frac{tt_1}{[1 - r \exp(-j\delta)](1 - r \exp j\delta)} = \frac{tt_1}{1 - r[\exp j\delta + \exp(-j\delta)] + r^2}$$

Therefore

$$I = \frac{ktt_1}{1 - 2r \cos \delta + r^2} \qquad (4.3)$$

or

$$I = \frac{ktt_1}{(1-r)^2} \times \frac{1}{1 + [4r/(1-r)^2] \sin^2(\delta/2)} \qquad (4.4)$$

where k is a constant.

If $t = t_1$, tt_1 may be replaced by t^2. Further, if it is assumed that there is no absorption of light in the reflecting surfaces and in the material,

$$1 - r^2 = t^2 \qquad (4.5)$$

Equation 4.3 for the intensity will be a maximum (I_{max}) when $\cos \delta = 1$, and a minimum (I_{min}) when $\cos \delta = -1$. Maxima and minima will therefore occur at $\delta = 2p\pi$ and $(2p+1)\pi$ respectively, where p is an integer. Thus

$$I_{max} = \frac{ktt_1}{(1-r)^2} \tag{4.6}$$

and

$$I_{min} = \frac{ktt_1}{(1+r)^2} \tag{4.7}$$

The variation of the intensity I (as a fraction of the maximum intensity I_{max}) with δ for various values of the reflection coefficient

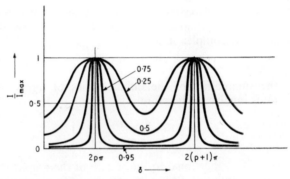

Fig. 4.2. Variation of intensity with phase difference for various reflection coefficients in fringes obtained on multiple-beam interference in transmitted light (the parameter is the coefficient r)

r is shown in Fig. 4.2. It is here assumed that the maxima have the same intensity irrespective of the magnitude of r. This will not be so in practice, because increasing the reflection coefficient of a surface by the deposition *in vacuo* of a film of silver or aluminium can only result in a decrease of the transmission coefficients t and t_1. Nevertheless, it is clear that the sharpness of the fringes increases with the reflection coefficient.

The ratio I_{max}/I_{min} is seen from Equations 4.6 and 4.7 to be

$$\frac{I_{max}}{I_{min}} = \left(\frac{1+r}{1-r}\right)^2 \tag{4.8}$$

which is independent of the transmission coefficients of the surfaces. The visibility V of the fringes is defined as

$$V = \frac{I_{max} - I_{min}}{I_{max} + I_{min}} = \frac{2r}{1+r^2} \tag{4.9}$$

and is also independent of the transmission coefficients. For an uncoated glass surface at normal incidence, r is 0·04. Then

$$V = \frac{0·08}{1+0·04^2} = 0·08 \text{ approx.}$$

A glass surface coated with pure silver by evaporation in a very good vacuum can have a reflection coefficient of 0·94 for an opaque layer. A value of 0·8 is possible with reasonable transmission. The visibility of the fringes with $r = 0·8$ would be

$$V = \frac{1·6}{1+0·64} = 0·975$$

Vacuum-deposited aluminium is preferred to silver, because it becomes coated with a tough adherent transparent film of aluminium oxide in air; its reflection coefficient is about 5% less than for silver for white light, but it is greater in the ultra-violet than that of silver.

4.2 The Fabry–Perot Etalon and Interferometer

The Fabry–Perot etalon consists of two plates of glass or quartz maintained in a holder with their facing accurately optically flat surfaces parallel and coated with a partially transmitting film of silver or aluminium having a reflection coefficient of about 0·8.

There are two main types of etalon: one type has a fixed separation (nominally 1 cm is frequently used, though other distances are available) between the reflecting surfaces on circular glass or silica plates separated by an accurately worked collar of fused silica; in the other arrangement, one plate is fixed and the other is movable on a precision micrometer screw, so that the separation can be varied whilst maintaining the reflecting surfaces accurately plane-parallel.

The Fabry–Perot etalon with a fixed separation has its inner plane parallel surfaces optically polished to be flat to $\lambda/50$ or even $\lambda/100$, where λ is the wavelength of the light used. The separator is a collar of silica with three optically polished feet spaced at 120° intervals around each of the circular edges [Fig. 4.3(a)]. The planes decided by each set of three feet are made accurately parallel. The reflecting circular glass or quartz plates are pressed in a metal holder by appropriate springs [Fig. 4.3(b)] which are brought to bear one on each side of the parallel planes decided by the feet on the collar. The final adjustment of the plates to be accurately plane-parallel is achieved by rotation by hand of screws mounted with respect to the springs and bearing members. A monochromatic source of light is observed by eye through the etalon. If the eye is focused at infinity—a

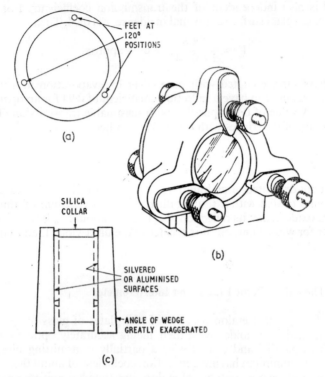

Fig. 4.3. The Fabry–Perot etalon with a fixed separation: (a) plan view of silica collar; (b) metal holder; (c) arrangement of plates

condition achievable by practice—concentric circular fringes are discerned. A telescope can be used to aid the eye in this observation. Exact parallelism is achieved when a lateral movement of the eye (or of the etalon) does not cause the fringes to open out or close in. The screws on the etalon mount are adjusted until this condition is obtained.

The outer unsilvered surfaces of the plates of the etalon are not parallel to one another but set so that the angle between them is from 1′ to 10′ [Fig. 4.3(c)]. This slight wedge shape given to each of the plates reduces the effect of the unwanted interference pattern which would be formed by these unsilvered outer faces. The plane-parallel 'slab' in which multiple-beam interference occurs is of air between the reflecting surfaces. The refractive index n is therefore very nearly unity; in very high precision work, the etalon space can be evacuated to ensure that n is exactly unity.

When two or more components of different wavelengths of a light source are observed by the Fabry–Perot etalon, equal-inclination concentric circular interference fringes due to each component are separately produced and are distinct from one another.

The optical path difference between neighbouring transmitted beams through the etalon is given by Equation 4.1 where $n = 1$. Multiple-beam interference in the transmitted parallel light occurs when these beams are brought to a focus by a lens, or on the retina of the relaxed normal human eye. Constructive interference will occur between neighbouring rays when

$$2d \cos R = p\lambda \qquad (4.10)$$

where p is an integer, λ is the wavelength of the light and d the axial separation between the etalon plates.

As the refractive index $n = 1$, the angle of refraction in the air between the plates will be the same as the angle of incidence θ and the angle of the emergent ray to the normal, presuming that the small difference between the refractive indexes of air and a vacuum is ignored. So the condition when

$$2d \cos \theta = p\lambda \qquad (4.11)$$

gives constructive interference.

The Fabry–Perot etalon is set up so that monochromatic light from an extended source S (Fig. 4.4) is rendered parallel by a converging lens L_1, traverses the etalon, and is then focused to a screen Z by a second converging lens L_2. In practice, S is frequently the illuminated slit of a spectrograph, L_1 the collimator lens; this is followed by the etalon, then a prism (usually of the constant-deviation type—Section 5.17) and finally a camera lens L_2 and the screen or photographic plate Z. The prism separates components of the incident light, but with limited resolving power; the multiple-beam interference in the etalon enhances the effective resolution enormously.

Considering first the extended source S (Fig. 4.4), it is seen that light from an axial point O on the source S will give an angle of

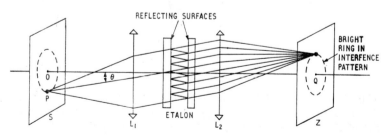

Fig. 4.4. With an extended source, parallel light incident upon a Fabry–Perot etalon produces focused concentric circular interference fringes at a screen

incidence $\theta = 0°$ at the etalon. At such normal incidence, $\cos \theta = 1$ and Equation 4.11 becomes

$$2d = p_0\lambda \qquad (4.12)$$

where p_0 is the order of interference for normal incidence.

For any other point such as P on the extended source S, the angle at which the collimated light is incident upon the etalon has a finite value θ. Now Equation 4.11 prevails and, for a given λ, constructive interference to give a maximum is when the order of interference p is an integer which is clearly less than p_0.

A given value of θ is obtained for points on a circle about the centre O of the extended source. The order of interference p will be a constant for the angle θ of emergence to the screen Z. The corresponding bright fringe (for constructive interference with p as an integer) will hence be a circle about the centre Q at the screen Z.

A concentric series of such circular bright fringes will correspond to p_0 at the centre (or very near the centre), $p_0 - 1$ for the next fringe, $p_0 - 2$ for the next further out, and so on. At the exact centre, where incidence is precisely normal, p_0 is not necessarily an integer because $2d$ is not necessarily an exactly integral number of wavelengths. Hence p_0 will be the order of interference for a bright ring very near the centre where θ is very small (and so $\cos \theta = 1$, with very small error). At the centre proper, strictly speaking the order of interference is $p_1 + \varepsilon$, where ε is a fraction; at this true centre there will therefore not, in general, be either a maximum or a minimum.

The bright rings will be separated by dark circular fringes where destructive interference occurs and

$$2d \cos \theta = \left(p + \tfrac{1}{2}\right)\lambda \qquad (4.13)$$

Differentiation of p_0 in Equation 4.12 with respect to λ gives

$$\frac{dp_0}{d\lambda} = \frac{d}{d\lambda}\left(\frac{2d}{\lambda}\right) = -\frac{2d}{\lambda^2}$$

Therefore

$$\frac{\lambda^2}{d\lambda} = -\frac{2d}{dp_0}$$

or

$$\frac{\lambda}{d\lambda} = -\frac{2d}{dp_0\lambda} = -\frac{p_0}{dp_0} \qquad (4.14)$$

The chromatic resolving power $\lambda/d\lambda$ of the Fabry–Perot etalon depends on the smallest change of wavelength $d\lambda$ which can be detected at a mean wavelength λ. From Equation 4.14, it is seen that this resolving power at the centre of the interference pattern is given by the smallest change of order p_0 which can be recognised.

This will depend upon the sharpness of the circular interference fringes. From Equation 4.4,

$$I = \frac{I_{max}}{1 + [4r/(1-r)^2] \sin^2 (\delta/2)} \qquad (4.15)$$

where I_{max} is the intensity at the central maximum in the concentric interference ray pattern (order p_0), and I is the intensity at a neighbouring position for light differing in phase by δ.

According to the Rayleigh criterion (Chapter 12 of Volume 1), the two maxima are resolved if the intensity at the midway point between two maxima is $8/\pi^2$ of the maximum intensity; the intensity

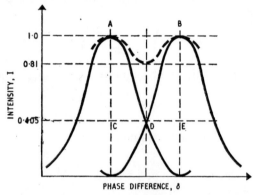

Fig. 4.5. The Rayleigh criterion for chromatic resolution

contributed by one bright fringe then only falls off to $4/\pi^2$ at this midway point (Fig. 4.5). Though this criterion as given in Volume 1 for a prism or diffraction grating does not strictly apply to the Fabry–Perot etalon because the peaks of intensity formed are considerably sharper, yet a simple—but pessimistic—estimate of the resolving power is given by putting $I/I_{max} = 4/\pi^2 = 0.405$ in Equation 4.15:

$$0.405 = \frac{1}{1 + F \sin^2 (\delta/2)}$$

where $F = 4r/(1-r)^2$ is known as the *coefficient of finesse*. Therefore

$$0.405 + 0.405F \sin^2 (\delta/2) = 1$$

Thus

$$\sin^2 (\delta/2) = \frac{0.595}{0.405F} = \frac{1.469}{F}$$

or

$$\delta = 2 \sin^{-1} \sqrt{\frac{1 \cdot 469}{F}}$$

This phase difference δ corresponds to CD in Fig. 4.5. The phase difference between neighbouring peaks A and B (i.e. CE) which can be recognised will be

$$2\delta = 4 \sin^{-1} \sqrt{\frac{1 \cdot 469}{F}}$$

As a change of order by unity corresponds to a phase change of 2π, the smallest change dp_0 of order p_0 that can be recognised is therefore given by

$$dp_0 = \frac{4 \sin^{-1} \sqrt{(1 \cdot 469/F)}}{2\pi}$$

From Equation 4.14 the resolving power is therefore given by

$$\frac{\lambda}{d\lambda} = -\frac{p_0}{dp_0} = -\frac{p_0\pi}{2 \sin^{-1}(1 \cdot 21/\sqrt{F})} \qquad (4.16)$$

With a reflection coefficient r of 0·8,

$$F = \frac{4r}{(1-r)^2} = \frac{3 \cdot 2}{0 \cdot 04} = 80$$

Therefore $\sqrt{F} = 8 \cdot 95$ and

$$\sin^{-1}\frac{1 \cdot 21}{\sqrt{F}} = \sin^{-1}\frac{1 \cdot 21}{8 \cdot 95} = 0 \cdot 135 \text{ rad}$$

This is small enough for the angle (in radians) to be taken instead of the sine. So Equation 4.16 can be approximated to

$$\text{resolving power} = -\frac{p_0\pi\sqrt{F}}{2 \times 1 \cdot 21}$$

Substituting $F = 4r/(1-r)^2$ gives the resolving power as

$$\text{resolving power} = -\frac{p_0\pi\sqrt{r}}{1 \cdot 21(1-r)} = -\frac{2 \cdot 6 p_0 \sqrt{r}}{1-r} \qquad (4.17)$$

It is seen that the resolving power is directly proportional to the maximum order of interference p_0 and depends on the reflection coefficient r of the surface films. An etalon of large separation d and highly reflecting surfaces is therefore required for high resolution.

If the etalon separation d is $1 \cdot 0$ cm and the reflection coefficient of each surface is $0 \cdot 8$, then for light of wavelength 5,000 Å,

$$p_0 = \frac{2d}{\lambda} = \frac{2}{5 \times 10^{-5}} = 4 \times 10^4$$

The resolving power is given by Equation 4.17 to be

$$\frac{\lambda}{d\lambda} = \frac{2 \cdot 6 \times 4 \times 10^4 \times \sqrt{0 \cdot 8}}{1 \cdot 21 \times 0 \cdot 2} = 2 \cdot 75 \times 10^5$$

At $\lambda = 5,000$ Å, therefore, it is possible to distinguish a change of wavelength $d\lambda$ equal to $5,000/(2 \cdot 75 \times 10^5) = 0 \cdot 0182$ Å. If an etalon of 10 cm separation were used, ten times this resolving power would be obtained, and wavelengths separated by only $0 \cdot 00182$ Å in 5,000 Å would be discerned. Measurements of the hyperfine structure of spectral lines can therefore be made. Such hyperfine structure determinations can be used to determine the effects on atomic spectra of the Zeeman effect, the presence of isotopes, nuclear spin and nuclear quadrupole moments.

If the etalon is used on a spectrograph between the prism and the collimator lens, the extended source of light will be a slit S, the prism of the spectrograph will produce separated lines at the camera plate, each line corresponding to the component wavelengths in the source; each line will be crossed by interference bands due to the multiple-beam interference in the Fabry–Perot etalon (Fig. 4.6).

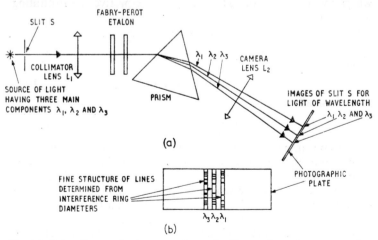

Fig. 4.6. Fabry–Perot etalon between prism and collimator lens of a spectrograph: (a) plan view; (b) appearance of photographic negative

4.3 The Method of Exact Fractions

If the separation d of the reflecting surfaces of a Fabry–Perot etalon is known approximately, for example to be 1·018 cm, and the wavelengths of three spectral lines are known accurately, the separation d can be determined to a very high degree of accuracy by the Benoît method of exact fractions; other wavelengths can then be measured to a similar high degree of accuracy.

For any wavelength λ_1, the order of interference p_0 at the centre of the Fabry–Perot fringes is not usually an integer so can be expressed as $p_1 + \varepsilon_1$, where p_1 is the order for the first bright ring, p_1 being an integer and ε_1 being a fraction. For other wavelengths λ_2, λ_3, λ_4, ... the corresponding values are p_2, p_3, p_4, ... for the integers and ε_2, ε_3, ε_4, ... for the fractions. As $\cos \theta$ in Equation 4.11 is unity in each case

$$2d = \lambda_1(p_1 + \varepsilon_1) = \lambda_2(p_2 + \varepsilon_2) = \lambda_3(p_3 + \varepsilon_3) \qquad (4.18)$$

To measure these fractions ε_1, ε_2 and ε_3 at the centre of the fringe systems, the etalon is placed between the prism and the collimator lens of a prism spectrometer. If j is the bright ring number (going out from the centre of the pattern) for a given wavelength and p is the order for the first bright ring, the order for the jth ring is $p - j + 1$. At this jth ring, θ will not be zero but equal to θ_j, say. From Equation 4.11, therefore,

$$2d \cos \theta_j = (p - j + 1)\lambda$$

where λ will be λ_1, λ_2 or λ_3 for ε_1, ε_2 or ε_3 respectively. Substituting

$$\frac{2d}{\lambda} = p + \varepsilon$$

gives

$$(p + \varepsilon) \cos \theta_j = p - j + 1 \qquad (4.19)$$

As θ_j is small,

$$\cos \theta_j = 1 - \tfrac{1}{2}\theta_j^2$$

The appearance in the telescope eyepiece or of the developed image on a photographic plate will be of a bright line, corresponding to a particular wavelength, crossed by the concentric circular interference fringes. The diameters of the bright rings at a given wavelength can be found by measurements with a travelling microscope on the photographic negative (Fig. 4.7).

If D_j is the diameter of the jth ring for a given wavelength,

$$KD_j = 2\theta_j$$

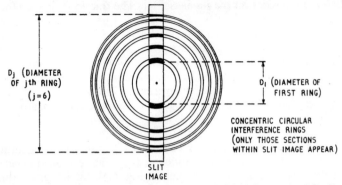

Fig. 4.7. *An image of the slit for a particular wavelength is crossed by fringes which are short sections of concentric circular interference fringes*

where K is a constant depending on the magnification produced by the camera lens. Therefore

$$\cos \theta_j = 1 - \tfrac{1}{8} K^2 D_j^2 \qquad (4.20)$$

From Equations 4.19 and 4.20 it follows that

$$(p + \varepsilon)\left(1 - \tfrac{1}{8} K^2 D_j^2\right) = p - j + 1$$

Therefore

$$\tfrac{1}{8}(p + \varepsilon) K^2 D_j^2 = j + \varepsilon - 1 \qquad (4.21)$$

When $D_j = 0$, $j + \varepsilon - 1 = 0$ so $j = 1 - \varepsilon$. Furthermore, a graph of D_j^2 against the ring number j is a straight line (Fig. 4.8) for

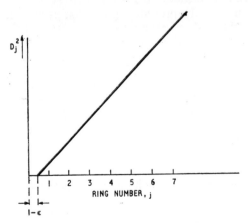

Fig. 4.8. *Plot of the square of the diameter of a bright interference ring (D_j^2) against the ring number j*

which the intercept on the j-axis is $1-\varepsilon$. The fraction ε is therefore determined for a particular wavelength λ. For accurately known wavelengths λ_1, λ_2 and λ_3, the fractions ε_1, ε_2 and ε_3 are found in this manner, each to an accuracy of $\pm 0{\cdot}01$.

For the separation d of, say, nominally $1{\cdot}018$ cm, $2d/\lambda_1$ gives the integer p_1 approximately. At this wavelength, ε_1 is known. Hence $\lambda_1(p_1+\varepsilon_1)$ in Equation 4.18 is apparently known. As λ_2 is also known, it is possible to calculate $p_2+\varepsilon_2$ from the relationship

$$\lambda_1(p_1+\varepsilon_1) = \lambda_2(p_2+\varepsilon_2)$$

The fraction ε_2 is then found because p_2 is necessarily integral; if this calculated value of ε_2 is different from that obtained experimentally (i.e. leading to a plot such as Fig. 4.8), the integral value of p_1 must be wrong. The procedure is then to find the correct value of the integer p_1 by exploring the range of values differing successively by $+1$, $+2$, $+3$, ..., $+p'$ and -1, -2, -3, ..., $-p'$ from the originally calculated value, where p' is an integer of 20–30 usually. Each time the corresponding value of ε_2 is calculated. When this value is the same as that determined experimentally at the wavelength λ_2, then the correct integer p_1 is known. To make sure, a third wavelength λ_3 is also explored in the same way. Now $p_1+\varepsilon_1$ is known precisely for the known wavelength λ_1, where p_1 is an exactly known integer and the fraction ε_1 is known to within $0{\cdot}01$. From the equation

$$2d = \lambda_1(p_1+\varepsilon_1)$$

the separation d is thus found to within about 10^{-7} cm.

For example, if d is normally $1{\cdot}018$ cm and λ_1 is exactly 5,000 Å, p_1 is initially estimated to be $2{\cdot}036/(5\times10^{-5}) = 40,720$. If it is eventually found by the procedure given that p_1 is, in fact, 40,728 whilst ε_1 is obtained by experiment to be $0{\cdot}03$, it follows that $p_1+\varepsilon_1$ is $40,728{\cdot}03$, and the exact length of the etalon is thus

$$d = \tfrac{1}{2}\times5\times10^{-5}\times40,728{\cdot}03 = 1{\cdot}01820075 \text{ cm}$$

to an accuracy of better than 1 part in 10^7.

Once the etalon separation d is found to this order of accuracy by use of the method of exact fractions, it is possible to determine with the same precision other wavelengths previously known only approximately.

4.4 The Fabry–Perot Etalon with Variable Separation

One accurately plane glass plate coated with silver or aluminium is fixed and the other is mounted on a nut on a micrometer screw so that it can be moved to alter the separation d. A convenient variable-separation etalon can be set up by removing the two full reflecting mirrors from a Michelson interferometer (Volume 1, Chapter 10) and setting up two partially reflecting mirrors parallel to each other with their silvered surfaces facing; one of these partially reflecting mirrors is fixed and the other is on the movable carriage controlled by the micrometer screw. Indeed, some commercial instruments are arranged so that they can be set up either as a Michelson interferometer or as a variable-thickness Fabry–Perot etalon.

The observer can view by eye, or with the aid of a telescope, a source of light directly through the two silvered plates and study the positions of the concentric circular interference fringes as the separation between the plates (i.e. the thickness or length of the etalon) is varied.

Suppose that there are two components, of wavelengths λ_1 and λ_2, in the light from the source and that $\lambda_1 > \lambda_2$. When the reflecting surfaces are nearly in contact (separation d is very small), the ring systems due to the two different wavelengths will almost coincide. As the separation d is increased, the rings separate. It is possible to judge when one set of rings is half-way between those of the other set. As d is then further increased, a position will be reached where the two ring systems coincide exactly, then separate out beyond this position to give a second half-way position and a second coincidence, and so on as d is increased progressively.

Let the separation be d_1 when the bright rings (i.e. the maxima) coincide in a direction θ near the centre of the field of view where θ is small; then

$$2d_1 \cos \theta = p_1\lambda_1 = q_1\lambda_2$$

Therefore

$$\frac{\lambda_1}{\lambda_2} = \frac{q_1}{p_1}$$

where p_1 and q_1 are the respective integral orders of interference.

At the next bright ring coincidence further from the centre, for the same separation d_1 but where θ has increased, p_1 becomes $p_1 - 1$ and q_1 becomes $q_1 - 1$; but $(q_1 - 1)/(p_1 - 1)$ is very nearly equal to q_1/p_1 because p_1 and q_1 are both very large numbers. Consequently, the coincidence of bright rings will be observed over the whole field of view.

The plate separation is then increased to d_2 at which the bright ring maxima due to λ_1 and λ_2 again coincide. This is achieved when p_1 is increased to p_2 and q_1 to q_2, so

$$2d_2 \cos \theta = p_2\lambda_1 = q_2\lambda_2$$

Therefore

$$2(d_1-d_2)\cos\theta = (p_1-p_2)\lambda_1 = (q_1-q_2)\lambda_2$$

Clearly, if $p_1-p_2 = m$, q_1-q_2 must equal $m+1$, where m is an integer. Therefore

$$2(d_1-d_2)\cos\theta = m\lambda_1 = (m+1)\lambda_2 = m\lambda_2+\lambda_2$$

Therefore

$$\lambda_1-\lambda_2 = \frac{\lambda_2}{m} \tag{4.22}$$

As $m = p_1-p_2 = 2(d_1-d_2)/\lambda_1$ near the centre of the fringe system when $\theta \rightarrow 0$ and $\cos\theta = 1$,

$$\lambda_1-\lambda_2 = \frac{\lambda_1\lambda_2}{2(d_1-d_2)} \tag{4.23}$$

If $\lambda_1-\lambda_2 = d\lambda$, where $d\lambda$ is very small, which is frequently the situation of interest, Equation 4.23 becomes

$$d\lambda = \frac{\lambda^2}{2(d_1-d_2)} \tag{4.24}$$

The possible procedures in practice are:

1. The number of fringes at wavelength λ_1 or λ_2 which appear from the centre of the field of view (for example, which pass the cross-wires in a viewing telescope eyepiece) is counted as the movable plate is moved from one coincidence of bright rings to the rest over the distance d_1 to d_2. This number is m in Equation 4.22, so λ_1/λ_2 is known, or λ_2 is found if λ_1 is known.
2. If the micrometer screw is accurately calibrated in centimetres, the traverse d_2-d_1 is directly measured and Equation 4.23 gives $\lambda_1-\lambda_2$, accurately provided that λ_1 and λ_2 are known approximately.

4.5 Brewster's Fringes: Two Fabry–Perot Etalons in Series

As has already been shown, with a single parallel plate a given interference fringe corresponds to a given value of $\cos\theta$; thus *constant inclination fringes* are formed which are at infinity and can be focused by an objective lens to give concentric alternately bright and dark rings in the focal plane of the lens. With two such parallel plates inclined at a small angle 2α to each other, *Brewster's fringes* are obtained in the focal plane of an objective lens when an extended source of light is viewed by transmission.

Suppose the two plates are of the same thickness d and have semi-silvered surfaces. In the case of chief interest, these 'plates' both consist of the air enclosed between the facing semi-silvered surfaces of an etalon; thus two etalons in series are involved, and the refractive index n of the medium is unity (Fig. 4.9).

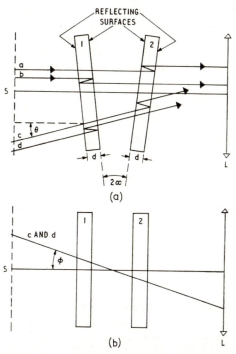

Fig. 4.9. *Brewster fringes formed on the transmission of light through two etalons in series and inclined at a small angle to each other: (a) plan view of etalons; (b) vertical elevation.*

Consider first horizontal rays such as a and b parallel to the axis (which is best defined as the axis of a viewing telescope, of which lens L is the objective). The etalons 1 and 2 are inclined at the small angle 2α and are symmetrically disposed about the normal to the axis in the plan view shown in Fig. 4.9(a). The angles of incidence of both rays a and b at etalons 1 and 2 will then be α.

The ray a has an additional path of $2d \cos \alpha$ in etalon 2, and the ray b has an additional path of $2d \cos \alpha$ in etalon 1. All such parallel rays can be divided into pairs, one of type a and the other of type b. In general, for a ray of type a there will be an even number m of reflections in etalon 1 and $m+2$ reflections in etalon 2; for a ray of type b, there will be $m+2$ reflections in etalon 1 and m in etalon 2. In the case illustrated in Fig. 4.9(a), m is taken to be zero for simplicity.

For horizontal parallel rays such as c and d inclined at an angle θ to the axis, the angle of incidence will be $\theta-\alpha$ at etalon 1 and $\theta+\alpha$ at etalon 2. For a ray of type c (which corresponds to type a) the additional path in etalon 2 is now $2d \cos (\theta +\alpha)$, whereas for a ray of type d (which corresponds to type b) there is a different additional path of $2d \cos (\theta-\alpha)$. The ray pairs such as c and d hence arrive at the focal plane of lens L with a phase difference δ given by

$$\delta = \frac{2\pi}{\lambda} 2d[\cos (\theta-\alpha)-\cos (\theta+\alpha)] = \frac{8\pi d}{\lambda} \sin \theta \sin \alpha$$

As expected, this is zero when $\theta = 0$, i.e. when the incident horizontal rays are parallel to the axis as for rays a and b.

From the extended source of light S, rays will not, of course, all be in or near the horizontal. Consider, therefore, the general case of rays which are inclined at angle ϕ to the horizontal and at θ to the vertical plane through the axis. The phase difference Δ between pairs such as c and d in Fig. 4.9(b) (not now in the horizontal plane containing the axis of the telescope) will be $\delta \cos \phi$, i.e.

$$\Delta = \delta \cos \phi = \frac{8\pi d}{\lambda} \sin \theta \sin \alpha \cos \phi \qquad (4.25)$$

where λ is the wavelength of the light from the extended source S.

Incident rays which lie in vertical planes parallel to the axis but which are at angle ϕ to the axis of the telescope will be those for which $\theta = 0$, so will arrive in phase at the focal plane of the telescope objective. For any particular value of ϕ, there will therefore be a bright point in the focal plane of lens L. For the range of values of ϕ for an extended source, the series of bright points will form a central vertical bright line in the focal plane. This will be observed both for monochromatic light and also for white light because $\Delta = 0$.

Incident rays for which θ is finite but with different values of ϕ will correspondingly be focused in a vertical line in the focal plane of lens L; however, there will now be a specific phase difference Δ between pairs of rays, depending on both θ and ϕ. In the usual practical situation, ϕ is small and $\cos \phi \simeq 1$, so that variation with ϕ is not significant. The focal plane of lens L, i.e. the field of view in a telescope of which L is the objective, will therefore be illuminated by a series of vertical interference fringes, known as *Brewster's fringes*.

Maxima, i.e. bright vertical lines, will appear in this system of interference fringes when $\Delta = 2p\pi$ or zero, where p is an integer. As ϕ is small in Equation 4.25, cos ϕ can be put equal to unity; thus maxima occur when

$$\frac{8\pi d}{\lambda} \sin \theta \sin \alpha = 2p\pi \text{ or zero} \qquad (4.26)$$

If the angles θ and α are also small, as is usual with Fabry–Perot etalons,

$$\theta = \frac{p\lambda}{4d\alpha} \qquad (4.27)$$

The angular separation of the maxima (bright line fringes) is therefore $\lambda/4d\alpha$.

To summarise, Brewster's fringes are obtained on viewing an extended source through two equal parallel plates in series, inclined at a small angle to one another. As observed in a telescope, these fringes consist of parallel bright lines interleaved by dark fringes which are vertical when the angle of inclination between the plates is in the horizontal plane. If the extended source of light is white, a central maximum bright white line flanked by coloured fringes is observed. With monochromatic light, a series of alternately light and dark fringes is observed for low orders of interference. At high orders, the fringes become curved.

With two Fabry–Perot etalons in series, the 'plate' or 'slab' is now simply of air. Brewster's fringes are seen if these two etalons are of the same thickness d, and also if the ratio of their thicknesses d_1 and d_2 is 2 : 1 or, in general, where d_1/d_2 equals the ratio of small integers.

4.6 Comparison of the Standard Metre with the Wavelength of Light by means of Fabry–Perot Etalons

In Volume 1 (Section 10.3) is described the determination of the wavelength of the red and other lines in the spectrum of a cadmium source in terms of the accepted standard metre. This pioneer work made use of the Michelson interferometer. Later work has utilised Fabry–Perot etalons. This was first undertaken in 1913 by Benoît, Fabry and Perot. More recent work is due to Sears and Barrell, and at the present time the red cadmium line ($\lambda = 6,440$ Å) has been discarded as the standard in favour of that from a discharge lamp containing the isotope of krypton of mass 86 ($\lambda = 6,060$ Å), which exhibits less hyperfine structure than the cadmium red.

To compare wavelengths with mechanical standards of length, of which the accepted international standard metre is the most important. Benoît, Fabry and Perot used five Fabry–Perot etalons (etalons 1, 2, 3, 4 and 5) of lengths (reflecting surface separations) 100 cm, 50 cm, 25 cm, 12·5 cm and 6·25 cm respectively. Sears and Barrell used only three etalons: etalon 1 of 1 m, etalon 2 of $\frac{1}{3}$ m and etalon 3 of $\frac{1}{9}$ m, where these lengths are precise as regards normal engineering standards but are nominal in relation to high-precision optical measurements.

In both series of experiments, the length of the shortest etalon was determined by the method of exact fractions using the red cadmium line (later the orange-red line of krypton 86); the number of wavelengths accommodated within the length of the etalon was thus found precisely. In the Fabry, Perot and Benoît procedure, the first part of the experiment was followed by a second part, in which the ratios of the lengths of the following etalon combinations were found: etalon 4/etalon 5; etalon 3/etalon 4; etalon 2/etalon 3; and etalon 1/etalon 2. To do this, specially calibrated thin air wedges between silvered glass plates were used. In the Sears and Barrell experiments, the ratios of the lengths of etalons 2 and 3 and of the lengths of etalons 1 and 2 were determined by a method depending on the observation of Brewster fringes (Section 4.5). The third and final part of both experiments was then to compare the longest etalon (etalon 1) of nominally 100 cm (but now of exactly known length in terms of the wavelenth of the light used) with the standard metre.

In both experiments, the apparatus was set up* so that the observation of the order of interference at the centre of the shortest etalon, the measurement of the ring diameters needed for the subsequent exact fraction calculation, the intercomparisons of the etalon lengths and the final comparison between the 100 cm etalon and the standard metre could all be made as quickly as possible. This was essential to avoid errors due to changes in atmospheric conditions. In the experiments of Sears and Barrell, the whole optical arrangement was maintained at constant temperature measured to an accuracy of 0·001 deg C; each etalon was specially constructed so that the space between its reflecting surfaces could be evacuated to low pressure so as to avoid errors resulting from the fact that the refractive index of air is not exactly unity.

The mean value of several measurements of the wavelength of the red line in the cadmium spectrum in terms of the standard metre is 6,438·4696 Å.

In 1960, the International Commission of Weights and Measures adopted the orange-red line of krypton 86 as the standard and defined the metre as 1,650,763·73 wavelengths *in vacuo* of this line.

---

* For fuller details see, for example: LONGHURST, R. S., *Geometrical and Physical Optics*, Longmans, Green, London (1957).

This line in the spectrum of light from a krypton 86 lamp is therefore the basic standard of length from which the metre is defined and, in particular, it is the reference wavelength in terms of which all other wavelengths in the electromagnetic spectrum are specified.

4.7 Interference Filters of the Fabry–Perot Type

Interference filters which transmit substantially monochromatic light with a much sharper cut-off than is possible with gelatine or coloured glass filters are made by vacuum-coating techniques. For example, a semi-transparent film of silver or aluminium is first deposited on a plane glass plate, on top of this is deposited a layer of a transparent dielectric such as cryolite, and finally a second semi-transparent film of silver or aluminium.

If d is the thickness of the dielectric film of refractive index n sandwiched between the reflecting metallic films, a Fabry–Perot etalon of very short length is produced. When a beam of collimated light is incident normally, maxima in the transmitted light will occur for those wavelengths λ which satisfy the equation

$$2nd = p\lambda$$

where p is an integer.

Cryolite evaporated in a vacuum will produce a durable transparent film, of refractive index about 1·34, on a substrate. If its thickness d is small, say 4×10^{-5} cm, comparable with visible light wavelengths, then

$$2 \times 1·34 \times 4 \times 10^{-5} = p\lambda$$

For $p = 1$, $\lambda = 10·72 \times 10^{-5}$ cm $= 10,720$ Å in the infra-red; for $p = 2$, $\lambda = 5,360$ Å in the visible and for $p = 3$ or more, λ is in the ultra-violet region. Consequently, the only visible light transmitted is at 5,360 Å in the green.

An interference filter with green transmission is thus available. However, the light transmitted will not only be of wavelength 5,360 Å, because there will be a distribution of light in wavelengths about the wavelength at the central maximum to an extent dependent upon the resolving power of the etalon (Fig. 4.5). From the analysis given in Section 4.2, it is seen that the intensity falls off to approximately 40% of that at the central maximum at wavelengths $\lambda - d\lambda$ and $\lambda + d\lambda$ where, from Equation 4.17,

$$\frac{\lambda}{d\lambda} = \frac{2·6 p_0 \sqrt{r}}{1 - r}$$

For $r = 0·9$

$$d\lambda = \frac{0·1\lambda}{2·6 p_0 \times 0·81} = \frac{0·0475\lambda}{p_0}$$

For the cryolite film of thickness 4×10^{-5} cm, $\lambda = 5.36 \times 10^{-5}$ cm and $p_0 = 2$, as shown above. Therefore,

$$d\lambda = \frac{0.0475 \times 5.36 \times 10^{-5}}{2} = 1.275 \times 10^{-6} \text{ cm}$$

Therefore, with a central maximum I_{max} at 5,360 Å, light of intensity $0.4\, I_{max}$ will be transmitted at wavelengths $(5,360 \pm 127.5)$ Å.

The width of the band of wavelengths passed by such an interference filter can be reduced to about 100 Å by increasing the reflection coefficient of the metallic surfaces to 0·94. It is then difficult to obtain sufficient transmitted light because, with metallic films, high reflectivity can only be obtained by thicker deposits of high light absorption.

This difficulty can be overcome by using enhanced reflecting layers formed by the vacuum deposition of transparent dielectrics on to glass instead of reflecting metallic films. In Section 9.4 of Volume 1, it is shown that a layer of transparent dielectric $\lambda/4$ thick on glass will produce enhanced reflection if this dielectric has a refractive index greater than that of the glass substrate. Suitable high refractive index dielectrics for this purpose are zinc sulphide, for which $n = 2.3$, and titanium dioxide of refractive index $n = 2.8$ at a wavelength 5,000 Å.

Interference filters of low absorption and good transmission of light can therefore be made by the deposition *in vacuo* on to a glass plate (which does not have to be optically flat because the deposited film follows contours accurately) of first a dielectric, such as titanium dioxide, to a thickness of $\lambda/4$ (where λ is the desired transmitted wavelength), then a thin layer of cryolite or, alternatively, magnesium fluoride, and finally a second layer $\lambda/4$ thick of titanium dioxide.

To obtain higher reflection coefficients than are possible with only one dielectric film (and so narrow down the band of wavelengths transmitted by the filter), dielectric films of alternately high and low refractive indices are vacuum deposited. With seven layers of zinc sulphide and cryolite, the reflection coefficient is 0·9.

The modern interference filter able to transmit a narrow band of wavelengths about a predetermined specific wavelength is a valuable device in optics, with considerable advantages in defined bandpass over the coloured gelatine filter. In recent developments, the vacuum coating procedure is programmed to give several layers of dielectric materials of controlled thicknesses. These layers are sandwiched between glass plates for protection, and the outer surfaces of the glass plates are bloomed (see Section 9.4 of Volume 1) to enhance light transmission and reduce back-reflection.

Reflection filters are also available: a dielectric layer of, say, cryolite is vacuum-deposited on to a mirror consisting of, for example, glass vacuum-coated with aluminium. A semi-transparent metallic film is then deposited on the dielectric. The mirror so made can be designed to have zero reflectivity at specific wavelengths.

4.8 The Lummer–Gehrcke Interferometer

The resolving power of a multiple-beam interferometer increases with the reflecting power of the separated surfaces. In 1901, Lummer devised a method of making an interferometer in which high reflection was obtained by utilising light internally reflected near the critical angle; in collaboration with Gehrcke, a new interferometer based on the principle was introduced in 1903. The reflecting surfaces did not require silvering or aluminising.

The Lummer–Gehrcke interferometer consists of an accurately plane-parallel plate of glass, or preferably quartz, with a small right-angled prism of the same material in optical contact at one end (Fig. 4.10). Light incident normally on the upright plane face of this prism is reflected at its hypotenuse face. The reflected light passes into the plane-parallel plate to be incident internally on its surface with air at an angle θ slightly less than the critical angle. The prism angle is predetermined to achieve this. At each successive incidence down the length of the plane-parallel plate, light is reflected and partially transmitted. The transmitted parallel beams are brought to a focus by a lens L.

The Lummer–Gehrcke plate is an alternative to the Fabry–Perot etalon, though it is little used nowadays because the latter has proved more versatile and is rather easier to construct. Like the Fabry–Perot etalon, it is usually set up between the collimator and prism on a constant-deviation spectrometer.

Multiple beam interference fringes of equal inclination are obtained in the focal plane of lens L. Two sets of identical fringe systems are produced symmetrically about the two sides of the plane-parallel plate.

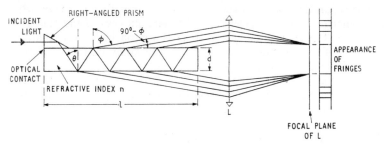

Fig. 4.10. The Lummer–Gehrcke interferometer

If n is the refractive index of the material of the plate of thickness d, maxima in the interference pattern occur when

$$2nd \cos \theta = p\lambda \qquad (4.28)$$

p being an integer. Let ϕ be the angle that the emergent light makes with the normal; then

$$n = \frac{\sin \phi}{\sin \theta}$$

Substituting for $\cos \theta$ in Equation 4.28,

$$2nd \sqrt{\left(1 - \frac{\sin^2 \phi}{n^2}\right)} = p\lambda$$

Therefore,

$$2d \sqrt{(n^2 - \sin^2 \phi)} = p\lambda \qquad (4.29)$$

or

$$\sin^2 \phi = n^2 - \frac{p^2 \lambda^2}{4d^2} \qquad (4.30)$$

To explore the variation of ϕ with order p (where n, d and λ are constant), differentiation of Equation 4.30 with respect to ϕ gives

$$2 \sin \phi \cos \phi = -\frac{\lambda^2}{4d^2} 2p \frac{\mathrm{d}p}{\mathrm{d}\phi} = -\frac{p\lambda^2}{2d^2} \frac{\mathrm{d}p}{\mathrm{d}\phi}$$

The angle $\Delta\phi$ between orders differing by Δp is therefore given by

$$\Delta\phi = -\frac{p\lambda^2 \, \Delta p}{2d^2 \sin 2\phi}$$

where $\Delta p = 1$ for successive orders. Substituting for $p\lambda$ from Equation 4.29, the angle $\delta\phi$ between successive orders is seen to be

$$\delta\phi = -\frac{\lambda \sqrt{(n^2 - \sin^2 \phi)}}{d \sin 2\phi} \qquad (4.31)$$

The separation between successive orders therefore increases with wavelength, varies inversely with the plate thickness d and increases as $\phi \to 90°$ (i.e. as grazing emergence is approached). Note that the length of the plate does not enter into this analysis: the separation is independent of this length.

For a given order p, the dispersion $\partial\phi/\partial\lambda$ is obtained by differentiating Equation 4.30 with respect to λ. Taking into account that the refractive index n is a function of wavelength λ,

$$\sin 2\phi \frac{\partial\phi}{\partial\lambda} = 2n \frac{\partial n}{\partial\lambda} - \frac{2p^2 \lambda}{4d^2}$$

Therefore

$$\frac{\partial \phi}{\partial \lambda} = \frac{4d^2 n(\partial n/\partial \lambda) - p^2 \lambda}{2d^2 \sin 2\phi}$$

Substituting for d from Equation 4.29 gives

$$\frac{\partial \phi}{\partial \lambda} = \frac{2\lambda n(\partial n/\partial \lambda) - 2(n^2 - \sin^2 \phi)}{\lambda \sin 2\phi} \tag{4.32}$$

The dispersion of the interferometer is therefore independent of the length and thickness of the plate, but it does depend on the dispersion $\partial n/\partial \lambda$ of the material of the plate, the wavelength and the angle of emergence ϕ.

A value of $\delta \phi$ obtained from Equation 4.31 and equated to the same value of $\delta \phi$ from Equation 4.32 will give $\delta \lambda$, the maximum difference of wavelength possible without overlap between successive orders. Thus,

$$\delta \phi = -\frac{\lambda \sqrt{(n^2 - \sin^2 \phi)}}{d \sin 2\phi} = \frac{2\lambda n(\partial n/\partial \lambda) - 2(n^2 - \sin^2 \phi)}{\lambda \sin 2\phi} \delta \lambda$$

Therefore

$$\delta \lambda = \frac{\lambda^2 \sqrt{(n^2 - \sin^2 \phi)}}{2d[n^2 - \sin^2 \phi - \lambda n(\partial n/\partial \lambda)]}$$

As $\sqrt{(n^2 - \sin^2 \phi)} = p\lambda/2d$, from Equation 4.29,

$$\delta \lambda = \frac{p\lambda^3/2d}{2d[(p^2 \lambda^2/4d^2) - \lambda n(\partial n/\partial \lambda)]}$$

or

$$\delta \lambda = \frac{p\lambda^2}{p^2 \lambda - 4d^2 n(\partial n/\partial \lambda)} \tag{4.33}$$

giving $\delta \lambda$, the difference of wavelength which a line in any order must have to coincide with the main fringe in the next order.

Equation 4.33 also applies to a Fabry–Perot etalon, for which $\partial n/\partial \lambda = 0$ (presuming the space between the etalon reflecting surfaces is evacuated to a low pressure).

The resolving power of the Lummer–Gehrcke plate interferometer may be estimated approximately by noting from Fig. 4.10 that the width of the beam entering the telescope or camera objective lens from the top (or bottom) surface of the plate is $l \cos \phi$, where l is the total length of the plate. The angle $d\phi$ between the central maximum and the first minimum of a beam of this width is $\lambda/(l \cos \phi)$, by comparison with diffraction at a slit. In accordance with the Rayleigh criterion this is the smallest angle resolvable.

From Equation 4.32,

$$d\phi = \frac{\lambda n(\partial n/\partial \lambda) - n^2 + \sin^2 \phi}{\lambda \sin \phi \cos \phi} \, d\lambda$$

Put $d\phi = \lambda/(l \cos \phi)$,

$$\frac{\lambda}{l \cos \phi} = \frac{\lambda n(\partial n/\partial \lambda) - n^2 + \sin^2 \phi}{\lambda \sin \phi \cos \phi} \, d\lambda$$

The resolving power $\lambda/d\lambda$ is hence given by

$$\frac{\lambda}{d\lambda} = \frac{l}{\lambda \sin \phi} \left(\lambda n \frac{\partial n}{\partial \lambda} - n^2 + \sin^2 \phi \right) \qquad (4.34)$$

Though useful, Equation 4.34 for the resolving power of a Lummer–Gehrcke interferometer is not strictly correct for two reasons:

1. The amplitude is only uniform over the wavefront entering the objective lens for grazing emergence of the light, which is only approachable in practice.

2. To calculate the resolving power exactly demands, as in the Fabry–Perot interferometer, an evaluation of the intensities in the parallel emergent beams. This computation is not easy because the series to be summed in adding up the successively decreasing intensities for the rays in the beam is not an infinite one as it is for the Fabry–Perot interferometer.

A useful approximation to the resolving power is available, however, from Equation 4.34 by putting $\phi = 90°$ (so $\sin \phi = 1$) and omitting the dispersion term $\partial n/\partial \lambda$, which makes a correction of only about 7%. The resolving power is therefore approximately evaluated from the equation

$$\text{resolving power} = \frac{\lambda}{d\lambda} = \frac{l}{\lambda} (n^2 - 1) \qquad (4.35)$$

The resolving power can therefore be taken to be between one and $n^2 - 1$ times the length of the plate measured in wavelengths.

The Lummer–Gehrcke plate is difficult to make and use because the surfaces need to be optically flat to within $\lambda/50$ to $\lambda/100$; the material must have an extremely uniform refractive index; mechanical strain in mounting must be avoided; and the temperature must be maintained constant to about ± 0.01 deg C.

Quartz plates are preferred because of their excellent thermal stability. To obtain the maximum possible reflection at the surfaces, the incident light is best linearly polarised with the electric vector perpendicular to the plane of incidence (Chapter 3), the extraordinary ray being made use of in a quartz plate.

Exercise 4

1. Give an account of the theory of *either* the Fabry–Perot interferometer *or* the Michelson interferometer, and describe in detail *one* application in metrology *or* spectroscopy of the instrument you have discussed. (M.P.)

2. Describe the optical arrangement used with a Fabry–Perot etalon and the fringe system observed with monochromatic light. How are the fringes produced and what factors determine the chromatic resolving power of the etalon? How may the difference in wavelength between a single spectral line of known wavelength λ and a close satellite of wavelength $\lambda + \delta\lambda$ be determined from measurements on their respective fringes of the same order n? (L.G.)

3. How would you determine the separation of two plane parallel plates about 1 cm apart to an accuracy of 1 in 10^5, given sources of standard wavelengths? Having found this separation, how would you determine precisely the separation of another pair of plates whose distance apart was almost twice that of the former pair? (L.P.)

4. Explain the formation of fringes by a Fabry–Perot interferometer, and describe, with the necessary theory, how the instrument can be used in the quantitative examination of the hyperfine structure of spectral lines in the visible region. Give a brief account of the experimental arrangements necessary for such an investigation, and explain how the resolving power is affected by the separation and reflecting power of the interferometer plates. (L.P.)

5. Describe the Fabry–Perot interferometer, discussing the features which give it a high spectroscopic resolving power.
It is desired to resolve two radiations emitted by a gas laser whose wave numbers differ by 0.005 cm^{-1}. What interferometer separation is required if the reflectivity of the plates is such that it is possible to resolve two fringes separated by a tenth of the separation between the orders? (L.P.)

6. Assuming that a narrow metal rod about 50 cm long, with highly polished plane ends is provided, suggest some interferometric method whereby the length may be measured with high precision in terms of wavelengths of light.
Give an account of the technique to be adopted and discuss the character of the light source to be used. (L.P.)

7. Spectrograms of the sun taken from opposite ends of the diameter perpendicular to its axis of rotation show that the corresponding Fraunhofer sodium lines have a relative displacement of 0.078 Å. Assuming that the diameter of the sun is 1.39×10^{11} cm, that the mean wavelength of the light is 5893 Å and that the velocity of light is 3×10^{10} cm sec^{-1}, obtain a value in days for the period of rotation of the sun about its axis. Derive any formula you use and suggest, with reasons, the type of spectrograph it would be necessary to use to obtain wavelength measurements of the required precision. (L.P.)

8. Give reasons for the choice of the wavelength of the orange line of krypton 86 as a standard of length. Is it likely that a standard of greater precision will become available in the future?
A spectrum line having two components is observed using a Fabry–Perot

interferometer with a 1 cm plate separation, and it is found that the angular separation of the two components is one-tenth that between orders. If the mean wavelength is $5 \cdot 0 \times 10^{-5}$ cm, calculate the wavelength difference between the components. (L.P.)

9. Write an account of interference filters designed to pass a fairly narrow band of wavelengths in the visible region of the spectrum.

Given that the refractive index of magnesium fluoride deposited *in vacuo* and subsequently baked in air is $1 \cdot 37$, calculate the thickness of a film of this material required to form an interference filter of the Fabry–Perot type which will selectively transmit light in a narrow region about the wavelength of 5,550 Å at which the human eye has its maximum sensitivity in daylight.

10. Describe the Lummer–Gehrcke interferometer plate and deduce an equation which gives approximately its chromatic resolving power.

Why has the Lummer–Gehrcke plate become almost obsolete in favour of the Fabry–Perot instrument?

11. Give the theory of the formation of fringes by the transmission of a plane monochromatic beam of light through two adjacent, parallel, optically-flat and partially reflecting surfaces.

It is desired to form an interference filter which will pass only substantially monochromatic radiation of wavelength 6000 Å. Describe a method of doing this and state, without mathematical detail, how the band-pass may be controlled. (Poly.)

CHAPTER 5

Spectroscopy

5.1 Emission Spectra

Bunsen and Kirchhoff did much of the original work in spectroscopy. In 1860, they gave the explanation of the Fraunhofer lines in the solar spectrum. They also invented a prism spectrometer incorporating an illuminated scale. Their most important discovery was that, under specified conditions, each element emitted light producing à definite spectrum characteristic of the element.

A main purpose of optical spectroscopy is the rapid analysis of materials by examination of either the emission or the absorption spectra. This book is concerned with spectroscopy utilising electromagnetic radiations in the visible, ultra-violet and infra-red regions. The important and rapidly developing sciences and techniques of X-ray spectroscopy, γ-ray spectroscopy and spectroscopy in the microwave radio region are not to be described. The ranges of wavelengths, frequency and photon energies of the radiations to be considered are shown in Table 5.1.

In the solid state, atoms and molecules are closely packed together. For example, tungsten wire is polycrystalline material in which atoms are locked in the lattice structure at separations of about the same size (1–2 Å) as those of the atoms themselves. Consequently, the energy levels occupied by the electrons in the atoms in a solid are affected by the proximity of neighbouring atoms. Isolated atoms (considered as atoms sufficiently far apart for their mutual influences on electronic structure to be negligible) will, when excited, emit a spectrum characteristic of the atom in the form of a series of lines of discrete frequencies. Atoms (or molecules) in solids, on the other hand, will have their energy levels so considerably modified by proximity that a continuous band of energy levels is concerned and not a series of specific separated ones.

Table 5.1.

ULTRA-VIOLET, VISIBLE AND INFRA-RED RADIATION

Radiation	Wavelength range (cm)	Frequency range (Hz)	Range of photon energies* (eV)
Ultra-violet	10^{-6} to 4×10^{-5}	3×10^{16} to $7 \cdot 5 \times 10^{14}$	124 to 3·1
Visible light	4×10^{-5} to 7×10^{-5}	$7 \cdot 5 \times 10^{14}$ to $4 \cdot 3 \times 10^{14}$	3·1 to 1·78
Infra-red	7×10^{-5} to 10^{-2}	$4 \cdot 3 \times 10^{14}$ to 3×10^{12}	1·78 to 0·0124

* Calculated from the equation energy = $h \times$ frequency, where $h = 6 \cdot 625 \times 10^{-34}$ J s is Planck's constant. The energy thus given in joules is converted into electron-volts on the basis that 1 eV = $1 \cdot 6 \times 10^{-19}$ J.

In a gas or vapour, the mean free paths between atoms (or molecules) are great enough except at high pressures for the atoms to be isolated from one another. For example, in nitrogen gas at s.t.p., the mean free path is $6 \cdot 6 \times 10^{-6}$ cm approx.—some 200 times the molecular diameter.

It is apparent, therefore, that the characteristic wavelengths in emission spectra are only obtained if the substance is in the vapour or gaseous state. Line spectra will be obtained for atoms; a band spectra for molecules.

The solid, when heated, will emit a continuous spectrum because of its continuous energy-band structure. This spectrum will not be characteristic of the material of the solid, but will depend on the temperature and emissivity. Thus the continuous spectrum in the light from a heated tungsten filament lamp is similar to that from a lamp with, say, a molybdenum filament.

Referring to Table 5.1, it is seen that energy must be made available to the vaporised atoms of a substance to excite them to states so that photons are emitted. The possible sources of radiation for this purpose are the flame, the discharge tube, the arc and the spark.

5.2 Flame Sources

A Bunsen burner flame is at a temperature T of about 1,200°K. The most probable energy of the particles in the flame is kT, where k is Boltzmann's constant = (1/11,600) eV deg^{-1} K. Therefore, the most probable energy in the Maxwell–Boltzmann distribution is about 0·1 eV, which is far too small to provide the necessary energies for photons in the visible region. Nevertheless, the alkali metals emit visible spectra when in a flame source, as is well-known for sodium chloride introduced into a Bunsen flame. Sufficient energy is available as a consequence of exothermic reactions that the substance undergoes with gases in the flame and the atmosphere. The alkali metals, in particular sodium, potassium and lithium, will emit some, but not all, of the lines in their characteristic spectra when heated in a Bunsen flame because these metals are strongly chemically active. Thus, sodium chloride will dissociate in the reactions taking place in a Bunsen flame and emit the characteristic spectrum of sodium.

For the majority of materials, however, a more effective source than a flame is necessary, and it is clear from Table 5.1 that this source of excitation needs to be more energetic the shorter the wavelength of the radiation emitted.

5.3 Discharge Tubes

The discharge tube contains gas at pressures ranging from about $0 \cdot 1$–10 mm Hg. Electrodes are sealed into opposite ends of the tube. A p.d. of several hundred volts maintained across these electrodes with a ballast resistance in series causes an electrical discharge to pass; the gas atoms and molecules are excited and ionised, and the glowing positive column in the discharge fills most of the tube. As compared with the arc source (Section 5.4), the glow discharge source operates with higher potential gradients in the gas and with smaller current densities.

An early example, still widely used in college laboratories, is the *Geissler tube* [Fig. 5.1(a)]. This consists of a capillary tube about 10 cm long and about 1 mm bore, between wider end tubes in which the electrodes are sealed. The capillary tube is aligned with the spectrometer slit with or without an intermediate focusing lens. The p.d. across the electrodes can be d.c. from an induction coil or a power pack or a.c. from a transformer. A ballast resistance is needed to limit the current in the discharge once the glow discharge is excited.

Such tubes are particularly suitable for the excitation of gases. The inert gases, particularly helium (He), neon (Ne) and argon (A), are monatomic and will emit their characteristic atomic line spectra. Other gases, such as nitrogen (N_2) and carbon dioxide (CO_2), will emit band spectra, but less stable molecules (for example, of hydrogen, H_2) are dissociated so that atomic line spectra are produced.

Elements which do not occur in the vapour state except at high temperatures can be excited in a Geissler tube by the use of an auxiliary gas, usually the inert gas argon. For example, the spectrum of iodine is emitted if this element is present within a Geissler

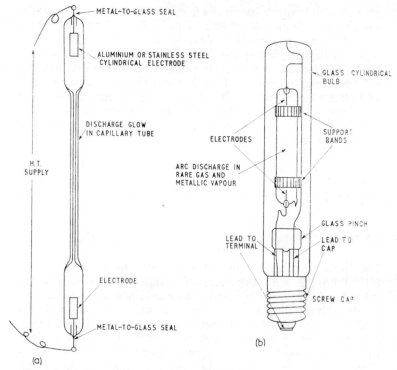

Fig. 5.1. Discharge tube sources of spectra: (a) Geissler tube; (b) commercial spectral lamp

tube containing argon. The spectra will, in general, result from both the atoms present and their positive ions, predominantly those which are singly charged.

If the tube is made of glass, ultra-violet radiation will be severely reduced by absorption. Quartz tubes will permit transmission of the ultra-violet down to about 2,000 Å.

Typical of more sophisticated discharge sources are commercial spectral lamps. These consist of a small discharge tube surrounded by an outer cylindrical bulb [Fig. 5.1(b)]. Within the discharge tube are electrodes sealed in at the two ends, and either a gas, a metallic vapour or a mixture of the two (for example, argon and sodium). This type of lamp is operated at considerably higher current density and higher pressure than the Geissler tube and has a much larger light output. Indeed, the discharge is a self-sustaining arc, rather than a discharge, in which fairly well-defined regions such as the positive column appear. For example, the range of spectral lamps obtainable from Philips Ltd have arc lengths of between 25 mm

and 40 mm, depending on the type, and operate at a current of
0·9 A. A typical power supply is an auto-leak transformer of which
the primary is connected across the a.c. mains at 240 V r.m.s.;
the secondary provides an open-circuit e.m.f. of 470 V r.m.s.,
which provides a suitable striking p.d. across the lamp electrodes.
When the arc strikes, this p.d. falls to about 10–50 V depending on
the nature of the element within the tube and the operating pressure.

The discharge tube and outer cylindrical bulb are of glass for
sources in the visible region of the spectrum, but of quartz for ultra-
violet down to 2,000 Å approx.

For college optical experiments, the most useful of these lamps
are those giving the spectra of cadmium, sodium, mercury, thallium
(which gives a line at 5,350 Å of width only 0·05 Å) and gallium
(giving intense sharp lines at 4,033 Å and 4,172 Å). Lamps of this
type with inert gas fillings (helium, neon, argon and krypton) are
also useful. Lamps with high-pressure fillings, particularly of
argon, xenon or krypton at 3–8 atm, give intense light outputs
through the visible spectrum in a continuum; on the other hand,
the lower-pressure lamps provide line spectra. The high-pressure
xenon lamp gives a continuous spectrum which is a good approximation to the solar spectrum.

Interference filters (Section 4.7) of the multi-layer dielectric
types are valuable adjuncts to these lamps. Placed within a beam
of collimated light from the lamp, such filters are available with
a narrow band-pass in appropriate regions to cut off all but the
selected lines required.

A hydrogen discharge lamp of special design is a useful source
of continuous radiation in the ultra-violet region. The discharge
takes place between a heated cathode and an enclosed anode. The
covering of the anode has a small opening of 1 mm diameter
through which the discharge is compressed to give a spot of high
radiation density. The striking p.d. is about 320 V and the operating
p.d. is 100 V. Automatic control of the anode current holds the
radiation output constant to $\pm 0·2\%$ for mains voltage changes
between 180 V and 240 V. With a quartz envelope, the radiation is
free of lines and is continuous between 2,000 Å and 3,500 Å.

A recent innovation in place of the hydrogen lamp is a discharge
lamp containing deuterium (the heavy isotope of hydrogen of mass
number 2). This gives more than twice the intensity of a hydrogen
lamp of corresponding size and power consumption. A version
(Ealing Scientific Ltd), with a special optical window made of
Suprasil, enables the continuous ultra-violet spectrum down to
1,650 Å to be transmitted.

The *Paschen hollow-cathode source* is a discharge tube in which
a cold cathode containing a cavity is used. The discharge is excited
in an inert gas at low pressure $(10^{-2}–10^{-1} \text{ mm Hg})$ by a high p.d.

established between this cathode and an anode. The cathode metal is sputtered by the impinging positive ions of the rare gas. The hollow-cathode design reduces the perturbing effects of electric fields and gas pressure on the breadth of the spectral lines. Sharp lines of the spectrum of the excited atoms of the metal sputtered from the cathode are therefore produced. These sharp lines are mostly due to the neutral atoms and their singly positively charged ions.

Electrodeless discharges are produced by surrounding a glass or quartz tube containing gas at a pressure of 10^{-2}–10^{-1} mm Hg by a coil carrying radiofrequency current. The tube does not require internal electrodes, and the electric field strengths set up by the radiofrequency electromagnetic radiation are moderate. The spectral lines produced are consequently primarily due to neutral atoms and are sharp relative to those from Geissler tube sources. Such electrodeless discharge sources can also be used to emit the line spectra of non-volatile elements: a vaporisable compound of the element is incorporated in the tube, which contains an inert gas. This compound dissociates in the discharge, and the spectra of the elements resulting are obtained.

To produce spectral lines which are extremely narrow, *atomic beam sources* are used. Such lines of very small breadth in wavelength are needed in studies of hyperfine structure with, for example, the Fabry–Perot interferometer. To ensure extreme sharpness, the thermal motion of the radiating atoms has to be minimised to reduce Doppler broadening (Section 5.8). A beam of atoms of the element whose spectrum is required is produced by evaporating the element in a small oven maintained at high temperature in a vacuum. The ejected atoms are collimated into a beam by passage through successive aligned apertures. The atoms in this beam are excited by electrons emitted from a thermionic filament and are accelerated to an anode on the opposite side of the beam. The spectrum emitted is observed in a direction perpendicular to that of the atomic beam. As the random motion of the atoms along this direction of observation is very small, Doppler broadening is small. The best practice is to excite the atomic beam by electrons directed at right angles to it and make observations from a direction perpendicular to both the atomic beam and the electron beam. The intensity of light in the spectrum is unfortunately unavoidably limited.

5.4 Arc Sources

Electric arcs in the atmosphere set up between electrodes of carbon or of certain metals are widely used in spectroscopic analysis as sources of characteristic radiation.

The d.c. carbon arc (Fig. 5.2) will now be described to illustrate the operation of arc sources. Two carbon rods are supported vertically in line within a support which enables the end of one rod to be moved against the other and then separated again. A source of e.m.f. (from a battery, the d.c. mains or a power pack of 50–240 V) is set up across the carbon rods with a ballast resistor in series—necessary because the arc has a negative resistance characteristic.

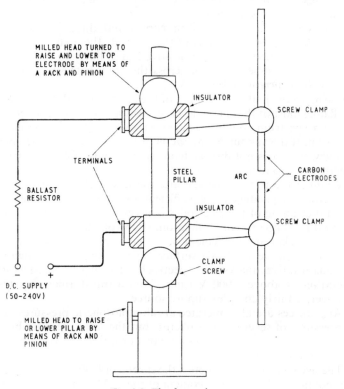

Fig. 5.2. The d.c. carbon arc

The ends of the rods are pushed together and then drawn apart gradually. A bright arc at a temperature of 3,000°–4,000°C is thereby produced across the ends, which are ordinarily at between 1 mm and 10 mm apart. As the arc current passes, the end of the positive carbon rod (usually the lower one) becomes hollowed out to a crater, whereas the end of the negative rod becomes pointed. The end of the positive rod is the hottest part and it emits a continuous spectrum. The vapour between the rods emits the many lines in the spectrum of carbon. Instead of the rods being moved, the arc may be ignited by momentary application of a high p.d. across the electrodes to cause an initiating spark.

To study, with the carbon arc, the line spectra of other elements, a small amount of the material in the form of the element of a suitable salt is placed in the crater of the lower positive rod or, better, the centre of this rod is bored with an axial hole which is fed with the material. The material dissociates (if a compound), volatilises and the excitation of its vapour in the arc produces the required emission spectrum.

For many metals, such as iron, copper and aluminium, the arc may be formed between rods of these metals themselves in place of the carbon electrodes. The positive rod is likely to melt if the current is too large. The p.d. across the arc is between 30 V and 60 V, with a current of 1·5–20 A.

Owing to the high temperature of the arc compared with that of the flame, most of the energy levels of neutral atoms are excited, so giving a spectrum containing many more lines than in the flame spectrum. If the vapour in the arc is of a particularly stable compound which does not dissociate at temperatures of 4,000°C, band spectra are produced.

The higher the p.d. across the arc, the less likely is flicker. The temperatures produced are sufficient to vaporise all materials. Careful cleaning of the electrodes is necessary to avoid unwanted spectral lines due to contamination. High-voltage a.c. arcs are less prone to flicker and movement of the point of contact of the arc over the negative electrode surface, so such arcs are preferable for quantitative analysis in spectrochemical work. Satisfactory operation at above 2,000 V r.m.s. from a transformer requires, however, a fairly complex supply source.

Arc sources are also operated at sub-atmospheric pressures and at pressures of several atmospheres, but the latter become high-pressure arc lamps giving a continuous or mixed spectrum rather than a line spectrum.

The arc method cannot detect the carbon or hydrogen in organic compounds, nor the oxigen content of rocks. Materials which melt and then do not vaporise can be mixed with powdered silica to prevent fusion. Powdered silica may also be soaked in a liquid to be analysed. Some components present in small quantities may disappear quickly and so must be recorded by photographic or photoelectric methods.

5.5 Electric Spark Sources

Electric spark sources are similar to arcs, except that the p.d. is intermittent and is much greater in the range 10–50 kV, and

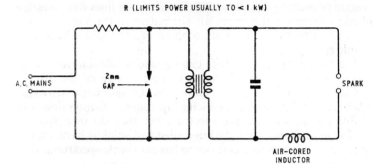

Fig. 5.3. The spark source

the current density is less. The spark is produced across the gap between electrodes by connecting them across the secondary of a transformer with an inductor in series (Fig. 5.3). When the p.d. across the gap rises to the value at which breakdown occurs, an oscillatory surge of ions and electrons passes between the electrodes, forming the spark. The oscillation frequency, and hence the repetition rate of the spark, depends on the inductance and capacitance in the circuit. At atmospheric pressure, the gap is 1–2 mm and the p.d. about 10 kV. Sources in which the spark is enclosed in a vessel at low pressure are also used, in which case the p.d. may be as much as 50 kV.

Temperatures of some 10,000°K are effectively produced in the spark, and the electrons produced are sufficiently accelerated in the intense electric field to ensure that atoms present are excited and ionised. The spectra emitted are therefore for high states of excitation and where a large fraction of the atoms become ionised. The ions will be singly charged or multi-charged (the atom losing more than one electron), but singly charged ions predominate usually.

The possible methods of obtaining the spectra of various materials are: to make the electrodes themselves of the appropriate metal or carbon; to allow liquids to drip from a funnel forming one electrode to a container forming the other electrode.

The extent of the excitation and ionisation of the material in the spark depends upon the duration of the spark and the phase in the applied p.d. at which it occurs. Some control over this extent is therefore possible by selection of the inductance and capacitance in the oscillatory circuit associated with the transformer secondary. Better control is achieved by electronic regulation of phase and spark duration.

Spark sources are useful in the visible and ultra-violet regions. Vacuum spark sources are particularly suitable in studies of the spectra of multiply ionised atoms. To eliminate lines due to atmospheric nitrogen and oxygen, an alternative to the vacuum spark is to run the spark in an atmosphere of hydrogen which has a simple spectrum.

The arc or the spark source can be used to obtain the emission spectra of 65 metallic elements; however, none of the 10 non-metallic elements (arsenic, antimony, boron, carbon, iodine, silicon, selenium, sulphur and tellurium) has satisfactory lines in the visible region with an arc spectrum but they do in a spark or discharge tube spectrum. All but iodine and sulphur have arc lines in the ultra-violet spectrum; boron has no visible spectrum.

5.6 Absorption Spectra

For many materials, emission spectra cannot be produced because the materials cannot readily be introduced into flame, gas discharge tube, arc or spark sources. The main difficulties are with liquids, some gases, and coopounds which dissociate. The technique of absorption spectroscopy is therefore practised extensively. The material in solid or liquid form is transparent to radiation in one or more of the ultra-violet, visible of infra-red regions. A sample of the material, usually in plate form or as a liquid in a transparent parallel-sided container, is placed between a radiation source and the slit of the spectrometer, so that the sample is in the continuous-spectrum beam from the source. The spectrum obtained is due to absorption of energy in lines, bands or a continuum, depending on the nature of the material: an absorption line spectrum is obtained for elements, a band spectrum for molecules, and a continuum for several dye-stuff and other materials. Certain parts of the continuous spectrum from the source will be absent or reduced in intensity in the recorded absorption spectrum. For example, the well-known doublet lines at 5,890 Å and 5,896 Å in the spectrum of sodium will appear as black lines against a continuum in an absorption spectrum.

The source of the continuous spectrum used in absorption spectroscopy is a tungsten filament lamp or a high-pressure xenon or krypton arc for work in the visible region, and a hydrogen or deuterium discharge lamp in the ultra-violet region.

5.7 Sources of Infra-red Radiation

In general, absorption spectroscopy is the usual technique for analysis in the infra-red region, particularly of the band spectra of liquid and gaseous compounds.

A source of continuous infra-red radiation is required. The ideal source is a black-body radiator; this is difficult to provide, but several other methods form satisfactory substitutes even though the emissivity of the material used is not unity.

The Nernst glower is a rod of zirconium oxide with the addition of yttrium oxide and rare earths. It is a non-conductor at temperatures below 800°C. It is raised to this temperature in a gas flame or by a surrounding electric heater and is then heated by the passage through the rod of electric current. The temperature may be varied, but the current must be sufficient to prevent the temperature decreasing below 800°C. The distribution of radiation with wavelength is Planckian with a peak energy at a wavelength of 22,700 Å for a temperature of 1,000°C (see Section 6.6 of Volume 1) and an emissivity of 0·6. This glower is operated in air, so the energy agaipts wavelength distribution will show the effect of carbon dioxide and water vapour absorption. *The globar source* is a silicon carbide rod heated electrically. (See also Section 5.36.)

5.8 Causes of Spectral Line Broadening

Instruments of low chromatic resolving power, such as a small prism spectrometer, are unable to reveal the fine structure of a spectral line. With a very narrow slit, the doublet structure of the yellow sodium spectral lines which differ in wavelength by approximately 6 Å can just be revealed. Instruments of high resolution not only show fine structure but reveal that the intensity of each line is greatest in the middle and decreases towards the edges and also that lines have different breadths.

The width of a spectral line is an indication of the temperature of the source—a fact of use in astronomy for the estimation of the temperatures of stars. This effect results from Doppler's principle and is known as *Doppler broadening*. Radiating atoms (and molecules) have velocities of translation, and these velocities will have components ranging from zero to well above the mean value in the line of sight. Atoms will continue to produce radiation of their characteristic frequencies, but their velocity will effect the wavelength measured so that all the radiation for a particular frequency will not be confined into one infinitesimally narrow spectral line. The broadening of the line resulting may be of such magnitude as to obscure the fine structure. Rayleigh states that the brightness of the line should be proportional to $\exp(-K\phi^2)$, where ϕ is the distance from the centre of the line in angular measure, and K is a constant which is larger the narrower the line. The value of K increases with decrease of the velocity of translation, which will diminish with the temperature and with the mass of the radiating atom (Fig. 5.4).

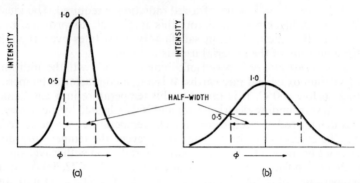

Fig. 5.4. Intensity distribution in a spectral line: (a) K large; (b) K small

At high pressure, interactions between radiating atoms in close proximity to each other will modify the frequencies of their radiation. The lower the pressure, the narrower the spectral line radiating. This effect is known as *pressure broadening*.

An atomic oscillator loses energy by radiation. The amplitude of the wave decreases as it is emitted and thus is no longer a simple harmonic wave of one frequency. Fourier analysis reveals that the apparently infinite wave train can be resolved into numerous component waves differing only very slightly in frequency from the fundamental frequency but sufficiently to produce an apparent broadening of the line. This effect is known as *radiation broadening*.

For purposes such as the study of fine and hyperfine structure, spectroscopically pure materials are necessary. Isotopically pure elements must therefore be used, because variations in the mass and the spin of the nucleus affect the frequency of the radiation (Section 2.5). The presence of a range of isotopes can so broaden a spectral line that other causes of line broadening are masked.

The ideal source is an isotopically pure material electrically excited at low pressure and at low temperature. The kinetic velocities of atoms are proportional to the square root of the absolute temperature. Cooling a source from 293°K (20°C) to the temperature of liquid nitrogen 77°K (−196°C), however, will only approximately halve the breadth of a spectral line caused by the kinetic motion of the radiating atoms.

5.9 Detection of Radiation

The detectors and principles of detection of radiation which are used in spectroscopy are listed.

The human eye: sensitivity extends from 4,000 Å to 7,000 Å approx., with peak sensitivity at 5,550 Å in bright light (Section 3.2 of Volume 1).

Photography: the common photographic emulsion is sensitive in the visible spectrum and in the ultra-violet; special emulsions for use in the ultra-violet and the infra-red are made.

Photoelectric devices: these include vacuum photocells, gas-filled photocells, photomultipliers, barrier layer cells, the photodiode and the phototransistor.

Photoluminescence: many substances emit radiation when photons are incident and where this radiation is of longer wavelength than that of the incident radiation. The luminescent emission persists after the excitation due to the photons in the incident radiation is removed. This emission decays exponentially in a manner depending on the life time of the state excited in the luminescent material. The exponentially decaying luminescence is known as *fluorescence*. Some luminescent materials also exhibit an afterglow which decays more slowly than the fluorescence and in a more complex manner; this phenomenon is called *phosphorescence*.

Thermal detectors: these include *the bolometer*, in which the increase of resistance of a metallic wire or strip with temperature rise brought about by incident radiation forms the basis of the sensing device; *thermistors*, which are mixtures of oxides (including those of iron, nickel, copper, zinc and manganese) which have large negative temperature coefficients of resistance and are therefore alternative sensors to the bolometer; the *thermojunction* and the *thermopile* which make use of the thermoelectric effect; and the *Golay cell*, in which incident thermal radiation increases the pressure of gas in an enclosure and where this pressure rise is indicated by the movement of a diaphragm. (See also Section 5.36.)

5.10 Photographic Emulsions

Both films and plates are used, but plates are usually preferred because of small changes in the dimensions of film due to shrinkage in processing.

Panchromatic emulsions are sensitive throughout the visible region and in the ultra-violet, but the spectral response is considerably different from that of the human eye (Fig. 5.5). Such emulsions can be used down to wavelengths of about 2,200 Å in the ultra-violet; the spectrograph has to be furnished with quartz optics. Below 2,200 Å, gelatine (a prime constituent of the usual photographic emulsions) absorbs ultra-violet radiation strongly and so normal photographic plates are useless. This problem can be over-come by smearing the photographic plates with paraffin oil, which is fluorescent and so converts the short wavelengths to longer ones which are not absorbed by the gelatine. After exposure, the paraffin is removed with acetone and the plates are processed normally. This method allowed Lyman to undertake spectrography in the ultra-violet down to wavelengths of 580 Å.

The more modern method is to use Schumann photographic plates, which are available commercially. These contain only a. trace of gelatine in the emulsion to bind the photosensitive silver bromide.

At wavelengths below about 1,800 Å, ultra-violet radiation is absorbed in air and absorption in quartz is considerable. The

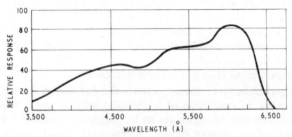

Fig. 5.5. Spectral response curve of a typical panchromatic photographic emulsion (a grating spectrometer was used with a tungsten lamp source at 2,850°K)

spectrograph therefore has to be evacuated. In vacuum spectrography, fluorite prisms and optics are used down to 1,200 Å; for shorter wavelengths than this, ultra-violet absorption in fluorite is pronounced so reflection-type diffraction gratings are used. With Schumann or Q emulsions in a vacuum grating spectrograph, records at wavelengths down to a few Ångstrom units (where the ultra-violet region overlaps the soft X-ray region in the electromagnetic spectrum) are possible.

The light sensitivity of photographic emulsions can be extended into the infra-red region of the spectrum by treating the emulsion with photosensitive dyes. Since 1930, panchromatic emulsions sensitive to wavelengths up to 14,000 Å have been made by incorporating polycarbocyanine dyes in the emulsion.

5.11 Photoelectric Detectors

The various photoelectric devices whose characteristics (including spectral response) are described in Section 6.18 of Volume 1 are all usable in spectroscopy. The semiconductor devices (the photodiode and the phototransistor) are tending more and more to replace the vacuum photocell in spectroscopy and spectrophotometry.

5.12 Use of Fluorescence

Many substances fluoresce when exposed to ultra-violet radiation. The light emitted is within the visible spectrum. A few examples are given in Table 5.2. Cadmium sulphide is strongly phosphorescent. After illumination with ultra-violet light, it emits a pale blue glow for about an hour.

Table 5.2.

SOME FLUORESCENT MATERIALS

Substance	Actual colour	Colour of fluorescent light emitted
Quinine sulphate	colourless	blue
Fluorspar	colourless	violet
Fluoroscein	brown	green
Vaseline	yellow	green
Barium platinocyanide	yellow	green
Uranium oxide	yellow	green
Chlorophyll	green	red

5.13 The Thermopile

Thermal detectors, unlike photographic plates and photocells, are non-selective; they absorb radiation over the entire spectral range from the ultra-violet to the infra-red. This is because the receiver of radiation is a black-body.

A useful type of thermopile in spectroscopy is that due to Schwarz (Fig. 5.6). This consists of a number of thermojunctions [between bismuth and silver in Fig. 5.6(a), but semiconductor materials are used in recent designs] in which alternate junctions are arranged in line, the line of hot junctions being behind a slit. In this linear thermopile, the hot junctions are blackened, usually of copper foil to which the bismuth and silver are soldered. Radiation incident upon the slit is absorbed by this line of hot junctions. The 'cold' junctions, also of foils to which silver and bismuth are connected, are shielded from the incident radiation and sufficiently separated from the hot junctions to ensure that they remain at constant temperature.

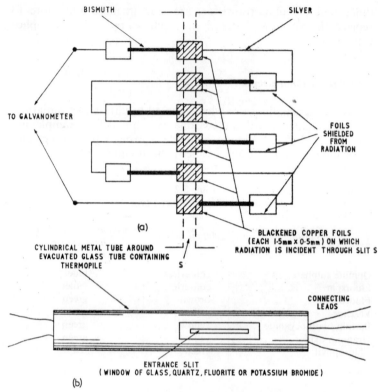

Fig. 5.6. Schwarz linear thermopile

Such linear thermopiles are mounted in air or in a vacuum. The vacuum linear thermopile is usually chosen for infra-red spectroscopy as it is much less susceptible to the effects of external radiation and much more sensitive than the air thermopile; however, it is less rapid in response.

The vacuum linear thermopile is mounted within an evacuated sealed-off glass tube with metal-to-glass sealed lead-in wires. This glass tube has in its wall opposite the line of hot junctions a narrow window of glass, quartz, fluorite, potassium bromide, caesium bromide or KRS 5 (see page 204) depending on the wavelength range in the radiation to be measured. The glass tube is within a metal tube with a slit opposite the window [Fig. 5.6(b)].

Typical of commercial vacuum linear thermopiles is the FT16 Schwarz type (Hilger and Watts Ltd). Each element has an area of 9.0 mm$\times 0.5$ mm, the series of hot junctions comprising one element (being behind the window and slit) and the cold element being shielded from radiation. Each element has a resistance of 200 Ω and has separate connecting leads so that connection of the elements may be either in series or in parallel opposition. The response time is 0·1 s, and the sensitivity is 25 $\mu V \mu W^{-1}$ (i.e. an output e.m.f. of 25 μV is produced for an incident radiation of 1 μW). Because the hot junction is blackened, this sensitivity is independent of wavelength. The calibrated linear thermopile thus forms an absolute instrument in that the incident radiation is measured directly in microwatts.

5.14 The Bolometer

The bolometer consists of two strips of metal, each about 5×10^{-5} cm thick and both blackened. One strip is exposed to the radiation, and the other is shielded from the radiation. These strips form two arms of a Wheatstone bridge. The sensitivity depends on the p.d. applied across the bridge and on the current sensitivity of the galvanometer. To avoid Joule heating, the p.d. applied must not cause too great a current to pass through the strips. Provided the temperature difference between the strips is small, the galvanometer deflection is proportional to the intensity of the radiation. A temperature change of 0·01°C can be measured.

Galvanometer amplifiers may be used, but they are limited because the magnitude of the thermoelectric current due to the small amount of energy in a single spectral line may be comparable with currents generated by motions of the galvanometer coil caused by Brownian motion.

5.15 The Thermal Golay Cell

The Golay cell, which utilises the expansion of a gas, is remarkably sensitive and it has become much used in recent work in infra-red spectroscopy, especially in the far infra-red (Section 5.36).

Radiation passes through a window transparent to infra-red radiation into a small cell filled with gas and containing an absorbing film of a few square millimetres in area. Heat is transferred to the gas in an amount depending on the modulation of the incident radiation by an interposed rotating sector S, which is motor driven. Increase of temperature of the gas causes a change in pressure which moves the flexible mirror forming the back of the cell. (Fig. 5.7)

The mirror is part of an optical system comprising a lamp, lens and line grating. With the optical set-up shown in Fig. 5.7, the grating is adjusted so that its image in the mirror coincides with

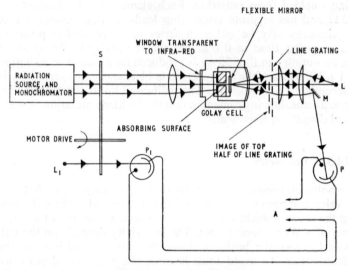

Fig. 5.7. Use of a Golay cell

the grating itself. On lateral movement of the grating, dark patches may be made to coincide with light portions of the grating so that the light cannot reach the photocell P via the plane mirror M. When the flexible mirror forming the back of the cell is bent as a consequence of a gas pressure increase in the cell, the grating image is moved relative to the grating itself so light reaches the photocell P. Therefore, the output of photocell P feeds to the electronic amplifier A an alternating p.d. of frequency equal to that of the rotating sector S, and of amplitude dependent on the extent to which the Golay cell mirror is flexed. The amplifier A is designed for this frequency. Any variation in p.d. applied to the lamp L, which illuminates the grating, will affect the photocell output and so spoil the accuracy of relative measurements. To avoid this, a second lamp L_1 is used on the same supply as L, but its light is chopped by the sector S. This light is incident on a second photocell P_1, and a comparison circuit ensures that the instrument response is independent of supply fluctuations.

The maximum response time is 30 ms, and the radiation intensity measurable is as small as 6×10^{-11} W.

5.16 Spectrometers and Monochromators

In spectroscopy, the essential requirement is the dispersion into a spectrum of the radiation from a source. This dispersion is achieved

either by a prism or a diffraction grating. To achieve greater resolution, an interferometer is used—generally in conjunction with
the spectroscope. With regard to the use of a prism or of a grating
to form a spectrum, equations for angular dispersion and chromatic
resolving power already developed in Chapter 12 of Volume 1
are important. For convenience, these results are repeated here
and further explanation given.

A prism is of material of refractive index n which varies with
the wavelength λ in accordance with the Cauchy equation

$$n = A + B\lambda^{-2} \tag{5.1}$$

where A and B are constants for a given material.

The angular dispersion of a prism is the change $d\theta$ of the angle of
deviation θ consequent upon a small change $d\lambda$ in the wavelength λ.
It is therefore $d\theta/d\lambda$. For a prism at minimum deviation and where
the whole of the prism face is illuminated uniformly by light
from a collimator, it is shown in Section 12.5 of Volume 1 that
the angular dispersion is given by

$$\frac{d\theta}{d\lambda} = -\frac{2bB}{a\lambda^3} \tag{5.2}$$

where b is the length of the base of an isosceles prism and a is
the width of the beam of incident collimated light. The angular
dispersion therefore increases with the length of the prism base
for a given value of a and increases with decrease of wavelength
(so is greater at the blue end of the spectrum). Also, with a given
width of the incident collimated beam, the angular dispersion is
doubled if two identical prisms are used in series. Note also that
the presence of the negative sign in Equation 5.2 is indicative of the
fact that the angle θ increases as λ decreases.

The chromatic resolving power of a prism, defined as $\lambda/\delta\lambda$ where
$\delta\lambda$ is the smallest change of wavelength discernable in accordance
with the Rayleigh criterion at a mean wavelength λ, is given by
the equation

$$\frac{\lambda}{\delta\lambda} = b\frac{dn}{d\lambda} = \frac{2bB}{\lambda^3} \tag{5.3}$$

where again the whole of the face of an isosceles prism is illuminated
uniformly by light incident from a collimator. The chromatic
resolving power therefore increases as the wavelength decreases
and also increases with length of the prism base.

The angular dispersion of a plane diffraction grating is the change
$d\theta$ of the angle of diffraction θ consequent upon a small change
$d\lambda$ in the wavelength λ. Equation 12.14 of Volume 1 shows that this

angular dispersion is given by

$$\frac{d\theta}{d\lambda} = \frac{p}{e \cos \theta} \tag{5.4}$$

where p is the integral order of the spectrum, and e is the separation between corresponding points on neighbouring rulings on the grating. The angular dispersion of a grating hence increases with the order p; thus in the second order it is double that in the first, and it increases with the number of grating rulings per centimetre (or $1/e$).

As regards the variation of $d\theta/d\lambda$ with λ, this will occur because $\cos \theta$ varies with wavelength. With normal incidence, θ is greater for the longer wavelengths so the dispersion is greater in the red end of the spectrum—which is opposite to the state of affairs obtained with a prism.

In several cases of practical interest, θ is near $0°$, so $\cos \theta = 1$. The angular dispersion is then almost independent of wavelength: thus a *normal spectrum* with a linear scale of wavelengths is obtained.

The chromatic resolving power R of a diffraction grating is shown in Section 12.6 of Volume 1 to be given by the equation

$$R = \frac{\lambda}{\delta\lambda} = pN \tag{5.5}$$

It therefore increases with the total number of rulings N and the order p; so in the third order, say, it is three times what it would be in the first order.

A spectroscope in which, by direct or indirect calibration, individual wavelengths in the spectrum are measured is a *spectrometer*. If the spectrum can be permanently recorded by photography—a specially designed camera is attached to the instrument which takes the place of the telescope—the instrument is called a *spectrograph*. Frequently, a given instrument can be used as either a spectrometer or a spectrograph.

After dispersion into a specrum, the instrument may be arranged or designed so that only a narrow band of wavelength emerges from its exit slit: the instrument is then known as a *monochromator* Generally, therefore, in a spectrometer or a spectrograph the object is to display the whole or a significant part of the spectrum, whereas in the monochromator the output is restricted to a narrow wavelength band (usually with facilities for selection of the mean wavelength desired). An instrument which is basically a spectrometer can be modified for use as a monochromator.

The same principles apply in the ultra-violet, visible and infra-red regions of the spectrum, but the techniques adopted for the various regions will differ as they have to take into account the problems of absorption and detection of the radiation in the instrument.

5.17 The Constant-deviation Spectrometer

A development from the simple prism spectrometer is the constant-deviation instrument. In the simple spectrometer, the telescope is moved so that various parts of the spectrum can be observed. In the constant-deviation instrument, a special prism is used: dispersion is obtained with the collimator and telescope permanently fixed at right angles to one another, and the prism is rotated to observe various parts of the spectrum.

The constant-deviation prism (Fig. 5.8) is a single specially out, ground and polished block of optical glass which is, in effect, three prisms ABC (30°, 60°, 90°), BCD (45°, 45°, 90°) and ADE (30°, 60°, 90°). The incident light from the collimator meets face AB at F, is refracted along FG, internally reflected at G at face BD to reach H where it emerges after refraction to the telescope.

For a particular wavelength λ, the image of the collimator slit is set on the cross-wires of the telescope. As the emergent beam HK has to be perpendicular to the incident beam IF because of the fixed collimator and telescope positions, the prism has to be rotated so that slit images for various values of λ are made to coincide with the cross-wires of the telescope eyepiece.

Within the 45° prism BCD, incidence along FG needs to be normal to face BC and emergence along GH normal to face CD. There will then be no refraction within prism BCD, only internal reflection through 90° at G. The refraction and dispersion therefore occur only in prisms ABC and ADE. With the conditions prevailing, the angle of incidence θ will be equal and opposite to the angle of emergence ϕ. The two refractions then cause no total deviation; all the deviation is due to reflection at G. The dispersions within prisms ABC and ADE will, however, be in the same sense.

As the angle of incidence θ and the angle of emergence ϕ are equal, the arrangement is equivalent to that of a 60° prism at minimum deviation. This deviation is effectively zero owing to refraction and 90° owing to reflection: it is constant irrespective of wavelength.

Referring to Fig. 5.8, let n be the refractive index of the material of the prism at a wavelength λ. Then $n = (\sin \theta)/(\sin R)$. As $\angle BFG$ is clearly 60°, angle R must be 30°. Therefore

$$\sin \theta = n \sin R = 0{\cdot}5n$$

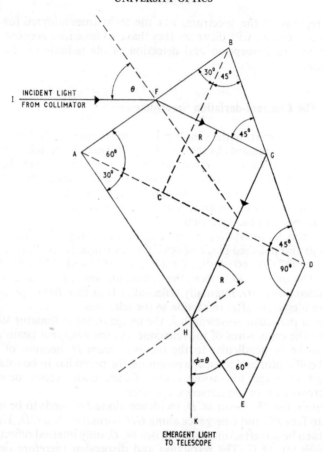

Fig. 5.8. The constant-deviation prism

If at wavelength λ the refractive index n is $1\cdot6412$, $\theta = \sin^{-1} 0\cdot8206$ = 55° approx. As n will depend upon wavelength, to bring the image of the collimator to coincide with the telescope eyepiece cross-wires, θ will need to be varied by small rotations imparted to the prism.

This rotation is imparted by a screw drive operated by turning a drum which is directly calibrated in wavelengths (Fig. 5.9). Rotation of this drum to a given position then enables light of a particular wavelength to be observed in the telescope. If, instead of the eyepiece, a slit is placed at the focus of the telescope objective, a constant-deviation monochromator is available. The telescope can alternatively be replaced by a camera so that the dispersed spectrum is photographed, giving a constant-deviation spectrograph.

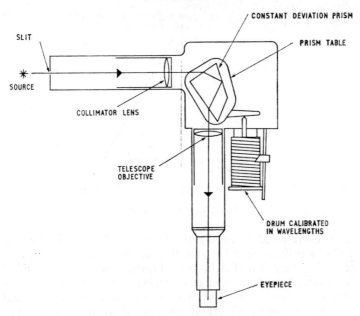

Fig. 5.9. The constant-deviation spectrometer

Commercial constant-deviation spectrometers are able in the visible region of the spectrum to achieve an accuracy of 1–3 Å in wavelength.

To obtain greater linear dispersion, a Littrow type of spectrometer or a grating spectrometer is used.

5.18 The Littrow Prism Spectrometer

The Littrow prism spectrometer can be adapted for use in the ultra-violet, visible and infra-red regions. Vacuum spectrographs of this type for use in the ultra-violet at wavelengths below 1,200 Å are also made.

The Littrow prism spectrometer is a double-pass instrument: dispersion is obtained by a triangular prism which is traversed twice by the light—which is thus doubly dispersed. It can be provided with a wavelength-calibrated drive which rotates the prism and can also be arranged so that it produces a spectrum on a photographic plate.

For use in the ultra-violet down to 2,000 Å approx., a quartz prism is necessary. When light traverses quartz, which is optically active, for each incident ray two circularly polarised light rays

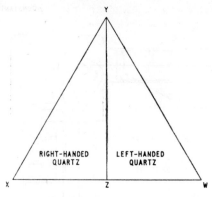

Fig. 5.10. A Cornu prism

emerge corresponding to slightly different refractive indices. In the Cornu prism (Fig. 5.10), this difficulty is overcome by making one half of the prism of right-handed quartz and the other half of left-handed. A single ray then emerges, because the phase difference introduced in the first half (prism XYZ) is balanced out by the equal and opposite phase difference introduced in the second half (prism ZYW). In the double-pass instrument of the Littrow type

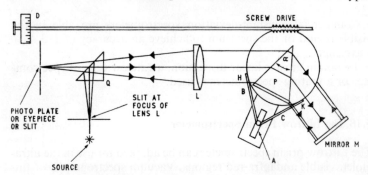

Fig. 5.11. A Littrow spectrometer (schematic plan view)

used in the ultra-violet, an ordinary quartz prism is satisfactory and the Cornu model is not needed because the phase difference introduced when the light traverses the prism in the forward direction is balanced out when the reflected light traverses the prism in the backward direction.

The light from the collimator lens L (Fig. 5.11) traverses the prism P of angle α to emerge after deviation and dispersion to a front-surface aluminised plane mirror M at which it is incident normally. The light is therefore reflected back to traverse the prism again, so that it is additionally dispersed, to be focused at the eye-piece, exit slit or a photographic plate. Lens L acts as both the colli-mator lens and the telescope or camera objective.

The entrance slit clearly needs to be outside the path of the light returning to the exit; it is therefore to one side of this path with a right-angled prism Q arranged to determine the path of the inci-dent light to the dispersing prism P. The mirror M is slightly tilted so that the returning rays pass over the prism Q.

The prism table can be rotated by means of the wavelength drum D and the screw drive. ABC is a mechanical device which automatically keeps the prism in a position of minimum deviation for light of wavelengths which are focused at the eyepiece cross-wires, the exit slit or the centre of the photographic plate. The ties B and C to pivots H and K form mechanical links whereby the mirror M is rotated through twice the angle of rotation of the prism when the drum D is turned.

The plano-convex achromatic lens L is of glass in the visible spectrum or of quartz and fluorite in the ultra-violet. In some de-signs, however, L is replaced by an aluminised concave mirror. The advantage of the mirror is that it does not introduce chromat-ism and, unlike a lens, does not absorb radiation. A monochrom-ator (exit slit) or a spectrograph (photographic plate at the exit) with a quartz prism and a concave mirror instead of lens L able to cover the wavelength range from 35,000 Å to 2,000 Å is made in this way. The optical paths are necessarily different with a mirror in place of lens L.

In a modification of the Littrow system, the right-handed compo-nent only of the Cornu prism is used. Component XYZ (Fig. 5.10) is used, and the face YZ is aluminised. Light entering the single right-handed component is then reflected back at face YZ. Then the clockwise circularly polarised vibrations incident upon YZ become anticlockwise components after reflection. These two components correspond to slightly different refractive indices, but the phase difference introduced in the incident path in the prism is balanced out by the opposite phase difference in the reflected path.

A monochromator based on the Littrow system, having a quartz prism and concave mirror focusing and covering the wavelength range 35,000–2,000 Å is often furnished with a Schwarz linear thermopile at the exit slit for recording in the infra-red and visible. In the ultra-violet and visible, this thermopile can be replaced by a small photomultiplier cell to obtain greater sensitivity but at the sacrifice of independence of sensitivity of wavelength.

To explore longer wavelengths in the infra-red than 35,000 Å, the quartz prism must be replaced by one of a different material. The choice is indicated by Table 5.3. All these materials are hygro-scopic and so their surfaces must be protected with a thin lacquer

Table 5.3.

CHOICE OF PRISM MATERIAL IN THE INFRA-RED

Material	Lithium fluoride	Calcium fluoride	Sodium chloride	Potassium bromide	Caesium bromide	Caesium iodide
Long wavelength limit (μm)	6·0	9·0	15·0	25·0	40·0	50·0

coating. A material known as KRS 5, which is 44% thallium bromide and 56% thallium iodide, is non-hygroscopic and can be used in the range 3–40 μm.

To explore wavelengths in the ultra-violet below 2,000 Å, the quartz prism is replaced by fluorite one which can be used for wavelengths down to 1,200 Å. Below 1,800 Å, the spectrometer would have to be evacuated to avoid undue absorption of the ultra-violet in air at atmospheric pressure.

5.19 The Grating Spectrometer

For a plane diffraction grating at which light of wavelength λ is incident normally, the equation

$$e \sin \theta = p\lambda \qquad (5.6)$$

gives the angles of diffraction θ at which principal maxima occur in the transmitted light for various orders $p = 1, 2, 3, \ldots$, where e is the separation between corresponding points on adjacent rulings in the grating (Section 11.6 of Volume 1). Each slit will produce a diffraction pattern in which the intensity distribution depends on the slit width. This combination of interference and diffraction effects has been considered analytically in Volume 1 (Section 11.6) but a restatement of results is useful here.

Suppose collimated light of wavelength λ is incident normally on a grating of parallel equidistant slits, each of width a much less than that of the opaque portions between slits. The separation between corresponding points on adjacent slits is e. The diffracted light is brought to a focus by a lens or the eye. The treatment of diffraction at a single slit gives the expression $R_\theta = (R_0 \sin \alpha)/\alpha$, where R_θ is the amplitude of the light vibration emerging in a direction at an angle θ to the incident direction, R_0 is the amplitude for $\theta = 0$, and $\alpha = (\pi a \sin \theta)/\lambda$. Therefore

$$R_\theta = R_0 \frac{\sin\left[(\pi a \sin \theta)/\lambda\right]}{(\pi a \sin \theta)/\lambda}$$

For N slits, the common phase difference between neighbouring clear slits is $(2\pi e \sin \theta)/\lambda$ and the resultant intensity I in the direction θ is decided by

$$I = k \frac{\sin^2 [(N\pi e \sin \theta)/\lambda]}{\sin^2 [(\pi e \sin \theta)/\lambda]}$$

where k is a constant. When

$$\frac{\pi e \sin \theta}{\lambda} = p\pi$$

the expression for I is indeterminate because the denominator is zero; the amplitude is therefore found by differentiating both numerator and denominator with respect to θ. Now

$$\frac{\mathrm{d}}{\mathrm{d}\theta} \left(\sin \frac{N\pi e \sin \theta}{\lambda} \right) = \frac{N\pi e}{\lambda} \cos \frac{N\pi e \sin \theta}{\lambda} \cos \theta$$

and

$$\frac{\mathrm{d}}{\mathrm{d}\theta} \left(\sin \frac{\pi e \sin \theta}{\lambda} \right) = \frac{\pi e}{\lambda} \cos \frac{\pi e \sin \theta}{\lambda} \cos \theta$$

Therefore the amplitude in direction θ is proportional to

$$\frac{N \cos [(N\pi e \sin \theta)/\lambda]}{\cos [(\pi e \sin \theta)/\lambda]} = \frac{N \cos Np\pi}{\cos p\pi} = \pm N$$

Hence the intensity I is proportional to N^2.

The resultant intensity in a direction θ is the consequence of both diffraction and interference terms. Therefore the intensity in direction θ is proportional to

$$\frac{\sin^2 [(\pi a \sin \theta)/\lambda]}{(\pi a \sin \theta/\lambda)^2} \frac{\sin^2 [(N\pi \varepsilon \sin \theta)/\lambda]}{\sin^2 [(\pi e \sin \theta)/\lambda]}$$

The variation of the second factor, the interference term, is such that maxima occur when $e \sin \theta = p\lambda$. This value can be substituted in the first factor, the diffraction term, to give the resultant intensities of the maxima as proportional to

$$\frac{\sin^2 (\pi ap/e)}{(\pi ap/e)^2}$$

where $p = 0, 1, 2, \ldots$ Calculation for $a = 0 \cdot 5e$ and $a = 0 \cdot 1e$ gives the results shown in Table 5.4. Both amplitudes and intensities are normalised to unity at $p = 0$. Note that when $a = 0 \cdot 5e$, the second, fourth, sixth, $\ldots$ orders of spectra disappear. When $a = 0 \cdot 1e$,

Table 5.4.

AMPLITUDE AND INTENSITY CALCULATIONS FOR $a = 0.5e$ AND $a = 0.1e$

		$p = 0$	$p = 1$	$p = 2$	$p = 3$	$p = 4$	$p = 5$
	Amplitude decided by	$\dfrac{\sin 0}{0} = 1$	$\dfrac{\sin (\pi a/e)}{(\pi a/e)}$	$\dfrac{\sin (2\pi a/e)}{(2\pi a/e)}$	$\dfrac{\sin (3\pi a/e)}{(3\pi a/e)}$	$\dfrac{\sin (4\pi a/e)}{(4\pi a/e)}$	$\dfrac{\sin (5\pi a/e)}{(5\pi a/e)}$
$a = 0.5e$	Amplitude	1	0.63	0	−0.21	0	0.13
$a = 0.5e$	Intensity	1	0.40	0	0.04	0	0.17
$a = 0.1e$	Amplitude	1	0.975	0.925	0.852	0.752	0.64
$a = 0.1e$	Intensity	1	0.95	0.86	0.73	0.57	0.41

the tenth order disappears, also the twentieth, thirtieth, and so on.

Diffraction gratings used in spectroscopy seldom have less than 3,000 lines per centimetre. With this number N, $e = 1/3,000$ and Equation 5.6 gives

$$\frac{\sin \theta}{3,000} = p\lambda$$

In the visible spectrum, the minimum value of λ is 4×10^{-5} cm and $\sin \theta$ can approach unity. The maximum possible order that can be observed in transmission is therefore

$$p = \frac{1}{3 \times 10^3 \times 4 \times 10^{-5}}$$

Therefore $p = 8$, to the nearest smaller integer. With $a = 0.1e$, the first missing order is the tenth. A grating with 3,000 lines per centimetre and $a = 0.1e$ would therefore not have missing orders.

5.20 Plane Grating in the Infra-red and the Ultra-violet

Glass absorbs radiation of wavelengths greater than about 3 μm (30,000 Å) and less than about 0.3 μm (3,000 Å). Although a quartz transmission grating could be used to extend this range, the best procedure is to employ a reflection grating. The reflection grating can be ruled on polished stainless steel or speculum alloy, but the usual practice is to make the ruling on optically polished glass and

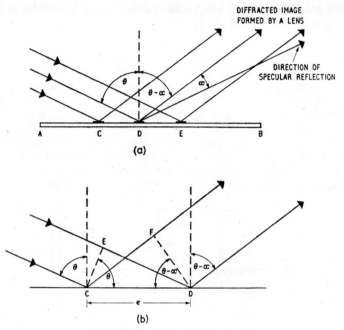

Fig. 5.12. The plane reflection grating

then coat it with an opaque layer of aluminium by deposition in a vacuum.

In Fig. 5.12(a) suppose collimated light of wavelength λ is incident at an angle θ on a reflection grating consisting of regularly spaced reflecting strips parallel to one another. Corresponding points on neighbouring strips are separated by e.

Consider light reflected from neighbouring strips C and D in the grating AB at an angle $\theta - \alpha$ to the normal. Constructive interference occurs between these neighbouring parallel rays (when they are brought to a focus by a lens or by the eye) when, in Fig. 5.12(b),

$$ED - CF = p\lambda$$

where p is an integer, CE is perpendicular to ED so is a wavefront in the incident beam, and DF is perpendicular to CF and thus forms a wavefront in the reflected beam. Therefore

$$CD \sin \theta - CD \sin (\theta - \alpha) = p\lambda$$

i.e.

$$e \left[\sin \theta - \sin (\theta - \alpha) \right] = p\lambda \qquad (5.7)$$

The general condition when light is diffracted on both sides of the specularly reflected image is

$$e\,[\sin\,\theta\pm\sin\,(\theta-\alpha)] = p\lambda \qquad (5.8)$$

In recent developments, rulings in the glass subsequently aluminised are cut at such an angle that most of the diffracted light is concentrated into one or two orders. They are called *blazed gratings*. Whereas small plane gratings of both the transmission and reflection types are usually plastic replicas from a master ruled grating and are mounted on a spectrometer table for students' experiments, the large plane grating of the blazed type is mounted in a spectrometer, monochromator or spectrograph of the Littrow pattern (Fig. 5.13). The quartz-fluorite achromatic lens L is used as both the

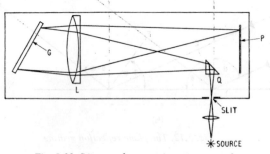

Fig. 5.13. Littrow plane grating spectrograph

collimator and camera lens in a Littrow spectrograph; the reflecting grating G is set at the appropriate angle, with appropriately angled blazed rulings to reflect the diffracted rays in the spectrum back to the lens L, which focuses them at the photographic plate P. An auxiliary small quartz prism Q is used to enable the slit illuminated by the source to be placed to one side of the main light paths.

5.21 The Rowland Concave Grating

The use of a lens in the collimator and telescope or camera inevitably introduces absorption of radiation in the ultra-violet and infrared regions. A valuable procedure, introduced by Rowland, is to rule the grating on a concave surface so that self-focusing can be achieved and lenses can be avoided.

The original Rowland grating was ruled on a concave mirror of speculum alloy. In present-day technique, the ruling is made on a concave polished glass surface, the diamond point being set to give the required blaze angle, and the ruling is aluminised. The ruled

lines are equally spaced along a chord and not an arc. The grating
is mounted with its rulings parallel to the slit (illuminated by the
source of radiation), so that diffraction and focusing are achieved
simultaneously.

In Fig. 5.14(a), the grating G is greatly exaggerated in size relative
to the circle (called the Rowland circle) for clarity. The radius of

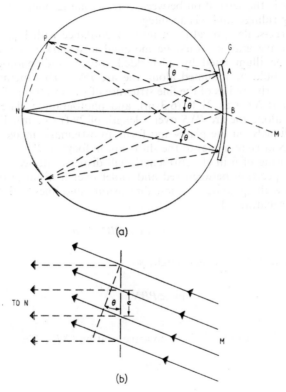

(a)

(b)

Fig. 5.14. The Rowland concave grating

curvature of the grating is equal to the diameter NB of the circle.
The points A, B, and C are on the grating. The circle touches the
grating at its midpoint B and passes through S, the slit illuminated
by the source of radiation. An image of the slit S is formed at P by
reflection in the concave grating. As ABC is, in practice, small compared with NB, the points A and C on the grating may be taken to
be on the circumference $PNSB$ of the circle.

Besides this reflected image at P, other images due to diffraction
will be formed along the arc PS.

Light from the slit S reflected to P will appear to come from the direction MB. The grating can be regarded, in effect, as a transmission type relative to light along MB. For light to be diffracted to N, it is seen from Fig. 5.14(b) that

$$e \sin \theta = p\lambda$$

where e is the separation between corresponding points on neighbouring rulings, and p is an integer.

In large-scale apparatus set up in accordance with Fig. 5.14(a), the concave grating would be mounted in a dark room, the slit would be illuminated by a shielded source, and photographic plates would be mounted along the arc PNS. This method was used in early studies of the fine structure of the spectrum of atomic hydrogen: NB was 21 ft (6·3 m), and photographic plates were erected along the arc PNS over a length of 29 ft (8·7 m). The rays fall obliquely on the plates and form an astigmatic image, so the line at S at right angles to the slit is not in focus at P.

A grating of 6 in (15 cm) length will disperse the second order visible spectrum between red and violet over a distance of 12 ft (3·6 m) with apparatus of these dimensions, and lines 0·03 Å apart can be separated. From Fig. 5.14(a)

$$e \sin \theta = e \sin \angle PBN = p\lambda$$

The angle NPB is a right angle, so

$$\sin \angle PBN = \frac{NP}{r}$$

where r is the radius of the concave grating (NB). Therefore

$$e \frac{NP}{r} = p\lambda$$

from which it is seen that the distance NP is proportional to λ in a given order p.

Suppose $r = 3-5$ m and the grating has 6,000 lines per centimetre. If the temperature changes by 1 degC, expansion of the grating will be such that de/e is about 2×10^{-5} deg^{-1} C, and there will be a corresponding error in the determination of λ. Accurate measurements of wavelengths therefore require a fine control of the environment.

Typical values of the dispersion for various sizes of grating and line spacing are given in Table 5.5.

Table 5.5.

DISPERSION VALUES FOR DIFFERENT GRATING SIZES AND LINE SPACINGS

Radius of curvature of the grating (m)	Lines per centimetre	First order (Å mm⁻¹)	Second order (Å mm⁻¹)
2·0	6,000	15·0	7·5
3·0	10,000	7·0	3·5
4·0	10,000	5·2	2·6
6·0	6,000	5·0	2·5
4·0	18,000	3·4	1·7
20·0	12,000	0·8	0·4

5.22 Mountings for Concave Gratings

Three mountings adapted to the Rowland circle are due to Paschen, to Rowland and to Eagle.

5.22.1 THE PASCHEN MOUNTING

The grating and slit are fixed, and a photographic plate with thin glass backing is curved in a mount to fit any desired part of the Rowland circle. In Fig. 5.15 are shown the approximate positions

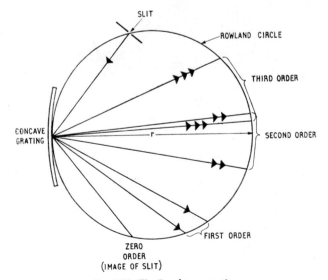

Fig. 5.15. The Paschen mounting

occupied by the zero and first three orders in the visible spectrum. This mounting is used considerably, but it requires a large dark room with pier mountings for the slit and grating and a specially erected circular track—the Rowland circle—on which firm mounting of the photographic plate holders is necessary.

5.22.2 THE ROWLAND MOUNTING

The concave grating G [Fig. 5.16(a)] and the photographic plate holder P are mounted at a distance r apart on a rigid beam, r being the radius of curvature of G, equal to the diameter of the Rowland circle (shown dotted). As the beam slides on the swivel trucks attached below G and P and mounted on the rigid perpendicular rails AB and AC, G and P clearly remain at the fixed distance r apart and are maintained on the Rowland circle.

Movement of G as its associated swivel truck is slid along AB will cause variation of the angle of incidence I of the light from the illuminated slit S mounted at the fixed junction A. On the other

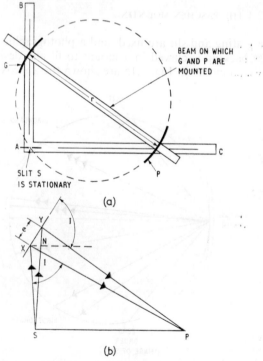

Fig. 5.16. The Rowland mounting

hand, the angle of diffraction θ, which is the angle between the diffracted rays reaching P and the normal to G along the axis of the beam between G and P, stays close to zero.

In Fig. 5.16(b), let X and Y be adjacent rulings on the concave grating separated by distance e. For light of wavelength λ, a maximum at an order of interference p will appear centrally on the photographic plate P when $XP = YP$ (which are each nearly equal to r) and the path difference between SY and SX equals $p\lambda$. As $\angle XSP$ is very nearly 90°,

$$SY - SX = YN = e \sin I$$

A maximum will appear at the centre P, therefore, when

$$e \sin I = p\lambda$$

As $\sin I = SP/r$,

$$\lambda = e \frac{SP}{pr}$$

In a given order p, therefore, λ is proportional to SP, which implies that, as S is fixed, the wavelength is very nearly proportional to the distance from some fiducial mark of the line recorded on the photographic plate (i.e. the spectrum is normal, to a close approximation).

As $\sin I = p\lambda/e$, it follows that $p\lambda/e$ cannot exceed unity. From this it is easily calculated that for a grating with 8,000 lines per centimetre, the maximum wavelength observable in the first order is 12,500 Å and 12,500/p in the pth order, where $p = 2, 3, 4, \ldots$.

5.22.3 THE EAGLE MOUNTING

A compact mounting similar to that in a Littrow spectrograph is due to Eagle; it is much used in all ranges of the spectrum, but is particularly convenient in the ultra-violet at wavelengths below 1,200 Å (where the container of the spectrograph has to be maintained under vacuum); moreover, the compact container involved facilitates temperature control.

The concave grating G and the curved photographic plate P are mounted at a distance apart (which can be varied) on a beam supported within the cylindrical container which can be evacuated, if required. Both G and P (which is curved) are on a Rowland circle (Fig. 5.17). The slit S is to one side of the beam within the container wall (or the slit and source of radiation are inside a separate attached container which can be evacuated together with the main chamber).

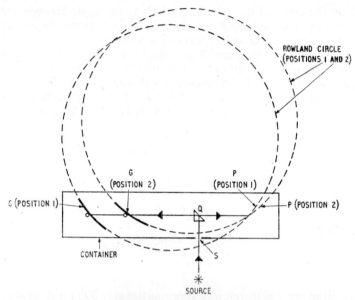

Fig. 5.17. The Eagle mounting (plan view)

The quartz prism Q directs radiation from the slit on to the grating G. In a vacuum spectrograph, Q is replaced by a plane mirror to avoid absorption of ultra-violet radiation.

The virtual image of the slit S formed by the prism Q (or plane mirror) is at the centre of the photographic plate P. The grating can be moved along the beam relative to the plate P. As it is moved, both G and P are rotated about a vertical axis so that they remain on a Rowland circle.

The angle of diffraction θ to the normal to the grating equals the angle of incidence I in this arrangement, so

$$2d \sin I = p\lambda$$

where p is an integer. As $\sin I$ has a maximum value of unity, the maximum wavelength observable is $2d/p$, which is twice that possible in the Rowland mounting.

The more recent *Wadsworth mounting* (Fig. 5.18) for a concave grating does not make use of the Rowland circle idea. Instead, radiation from the slit S is collimated by the aluminised front-surface concave mirror M to be incident on the concave grating G which can be rotated to vary the angle of incidence. The centre of the curved photographic plate P is maintained on the normal to the grating G. As G is rotated, therefore, P has to be moved.

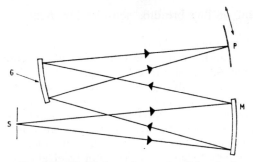

Fig. 5.18. The Wadsworth mounting (plan view)

With the compact Wadsworth set-up, spectrographs of larger aperture and improved definition (as a result of reduced aberration in the optical system) are possible, leading to more intense sharp lines at the plate P with the consequent improvement that exposure times required are reduced.

5.23 High-resolution Spectrometry

A spectrometer or monochromator based on the use of a prism is capable of a chromatic resolving power of about 50,000, so a spectral line of wavelength 5,000 Å can be measured to an accuracy of 0·1 Å approx. To achieve much greater resolution would demand excessively large prisms or a number of prisms in series to give a large value of b, the length of the base, in Equation 5.3.

The use of a grating can lead to higher chromatic resolving power. Reference to Equation 5.5 shows that a large number N of rulings is required in the width of the grating encountered by the wavefront in the incident collimated light, and/or the spectrum must be recorded in a higher order p. Unless the grating were very large (demanding correspondingly a very wide uniform beam of incident collimated light) which would be very difficult and expensive to achieve, about the maximum possible value of N is 100,000. The limitation is determined by the number of rulings per centimetre possible; the ruling is done by a diamond cutter attached to a dividing engine; the very small point on the diamond required to achieve an excessively fine ruling would wear unduly. In the second order ($p = 2$), a chromatic resolving power of about 200,000 is possible with a ruled grating.

In the visible spectrum, therefore, wavelength determination to 0·1 Å is possible with a prism spectrometer and possibly 0·025 Å with a large grating spectrometer. In high-resolution work aimed at determining the hyperfine structure of spectral lines and the measurement of line breadth, considerably greater accuracy is required.

For this very high resolution, the instruments available are the Fabry–Perot interferometer (Section 4.2), the Lummer–Gehrcke plate (Section 4.8) and the echelon grating. The Fabry–Perot interferometer is usually placed between the collimator and the prism of a constant deviation spectrograph. Without the Fabry–Perot interferometer, the spectrograph will produce lines in the focal plane of its camera lens if the source gives an atomic spectrum. For two wavelengths λ and $\lambda + \Delta\lambda$ in the radiation from the source which are so close together that $\Delta\lambda$ is not resolvable by the prism, the two lines will appear as one. On insertion of the Fabry–Perot interferometer, very narrow bright rings alternating with dark ones result. Though the spectral lines appear as one, the ring systems on each are clearly distinguishable. Measurement of their diameters now enables $\Delta\lambda$ to be determined. Provided that the line wavelengths are initially known to the nearest $0 \cdot 1$ Å, the introduction of the Fabry–Perot interferometer enables the wavelength to be found to at least three decimal places. The resolving power now obtainable depends on the length of the etalon and the reflection coefficient of its surfaces (Section 4.2).

Usually, the examination of the fine structure of a spectral line by the use of a Fabry–Perot interferometer necessitates isolation of the line by a prism or grating to avoid confusion. In some instances, however, a variable-length interferometer can be used to examine fine structure precisely without the use of a prism spectrometer, provided that the source of radiation is nearly monochromatic. When the interferometer separation is altered, the ring systems due to each component wavelength move relatively to one another. For example, measurement of the distance between successive coincidences of the ring systems due to each component of the yellow sodium doublet allows their difference in wavelength of $5 \cdot 97$ Å to be readily determined (Section 4.4).

The Lummer–Gehrcke plate (Section 4.8) is an alternative to the Fabry–Perot interferometer. It is used between the collimator and prism of a spectrometer. As described in Section 4.8, the Lummer–Gehrcke plate is usually 130 mm long, 15 mm wide and has a thickness of less than 1 cm. Its resolving power is equal approximately to the length of the plate in wavelengths. It produces sharp bright line interference fringes on a dark background, whereas the Fabry–Perot interferometer produces bright circular fringes.

The development of the Fabry–Perot interferometer has rendered obsolete the Lummer–Gehrcke plate, which is more difficult to make.

Another instrument of very high resolving power is the echelon grating, introduced by Michelson in 1898. The simple but ingenious idea put forward relates, in effect, to a consideration of Equation 5.5 for the chromatic resolving power R of a diffraction grating:

$$R = \frac{\lambda}{\delta\lambda} = pN$$

Whereas N cannot readily be made to exceed 100,000 and p is limited to three or four with plane gratings, Michelson's suggestion was to make N equal to 20–40 but increase p to several thousand. To achieve this, he used a pile of parallel plane plates staggered to simulate the steps of a staircase (the word échelon is the French for step). With 40 plates (i.e. $N = 40$) and a step of 1 cm height, the order of interference p could be made 40,000 at a wavelength of 5,000 Å, giving a resolving power of $40 \times 40,000$ (i.e. 1.6×10^6).

The echelon grating can be made as a transmission or a reflection type. The former is very difficult to make as it demands not only optically flat and plane-parallel blocks of glass but also the use of glass of exceptional homogeneity. As it cannot achieve as high a resolving power as the Fabry–Perot interferometer, the transmission type is obsolete. The reflection echelon grating forms, however, an important very high resolution instrument for work over a wide range of wavelengths from the ultra-violet, through the visible, into the infra-red. Though difficult to construct, homogeneity in refractive index of the glass is now not necessary. Also, being a reflection device, loss due to absorption in the ultra-violet and the infra-red is of no concern as it would be in, for example, a Fabry–Perot etalon constructed with quartz plates.

5.24 The Reflection Echelon Grating

An echelon grating is constructed from a number N of plane-parallel plates which each has the same thickness t. These plates have to be very accurately plane, so that they can be wrung together in optical contact to form a pile with an off-set step, the height of each step being s. The optical working demanded is of a very high precision to ensure that the plates will go into optical contact and that their thicknesses t are equal to within 0.05λ, where λ is a mean wavelength of about 5,000 Å.

For a transmission echelon, it is essential that all the plates be cut from the same extremely homogeneous piece of optical glass. For the reflection echelon homogeneity in refractive index is unimportant. Fused silica is usually employed for the reflection type, as it has a low thermal expansion coupled with a relatively high thermal conductivity compared with glass; these factors assist towards ensuring a high standard of optical polishing.

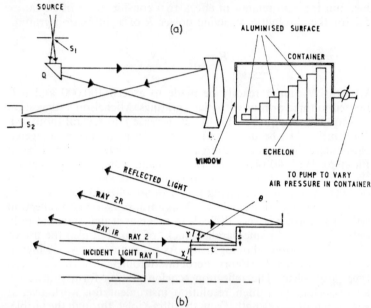

Fig. 5.19. The reflection echelon grating

The pile of plates in a reflection echelon is supported in a mount within a container furnished with a window; the container can usually be connected to a vacuum pump so that the pressure (and hence refractive index) of the air surrounding the echelon can be reduced at will. After the plates have been mounted but before insertion in the container, the front-surface of the pile of step formation is aluminised.

The reflection echelon is frequently set up in a Littrow type of arrangement. Light from the illuminated slit S_1 [Fig. 5.19(a)] is directed via the right-angled prism Q (or alternatively a mirror) on to the lens L. With S_1 in the focal plane of L, collimated light is incident on the aluminised front-surface of the echelon normal to the front-surface planes of the plates. The reflected and diffracted light from the echelon is focused by the lens L on to the slit S_2 of a spectrograph.

Each 'mirror' of step width s acts like the reflecting ruling of a plane diffraction grating, and there are N such steps. In Fig. 5.19(b), consider neighbouring parallel rays 1 and 2 in the incident beam, which give rise to parallel rays $1R$ and $2R$ in the reflected light leaving at an angle of diffraction θ to the normal. Ray 2 has to travel a distance t greater than ray 1 to reach the echelon surface. Ray $2R$ has to travel a distance $t \cos \theta$ to reach the wavefront

XY (drawn perpendicular to rays 1*R* and 2*R* through the corner of a step). Ray 1*R* has to travel a distance $s \sin \theta$ from the reflecting surface to reach *XY*. The path difference between rays 1*R* and 2*R* is therefore

$$t + t \cos \theta - s \sin \theta$$

For light of wavelength λ diffracted through an angle θ to give a principal maximum in the focal plane of the lens *L*, this path difference must be an integral number of wavelengths *p*. Therefore

$$t(1 + \cos \theta) - s \sin \theta = p\lambda$$

where *p* is an integer. As θ is a small angle,

$$2t - s\theta = p\lambda \qquad (5.9)$$

Taking into account that the refractive index *n* of the air is not exactly unity and can be varied by varying the pressure, Equation 5.9 becomes

$$(2t - s\theta)n = p\lambda \qquad (5.10)$$

With a thickness *t* of 1·0 cm, for light of wavelength 5,000 Å (5×10^{-5} cm) and order of interference *p* and for small angles θ, (i.e. the diffracted light being very near the normal), it is seen from Equation 5.9 that

$$p = \frac{2t}{\lambda} = \frac{2·0}{5 \times 10^{-5}} = 40,000$$

If there are 30 plates in the pile, $N = 30$, corresponding to 30 steps or 'rulings' in the grating. The resolving power *R* will therefore be (Equation 5.5)

$$R = \frac{\lambda}{\delta\lambda} = 4 \times 10^{4} \times 30 = 1·2 \times 10^{6}$$

Assuming $n = 1$ and ignoring the dispersion of air, the angular dispersion $d\theta/d\lambda$ is obtained from Equation 5.9, which may be rearranged to give

$$\theta = \frac{2t}{s} - \frac{p\lambda}{s} \qquad (5.11)$$

Therefore

$$\frac{d\theta}{d\lambda} = -\frac{p}{s}$$

As $p = 2t/\lambda$ for small angles θ, therefore

$$\frac{d\theta}{d\lambda} = -\frac{2t}{\lambda s} \qquad (5.12)$$

For $t = 1\cdot0$ cm and $s = 0\cdot6$ cm, the value of the angular dispersion $d\theta/d\lambda$ at and near the normal is therefore $2/(5\times10^{-5}\times0\cdot6) = 66{,}667$ for light of wavelength 5,000 Å.

The angular separation between neighbouring orders is given by evaluating $d\theta/dp$ and putting $dp = 1$. From Equation 5.11

$$\frac{d\theta}{dp} = -\frac{\lambda}{s} \tag{5.13}$$

The value of the angular separation between neighbouring orders is therefore λ/s, which is very small. The echelon can thus only be used to examine a narrow range of wavelengths at any one

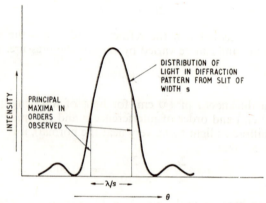

Fig. 5.20. The intensities of neighbouring orders observed with a reflection echelon grating

time. This is ideal for the study of the hyperfine structure of lines or the splitting of lines in the Zeeman effect. The source of light to be examined—for example that illuminating slit S_1 in Fig. 5.19(a)—is therefore best substantially monochromatic.

As neighbouring orders have an angular separation of only λ/s, which is half the width of a diffraction pattern due to a face of width s, only two orders are observed with any intensity (Fig. 5.20).

The echelon grating can be regarded as one with a very effective 'blaze', in that almost all the light giving rise to diffraction maxima is confined to small angles to the normal and within two orders. Harrison introduced in 1949 the *echelle grating* (Fig. 5.21) which is, in effect, a blazed grating half-way in operation between the ruled plane grating and the echelon. The echelle grating has wide shallow grooves designed to reflect light incident at an angle usually exceeding 45°, but normal to the shallow side of the step.

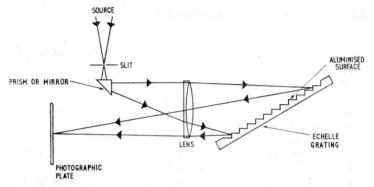

Fig. 5.21. The echelle grating in a Littrow arrangement (the grating has 40–400 steps per centimetre, and step depths in the range 0·06–0·25 mm)

5.25 Standards of Wavelength

The absolute standard is the metre, defined as 1,650,763·73 wavelengths of a particular line in the orange of the spectrum of a krypton 86 discharge lamp operated at low temperature (Section 4.6). The primary standard of wavelength is therefore the krypton 86 orange line, determined in relation to the metre to an accuracy of one part in 10^8.

Other primary standards of wavelength used prior to that of the krypton 86 radiation are the cadmium red line of wavelength 6438·4696 Å, and the mercury 198 green line of wavelength 5460·740 Å.

Precision measurements of other wavelengths are made by comparison with a primary standard, usually by means of a grating spectrometer and a Fabry–Perot etalon spectrometer. From such comparisons, useful secondary standards of wavelength have been established. In particular, the spectra of iron, neon and krypton are valuable.

Thousands of lines of wavelengths between 2,101 Å and 10,216 Å in the arc spectrum of iron have been measured. With the operating conditions of the iron arc carefully specified, 306 secondary standards of wavelength between 2,447 Å and 6,677 Å have been adopted.

The neon spectrum is especially rich in red lines, several of which are used as secondary standards. The wavelengths in the spectrum of natural krypton are useful secondary standards as they agree to within one part in 10^6 or better with those from the isotopes krypton 84 and krypton 86, the last of which is the fundamental standard.

5.26 The Calibration of a Spectrometer

In the *ultra-violet region* between 4,000 Å and 2,000 Å, a number of lines of known wavelengths are employed for calibration of a spectrometer or spectrograph. In Ångstrom units to four significant figures, where the element giving the spectrum is noted in brackets, these lines are 3,902 (molybdenum), 3,719 (iron), 3,515 (nickel), 3,453 (cobalt), 3,067 (bismuth), 2,881 (silicon), 2,496 (boron) and 2,348 (beryllium).

For calibration in the *visible region*, the usual choice is the cadmium lamp spectrum in which convenient lines occur at 6,438 Å, 5,086 Å, 4,800 Å, 4,678 Å and 4,413 Å.

If the spectrum to be determined is photographed beside that of the cadmium spectrum on the same photographic plate, a travelling microscope or comparator is used to measure the distance x' of the line of unknown wavelength λ' from, say, the cadmium line at 6,438 Å. The Hartmann dispersion equation is

$$\lambda = \lambda_0 + \frac{A}{B+x} \qquad (5.14)$$

where λ_0 is a constant wavelength, and A and B are constants for a given spectrograph. These constants A, B and λ_0 are found by determining x for three known lines in the cadmium spectrum, corresponding to three known values of λ. For the line of wavelength λ', $x = x'$ and use of Equation 5.14 in which A and B are now known enables λ' to be found.

In the *infra-red region*, a convenient practice is to determine the irregularities in an intensity–wavelength graph for the energy received by a spectrometer (with thermopile recording, for example) from a continuous source of radiation. These irregularities are caused by carbon dioxide and water vapour, which absorb specific wavelengths.

5.27 Calibration of a Spectroscope by the Edser–Butler Method

A convenient simple method for a calibrating a spectroscope in the visible region is due to Edser and Butler. It is capable of an accuracy of 3–5 Å. Though the procedure forms an interesting students' laboratory experiment, it is only seldom used in spectroscopy.

A slit S_1 is illuminated by white light, and an image of it is formed by a lens L on the slit S_2 of the spectroscope [Fig. 5.22(a)]. A continuous spectrum is observed in the telescope of the spectroscope. The Edser–Butler arrangement consists of two plane glass plates placed one on top of the other but separated by a small distance d by means of suitable spacers. A suitable device for a students' experiment is to use two small sheets of plate glass separated by strips of paper at their edges and held in a simple clamp or holder. In order to render these plates parallel, a distant small illuminated aperture is viewed through the plates which are then pressed together until the aperture and its images coincide.

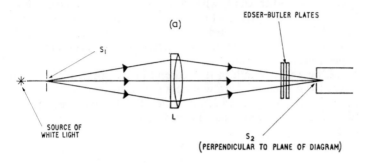

(a)

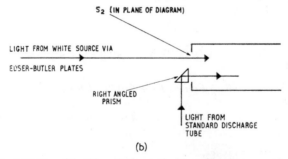

(b)

Fig. 5.22. Use of the Edser–Butler method for calibrating a spectroscope

The preferable commercial instrument consists of a thin air film between two parallel semi-aluminised plates in a holder with three adjusting screws: in effect, an etalon with a very small length d.

The Edser–Butler plates are usually placed near the spectroscope slit within the beam of incident white light. The angle of incidence equals the angle of refraction R within the air film. With the plates normal to the incident beam, the angle R is zero. From the study of the interference of light in plane parallel-sided plates (Section 9.1 of Volume 1) in the transmitted light, for a maximum

$$2nd \cos R = p\lambda \tag{5.15}$$

and for a minimum

$$2nd \cos R = \left(p + \tfrac{1}{2}\right)\lambda \tag{5.16}$$

where p is an integer and n is the refractive index of the parallel-sided film between the plates. The refractive index $n = 1$, as the film is air.

There is a continuous range of values of λ in the radiation from the white light source. At any wavelength in this continuum at which Equation 5.16 is satisfied, a dark band will appear across the spectrum in the field of view of the telescope of the spectroscope. On the other hand, when Equation 5.15, is satisfied there will be a maximum, giving a bright band. The continuous spectrum observed is therefore crossed by a series of parallel dark bands alternating with bright ones perpendicular to the direction in which the spectrum is traversed.

Let λ_r be a wavelength in the red end of the spectrum at which a bright band occurs. There will be a series of wavelengths λ_1, λ_2, λ_3, ..., λ_k (all shorter than λ_r), at which bands numbered successively 1, 2, 3, ..., k will occur. From Equation 5.15, putting $n = 1$ and $R = 90°$,

$$2d = p_r \lambda_r$$

where p_r is the order of interference producing the bright band at wavelength λ_r, and

$$2d = p_k \lambda_k$$

where $p_k = p_r + k$, and λ_k is the wavelength corresponding to the kth band. Therefore

$$2d = p_r \lambda_r = p_k \lambda_k = (p_r + k)\lambda_k$$

Therefore

$$\lambda_r = \lambda_k + \frac{k\lambda_k}{p_r}$$

But $p_r = 2d/\lambda_r$. Therefore

$$\lambda_r = \lambda_k + \frac{k\lambda_r\lambda_k}{2d}$$

Thus

$$\frac{1}{\lambda_k} = \frac{1}{\lambda_r} + \frac{k}{2d} \tag{5.17}$$

or

$$\bar{\nu}_k = \bar{\nu}_r + \frac{k}{2d} \tag{5.18}$$

where $\bar{\nu} = 1/\lambda$ is the wave number. As $2d$ is a constant and k is an integer, it is seen that successive bright bands (and correspondingly intervening dark bands) cross the spectrum at equal intervals of wave number $\bar{\nu}$.

It is necessary to select two known wavelengths: one λ_r (preferably in or near the red) and the other $\lambda_k = \lambda_b$ (near or in the blue) in order to determine the wavelengths λ_k at which intermediate bright bands occur, where $k = 1, 2, 3, \ldots$. The procedure is to observe two spectra at the same time. One is the continuous spectrum interrupted by bands due to the Edser–Butler plates and brought about by white light illuminating the top half of the spectroscope slit. The other is a line spectrum (from a discharge tube) containing lines of two known wavelengths λ_r and λ_b of the light which illuminates the bottom half of the slit. Fig. 5.22(b) shows a typical method of achieving this dual observation. The lines of known wavelengths λ_r and λ_b will not, in general, coincide exactly with positions of maxima in the Edser–Butler fringes, so it is necessary to estimate a fraction of a fringe in estimating the value of k in Equation 5.17 which corresponds to where $\lambda_k = \lambda_r$ or λ_b.

Given specific values of λ_r and λ_b separated by a counted number of fringes k, substitution in Equation 5.17 gives d, the thickness of the air-film between the Edser–Butler plates. With the collimator and prism positions fixed, the telescope can now be rotated from the position where light of wavelength λ_r is focused on the eyepiece cross-wires to the successive bright bands corresponding to $k = 1$, $2, 3, \ldots$. At each position, the angle of setting of the telescope is noted against a divided circle and the corresponding wavelengths $\lambda_k = \lambda_1, \lambda_2, \lambda_3, \ldots$ are calculated by putting $k = 1, 2, 3, \ldots$ successively in Equation 5.17. Alternatively, the collimator and telescope positions can be kept fixed, and the angle of setting of the prism plotted against wavelength.

The method also lends itself readily to a linear plot of various values of $\bar{v}_k$, the wave number, against k, as is seen from Equation 5.18.

5.28 Checking the Chromatic Resolving Power of a Spectrometer

In the visible spectrum, a number of elements give spectra containing convenient doublet lines useful in making a quick approximate check on the resolving power of a prism or small grating spectrometer. These doublets are given in Table 5.6.

5.29 Spectrophotometry

A spectrophotometer is an instrument for measuring the distribution of the energy of radiation through part of the spectrum. This energy may be directly from a source of radiation, or from a

Table 5.6.

DOUBLETS CONTAINED IN THE SPECTRA OF A NUMBER OF ELEMENTS

Element	Titanium	Iron	Titanium	Iron	Titanium	Iron	Sodium	Iron	Magnesium	Iron
Wavelengths of doublet lines (Å)	5,036·4 5,035·9	6,137·6 6,136·6	5,038·4 5,036·4	5,269·5 5,266·5	5,020·0 5,016·1	5,435·5 5,429·6	5,895·9 5,889·9	4,619·2 4,611·2	5,183·6 5,172·6	5,191·4 5,171·5
Separation (Å)	0·5	1·0	2·0	3·0	3·9	5·9	6·0	8·0	11·0	19·9

surface which reflects or scatters radiation directed on to it from a primary source, or from a material (solid, liquid or gas) which transmits radiation directed on to it. In general, a spectrophotometer does not measure the energy in a given narrow region of the spectrum in absolute units. Rather, the purpose is to compare outputs obtained when first the radiation concerned is incident directly on the spectrophotometer slit and then record this output when a reflecting surface or absorbing material is placed between the radiation source and the slit.

The output is measured photographically, or by some kind of phototransducer which converts the radiation usually into an electrical signal, the commonest form of such transducer being a photocell.

Usually, the radiation incident upon the slit of the spectrophotometer is divided into two parts: directly or otherwise from the luminous source; and after reflection from a surface or transmission through a material. There are consequently two simultaneous output signals from the spectrophotometer and these are compared.

The spectrophotometer must be based on a dispersive system adapted to the spectral region concerned. Much work is done with prism and grating instruments in the visible spectrum, but instruments for operation in the infra-red and ultra-violet are made and continual development has been undertaken and is still in progress to enable the far infra-red and far ultra-violet regions to be quantitatively explored.

In the visible region, the reflectance at various determined wavelength intervals in the spectrum (i.e. the *spectral reflectance*) from the surface of a sample of opaque material is frequently determined by comparing with a suitable spectrophotometer the amount of light reflected by the sample with that from a standard white surface which reflects all the light incident upon it.

The most important application is absorption spectrophotometry. In general terms, the purpose is to measure the transmission of a transparent material for radiation in various selected regions of the spectrum. Quantitative work is then based on two laws: Lambert's law and Beer's law.

Lambert's law relates the transmitted intensity I to the incident intensity I_0 in terms of the length l of the radiation path through the absorber and the absorption coefficient μ of the material. This law is

$$I = I_0 \exp(-\mu l) \tag{5.19}$$

Beer's law states that

$$I = I_0 \exp(-cl) \tag{5.20}$$

where c is the concentration of an absorbing solution.

These two laws are usefully combined to give

$$I = I_0 \exp\left(-\frac{Kcl}{d}\right) \tag{5.21}$$

where K is another constant which depends on d, the size of any particles in suspension in a solution, and the wavelength λ of the radiation. Except when d is very small, Equation 5.21 becomes

$$I = I_0 \exp\left(-K_1 cl\right) \tag{5.22}$$

or

$$K_1 cl = \log_e \frac{I_0}{I} \tag{5.23}$$

The term $\log_e\left(I_0/I\right)$ is known as the *absorbance*, and K_1 is the *molar absorptivity*.

Automatic self-balancing spectrophotometers readily measure the transmittance I/I_0, which is an inconvenient measurement for subsequent use as it is not related linearly to concentration and the length of the cell containing the solution. Modern instruments measure the absorbance, which is related directly to K_1, c and l.

Deviations can occur from the Lambert–Beer law when light is scattered as well as absorbed by the material and also when fluorescence is induced in the solution by the incident radiation. Deviations can be experienced which depend on the concentration of the solution: thus Beer's law may not be valid if partial or complete dissociation of the solute occurs.

5.30 The Use of Photographic Emulsions in Spectrography and Spectrophotometry

A much used procedure is to record on a photographic plate in a spectrograph the spectrum of the radiation from a source. The optical density of the silver deposit in the subsequently processed emulsion is then recorded at various known wavelengths throughout the spectrum. This optical density is measured by a microphotometer.

This kind of technique can be used in two main ways. In the first, the spectrum of the radiation from a luminous source (which may, for example, be the continuous spectrum of the light from a tungsten lamp or the line spectrum from a discharge lamp or an arc) is recorded; on the same photographic plate is recorded (usually simultaneously, by means of a beam-splitter device in front of the spectrograph slit) the spectrum resulting when this radiation is transmitted through an absorbing material. From the measurement of the two sets of optical densities of the photographic deposit at various wavelengths, the transmittance and absorbance at these wavelengths of the absorbing material may be found. In the second method, typical practice is to photograph the arc or spark spectrum for a metallic alloy 1 having a known constituent (for example, a known percentage of aluminium in a steel). The arc or spectrum of a second metallic alloy 2 in which the percentage of, say, aluminium is unknown is also photographed. By comparing the measured optical densities at certain wavelengths in the two spectra, the percentage of aluminium in the second alloy can be found.

To examine the validity of the use of photographic emulsions in spectrography and spectrophotometry, an outline of a theory of the photographic process due to Mott and Gurney in 1938 is given.

Photographic emulsions, consisting essentially of silver halide in gelatine, are more sensitive to light if they contain sulphur compounds (thiocarbamides). Thus, the formation of silver sulphides in the silver bromide grains in the emulsion seems possible. Silver bromide has an ionic lattice structure. When exposed to light, mobile electrons are liberated from the bromine negative ions by the incident photons, the reaction being

$$Br^- + h\nu \rightarrow Br + e^-$$

where ν is the frequency of the incident radiation and h is Planck's constant. These electrons will be trapped near the sulphides. The silver sulphide spots are therefore negatively charged.

Positive silver ions Ag^+ (smaller than bromine ions) that have been displaced by thermal processes are mobile and move towards the negatively charged sulphide spots. On arrival, collections of silver atoms are formed around the silver sulphide spots in the grains; these spots grow as the process proceeds. The reaction is

$$Ag^+ + e^- \rightarrow Ag$$

The latent image is thus formed. When the exposed photographic emulsion is placed in the chemical developer (a mild reducing agent), electrons are supplied to the silver nuclei. The spots become charged negatively, and so more positive silver ions are discharged from the grain. Development increases the free silver in the exposed grains by a factor of about 10^5. The emulsion is fixed after development and washing by immersion in 'hypo'—sodium thiosulphate—which reacts with the residual silver bromide but affects only slightly the black silver in the exposed grains. The complex argentothiosulphates formed are more or less unstable and are subsequently removed from the emulsion by washing, leaving behind the black silver deposits which are denser the greater the initial incident light exposure.

With low incident light intensities, the modest supply of photons means that the rate of arrival of electrons will be small at the sensitive silver sulphide spots, and these spots will hardly change because they lose electrical charge by leakage. At the other extreme, with high light intensities, large numbers of electrons are produced by the plentiful photons, but each sulphide spot can take only a certain charge at a time because of its small capacitance. Between these two extremes, the influx of electrons takes place at a rate such that they are all captured in silver sulphide spots. The developed and fixed plate will then exhibit blackened silver deposits in which the degree of blackening is directly proportional to the exposure.

The exposure is the product of illumination E and the time t. The emulsion blackening is expressed by its *optical density* D:

$$D = \log_{10} \frac{I_0}{I}$$

where I_0 is the incident light intensity, I is the transmitted light intensity and $I_0/I = $ *opacity* O (the reciprocal of the *transmittance*). If a film transmits half the light intensity incident upon it, the opacity $O = 2$ and $D = 0\cdot3$. Similarly, films which transmit $0\cdot1$, $0\cdot01$ and $0\cdot001$ of the incident light have opacities of 10, 100 and 1,000 and optical densities of $1\cdot0$, $2\cdot0$ and $3\cdot0$ respectively.

The optical densities are measured photometrically (the instrument used in spectroscopy is the microphotometer). If these densities are plotted against the logarithm of the exposures (Et, where E is the illumination and t the time) that have produced them, the characteristic curve (blackening or sensitometric curve) for the photographic emulsion concerned is obtained. Such curves have three distinct regions (Fig. 5.23): the curved portion with underexposure, the linear region with correct exposure, and the markedly curved region with over-exposure leading to reversal or the solarisation region.

In the central linear region over which the exposure is correct, the equation of the characteristic is easily seen to be

$$D = \gamma (\log Et - \log i) \qquad (5.24)$$

where $\gamma = \tan \alpha$ is the tangent of the gradient of this linear section. The term γ is related to contrast, but γ is not the only deciding factor. As shown in Fig. 5.23, the inertia i is the intercept on the log Et axis, decided by the tangent to the straight section of the characteristic. For fast photographic emulsions, which are very sensitive to light, γ is about $1\cdot4$; for slow insensitive emulsions, γ is about $3\cdot2$.

The characteristic curve is determined in an internationally adopted manner. The light source is a tungsten filament lamp operated

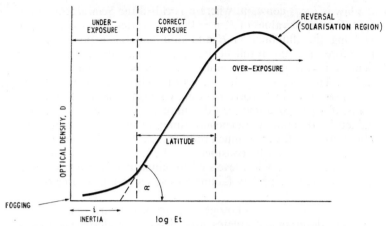

Fig. 5.23. Characteristic curve for a photographic emulsion (negative material)

at a colour temperature of 2,360°K and screened with a filter to give the light the quality of noon sunlight (colour temperature, 5,400°K). (The colour temperature of an incandescent source is the temperature at which a black-body radiator would have to operate in order to match visually the light from the source.) A set of graded exposures is produced by using various times t with constant illumination E, and the optical density D is determined photometrically.

The constants γ and i will be specific values for light specified in this way. However, both γ and i will vary considerably with wavelength λ. The value of γ for the emulsion will depend on the nature of the developer and on the time and temperature with a given developer. As development time increases, γ increases to a limited maximum value γ_{max}. The inertia i remains unchanged when bromide-free developers are used, but varies with different developers.

Light absorption takes place over the whole silver bromide grain. A grain must absorb at least 100 photons to become developable. Photographic materials differ in graininess: this increases with fast emulsions, which are very sensitive to light. The resolving power of an emulsion is measured by the number of lines per millimetre which can be distinguished in the processed negative. Values range from 40 lines to 50 lines per millimetre for fast emulsions, and reach several hundred lines per millimetre for slow emulsions.

The effect of Et, the exposure, is a constant for some photochemical reactions; i.e. if E is multiplied by n and if t is divided by n, the exposure Et is the same. This is known as *Bunsen and Roscoes's reciprocity law*, enunciated in 1862. For photographic emulsions, the law is Et^p = constant, where p is called the *Schwarzchild exponent*. For small values of E, $p = 0.8$, but varies with the emulsion. Halving the illumination E and doubling the exposure time t, therefore, does not result in the same optical density of the silver deposit in the processed emulsion. This is known as *reciprocity failure*. The exponent p diminishes the effect of time in exposure; with low values of E, correspondingly longer times t are necessary. Thus, if a photographic record cannot be obtained in 2 h, little is gained by doubling the exposure time; an increase by a factor of about 10 is needed. For much ordinary photography, however, the reciprocity law can be considered to be true; it is only with very high levels and very low levels of illumination of the photographic emulsion that reciprocity failure presents a serious source of difficulty.

Other problems in photographic recording are: shrinkage of film on development (plates are therefore preferred); turbidity whereby an emulsion on development displays a variation in optical transmission over non-exposed portions (this appears as chemical fogging); agitation of the developer is important in processing to avoid local variations across the emulsion in developer concentration.

This brief account of the photographic process clearly stresses the need for very accurate control in the use of photographic plates in spectrophotometry. Even with the best procedure, it is not easy to ensure accuracy to better than $\pm 5\%$. The factors which demand careful regulation are:

1. Selection of photographic plates of appropriate speed, γ and spectral sensitivity. In any comparison between recorded spectra, it is preferable to record the spectra concerned alongside one another on the same plate because, in general, there will be too great a variation of characteristics between one plate and another, even amongst those from the same box of plates.
2. The exposure must be arranged to ensure as far as practicable that the linear portion only of the characteristic curve for the emulsion is utilised.
3. The development must be carefully standardised as regards choice of developer, temperature at which development is undertaken and time of development. Agitation should be practised in a regulated manner.
4. The subsequent washing, fixing and final washing procedures must be regulated, but the demands on control are not so severe as in development.

With such careful attention to photographic procedures, it is clearly possible to determine the absorption spectrum of a material or to compare the emission spectra from various luminous sources. The photographic method in spectrophotometry is chiefly of value in the visible region of the spectrum and the near ultra-violet.

5.31 The Hilger–Nutting Spectrophotometer

The Hilger–Nutting spectrophotometer (Fig. 5.24) is used chiefly to measure the absorption of visible light of various wavelengths in a liquid. It employs polarisation methods to compare the intensities of two beams of light. It is used in conjunction with a spectrometer, the combination forming a spectrophotometer.

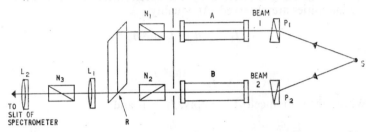

Fig. 5.24. Optical system of a Hilger–Nutting photometer (beams reaching R from A and B are polarised in planes at right angles to one another by the two Nicol prisms N_1 and N_2)

Light from the source S is deviated into two parallel beams 1 and 2 by the achromatic prisms P_1 and P_2. Beam 1 traverses absorption cell A, whereas beam 2 traverses an identical cell B. A and B are usually glass cylinders terminated by plane-parallel end windows and can be filled with the fluid to be examined. Often cell A is empty (contains air) and cell B is filled with the liquid of which an absorption study is required.

Beam 1 traverses Nicol prism N_1, whilst beam 2 traverses Nicol prism N_2; these Nicols are set so that light in beam 1 emerging from N_1 is polarised in a plane perpendicular to that of beam 2 emerging from N_2. Subsequently in the optical paths, the rhomboidal prism R brings the beams 1 and 2 close together but so that they can still be seen separately. These adjacent beams are collimated by lens L_1 before they traverse the analysing Nicol prism N_3, which is mounted within a divided circle so that its rotation in degrees can be determined. The lens L_2 focuses the exit edge of the rhomboidal prism R on the entrance slit of the spectrometer (usually a constant-deviation instrument). This edge forms the dividing line between the two adjacent beams as seen in the eyepiece of the spectrometer telescope.

The intensities of the two beams 1 and 2 are equal before they enter cells A or B. Let this intensity be I_0. Within cell A, the intensity of beam 1 is reduced to I_1; within cell B, the intensity of beam 2 is reduced to I_2. Suppose θ is the angle through which the analysing Nicol prism N_3 is rotated from the direction of the linearly polarised light emerging from Nicol prism N_1 in beam 1. The intensity of beam 1 after emerging from N_3 is therefore decreased to $I_1 \cos^2 \theta$ (absorption of light in the Nicol prisms and the rhomb R being neglected). The intensity of beam 2 after emerging from N_3 will be increased from zero (when $\theta = 0$, N_3 is crossed with respect to N_2) to $I_2 \cos^2 (90° - \theta) = I_2 \sin^2 \theta$. The Nicol N_3 is rotated until these intensities are equal. This observation of equality is made at a given wavelength selected by the spectrometer through which the intensities are observed. At equality,

$$I_1 \cos^2 \theta = I_2 \sin^2 \theta$$

or

$$\frac{I_1}{I_2} = \tan^2 \theta$$

Where absorption cell A is empty, $I_1 = I_0$ and

$$I_2 = \frac{I_0}{\tan^2 \theta}$$

The divided circle attached to the analysing Nicol prism N_3 is usually marked both in degrees and also in optical densities D, where

$$D = \log_{10} \frac{I_0}{I_2}$$

A curve can be plotted of the transmittance I_2/I_0 against wavelength (as set by the spectrometer), or of optical density D against wavelength. This will give the absorption spectrum of the liquid in cell B.

This instrument can be adapted to measure at various wavelengths the transmittance (or optical density) of a transparent solid (such as a light filter) by placing a plane-parallel slab of the solid in beam 2 in place of absorption cell B and omitting cell A. Also, if prisms P_1 and P_2 and cells A and B are removed, the intensities of two sources of light can be compared at various wavelengths through the spectrum.

5.32 Modern Spectrophotometers

The technology of the several kinds of advanced spectrophotometers and absorption spectrophotometers used in modern practice in the infra-red, visible and ultra-violet regions is beyond the scope of this book. For example, double-beam diffraction grating recording spectrophotometers with photoelectric detectors, amplifiers and pen recorder output giving the absorption spectrum directly make use of automatic drive of the grating setting in conjunction with a servomechanism to control the slit width.

A Féry prism of quartz which has a concave entrance-surface and a fully aluminised concave back-surface is used in the 'Unicam' prism absorptiometer (Fig. 5.25). This type of prism is self-focusing. It is mounted on an arm coupled to a drum directly calibrated in wavelengths. Rotation of the drum orients the prism to a position

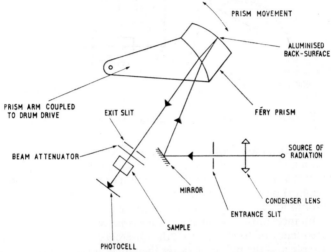

Fig. 5.25. Optical paths in a Unicam prism absorptiometer

at which the radiation traversing the exit slit is monochromatic of known wavelength. This monochromatic radiation passes through the sample or a standard. The sample is a liquid in a parallel-sided cell, often of 1 cm length, or it may be a plane-parallel slab of a solid. The standard is usually a pure solvent of known absorption characteristics. The light emerging from the sample is incident upon a photocell. The ratio of the outputs from the photocell (which must have a linear response) with and without the sample in position gives the transmission of the sample at the selected wavelength.

Spectrophotometry practice in the near infra-red is illustrated in outline by Fig. 5.26. Radiation from a Nernst filament is dispersed by a quartz prism (for wavelengths exceeding 35,000 Å, a prism of a material selected from those listed in Table 5.3 may be used) which can be rotated so that a small range of wavelengths passes through a slit of adjustable width. The beam of monochromatic light thus obtained is incident upon a beam-splitter (a thin pellicle of plastic material vacuum-coated with a semi-transparent aluminium layer may be used) so that one half of the radiation passes through a reference optical density to detector 1 and the other half via a mirror through an absorption cell to detector 2.

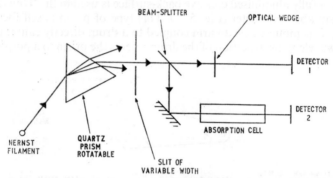

Fig. 5.26. Outline of arrangement for spectrophotometry in the near infra-red

These detectors are Golay air cells. The reference optical density may be a neutral optical wedge (a plate along which the optical density varies with distance in a known manner and independently of wavelength) or a rotating sector.

Automatic recording may be introduced by rotating the prism by a cam mechanism, while at the same time switching the detectors at a frequency of 10 Hz (10 c/s); the difference in intensity between the sample and the reference beam then gives a proportional 10 Hz alternating output e.m.f. The neutral optical wedge may be circular and rotated by a servomechanism so that there is no difference in output between the two detectors. The servomechanism also controls the position of a pen recorder or a print-out mechanism; thus, as the prism is rotated by the cam mechanism to produce a change in wavelength, the transmittance of the sample is recorded continuously on paper.

Indicative of the sophisticated techniques used in modern practice in the far infra-red region of the spectrum is the outline given in Section 5.36.

5.33 Microphotometers

A microphotometer or microdensitometer is used for such work as the measurement of the optical densities of the black lines on a photographic negative which has been exposed in a spectrograph. The variation of density over the plate is large over very short distances. In a microphotometer, there must therefore be produced a beam of light of very small cross-sectional area. This beam is passed through the photographic negative, and the reduction in its intensity due to the silver deposit in various locations in the negative is measured, usually by a photocell.

To provide the narrow beam of light, a microscope objective is used. Frequent practice adopted is to project via this objective an image of an illuminated slit on to the photographic negative. The light transmitted through the negative impinges on a phototransducer (often a photovoltaic cell or a phototransistor) placed close to the negative. The beam of light is usually vertical, with the negative supported horizontally in a mount; the phototransducer is immediately beneath the negative under the microscope objective above. With a linear photocell, the output reading with clear glass in the photographic plate is proportional to intensity I_0 and with the black silver deposit inserted this intensity is reduced to I, giving a corresponding photocell output. The optical density D of the area of the negative explored is then given by the value of $\log_{10} (I_0/I)$.

The slit-shaped area of the photographic negative explored may be as small as 0·001 cm in width. The negative is supported firmly in a mount which can be moved across the light beam by a micrometer screw drive such that the exact position of the area of the negative can be read on a calibrated scale. Motion of a spectrogram in one direction across the light beam is usual, but in some microphotometers a drive to impart motion in two perpendicular directions is provided.

A precision instrument needs stabilised power supplies so that the current through the light source (which illuminates the slit) and any p.d. used in the photocell circuitry are both independent of fluctuations in the mains supply voltage. In more expensive microphotometers, the phototransducer output and the monitoring of the position of the negative holder (which is made to traverse slowly through the beam of light by a motor drive) are displayed on a pen recorder; a plot of optical transmission or density against wavelength is thus obtained directly and automatically.

When the spectrograph used has adequate dispersion and chromatic resolving power, the exploration of the spectrogram by a microphotometer is able to record fine structure invisible to the eye. A microphotometer capable of recording or detecting very small differences in light transmission must be contained in a light-tight housing, and care must be taken that only the light transmitted through the photographic plate is incident upon the phototransducer.

5.34 Outline of Applications of Absorption Spectrophotometry

5.34.1 THE CONCENTRATION OF A SOLUTION

The concentration c of a solution may be found by determining at a suitable wavelength λ at which absorption is significant the optical density D. If, for the same solute and solvent and the same wavelength λ, the optical densities D_1 and D_2 of solutions of known concentrations c_1 and c_2 are found, the unknown concentration is given from

$$\frac{c-c_1}{c-c_2} = \frac{D-D_1}{D-D_2}$$

This technique may be extended to a solution containing a number of different solutes. For each of the different solutes a suitable wavelength is chosen at which the absorption of radiation is pronounced, and this leads to the determination of the various concentrations.

5.34.2 THE INVESTIGATION OF CHEMICAL STRUCTURE

One of the main fields of application of absorption spectrophotometry is the investigation of chemical structure. Absorption spectra resulting from electronic transitions are associated with photons of wavelengths in the visible and ultra-violet regions. At wavelengths above about 8,000 Å in the infra-red, the energies of the photons in the incident radiation are insufficient to produce changes in electron energy levels; however, energy transitions associated with molecular vibrations and rotations are excited, in some cases far into the infra-red.

If the specimen is gaseous, the atoms or molecules are relatively far apart except at high pressures. They may be considered isolated from one another in that the energy levels in one atom or molecule are scarcely affected by its neighbours. Fine details in the absorption spectra are therefore observable. For specimens in the condensed state (liquid, solid or in solution) the proximity effect of atoms or molecules on their neighbours becomes pronounced: energy levels are no longer discrete but overlap. The absorption spectrum detail is therefore no longer fine because lines become spread out into overlapping bands.

Ultra-violet absorption spectroscopy is used considerably in studies of electronic transitions in organic chemistry. In the visible region, spectrophotometry is applied to dye-stuffs, light filters and studies of gaseous discharges. A famous application in astronomy is the investigation of the Sun's chromosphere. Over 500 absorption lines—the Fraunhofer lines—have been identified in the continuous solar spectrum, and these have led to a detailed knowledge of the constituents in the Sun's chromosphere.

Gases and liquids absorb radiation of certain wavelengths characteristic of the substance, especially in the infra-red region. This allows rapid chemical analysis in the identification of substances and, as noted in Section 5.34.1, the quantitative estimation

Table 5.7.

SMALLEST CONCENTRATION OF GASES WHICH CAN BE MEASURED WITH NOT MORE THAN 2% ERROR

Gas	CO	CO_2	CH_4	C_2H_2	C_2H_4	C_2H_6	Vapours of solvents
Concentration (vol. %)	0·05	0·005	0·1	0·1	0·05	0·1	0·1

of the amounts of these substances. Infra-red gas analysers make use of this principle. Table 5.7 gives the smallest concentration of certain gases which can be measured with not more than 2% error.

Infra-red radiation of a wavelength selected as being suitable for a particular gas is divided so that a portion passes through an absorption cell filled with dry air while the other portion is passed through a similar absorption cell into which the gas sample is passed. Radiation detectors at the exit of each cell may be so connected that their combined output is fed to a meter calibrated directly in gas concentration. Variations in the carbon dioxide content of the atmosphere (normally about 0·03%) due, for example, to sunlight, to bacterial action in soils or to plant life, may be satisfactorily investigated. Combustion processes in petrol and diesel motors can be recorded.

Infra-red absorption methods are also used to investigate organic compounds of biochemical and biological interest. As a qualitative example, plant pigments in minute quantities can be identified. As a quantitative example, the strength of a penicillin solution may be found by absorption.

The interpretation of data on chemical constitution is not always easy, as several groups may have close absorption frequencies extending over a range which makes their resolution difficult. The type of solvent can sometimes affect the solute absorption wavelengths and, for example, the absorption wavelengths

Table 5.8.
SOME CHARACTERISTIC ABSORPTION WAVELENGTHS

Chemical	Free OH	N—H	Triple bond —C≡C—	C=N	Water	O—H	Acetyl group	Substitute in an aromatic compound		
								para	ortho	meta
Absorption wavelength (μm)	2·75	3·0	4·6	6·2	6·2	9·5	16·1	12·1	13·4	12·8

due to a double bond may not be the same for an aldehyde as for a ketone. Halogens, sulphur, silicon and phosphorus in organic compounds can be identified, and a whole range of compounds (such as pyridine, naphthalene, anthracene and olefins) have characteristic absorption wavelengths. Some characteristic absorption wavelengths are given in Table 5.8.

5.34.3 FLASH PHOTOLYSIS

The progress of chemical reactions with time may be followed by absorption spectrophotometry. A useful technique is that of flash photolysis: an intense flash of activating radiation impinges on the chemical; the photochemical products resulting are short-lived; they are identified, and their decay is studied by recording absorption spectra.

5.35 Astronomical Applications of Spectroscopy

Spectral observations have been of immense value to astronomers. Much of the information on the nature of the Universe is a consequence of the precision with which astrophysicists have been able to measure the wavelengths of spectral lines.

Information on stellar and solar velocities is obtained from measurements of the Doppler effect. The velocity of light in free space c is constant. A radiating body which is receding from the Earth at a velocity v will radiate wavelengths appropriate to its composition, but these wavelengths will be longer than those radiated from the same elements on Earth. The apparent wavelength λ is given by

$$\lambda = \lambda_0 \left(1 \pm \frac{v}{c}\right)$$

where λ_0 is the wavelength measured when $v = 0$. Observations of this 'red shift' show that the more distant nebulae are moving away from the Earth faster than near nebulae. This leads to the conclusion that the Universe is expanding more rapidly at its extremities. Red shifts of 200 Å have been observed.

By observing periodic variations in the wavelength of light from double stars, their velocity and period of rotation can be measured. Similarly, the rings of Saturn are shown to be non-rigid as spectroscopy evinces that the inner portions move faster than the outer ones.

The temperature of stars may also be estimated from the broadening of spectral lines due to Doppler effect. Atoms radiating at high temperatures exhibit broader spectral lines than those at low temperature, because they have greater translational velocities. An atom moving at a speed of 3 km s^{-1} will appear to have a wavelength differing by one part in 100,000 from the radiation from a stationary atom. This is equivalent to 0·059 Å for the sodium 5,896 Å spectral line. Thus r.m.s. speeds, which are proportional to temperature, may be calculated for elements in the star from the width of their spectral lines and the temperature may be compared with that estimated from the radiation laws.

Measurements of the wavelengths in the emission spectra of stars permit their constituent elements to be determined. From the absorption spectra, the composition of the atmospheres of stellar bodies is found.

The splitting of spectral lines due to the Zeeman effect is utilised to investigate distant magnetic fields in space. The Stark effect can be used to detect strong electric fields near radiating atoms: a potential gradient of the order of 10^5 V cm^{-1} is necessary before a measurable change in wavelength occurs.

A slight shift in the position of spectral lines gives information on high stellar densities. Otherwise, density can only be estimated from observations on the motion of double stars.

5.36 Advances in Spectroscopy in the Far Infra-red

It is not possible to be specific about the limits of the far infra-red region, but generally it is considered to lie between wavelengths of 40 μm and 2,000 μm. Spectroscopists prefer to specify wave numbers ($\bar{\nu} = 1/\lambda$) rather than wavelengths, so in wave numbers the region is between 250 cm^{-1} and 5 cm^{-1}. Though studies in this spectral region began more than 50 years ago, progress was slow, primarily because of the lack of an intense broad-band source for absorption spectroscopy. In this region, the radiation suffers massive absorption in water vapour. Spectrometers used must therefore be evacuated.

Suitable detectors for far infra-red radiation were lacking until the Golay cell (Section 5.15) appeared in the 1950s; from then onwards, progress has been rapid. Impetus to research comes from the fact that simple solids and molecular compounds exhibit important spectra in this region. Current research arising from such spectral studies includes investigations of: the lattice vibrational properties of crystals as functions of temperature and pressure; the optical and dielectric properties of solids; the rotational spectra of molecules; the intermolecular motions of large molecules; exchange interactions between magnetic ions; ferroelectric transitions; semiconductors and superconductors; and the vibrational spectra of liquids.

The region has been approached in two ways: from the shorter wavelength end by the extension of infra-red techniques and from the longer wavelength end by the extension of microwave radio methods. The former has the advantage over conventional spectroscopy that the precision demanded of the optical components is not so great as in the visible region, but the disadvantage that suitable transparent materials are few in number and have poor dispersion properties. The use of radio methods, necessitating very small resonant cavities for submillimetre wavelengths, is more demanding on precision than work at normal millimetre and centimetre wavelengths. The region in which the optical and microwave 'radio' methods merge employs techniques known as 'quasi-optical'. Submillimetre methods utilising tuned cavities, waveguides and electron beam sources are not to be described in this book.

Apart from the submillimetre microwave methods, the two techniques practised in far infra-red spectroscopy are the use of diffraction gratings in the form of echelles and echelettes (Section 5.24), and Fourier transform spectroscopy utilising interferometers.

5.37 Grating Spectroscopy in the Far Infra-red

The broad-band source of radiation used is a hot body with blackbody type spectral distribution. The most effective is the quartz-enveloped mercury arc lamp. At wave numbers above 100 cm^{-1} the radiation is emitted by the hot quartz envelope; at wave numbers below 100 cm^{-1}, the radiation is predominantly from the mercury discharge.

A typical monochromator is that due to Czerny and Turner (Fig. 5.27), and Littrow models are also used. The echelle diffraction grating employed is usually $10 \text{ cm} \times 10 \text{ cm}$, blazed at an angle of $20°$ and with 15–120 rulings per centimetre. The spherical mirrors for the 'collimator' and 'telescope' are coated with gold, silver or aluminium and have a reflectivity of 98.5% in the far infra-red region. Window materials (and in further developments, lenses, light pipes and light cones) transparent to the radiation are frequently of polyethylene, but quartz, diamond, alkali halides and other ionic crystals (Section 5.18) are used over select regions with silicon and germanium at low wave numbers.

The dominant problem is to prevent the detector from responding to unwanted radiation and ensure that it receives only radiation from the source. Such unwanted radiation arises from the components and walls of the spectrometer; furthermore, high-energy radiation from higher orders appearing in the first order (the one normally used) of the diffraction pattern is a particular source of difficulty.

To avoid this unwanted radiation, two procedures are adopted. The first is to chop mechanically the radiation from the source (usually done at 13 Hz) and tune the detector amplifier to respond only to signals at this frequency. This avoids output signals due to radiation other than from the source itself. The second is to employ filters to reduce the unwanted radiation from higher orders,

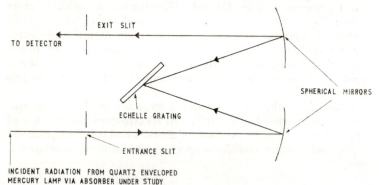

Fig. 5.27. Outline of a Czerny–Turner monochromator for the far infra-red

which may reach the first order. Such filters are: absorption or transmission types which make use respectively of the strong absorption bands in ionic crystals or the scattering and diffraction properties of polyethylene transmission gratings for wavelengths less than the grating space; gratings and metal meshes for which radiation of wavelength greater than the mesh spacing is specularly reflected; Reststrahlen types which utilise the strong reflection band of ionic crystals; and Fabry–Perot types made of parallel metal meshes which can be made to isolate a narrow spectral region.

The Golay cell is widely used. Other detectors employed include photoconductive indium–antimony or germanium at 4·2°K, point-contact crystal rectifiers, bolometers, superconducting Josephson tunnel diodes, and pyroelectric thermal devices.

5.38 Fourier Spectroscopy

This sophisticated and expensive technique for obtaining the power spectrum of radiation was first used in 1911 by Rubens and has been reborn following the work of Fellgett in 1951. It is tending to overhaul grating spectroscopy because of the following advantages:

1. The resolution of the grating spectrometer in the far infra-red is limited by slit width; this does not apply to Fourier spectroscopy, so much higher resolution is achievable.
2. At any one time, the whole spectral range is incident on the detector in Fourier spectroscopy whereas in grating methods only a narrow width of the spectrum is incident. Not only does this mean a greatly improved signal-to-noise ratio, but it also enables recording to be much more rapid.
3. The filtering of unwanted radiation is not so stringent as in grating spectroscopy.

Disadvantages are that the spectrum is not measured directly, that the procedure is not very suitable for very narrow range investigations, and that the technique is expensive.

A two-beam interferometer is used, usually with a beam-splitter made from a melinex membrane. The flux I_x of infra-red radiation reaching the central fringe is a function of the path difference x between the two beams. (This compares with the use of the Michelson interferometer to determine the fine structure and breadth of spectral lines by the 'visibility' technique.) This function contains a constant term and an oscillatory term F_x. The flux I_x is called the *interferogram*. This interferogram is characteristic of the incident spectrum of radiation and can be analysed to yield the spectral distribution.

This procedure is known as the 'multiplex' method, implying the simultaneous detection of a broad spectral region of undispersed radiation with a single detector. The intensity of each spectral component of width $\delta\bar{\nu}$ cm^{-1} (in wave numbers) in a broad spectrum is coded by the specific orthogonal code of sine and cosine simple harmonic functions. The intensity of each spectral component is therefore modulated sinusoidally at a frequency proportional to its wave number $\bar{\nu}$ cm^{-1}. The width of the component depends on the duration of the modulation.

Amplitude division, wavefront division and polarising interferometers have all been used for multiplexing. From such instruments, the observed interferogram is a spatial frequency representation of the spectral function. Consequently, analogue or digital computer Fourier transformation must be undertaken to obtain the power function.

If a two-beam interferometer is illuminated with monochromatic radiation of intensity I_0 and frequency ν,

$$I_x = I_0(1 + \cos 2\pi\nu x)$$

For a spectral input represented by $I(\nu)$

$$I_x = \int_0^\infty I(\nu)(1 + \cos 2\pi\nu x)\,d\nu = \tfrac{1}{2}I(0) + \int_0^\infty I(\nu)\cos 2\pi\nu x\,d\nu$$

where $I(0)$ is the intensity at zero path difference. Application of the Fourier integral theorem for the even function I_x gives the spectrum

$$I(v) = 4 \int\limits_0^\infty \left[I_x - \tfrac{1}{2} I(0) \right] \cos 2\pi v x \, \mathrm{d}x$$

in terms of the measured I_x. This is the fundamental relation of Fourier spectroscopy. The interferogram is measured as a function of path difference, and the spectrum is computed by analogue or digital means.

In the *periodic method*, the path difference is varied rapidly with a saw-tooth motion of period $2T_0$. Each resolution width of the spectrum appears as an audiofrequency harmonic of fundamental frequency $1/T_0$. The spectrum is recovered by passing the signal from the far infra-red detector through an amplifier of bandwidth less than $1/T_0$, and which is tuned to each harmonic in turn. Such spectrometers lack the advantage of obtaining the whole spectral range of interest at one time (called the *multiplex advantage*), because they sample only one harmonic in the interferogram at a time.

The alternative *aperiodic method* is preferred. The interferogram is recorded once, and the spectrum computed. The interferogram is sampled at small uniform intervals of path difference. The Fourier integral is approximated by a sum in the computer.

Exercise 5

1. Write an account of the chief characteristics of photographic emulsions in relation to their use in recording radiation.

2. Write an essay on the various techniques used in spectroscopy to record infra-red radiation.

3. Describe, with a diagram, a thermal Golay cell for measurements of infra-red radiation and compare its performance with that of the bolometer and of the thermopile.

4. Describe briefly the factors in spectroscopic sources which give rise to line broadening and show how each factor may be minimised.
   Describe a source and a dispersive instrument capable of resolving the hyperfine structure of the sodium D lines. (Poly.)

5. Explain how a plane diffraction grating is used in spectroscopy and derive the relation which gives the angular positions of the principal maxima when monochromatic light is incident obliquely.
   A wide reflection grating having 3000 lines cm^{-1} is used in a monochromator, the angle between the incident beam and the diffracted beam being fixed at 10°. The grating which is adjusted to be normal to the incident beam is illuminated with white light and a lens of focal length 50 cm is used

to focus the diffracted beam on the exit slit which is 0·1 cm wide. Determine the mean wavelength and range of wavelengths of the visible light emerging from the slit.   (L.G.)

6. Describe one form of prism spectrograph suitable for use in the UV down to 2300 Å. Explain the choice and use of the prism and any lens included. Explain the use of such an instrument with photographic plates either to identify elements present in a metal alloy or to determine the proportion of a particular element present in each of a series of closely similar alloys.
                                                                         (L.Anc.)

7. Write a short essay on the precise measurement of the wavelength of a standard line in the spectrum.   (L.G.)

8. Explain the formation of a spectrum by means of a plane diffraction grating used either for transmission or for reflection. Describe the arrangement of a grating spectrometer for the examination of absorption spectra in the infra-red region explaining the function of each part. Mention (a) a suitable source and (b) a suitable detector for the radiation.   (L.Anc.)

9. Write an essay on spectroscopic techniques used in *either* (a) the ultra-violet *or* (b) the infra-red regions of the spectrum.   (L.P.)

10. Give a general account of the methods used for obtaining emission spectra, including the investigation of fine structure. What is the significance of the breadth of the lines?   (L.Anc.)

11. Parallel light is incident on a parallel-sided block of thickness t and refractive index μ. If the angle of refraction in the medium is r show that the phase difference between the directly transmitted ray and the ray reflected once at each surface is $4\pi\mu t \cos r/\lambda$ where λ is the wavelength *in vacuo*.
   Describe briefly a method of calibrating a spectroscope by the use of a thin air film between parallel plates. How may fringes of good visibility be obtained? For a film of thickness 0·01 mm, a bright fringe coincides with light of wavelength 6250 Å. At what shorter wavelengths will the 1st and 10th fringes from 6250 Å occur?   (L.G.)

12. Give a brief account of the ways by which the spectroscopy of electromagnetic radiation has been extended to regions beyond the visible. Describe in detail the techniques involved in *one* region.   (L.P.)

13. Give an account of some form of infra-red spectrometer including a description of (a) the method of recording the spectrum, (b) the determination of wavelength. Discuss briefly one important application of investigations in the infra-red.   (L.G.)

14. Write an essay on the methods used in infra-red spectroscopy, and the information about molecules that can be obtained from infra-red absorption spectra.   (L.Anc.)

15. Explain how the Doppler effect influences the radiation received from terrestrial and astronomical sources.
   What steps can be taken to minimise its effect in terrestrial sources and to what useful information does its presence lead in astro-physics?   (L.P.)

16. How may an interferometer be used for accurate determination of the wavelengths of spectral lines from a source which has many lines in the visible region? Give a careful sketch of the apparatus including the approximate physical dimensions of all components of the system assuming that 10^{-2} Å resolution is required.

Calculate the approximate size of diffraction grating which would give the same resolution. (M.P.)

CHAPTER 6

More Advanced Treatment of Diffraction and Interference

6.1 The Diffraction of Electromagnetic Waves

If it is assumed that radiation is propagated in straight lines in a uniform isotropic medium, an obstacle placed between a source of radiation and a receiving screen will result in a shadow at this screen of shape and dimensions decided by simple geometrical considerations. Taking into account that the radiation has a finite wavelength, however, it is established that the radiation spreads into this geometrical shadow because of the phenomenon of diffraction. This is explained in the simplest instances by Huygens' principle (Section 7.6 of Volume 1). It is assumed that all points on the wavefront in an aperture (or around an obstacle) act as secondary sources from which the energy is radiated in the form of secondary wavelets without phase change to points on the side of the aperture (or obstacle) remote from the primary source. This gives rise to an intensity distribution which forms the spatial diffraction pattern for the particular aperture or obstacle and wavefront.

In a more general sense, an electromagnetic wave incident on a shield containing an aperture will give rise to effects both within the aperture and on the shield. The secondary sources within the aperture will radiate in a complex manner with differing amplitudes, states of polarisation and phases not only on the side of the aperture remote from the primary source but also on the primary source side as well. A complete treatment of diffraction to deduce the spatial intensity distribution of light requires that all these effects be taken into account. Fortunately, in practice, it is only necessary to determine effects very close to a shield or aperture.

If far-field paraxial effects with a symmetrical aperture are being considered, as often happens in practice, polarisation and shield effects can be neglected and adequate results obtained by the method of Kirchhoff (Section 6.15). This method takes into account the phase change on re-radiation (i.e. from the secondary sources) and the obliquity of a secondary source with respect to the point at which intensity is to be determined. If the former of these factors—the phase change—is also neglected and allowance is made in only a general and approximate manner for the latter factor—the obliquity—the comparatively simple Fresnel treatment is valid. This Fresnel procedure is nevertheless adequate for most optical diffraction in the visible region. The Fresnel method is therefore described first, and the more advanced procedures which take into account shield effects, phase and polarisation changes are left till later.

6.2 Fresnel's Treatment of a Plane Wavefront in a Circular Aperture

A uniform collimated beam of monochromatic radiation of wavelength λ is incident normally on a circular aperture in a shield. The wavefront within this aperture is therefore plane. Let O be the centre of the aperture, and P a point on the axis at a distance b beyond the aperture centre (Fig. 6.1). It is required to find an

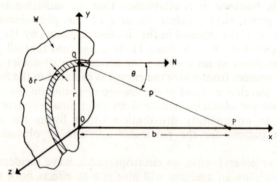

Fig. 6.1. Fresnel's treatment of a plane wavefront in a circular aperture

approximate value for the amplitude of the wave at P. This amplitude will arise from the interference of wavetrains from uniformly distributed secondary sources over the wavefront W in the plane yOz, where Ox is the direction of the incident light.

The wavefront may be conveniently divided into very narrow concentric annuli about the point O. For a particular annulus (shown shaded in Fig. 6.1), its contribution to the amplitude at P will depend on the area of the annulus and the amplitude at the wavefront W, and on the distance p from any point Q on this annulus to P, where intensity (proportional to the square of the amplitude) falls off in accordance with the inverse square law.

The phase of the wavetrain from this annulus may be conveniently measured relative to the phase of a wavetrain from a very small area at O. It will thus be $(2\pi/\lambda)(p-b)$.

The obliquity of any point Q in the wavefront W with respect to the point P is measured by the angle θ between the line QP and the normal NQ to the wavefront at Q. If this angle θ is not too large for a particular annulus, its effect may be neglected; furthermore, the inverse square law effect will be constant, as will be the amplitude over the wavefront.

Thus, in estimating the relative effect at P due to the annulus, a vector may be drawn having a length directly proportional to the area of the annulus and a phase angle of $(2\pi/\lambda)(p-b)$. For a continuous range of such annuli, the vectors representing the amplitude at point P due to the very thin annuli become part of the arc of a circle. The resultant effect is then represented by the chord which joins the ends of the arc.

As a matter of convenience, Fresnel divided the wavefront into 'half-period' zones. The distance p to the extremity of each succeeding half-period zone from the centre outwards increases by half a wavelength [Fig. 6.2(a)]. The effects of the very thin annuli at the extremities of a given zone thus differ in phase angle by π. The diagram representing the addition of the successive vectors for the very thin annuli comprising such a half-period zone is shown in Fig. 6.2(b).

The area of an annular zone with an inner radius r and outer radius $r+\delta r$ and where p increases to $p+\delta p$ (Fig. 6.3) is $2\pi r\,\delta r$. Now

$$r^2 = p^2 - b^2$$

Differentiating with respect to r, where b is constant,

$$2r = 2p\,\frac{\mathrm{d}p}{\mathrm{d}r}$$

Therefore

$$r\,\delta r = p\,\delta p$$

Hence the zone area $= 2\pi p\,\delta p$.

For the nth Fresnel half-period zone,

$$p = b + \frac{n\lambda}{2}$$

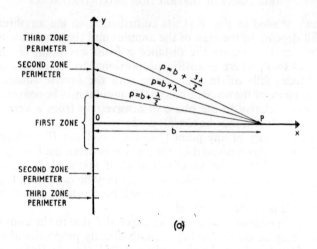

THIRD ZONE
PERIMETER

SECOND ZONE
PERIMETER

FIRST ZONE {

SECOND ZONE
PERIMETER

THIRD ZONE
PERIMETER

$p = b + \frac{3\lambda}{2}$

$p = b + \lambda$

$p = b + \frac{\lambda}{2}$

(a)

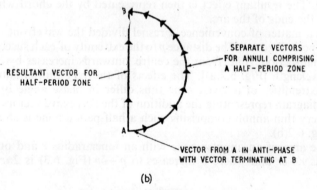

RESULTANT VECTOR FOR
HALF-PERIOD ZONE

SEPARATE VECTORS
FOR ANNULI COMPRISING
A HALF-PERIOD ZONE

VECTOR FROM A IN ANTI-PHASE
WITH VECTOR TERMINATING AT B

(b)

Fig. 6.2. Fresnel's half-period zones

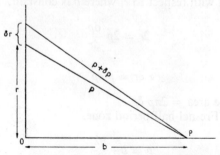

δr

r

$p + \delta p$

p

b

Fig. 6.3. The areas of Fresnel zones

and

$$\delta p = \frac{\lambda}{2}$$

The area δS of the nth zone is therefore given by

$$\delta S = 2\pi \left(b + \frac{n\lambda}{2}\right)\frac{\lambda}{2}$$

If the term in λ^2 is neglected,

$$\delta S = \pi b\lambda \tag{6.1}$$

which is a constant to the first order of small quantities.

As the effects of neighbouring half-period zones differ in phase by π and their areas are equal, it follows that the resultant effect of adjacent zones will be nearly equal and opposite. In fact, as n increases, the zone areas increase slightly, but they become progressively farther away from P; these two factors can be shown to balance out. Therefore, apart from the obliquity factor, each zone does give at P a contribution of the same amplitude. The effect of the obliquity factor is to cause the amplitudes due to successive zones to decrease gradually. If, therefore, the amplitudes of the vibration at P due to zones 1, 2, 3, ..., n are A_1, A_2, A_3, ..., A_n, the total amplitude A due to n zones at P will be given by

$$A = A_1 - A_2 + A_3 - A_4 + \ldots \pm A_n \tag{6.2}$$

The alternation of signs is due to the fact that the amplitude contributions from successive zones are in anti-phase.

If n is odd, this series is conveniently rearranged to become

$$A = \frac{A_1}{2} + \left(\frac{A_1}{2} - A_2 + \frac{A_3}{2}\right) + \left(\frac{A_3}{2} - A_4 + \frac{A_5}{2}\right) + \ldots + \frac{A_n}{2} \tag{6.3}$$

or

$$A = A_1 - \frac{A_2}{2} - \left(\frac{A_2}{2} - A_3 + \frac{A_4}{2}\right) - \left(\frac{A_4}{2} - A_5 + \frac{A_6}{2}\right) - \ldots$$

$$- \frac{A_{n-1}}{2} + A_n \tag{6.4}$$

As the terms A_1, A_2, A_3, ... decrease progressively, each term is greater than the mean value of the terms preceding and following it. The quantities in brackets in Equations 6.3 and 6.4 are therefore all negative. It follows that

$$\frac{A_1}{2} + \frac{A_n}{2} > A > A_1 - \frac{A_2}{2} - \frac{A_{n-1}}{2} + A_n$$

As A_1 and A_2 are very nearly equal, as also are A_{n-1} and A_n,

$$A = \frac{A_1}{2} + \frac{A_n}{2} \qquad (6.5)$$

The same argument and result applies if the value of n is taken to be even.

The conclusion is that the resultant amplitude A at P due to n zones is equal to half the sum of the amplitudes contributed by the first and the nth zone, where the nth zone will be the last one in a given aperture.

Two cases of particular interest arise:

1. The radius of the aperture is of significant size compared with the distance OP, so the number of half-period zones n is vary large. As the angle θ (Fig. 6.1), which decides the obliquity factor for this final zone, will be large, the contribution of the nth zone is very small compared with that of the first one (i.e. $A_n \ll A_1$). Equation 6.5 shows that the resultant amplitude at P will then be only slightly larger than half the amplitude due to the first zone alone.

2. The radius of the aperture is small compared with the distance OP so that the number of half-period zones n is not very large. Equation 6.5 will apply. If, however, the number of zones n is even, A_n will lie in the opposite direction to A_1, (i.e. A_n and A_1 are in anti-phase), so

$$A = A_1 - A_n$$

and as A_n is not much smaller than A_1, A will be small. On the other hand, if n is odd, A_n will be in the same direction as A_1 (A_n and A_1 are in phase) so

$$A = A_1 + A_n$$

and A will be large.

For an aperture of given radius, the variation of amplitude with distance $b = OP$ as the point P in question on the axis moves away from O is represented by Fig. 6.4. Maxima will occur on this graph wherever P is at such a distance that n is odd, and minima will occur whenever n is even. The same variation in amplitude will be obtained at a fixed point P on the axis as the radius of the aperture is gradually altered.

For an off-axial point P' (Fig. 6.5), the amplitude may be determined by considering the zones and parts of zones effective within the aperture.

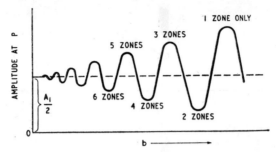

Fig. 6.4. Plot of the amplitude of the resultant vibration at P as the distance b is increased (A_1 is the amplitude due to the first zone only)

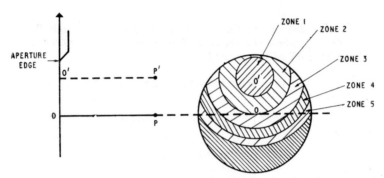

Fig. 6.5. How the amplitude of an off-axial point P is related to the zones and parts of zones within the aperture

6.3 A Spherical Wavefront in a Circular Aperture

The radiation incident upon the circular aperture is from a point source in a homogeneous medium, so the aperture contains a spherical wavefront. This spherical surface may be divided into Fresnel zones in the same way as for the plane wavefront (Section 6.2) and the amplitude at an axial point P beyond the aperture determined. However, the obliquity factor is more pronounced, as also is the variation in the distance p from a point Q in the wavefront as Q moves from the pole of the wavefront at O to the extremity E of the aperture (Fig. 6.6). The results obtained from Fresnel's theory are thus only strictly applicable to small apertures.

To find the area of a half-period zone in a spherical wavefront, let AB be such a zone (Fig. 6.7), where S is the point source of radiation at distance a from the wavefront and the point P is at distance b beyond the wavefront. Let x be the distance along the axis of symmetry SP to the extremity of the zone through A, and

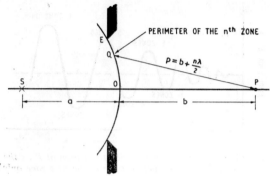

Fig. 6.6. A spherical wavefront in a circular aperture

$x+\delta x$ this distance to the extremity of the zone through B. Let $\angle BSO = \phi$, where O is the pole of the wavefront and $\angle BSA = \delta\phi$ The area δS of the zone AB is given by

$$\delta S = a\,\delta\phi\,2\pi a \sin\phi = 2\pi a^2 \sin\phi\,\delta\phi$$

Also,

$$BP^2 = p^2 = a^2 + (a+b)^2 - 2a(a+b)\cos\phi$$

Therefore

$$p\,\delta p = a(a+b)\sin\phi\,\delta\phi$$

Thus

$$\delta S = \frac{2\pi a p\,\delta p}{a+b}$$

If AB is the nth Fresnel zone from the centre, $p = b+(n\lambda/2)$ and $\delta p = \lambda/2$. Therefore

$$\delta S = \frac{2\pi a}{a+b}\left(b+\frac{n\lambda}{2}\right)\frac{\lambda}{2}$$

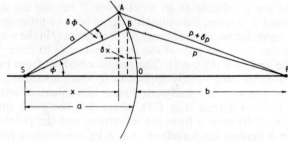

Fig. 6.7. Area of a half-period zone in a spherical wavefront

If terms in λ^2 are neglected, then

$$\delta S = \frac{\pi ab\lambda}{a+b} \qquad (6.6)$$

This reduces to the expression for the area of a zone in a plane wavefront (Equation 6.1) when $a \to \infty$ because, as $a \to \infty$,

$$\frac{\pi b\lambda}{1+(b/a)} \to \pi b\lambda$$

This would be expected, as a spherical wavefront becomes a plane one when its radius is infinitely long.

The radius r_n of the nth Fresnel zone is given by

$$r_n^2 = p^2 - b^2$$

where $p = b + (n\lambda/2)$. Therefore

$$r_n = \sqrt{\left[\left(b+\frac{n\lambda}{2}\right)^2 - b^2\right]} = \sqrt{\left(bn\lambda + \frac{n^2\lambda^2}{4}\right)}$$

If n is not too large, the term involving λ^2 may be neglected. As b and λ are constants

$$r_n \propto \sqrt{n} \qquad (6.7)$$

For a particular position of the axial point P beyond the wavefront, it is seen that the radii of the successive Fresnel zones are proportional to $\sqrt{n}$.

6.4 The Zone Plate

As the effects of adjacent Fresnel zones at an axial point P are in anti-phase, the resultant amplitude at P is due to the effect of half the first and half the last zones only. If, however, alternate zones are rendered ineffective, the amplitude at P will result from half the total number of zones and will consequently be greatly increased.

The zone plate is a transparent plane sheet of glass at which alternate Fresnel zones are made opaque. A simple method of making such a zone plate is first to draw in black ink on a white card a set of concentric rings having radii proportional to the square roots of the natural numbers 1, 2, 3, . . . (Equation 6.7). Every other zone between rings is made black. This card is photographed. The glass plate negative contains about 30 transparent zones which

Fig. 6.8. A zone plate (about six times usual size)

alternate with black opaque ones in a diameter of about 1 cm (Fig. 6.8).

This zone plate has a focusing action rather like that of a converging lens. Thus suppose a zone plate Z is set up normal to an axis between a point source S and a point P, where $SZ = a$ and $ZP = b$ (Fig. 6.9). Suppose the radius of the first transparent circular region of the zone plate is r. Let point P be at such a position that there is an odd number of zones $(2k+1)$ effective at P

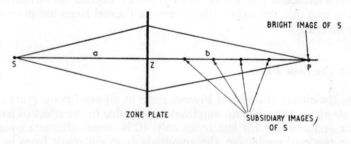

Fig. 6.9. Action of a zone plate

from this first transparent region, where k is an integer. This odd number will give a maximum amplitude at P (Section 6.2). As the transparent region has an area of πr^2 and each Fresnel zone within it has an area $\pi ab\lambda/(a+b)$ (Equation 6.5), it follows that

$$\frac{\pi r^2}{\pi ab\lambda/(a+b)} = 2k+1$$

Therefore

$$\frac{1}{a} + \frac{1}{b} = \frac{(2k+1)\lambda}{r^2} = \frac{1}{r^2/(2k+1)\lambda} \qquad (6.8)$$

This equation is similar to that relating the real object and image distances x and x' for a converging thin lens of focal length f, i.e.

$$\frac{1}{x} + \frac{1}{x'} = \frac{1}{f} \qquad (6.9)$$

By analogy, a is the object distance and b the image distance. As all the alternate transparent regions in the zone plate act like the first one and all give amplitudes at P in phase, there will be a bright image at P. The focal length of the zone plate is seen by comparison of Equation 6.8 and Equation 6.9 to be given by

$$f = \frac{r^2}{(2k+1)\lambda}$$

There will therefore be a set of focal lengths corresponding to various values of the integer k and for a given wavelength λ. Correspondingly, for a given object distance a, there will be a set of image distances b.

If the zone plate were not present, the amplitude at point P due to the unimpeded wavefront would be $A_1/2$—half that due to the first Fresnel zone alone. With the Fresnel zone plate present, suppose P is at such a position that a small odd number of Fresnel zones exist in the first transparent region, i.e. $2k+1$ is small. From Section 6.2, it is seen that the amplitude at P due to this first region only is $A_1 + A_n = 2A_1$. But there are several such regions in the zone plate, all producing the same additive effects at P because the anti-phase regions are opaque. If this number of transparent zone plate regions is 10, the amplitude at P will be $20A_1$. The intensity at P is therefore 400 times that which would be obtained if the zone plate were absent.

The intensity at P will be greatest when the transparent regions of the zone plate each transmit three Fresnel zones. This will correspond to a primary focal length of the zone plate. There will be shorter focal lengths corresponding to five, seven, nine, ... Fresnel zones within each transparent region at which subsidiary maxima in intensity will occur. Between maxima, much smaller disturbances will exist corresponding to the situation where each transparent region of the plate contains an even number of Fresnel zones (Section 6.2).

An even more efficient zone plate has been made in which the non-active regions of the plate are replaced by transparent crystalline deposits which introduce a phase change of π. All the regions of the plate are now operative in phase. Ideally, such a plate will give four times the intensity due to that of the conventional zone plate.

6.5 The Cylindrical Wavefront; The Fresnel Integrals

The treatment of a cylindrical wavefront by Fresnel zone methods is more complicated than for plane and spherical wavefronts. This is because the Fresnel half-period zones are parallel strips not having circular symmetry about an axis as do the annular zones employed in the analysis for plane and spherical wavefronts.

A slit source S of monochromatic radiation of wavelength λ produces a cylindrical wavefront at a distance a in a rectangular aperture which can be divided into half-period zone strips as shown

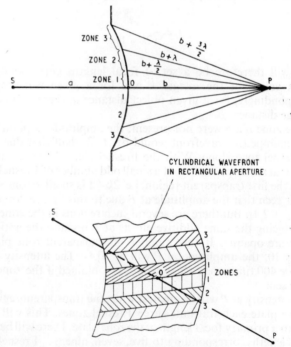

Fig. 6.10. Cylindrical wavefront in a rectangular aperture

in Fig. 6.10; the outer extremities of these zones are successively at distances $b+(\lambda/2)$, $b+\lambda$, $b+(3\lambda/2)$, ... from the axial point P, which is at a distance b on the axis SP beyond the pole of the wavefront at O.

Consider a strip AB on the cylindrical wavefront at a distance q along the arc from O, where the width of the strip is δq (Fig. 6.11). Let $\angle OSA = \phi$, $\angle ASB = \delta\phi$ and A be at a distance p from the axial point P beyond the wavefront about 0.

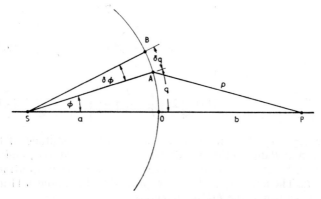

Fig. 6.11. A cylindrical wavefront from a slit source

The magnitude δU of the vibration at point P at time t due to the strip AB is given by

$$\delta U = k\,\delta q \sin 2\pi\left(\frac{t}{T} - \frac{p}{\lambda}\right) \tag{6.10}$$

where T is the period of the propagated wave motion and k is a constant of proportionality, and provided that the angle ϕ is small so that the vibration at the wavefront is proportional to $\sin(2\pi t/T)$. Putting $p - b = \Delta$, Equation 6.10 then becomes

$$\delta U = k\,\delta q \sin 2\pi\left(\frac{t}{T} - \frac{b}{\lambda} - \frac{\Delta}{\lambda}\right)$$

$$= k\left[\sin 2\pi\left(\frac{t}{T} - \frac{b}{\lambda}\right)\cos\frac{2\pi\Delta}{\lambda} - \cos 2\pi\left(\frac{t}{T} - \frac{\Delta}{\lambda}\right)\sin\frac{2\pi\Delta}{\lambda}\right]\delta q$$

If the magnitude of the vibration at P due to the wavefront between limits q_1 and q_2 (provided that ϕ is small) is U,

$$U = k\left[\sin 2\pi\left(\frac{t}{T} - \frac{b}{\lambda}\right)\int_{q_1}^{q_2}\cos\frac{2\pi\Delta}{\lambda}\,dq\right.$$

$$\left. -\cos 2\pi\left(\frac{t}{T} - \frac{b}{\lambda}\right)\int_{q_1}^{q_2}\sin\frac{2\pi\Delta}{\lambda}\,dq\right]$$

For convenience, put

$$I_1 = \int_{q_1}^{q_2} \cos \frac{2\pi \Delta}{\lambda} \, dq = A \cos \alpha \qquad (6.11)$$

and

$$I_2 = \int_{q_1}^{q_2} \sin \frac{2\pi \Delta}{\lambda} \, dq = A \sin \alpha \qquad (6.12)$$

Then

$$U = kA \sin \left[2\pi \left(\frac{t}{T} - \frac{b}{\lambda} \right) - \alpha \right] \qquad (6.13)$$

where $A^2 = I_1^2 + I_2^2$, $\tan \alpha = I_2/I_1$ and A is the amplitude of the vibration at P due to the cylindrical wavefront between q_1 and q_2. The intensity at P is proportional to A^2 and is hence proportional to $I_1^2 + I_2^2$. The terms I_1 and I_2 as expressed by Equations 6.11 and 6.12 are known as the *Fresnel integrals*.

From Fig. 6.11,

$$p^2 = a^2 + (a+b)^2 - 2a(a+b) \cos \phi$$

or, as ϕ is assumed to be small,

$$p^2 = a^2 + (a+b)^2 - 2a(a+b) \left(1 - \frac{q^2}{a^2} \right)$$

$$= b^2 + \frac{2(a+b)q^2}{a}$$

Therefore

$$p^2 - b^2 = \frac{2(a+b)q^2}{a} \qquad (6.14)$$

Putting $p + b = 2b$, on the basis that q is small, and $p - b = \Delta$, Equation 6.14 becomes

$$2b \, \Delta = \frac{2(a+b)}{a} q^2$$

Therefore

$$\Delta = \frac{a+b}{ab} q^2 \qquad (6.15)$$

It is convenient to put

$$\frac{2\pi \Delta}{\lambda} = \frac{\pi v^2}{2}$$

Therefore

$$\Delta = \frac{a+b}{ab}\, q^2 = \frac{\lambda v^2}{4} \qquad (6.16)$$

For given values of λ, a and b, it follows on differentiating with respect to q that

$$2q \propto 2v\,\frac{dv}{dq}$$

or

$$q\, dq \propto v\, dv$$

The integrals I_1 and I_2 (Equations 6.11 and 6.12) may therefore be written in the forms

$$I_1 = \int_{v_1}^{v_2} \cos\frac{\pi v^2}{2}\, dv \qquad (6.17)$$

$$I_2 = \int_{v_1}^{v_2} \sin\frac{\pi v^2}{2}\, dv \qquad (6.18)$$

and

$$A^2 \propto I_1^2 + I_2^2 \qquad (6.19)$$

where now the integrals in Equations 6.17 and 6.18 are standard forms and may be evaluated from mathematical tables for any range $0 \to v$, corresponding to a range $0 \to q$ along the wavefront as given by Equation 6.16.

The results obtained may be regarded as approximately true for larger rectangular apertures.

6.6 The Cornu Spiral

The effect of the Fresnel zones, subject to the limitations already mentioned, may be obtained from vector plots based on the Fresnel integrals. A curve is plotted on Cartesian axes defined by the parametric equations

$$x = I_1 \quad \text{and} \quad y = I_2 \qquad (6.20)$$

On this curve, an element of length δs at any point is related to δx and δy by the equation

$$(\delta s)^2 = (\delta x)^2 + (\delta y)^2$$

But $x = I_1$ is given by Equation 6.17, and $y = I_2$ is given by Equation 6.18. Therefore,

$$(\delta s)^2 = \left(\cos^2 \frac{\pi v^2}{2} + \sin^2 \frac{\pi v^2}{2}\right)(\delta v)^2 = (\delta v)^2$$

Therefore

$$s = v$$

The curve plotted is therefore from the equations

$$x = I_1 = \int_0^s \cos \frac{\pi s^2}{2}\, ds \qquad (6.21)$$

and

$$y = I_2 = \int_0^s \sin \frac{\pi s^2}{2}\, ds \qquad (6.22)$$

The intrinsic equation of this curve is readily obtainable because

$$\frac{dy}{dx} = \tan \frac{\pi s^2}{2} = \tan \psi$$

where ψ is the angle which the tangent to any element ds on the curve makes with the x-axis. Hence

$$\psi = \frac{\pi s^2}{2} \qquad (6.23)$$

is the intrinsic equation required. It represents a spiral, known as *Cornu's spiral* (Fig. 6.12), with asymptotic points L_1 and L_2 having (x,y) coordinates given by

$$x = y = \pm\int_0^\infty \cos \frac{\pi s^2}{2}\, ds = \pm\int_0^\infty \sin \frac{\pi s^2}{2}\, ds = \pm\frac{1}{2}$$

On Cornu's spiral, any element of length δs is a vector of length proportional to the contribution δA to the amplitude at the point P (Fig. 6.11) brought about by an elemental zone on the cylindrical wavefront. The whole spiral is the 'polygon' of infinitesimally short successive vectors due to all the elemental zones into which the wavefront may be divided. If, therefore, the wavefront is limited (for example, by a rectangular aperture) so that the zone vectors concerned are between points Q_1 and Q_2 on the Cornu spiral

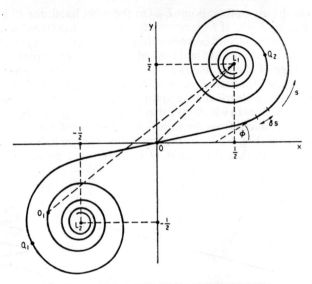

Fig. 6.12. Cornu's spiral

(Fig. 6.12), the addition of all these vectors gives a resultant decided by the straight line Q_1Q_2. The resultant amplitude of the radiation at point P beyond the limited wavefront is therefore proportional to Q_1Q_2 and the intensity at P is proportional to $(Q_1Q_2)^2$.

6.7 The Diffraction of a Cylindrical Wave by a Straight Edge

The cylindrical wavefront at W from the line source S is limited by a straight edge OC so that the portion of the wavefront to one side of O is shielded. It is required to determine the nature of the diffraction pattern in a plane through P perpendicular to the axis SOP and beyond the wavefront W (Fig. 6.13).

At the point P, only half the wavefront W is effective. The resultant amplitude of the vibration at P due to the radiation from S is therefore represented by the straight line OL_1 on the Cornu spiral (Fig. 6.12). For a point such as P_1, above P, the pole of the wavefront W is at O_1. Now one half of the wavefront is effective plus the part OO_1 of the other half. The appropriate vector representing the resultant amplitude at P_1 is now the straight line O_1L_1 on the Cornu spiral (Fig. 6.12).

If the point P_1 is further removed from P, i.e. the distance l is increased (Fig. 6.13), so the pole O_1 moves further along the unobstructed half of the wavefront W, and correspondingly point O_1 on the Cornu spiral (Fig. 6.12) moves further around the lower spiral towards the asymptotic point L_2. On the other hand, for P_1 below P in Fig. 6.13 (i.e. if l becomes negative), the wavefront pole O_1 moves to below O, and correspondingly the point O_1 on the Cornu spiral moves into the top half towards the asymptotic point L_1.

The edge of the 'geometrical' shadow of the straight edge is at P on a screen through P perpendicular to the axis SOP. There is not, however, a clear-cut edge to this shadow because of the diffraction. The manner in which the intensity of light varies in the shadow about P is deduced from the variation in position of point O_1 on the Cornu spiral (Fig. 6.12). As O_1 moves into the top half of this spiral, it is clear that the vector O_1L_1 diminishes progressively in

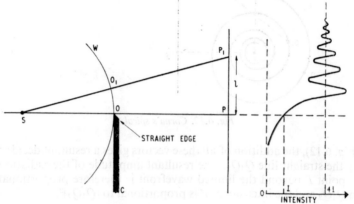

Fig. 6.13. The diffraction of a cylindrical wave by a straight edge

length; the intensity, proportional to $(O_1L_1)^2$, will likewise diminish progressively to become zero when O_1 reaches L_1. As O_1 moves into the bottom half of the Cornu spiral, it is seen that the intensity is always greater than that represented by $(OL_1)^2$, increases at first, and then fluctuates as O_1 moves around the turns of the lower spiral until L_2 is reached. Eventually the intensity is represented by $(L_1L_2)^2$, four times that at the geometrical edge of the shadow at P.

This variation in light intensity with position of the point P_1 is shown in Fig. 6.13. Note that within the diffraction bands near the point P but above it, the intensity maxima are greater than the intensity well outside the shadow.

6.8 The Diffraction of a Cylindrical Wave by a Rectangular Aperture

For a cylindrical wave diffracted by a rectangular aperture, a *fixed* length of the arc of the Cornu spiral, decided by the effective section of the wavefront W in the aperture (Fig. 6.14), moves around the

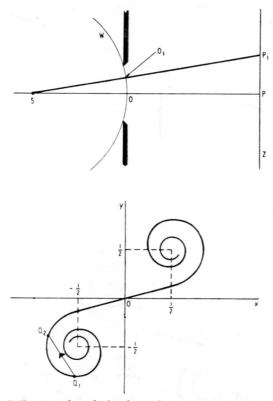

Fig. 6.14. Diffraction of a cylindrical wave by a rectangular aperture (arc Q_1Q_2 is constant, but vector Q_1Q_2 depends on the positions of points Q_1 and Q_2 on the Cornu spiral)

spiral as the pole O_1 on the wavefront moves with the point P_1 on the screen Z. The corresponding vector Q_1Q_2 will have a length depending on the position on the spiral of the arc Q_1Q_2. Whereas the arc length Q_1Q_2 is constant, the straight line Q_1Q_2 will vary in length. The magnitude of $(Q_1Q_2)^2$ will be proportional to the intensity at the point P_1 on the screen Z.

The diffraction pattern obtained is generally complex and will depend on the aperture width.

6.9 The Diffraction of a Cylindrical Wave by a Rectangular Obstacle

If the rectangular aperture (Section 6.8) is replaced by a rectangular shield obstructing the central part of the wavefront (Fig. 6.15), only the two outer regions of the wavefront are effective. These

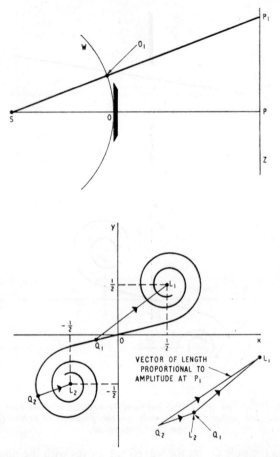

Fig. 6.15. Diffraction of a cylindrical wave by a rectangular obstacle

regions will be represented by vectors Q_1L_1 and Q_2L_2 on the Cornu spiral, where the positions of Q_1 and Q_2 depend on the position of point P_1 on the screen. The two separate vectors Q_1L_1 and Q_2L_2 are added to give a resultant vector of length proportional to the amplitude at P_1.

6.10 Fraunhofer or Far-field Diffraction

There is a range of phenomena in which the distances of the object and image from the aperture or apertures are large compared with the wavelength of the radiation and the aperture dimensions. This means that the wavefronts in the aperture are virtually plane, and parallel bundles of rays are involved. Such diffraction is termed Fraunhofer, in contrast to the type of diffraction already discussed, known as Fresnel.

Whilst this division between Fraunhofer and Fresnel diffraction is generally agreed upon, there is not an arbitrary dividing line between the two types of diffraction phenomena. In practice, the dividing line will be determined by the resolving power of the recording apparatus.

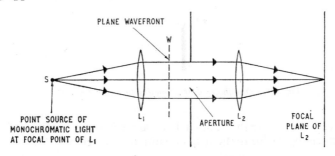

Fig. 6.16. Arrangement for producing far-field diffraction

For example, if the pattern in the second focal plane of lens L_2 (Fig. 6.16) is recorded by some means, the result might be termed an ideal Fraunhofer pattern because both object and image are in effect at infinity. A number of phenomena occur in this way, and no doubt arises. On the other hand, exactly the same pattern may be observed as in the position of the focal plane of lens L_2 if no lenses are present at all but if the object and image distances from the aperture are large enough for the recording method to be incapable of detecting a difference between Fraunhofer and Fresnel diffraction. It is thus simpler to refer to all diffraction effects involving parallel diffracted rays as Fraunhofer or far-field effects, and any other as Fresnel. This distinction is used in this text.

6.11 Fraunhofer Diffraction Due to a Single Narrow Slit

The analysis of Fraunhofer diffraction due to a single narrow slit has been given in Section 11.2 of Volume 1 but is repeated here in modified form.

The slit of width a is uniformly illuminated by normally incident collimated light which is monochromatic of wavelength λ. The slit is considered to be divided into equal elements parallel to the length of the slit and each of width dx (Fig. 6.17). If R_0 is the amplitude of the wave in the plane of the slit, then the amplitude dR_θ in the

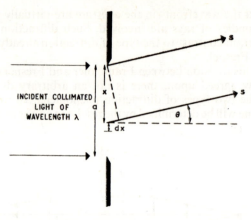

INCIDENT COLLIMATED
LIGHT OF
WAVELENGTH λ

Fig. 6.17. Fraunhofer diffraction due to a single narow slit

direction s (where the vector s is at angle θ to the direction of the
incident light) due to the strip of width dx is given by

$$dR_\theta = R_0 \exp (jkx \sin \theta)\, dx$$

where $k = 2\pi/\lambda$. For the whole slit of width a, therefore,

$$R_\theta = R_0 \int_0^a \exp (jkx \sin \theta)\, dx = \frac{R_0}{jk \sin \theta} [\exp (jka \sin \theta) - 1]$$

The intensity I_θ is given by

$$I_\theta \propto R_\theta \bar{R}_\theta$$

where $\bar{R}_\theta$ is the complex conjugate of R_θ. Therefore

$$I_\theta \propto \frac{R_0^2[\exp (jka \sin \theta) - 1] [\exp (-jka \sin \theta) - 1]}{-k^2 \sin^2 \theta}$$

or

$$I_\theta \propto \frac{R_0^2 \sin^2 [(ka \sin \theta)/2]}{-k^2 \sin^2 \theta}$$

As a is a constant,

$$I_\theta \propto \frac{R_0^2 \sin^2 [(ka \sin \theta)/2]}{[(ka \sin \theta)/2]^2}$$

But $I_0 \propto R_0^2$. Therefore, substituting $k = 2\pi/\lambda$,

$$\frac{I_\theta}{I_0} = \frac{\sin^2 [(\pi a \sin \theta)/\lambda]}{[(\pi a \sin \theta)/\lambda]^2} = \frac{\sin^2 \alpha}{\alpha^2} \qquad (6.24)$$

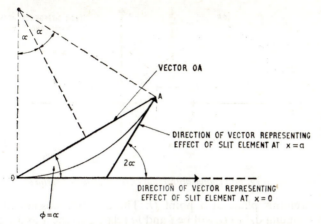

VECTOR OA

A

DIRECTION OF VECTOR REPRESENTING
EFFECT OF SLIT ELEMENT AT x = a

2α

DIRECTION OF VECTOR REPRESENTING
EFFECT OF SLIT ELEMENT AT x = 0

$\phi = \alpha$

Fig. 6.18. Vector diagram showing summation of effects due to elements into which a single slit is divided (see also Fig. 11.2 of Volume 1); the vector OA represents R, the resultant of an infinite number of vectors along the arc OA)

where $\alpha = (\pi a \sin \theta)/\lambda$. Also

$$\frac{R_\theta}{R_0} = \frac{\sin \alpha}{\alpha}$$

The complex amplitude will involve the phase angle ϕ, as shown by the vector diagram of Fig. 6.18 (see also Fig. 11.2 of Volume 1); as $\phi = \alpha$, the complex amplitude is given by $R_0[(\sin \alpha)/\alpha] \exp j\alpha$.

6.12 Fraunhofer Diffraction Due to a Rectangular Aperture

If the width of the slit is comparable with its length, two-dimensional Fraunhofer diffraction by a rectangular aperture is concerned. Suppose such an aperture has a corner at the origin O of perpendicular axes Ox and Oy and has sides of length a along the x-axis and b along the y-axis [Fig. 6.19(a)]. Let dA be a small element of area in the aperture in the plane xOy having a reference vector r with respect to the origin O. In Fig. 6.19(b), s is a unit vector in the diffraction direction considered. If the direction cosines of s relative to the x, y and z axes are respectively l, m and n, the path difference between the parallel wavetrains 1 and 2 is $r.s$ and the corresponding phase difference is $kr.s$, where $k = 2\pi/\lambda$. Note that the scalar product $r.s$ has a magnitude $rs \cos (r, s)$ where (r, s) is the angle between vectors r and s.

The vector s prolonged to a far plane beyond the rectangular aperture, where this distant plane is parallel to the aperture plane,

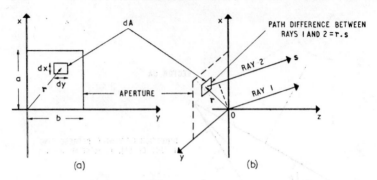

Fig. 6.19. Fraunhofer diffraction at a rectangular aperture

will meet this plane at a point Q. The direction cosines of the vector joining dA to Q will be l and m relative to the x and y axes respectively; the direction cosine n with respect to the z-axis will be zero, because the z-axis is normal to both the aperture plane and the far plane. The complex amplitude at this distant point Q is $R_{l,m}$ given by

$$R_{l,m} \propto \int_0^A dA \exp(jk\mathbf{r}.\mathbf{s})$$

where A is the area of the aperture. This expression becomes in Cartesian coordinates

$$R_{l,m} \propto \int_0^a \int_0^b \exp[jk(lx+my+nz)] \, dx \, dy$$

$$\propto \int_0^a \left\{ \frac{\exp[jk(lx+my)]}{jkm} \right\}_0^b dx$$

$$\propto \int_0^a \frac{\exp(jklx)}{jkm} [\exp(jkmb)-1] \, dx$$

$$\propto \left[\frac{\exp(jklx)}{-k^2ml} \right]_0^a [\exp(jkmb)-1]$$

$$\propto \frac{-[\exp(jkla)-1][\exp(jkmb)-1]}{k^2ml}$$

Therefore

$$|R_{l,m}|^2 = R_{l,m} \bar{R}_{l,m} \propto \frac{\sin^2 \alpha_1 \sin^2 \alpha_2}{(k^2ml)^2}$$

where $\alpha_1 = \pi la/\lambda$ and $\alpha_2 = \pi mb/\lambda$. Therefore, as a, b and λ are all constants,

$$|R_{l,\,m}|^2 \propto \frac{\sin^2 \alpha_1}{\alpha_1^2} \frac{\sin^2 \alpha_2}{\alpha_2^2} \tag{6.25}$$

For a maximum intensity in the diffraction pattern,

$$\alpha_1 = (2p+1)\frac{\pi}{2}$$

and

$$\alpha_2 = (2q+1)\frac{\pi}{2}$$

where p and q are integers. Thus

$$la = (2p+1)\frac{\lambda}{2} \tag{6.26}$$

and

$$mb = (2q+1)\frac{\lambda}{2} \tag{6.27}$$

Considering diffracted rays from the corners O, A and B of the aperture (Fig. 6.20), it is seen from Equations 6.26 and 6.27 that the condition for a maximum in the direction s, apart from the central maximum, is given by

$$a.s = (2p+1)\frac{\lambda}{2}$$

and

$$b.s = (2q+1)\frac{\lambda}{2}$$

because $l = \cos \psi_a$, $m = \cos \psi_b$ and s is a unit vector.

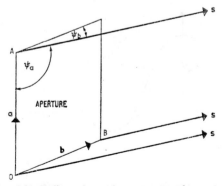

Fig. 6.20. Diffracted rays from a rectangular aperture

274 UNIVERSITY OPTICS

6.13 Fraunhofer Diffraction Due to a Circular Aperture

The circular aperture centre O is illuminated uniformly by mono-chromatic light of wavelength λ incident along the axis Oz normal to the aperture. The Fraunhofer amplitude R_s in the direction of the unit vector s [Fig. 6.21(a)] is given by

$$R_s = \int^{A} R_0 \exp{(jk r . s)}\, dA$$

where dA is an element of area about point P in the aperture, $k = 2\pi/\lambda$, OP is a vector of length r in the plane of the aperture, R_0 is the amplitude of the wave in the plane of the aperture, and A is the area of the aperture.

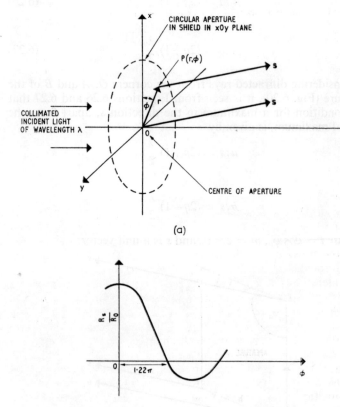

(a)

(b)

Fig. 6.21. Fraunhofer diffraction at a circular aperture

Choosing cylindrical coordinates so that point P has coordinates $(r, \phi, 0)$ with respect to the centre O of the aperture,

$$R_s = \int\limits_0^{2\pi} \int\limits_0^a R_0 \exp\left(jk\mathbf{r}.\mathbf{s}\right)r \, d\phi \, dr$$

The solution of this integral is of the form

$$R_s \propto \frac{J_1(\phi)}{\phi}$$

where $J_1(\phi)$ is the first order Bessel function and $\phi = (2\pi a \sin \theta)/\lambda$.

A plot of R_s/R_0 against ϕ is shown in Fig. 6.21(b). Note that R_s is zero at an angle ϕ given by $1 \cdot 22\pi$.

6.14 The Babinet Principle of Complementary Screens

Suppose a screen D_1 contains any distribution of opaque and transparent portions (for example, D_1 may be a flat opaque sheet containing a number of holes). The screen D_2 complementary to D_1 has the opaque portions where D_1 has transparent ones and vice versa. Thus an example of D_1 as a flat opaque sheet containing a series of holes would have complementary screen D_2 in the form of a transparent glass plate containing a like series of opaque patches where there were holes in D_1.

Let Q be a point in a field viewed by an observer. A source of radiation exists which illuminates this observed field, but the disturbance due to this radiation at Q is zero. For example, Q may be just outside the direct light produced by a luminous source.

The diffracting screen or shield D_1 is introduced between the source of radiation and the field of view. As a consequence, a disturbance of amplitude R_1 is produced at Q; point Q becomes illuminated because of diffraction due to D_1, even though with D_1 absent there is no illumination at Q. Babinet's principle states that the intensity at Q due to the introduction of D_1 is the same as that which would be produced by the introduction, instead, of the complementary screen D_2.

This principle is easily proved. Thus, suppose the disturbance at Q due to the introduction of diffracting screen D_2 has an amplitude R_2. Any radiation received at Q must be through the transparent portions of the screen. If the transparent portions of both screens D_1 and D_2 were imagined to be present simultaneously, the radiation would be unimpeded and the disturbance at Q would be zero. It follows that $R_2 = -R_1$ and $R_2^2 = R_1^2$. Complementary screens therefore produce identical diffraction patterns in those regions of the field of view outside the direct light from the source.

6.15 Kirchhoff's Formulation of Huygens' Principle

As stated at the beginning of this chapter, the Fraunhofer and the Fresnel elementary treatments of diffraction are both approximate, because they do not take into account changes of phase on re-radiation from a Huygens' secondary source and give no exact analysis of obliquity. The Kirchhoff treatment accounts for both these factors, but ignores polarisation; it is therefore only strictly true for longitudinal waves or for electric vectors all acting in the same directions. Furthermore, no account is taken of diffraction effects at a field of view very close to the diffracting obstacle. The Kirchhoff analysis is thus not a full one and may be considered as a mathematical formulation of ideas which were already held by Fresnel.

The problem is to find the disturbance at a point Q in terms of the integrated disturbances over the wavefront W arising from a source of radiation S [Fig. 6.22(a)]. The analysis involves the use

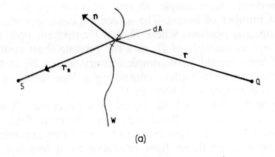

(a)

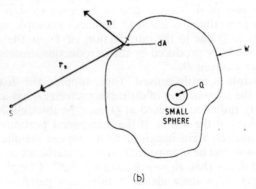

(b)

Fig. 6.22. Kirchhoff's theory of diffraction

of Green's theorem, expressed in the form:

$$\int_A (u \text{ grad } v - v \text{ grad } u) . \, dA = \int_\tau (u \nabla^2 v - v \nabla^2 u) \, d\tau \quad (6.28)$$

Here, u and v are two scalar quantities assumed to be single-valued and continuous in a given volume τ, where $d\tau$ is an element of volume within τ. The element of area dA is on the bounding surface of the total area A enclosing the volume τ, and the vector $dA = n \, dA$, where n is a unit vector drawn in the outward normal direction at dA.

It is assumed than that the wave surface W completely surrounds the point Q and that the source S is outside it [Fig. 6.22(b)]. The functions u and v are chosen as spherical wave amplitudes satisfying the wave equation as follows:

$$u = \frac{\exp(-jkr_s)}{r_s} \quad (6.29)$$

and

$$v = \frac{\exp(-jkr)}{r} \quad (6.30)$$

where $k = 2\pi/\lambda$, the distance r is measured from point Q to any point in the surface enclosing the volume, and the distance r_s is measured from point S to any point in the enclosing surface. Since $v \rightarrow \infty$ as $r \rightarrow 0$, which is inadmissible, the point Q must be excluded from the region of integration. To do this, Q is surrounded by a sphere of very small radius; over the surface of this sphere, the amplitude of the disturbance is assumed to be constant and equal to the amplitude u_q at Q which it is required to find.

As there are no sources of radiation within the volume τ, Poisson's equation gives

$$\nabla^2 u = \nabla^2 v = 0 \quad (6.31)$$

Equation 6.28 therefore becomes simply

$$\int_A (u \text{ grad } v - v \text{ grad } u) . \, dA = 0 \quad (6.32)$$

Consider first the value of this integral when the enclosing surface W is a sphere of radius r around point Q. The element of area dA is then $r^2 \, d\omega$, where $d\omega$ is the solid angle subtended by dA at Q. Then,

$$I = \int_{\text{sphere}} (u \text{ grad } v - v \text{ grad } u) . \, dA$$

$$= \int_{\text{sphere}} \left[u \frac{\partial v}{\partial r} (-n) - v \text{ grad } u \right] . \, nr^2 \, d\omega \quad (6.33)$$

because n and r are in opposite senses so that the unit vector along grad v is $-n$. Differentiating Equation 6.30 with respect to r gives

$$\frac{\partial v}{\partial r} = \frac{-jkr \exp(-jkr) - \exp(-jkr)}{r^2}$$

Substitution in Equation 6.33 gives

$$I = \int_{\text{sphere}} [r \exp(-jkr)(jku - \text{grad } u.n) + u \exp(-jkr)] \, d\omega$$

For the sphere of very small radius around point Q over the surface of which $u = u_q$ is a constant (i.e. $u \to u_q$ as $r \to 0$), the integral I becomes I' given by

$$I' = \int_{\substack{\text{sphere} \\ r \to 0}} u_q \, d\omega = 4\pi u_q \tag{6.34}$$

The total integral for a wavefront W of any shape enclosing point Q is therefore given by I' for the small sphere around Q plus the integral given by Equation 6.32 for the surface W. So the appropriate expression is

$$4\pi u_q + \int_W (u \text{ grad } v - v \text{ grad } u).dA = 0$$

Therefore

$$u_q = \frac{1}{4\pi} \int_W (-u \text{ grad } v + v \text{ grad } u).dA \tag{6.35}$$

or, substituting for u and v from Equations 6.29 and 6.30 respectively,

$$u_q = \frac{1}{4\pi} \int_W \left\{ \frac{-\exp(-jkr_s)}{r_s} \text{ grad} \left[\frac{1}{r} \exp(-jkr) \right] \right.$$

$$\left. + \frac{1}{r} \exp(-jkr) \text{ grad} \left[\frac{1}{r_s} \exp(-jkr_s) \right] \right\}.dA \tag{6.36}$$

This is Kirchhoff's formula giving u_q, the amplitude of the disturbance at point Q in terms of the integrated disturbances over a closed wave surface W enclosing Q. The function u is the complex amplitude of the disturbance arriving at W from the source of radiation S, and the integral is the summation of the wavelets from W to Q.

This theory may be applied to optical problems involving transverse waves when the source S and the point Q both lie on the axis of a circular aperture in an opaque screen. In this special situation, the amplitude and phase are both independent of polarisation and Equation 6.35 is identical for longitudinal and transverse waves. Equation 6.35 may be written in the form

$$u_q = \frac{1}{4\pi} \int_W \left(v \frac{\partial u}{\partial n} - u \frac{\partial v}{\partial n} \right) dA \qquad (6.37)$$

because

$$\text{grad } u.dA = \frac{\partial u}{\partial n} dA$$

and

$$\text{grad } v.dA = \frac{\partial v}{\partial n} dA$$

Substituting for u and v from Equations 6.29 and 6.30 respectively, therefore,

$$u_q = \frac{1}{4\pi} \int_W \left\{ \frac{1}{r} \exp(-jkr) \frac{\partial u}{\partial n} - u \frac{\partial}{\partial n} \left[\frac{1}{r} \exp(-jkr) \right] \right\} dA$$

i.e.

$$u_q = \frac{1}{4\pi} \int_W \left[\frac{1}{r} \exp(-jkr) \frac{\partial u}{\partial n} + \frac{jku \exp(-jkr)}{r} \frac{\partial r}{\partial n} \right.$$

$$\left. - u \exp(-jkr) \frac{\partial}{\partial n} \left(\frac{1}{r} \right) \right] dA \qquad (6.38)$$

6.16 Kirchhoff's Theory of the Diffraction of a Spherical Wave by a Circular Aperture

The surface of integration is made the part of the spherical wavefront AOB in the circular aperture, the opaque screen containing this aperture and an infinitely distant hemisphere (Fig. 6.23). The contributions due to the opaque screen and the hemisphere are assumed to be zero leaving the wavefront in the aperture only. Let the complex amplitude of the vibration in the circular aperture be

$$u_o = \frac{\exp(-jkr_s)}{r_s}$$

where r_s is the distance from the point source S to the spherical wavefront in the aperture.

For an element of area dA in this wavefront, let the distance to an axial point P beyond the aperture be r. The centre of the aperture is at O and the axial distance $OP = r_p$.

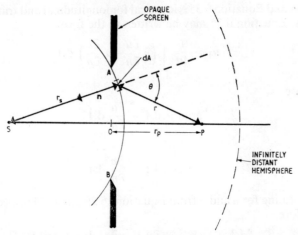

Fig. 6.23. Diffraction of a spherical wave by a circular aperture

The normal **n** to the wavefront drawn outwards from the closed surface is towards the source. If the angle between this normal and the radius vector **r** is θ, then

$$\frac{\partial r}{\partial n} = \cos\theta$$

Substituting in Equation 6.38, but for u_p (the complex amplitude of the disturbance at point P),

$$u_p = \frac{1}{4\pi} \int_{\text{aperture}} \left\{ \frac{1}{r} \exp(-jkr) \frac{\partial}{\partial n}\left[\frac{\exp(-jkr_s)}{r_s}\right] \right.$$
$$\left. + \frac{jku_0 \exp(-jkr)}{r}\cos\theta - u_o \exp(-jkr)\frac{\partial}{\partial n}\left(\frac{1}{r}\right) \right\} \, dA$$

In this expression

$$\frac{\partial}{\partial n}\left[\frac{\exp(-jkr_s)}{r_s}\right] = \frac{-jkr_s \exp(-jkr_s) - \exp(-jkr_s)}{r_s^2} \frac{\partial r_s}{\partial n}$$

As

$$u_o = \frac{\exp(-jkr_s)}{r_s}$$

and

$$\frac{\partial r_s}{\partial n} = 1$$

therefore

$$\frac{\partial}{\partial n}\left[\frac{\exp(-jkr_s)}{r_s}\right] = jku_o - \frac{u_o}{r_s}$$

Thus

$$u_p = \frac{u_o}{4\pi}\int_{aperture}\left[\frac{1}{r}\exp(-jkr)\left(jk - \frac{1}{r_s} + jk\cos\theta + \frac{1}{r}\frac{\partial r}{\partial n}\right)\right]dA$$

As

$$\frac{dr}{dn} = \cos\theta$$

then

$$\frac{u_p}{u_o} = \frac{1}{4\pi}\int_{aperture}\left[\frac{jk\exp(-jkr)(1+\cos\theta)}{r}\right.$$

$$\left. - \frac{\exp(-jkr)}{rr_s} + \frac{\exp(-jkr)\cos\theta}{r^2}\right]dA \qquad (6.39)$$

The physical interpretation of this Equation 6.39 is that there are, in effect, three wavelets emanating from a Huygens' secondary source:

1. A wavelet depending on the area dA, $1/r$ and an obliquity factor $1+\cos\theta$ in interpretation of the term $[jk\exp(-jkr)(1+\cos\theta)]/r$;
2. A wavelet depending on the area dA and $1/r$ but with no obliquity, decided by the term $[\exp(-jkr_s)]/rr_s$, where r_s is the separation between source and aperture;
3. A wavelet depending on the area dA and varying inversely with r^2 and with an obliquity factor $\cos\theta$, given by the term $[\exp(-jkr)\cos\theta]/r^2$.

The wavelets in the first two of these cases, in which obliquity factors are involved, are illustrated in Fig. 6.24.

Note also that the term $[jk\exp(-jkr)(1+\cos\theta)]/r$ involves a phase change of $\pi/2$ on radiation from the secondary source. This change in phase on radiation from a point source has been observed in microwave experiments involving interference between plane and spherical waves. It was first noted by Gouy in 1890 using interference in the visible region.

In the simple Fresnel treatment, r and r_s are both large compared with the wavelength, and the obliquity angle θ is small. Hence only the term $[jk\exp(-jkr)(1+\cos\theta)]/r$ is effective, involving the phase change of $\pi/2$. The obliquity factor with θ small becomes $1+\cos\theta = 2$.

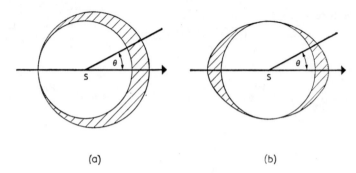

(a)   (b)

Fig. 6.24. Effect of obliquity factors on wavefronts from a point source: (a) Huygens' source with obliquity factor $1 + \cos \theta$; (b) Huygens' source with obliquity factor $\cos \theta$

6.17 Interference and Associated Phenomena

In the previous sections on diffraction, the spatial amplitude distribution arising from a given wavefront in a given aperture of finite dimensions is considered. In the following sections, the concern is the spatial amplitude distribution arising from a number of separated coherent sources. Two sources of radiation are coherent if they send out wavetrains having a phase difference which is independent of time. The coherent sources may be a set of apertures which are not necessarily identical, and the problem of finding the spatial amplitude distribution then involves both diffraction and interference. The diffraction problem is solved by determining the diffraction effect of each aperture at the point in the field of view considered, and the interference problem by considering the effect at this point of separated wavetrains from different apertures. The final effect is found by considering the two phenomena together. A full treatment is beyond the present scope. To limit the scope, the important cases discussed are those where identical sets of coherent sources in two dimensions are involved and the diffraction is of the Fraunhofer type. Interference may also arise from a set of coherent scatterers in one, two or three dimensions (for example, in X-ray diffraction).

6.18 Coherence

Suppose a set of sources of radiation gives rise to wavetrains which interfere, but that the diffraction effects are uniform in all directions so need not be considered. Let the complex amplitudes u_1, u_2, u_3,

..., u_n from sources 1, 2, 3, ..., N be represented by

$$u_1 = R_1 \exp (j\phi_1)$$
$$u_2 = R_2 \exp (j\phi_2)$$
$$u_3 = R_3 \exp (j\phi_3)$$
$$\dots\dots\dots\dots\dots\dots$$
$$u_n = R_n \exp (j\phi_n)$$

where the time factor is omitted, and all the vibrations are of the same frequency and assumed to be in the same direction.

By the principle of superposition, these amplitudes may be added vectorially in the usual way (Fig. 6.25) to give the resultant R. Clearly,

$$R^2 = \left(\sum_{n=1}^{n=N} R_n \sin \phi_n\right)^2 + \left(\sum_{n=1}^{n=N} R_n \cos \phi_n\right)^2 \qquad (6.40)$$

or

$$R^2 = \sum R_n^2 + 2 \sum_{n \neq m} R_n R_m (\sin \phi_n \sin \phi_m + \cos \phi_n \cos \phi_m) \qquad (6.41)$$

Assume that the angles ϕ_n have random values, so that the phase angle $\phi_m \sim \phi_n$ between any two wavetrains n and m also takes on random values over a period of time. As all values of ϕ_n may be assumed to be equally probable, the mean value $\bar{R}^2$ of R^2 over a finite time is given by

$$\bar{R}^2 = \sum_{n=1}^{n=N} R_n^2$$

because $\sin \phi_n \sin \phi_m$ and $\cos \phi_n \cos \phi_m$ in Equation 6.41 average out to zero over an integral number of complete cycles. It follows

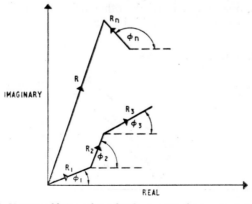

Fig. 6.25. Vector addition of amplitudes to give the resultant amplitude

that if $\phi_n \sim \phi_m$ has random values, the resulting intensity proportional to $\bar{R}^2$ is equal to the sum of the individual intensities. The effect at any point is therefore simply a photometric scalar effect, and no interference occurs. Sources such as these are termed incoherent.

For coherent sources, $\phi_n \sim \phi_m$ must be independent of time and depend only upon the spatial coordinates of the point at which interference takes place.

6.19 The Classification of Interference Phenomena

In all interference phenomena, two or more wavetrains, which interfere spatially, are involved. An obvious means of classification is based on the methods used to produce the necessary coherent Huygens' sources which give rise to these wavetrains. In all methods a single wavefront is used to form two or more secondary sources.

In *division of wavefront* methods, a section of an extended source is used to give a plane wave having as high a degree of coherence as is compatible with reasonable intensity. This plane wavefront is divided by apertures in a screen which then form the interfering sources. A spatial interference pattern is established beyond the screen and is modulated by the diffraction effect at the separated apertures. The result may be regarded as a 'pure' interference effect if the apertures have infinitely small dimensions so that the diffraction effects will tend towards uniformity in all directions. An example is the plane transmission diffraction grating, which comprises a large number of parallel close thin slits in a plane screen. A plane wavefront falling normally on these slit apertures gives rise to interfering sources.

In *division of amplitude*, a given wavetrain is divided into two wavetrains, one reflected and the other refracted at the boundary between two optical media. If the wavetrains are superimposed

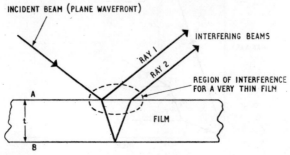

Fig. 6.26. Interference of light in a thin film

after travelling through different optical paths, then interference takes place between them. An example is interference in thin films. Referring to Fig. 6.26, note that the film must be very thin if the reflected and refracted wavefronts are to be superposed; indeed the film thickness must be of the order of the wavelength of the interfering light.

If the reflecting surfaces A and B in Fig. 6.26 are separated by a distance appreciably greater than the wavelength of the radiation, the emergent rays 1 and 2 are separated. Now there is both *division of wavefront and of amplitude*.

6.20 The General Forms of Fringes due to Interference in Thin Films

Let A and B (Fig. 6.27) be two reflecting surfaces at a small angle α to one another and enclosing a thin film which, for simplicity, is assumed to be air of refractive index $n = 1$. A ray from an extended source meets the surface A at P and is reflected along PE. The same incident ray will also traverse the thin film and be reflected from the surface B to give rise to a ray (not shown in Fig. 6.27) exceedingly close to PE which will interfere with the reflected ray from A provided that the angle α and the film thickness are both very small.

An observer at E will thus see a localised interference effect in the region of P. Let EO be normal to the surface A at point O. Taking O to be the origin of Cartesian axes Ox and Oy, the coordinates of

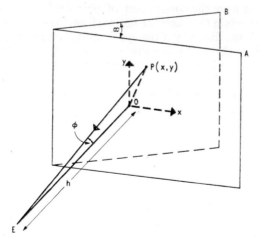

Fig. 6.27. Interference on reflection from a thin film (the film thickness and angle α are both greatly exaggerated; EO is normal to the surface A)

point P are (x, y) and $OP = \sqrt{(x^2+y^2)}$. The path difference Δ between the two interfering wavetrains reaching E is given (from Equation 9.1 of Volume 1) by

$$\Delta = 2t_p \cos \phi \qquad (6.42)$$

where t_p is the thickness of the film at point P, and ϕ is the angle of refraction in the film which, for an air film, is the same as the angle of reflection of the ray PE. This angle to the normal EO is $\angle PEO = \phi$. As $\angle POE$ is a right angle, it follows that

$$\cos \phi = \frac{h}{EP} = \frac{h}{\sqrt{(EO^2+OP^2)}} = \frac{h}{\sqrt{(h^2+x^2+y^2)}} \qquad (6.43)$$

If the thickness of the film at O (i.e. along the normal to the film) is t_o,

$$t_p = t_o + x\alpha \qquad (6.44)$$

provided that the y-axis is parallel to the line of intersection of surfaces A and B and the perpendicular x-axis is in the plane A. Substituting from Equations 6.43 and 6.44 into Equation 6.42 gives

$$\Delta = \frac{2(t_o+x\alpha)h}{\sqrt{(h^2+x^2+y^2)}}$$

The locus of a given interference fringe is hence given by

$$x^2(\Delta^2-4h^2\alpha^2) + y^2 \Delta^2 - 8t_o\alpha h^2 x + h^2(\Delta^2-4t_o^2) = 0 \qquad (6.45)$$

where x and y are the coordinates of points on the locus with respect to the origin O (where the normal from the eye meets the surface A), h is the distance of the eye from this origin, α is the small angle between the reflecting surfaces A and B, t_o is the thickness of the film at the origin O, and Δ, the path difference, is a constant for a given fringe.

In general, Equation 6.45 is that of a conic section and takes the following forms:

1. An ellipse if $\Delta^2 > 4h^2\alpha^2$;
2. A hyperbola if $\Delta^2 < 4h^2\alpha^2$;
3. A parabola if $\Delta^2 = 4h^2\alpha^2$;
4. A circle if $\alpha = 0$;
5. A pair of straight lines if $\Delta = 0$.

The path difference Δ is small for very thin films (t_p small), in which case the fringe forms will be hyperbolic or circular; they will in fact be circular if the film surfaces are accurately parallel ($\alpha = 0$), giving the Haidinger-type fringes of equal inclination already described in Chapter 9 of Volume 1.

The eccentricity of the hyperbola will increase with decreasing path difference Δ until the limiting case where Δ approaches zero, when the fringes will be straight lines.

6.21 Fizeau Fringes

An imperfectly collimated beam of monochromatic light is incident upon a thin film at a point P (Fig. 6.28). If δI is the angle between extreme rays in the cone of light, a range of angles of incidence to the normal exists between I and $I+\delta I$. If the interference in the reflected light fringe in the region of P is dark, for the pth order

$$p\lambda = 2nt \cos R \qquad (6.46)$$

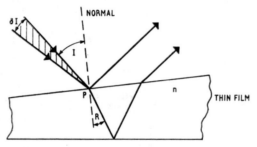

Fig. 6.28. Incidence of imperfectly collimated light on a thin film (the film thickness is greatly exaggerated)

where λ is the wavelength of the light, n is the refractive index of the material of the film, R is the angle of refraction in the film, and t is the thickness of the film at point P (see Equation 9.3 of Volume 1).

But there is not only a single value of the angle of refraction R: a range of values exist because of the range of angles of incidence from I to $I+\delta I$. The effect of the range of angles of incidence is to move the order p at P through a range corresponding to a change of thickness of the film from t to $t+\delta t$.

For a given order of interference p, $p\lambda$ is a constant. Differentiation of Equation 6.46 therefore leads to

$$0 = 2nt \cos R \; \delta t - 2nt \sin R \; \delta R$$

where δR is the range of values of R corresponding to δI. Thus

$$\delta t = t \tan R \; \delta R \qquad (6.47)$$

From Equation 6.47, it is seen that fringes of the thin film type can be produced when t is large provided that $\tan R$ is small (i.e. the incident beam is along or near the normal) and δR is small (i.e. the incident beam is highly collimated).

Fringes of this type are called Fizeau fringes; they are widely used in testing optical components. The essential features of the necessary optical system are two separated non-silvered surfaces, which may be widely separated, and a small point source of light at the focal point of a highly corrected converging lens and thus giving a plane wavefront incident nearly normally on one of the surfaces.

An arrangement for observing Fizeau fringes [Fig. 6.29(a)] comprises a small point source S of monochromatic light at the

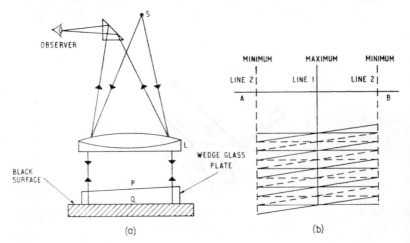

Fig. 6.29. Observation of Fizeau fringes

focal point of a highly corrected collimator lens L. The collimated light from L is incident slightly away from the normal upon a thick glass plate PQ on a black table. Suppose this glass plate has plane surfaces P and Q inclined to one another at a small angle, forming a wedge. Two plane waves leave this wedge, one reflected from its front-surface P and the other from its back-surface Q. The crests and troughs in these reflected waves before they enter the lens L are represented by full lines and dashed lines respectively in Fig. 6.29(b). It is seen that along lines such as line 1, the crests and troughs in one reflected wave coincide with those in the other and so produce constructive interference; along lines such as line 2, crests coincide with troughs to give destructive interference. In a plane such as AB, a fringe system is observed with maxima and minima where it is intersected by the loci of line 1 and line 2. These loci intersect the glass plate at thicknesses of $2nt = (p+\frac{1}{2})\lambda$ for maxima and $2nt = p\lambda$ for minima.

The plane wavefronts in the reflected light become spherical after traversing the lens L. The eye placed to receive the light emerging from L is able to discern, in relation to these fringes, departures from flatness of the surfaces P and Q of the glass plate and lack of parallelism between P and Q.

6.22 Fraunhofer Diffraction Treated by Fourier Methods

A powerful theoretical method in dealing with problems of diffraction makes use of the Fourier transform. An introduction only to the fundamental ideas involved is given here.

In the most general case, the analytical problem in diffraction can be stated in the form that, in the propagation of radiation, the amplitude and intensity distribution are known at a given region and it is required to find the amplitude and intensity distribution at a separate region. For Fraunhofer diffraction, the known distribution is where the diffracting obstacle (such as an aperture) is placed (a region sometimes called the 'object space', not to be confused with the use of this term in relation to lenses), and it is required to evaluate the distribution at a large distance in the image or Fraunhofer space where the diffraction pattern of interest is formed.

As the Fraunhofer space is at a large distance compared with the dimensions of the diffracting obstacle and the wavelength of the radiation, the interfering wavetrains that give rise to the diffraction pattern may be considered as parallel bundles of radiation leaving volume elements in the object space in a specified direction. In Fig. 6.30, therefore, let P and Q be the centres of two small equal volume elements δV in the object space (i.e. where the specified distribution is known in relation to a diffracting obstacle at this position). Suppose that δV is small enough to contain a uniform density of radiating Huygens' sources of secondary wavelets. P and Q are in positions relative to an origin O decided by the vectors r_p and r_q respectively, and r is the vector joining P and Q. The magnitudes

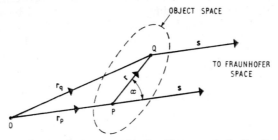

Fig. 6.30. Specification of poistions within the object space in the Fourier treatment of Fraunhofer diffraction

r_p, r_q and r of these vectors are all small, because the diffracting obstacle dimensions are small compared with the distance to the Fraunhofer space.

Assume that the specified spatial amplitude distribution at a point such as P in the object space is given by

$$u = f(r_p, \theta, \phi) \qquad (6.48)$$

where r_p, θ and ϕ are the polar coordinates of P with respect to the origin at O, and f is a specified continuous function. The Huygens' source of secondary wavelets at P will produce at any point R at a distance r' from P a spatial amplitude distribution given by

$$u' = g'(r', \theta', \phi')$$

where g' is a continuous function, and r', θ' and ϕ' are the polar coordinates of R with respect to an origin at P. At unit distance from P, $r' = 1$ and

$$u' = g'(\theta', \phi')$$

Suppose the point R is in the direction of a unit vector s emanating from P. Then the specification of s corresponds to the specification of θ' and ϕ', so u' may be written as

$$u' = g(s) \qquad (6.49)$$

where g is a continuous function.

This radiation from P in the direction determined by s will interfere with the parallel radiation from Q in the direction s. It will be this interference (which may in practice only occur via the action of a lens focusing the Fraunhofer diffraction pattern at a screen) which decides the resultant amplitude in the Fraunhofer space (i.e. in the diffraction pattern at, or because of the focusing lens effectively at, a large distance) due to P and Q combined. However, the radiation in the direction of s from Q differs in path by $r \cos \alpha$ from that produced by P, where α is the angle between r and s (Fig. 6.30). The corresponding phase difference will be $kr \cos \alpha$, where $k = 2\pi/\lambda$, λ being the wavelength of the radiation. Therefore, whereas the amplitude of the electric vector in the radiation due to P is proportional to $g(s)$ and is perpendicular to s, that due to Q will also be $g(s)$ but at angle α to s. The complex amplitude resulting from the addition of the two is hence proportional to $g(s) \exp(jkr.s)$, where $r.s$ is the scalar product of r and s of magnitude $rs \cos \alpha$.

As the specified spatial amplitude distribution at P is given by Equation 6.48 and there is a uniform density of Huygens' sources in the small volume element δV, it follows that the complex amplitude in the Fraunhofer space due to P and Q is given by

$$\delta U' = a f(r_p, \theta, \phi) g(s) \exp (jkr \cdot s)\, \delta V$$

where a is a constant of proportionality.

Assuming that there are no discontinuities in the radiation between the diffracting obstacle and the Fraunhofer space, the resultant complex amplitude U due to all the volume elements δV around all points such as P and Q in the diffracting obstacle is given by

$$U = g(s) \int_{-\infty}^{\infty} f(r_p, \theta, \phi) \exp (jkr \cdot s)\, dV \qquad (6.50)$$

for a given direction s. Note that $g(s)$ is outside the integral sign, which is justifiable on the basis that it is dependent only on the fixed direction decided by s.

In the Appendix (page 362) it is shown that the integral

$$\int_{-\infty}^{\infty} f(r_p, \theta, \phi) \exp (jkr \cdot s)\, dV$$

is the Fourier transform of $f(r_p, \theta, \phi)$.

It is helpful to use Cartesian coordinates, in which event $r \cdot s = (x_q - x_p)l + (y_q - y_p)m + (z_q - z_p)n$, where P is the point (x_p, y_p, z_p) with reference to the origin at O, and the direction cosines of s are l, m and n with respect to a right-handed set of Cartesian axes at O. The integral then becomes

$$\iiint_{-\infty}^{\infty} f(x, y, z) \exp [jk(lx + my + nz)]\, dx\, dy\, dz$$

and U is a function of l, m and n.

This general treatment shows that a very simple relationship exists between the Fraunhofer object and image spaces in that the amplitude distributions are Fourier 'mates'. Thus, in the analysis, U in Equation 6.50 is the Fourier transform of $g(s) f(r_p, \theta, \phi)$ and, similarly, the whole process may be reversed to consider the distribution in the object space if that in the image space is specified.

6.23 The Aperture Function: Fraunhofer Diffraction due to a Single Slit

The value of $g(s) f(r_p, \theta, \phi)$ gives the amplitude due to P only at a unit distance along the direction of vector s. This is known as the aperture function A. If the Huygens' wavelets from such a point as P have spherical wavefronts, $g(s)$ is a constant, having the same

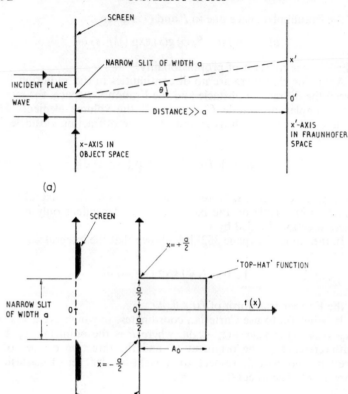

Fig 6.31. The 'top-hat' distribution corresponding to a plane wave incident upon a
single narrow slit in a screen

magnitude irrespective of the direction of s. The aperture function
A is then given by

$$A = \text{constant} \times f(r_p, \theta, \phi)$$

and Equation 6.50 becomes

$$U = \int_{-\infty}^{\infty} A \exp(jk\mathbf{r}.\mathbf{s}) \, dV$$

which is evaluated from the equivalent result

$$U = \int_{-\infty}^{+\infty} A \, (\text{Fourier transform of } A) \, dV \qquad (6.51)$$

Consider a plane wave of monochromatic radiation of wavelength λ incident upon a narrow slit in a screen [Fig. 6.31(a)]. Within the slit itself, the spatial distribution of amplitude is a constant irrespective of position (presuming that the slit is uniformly illuminated). Hence $f(r_p, \theta, \phi)$ is a constant and, presuming that the Huygens' secondary wavelets are spherical, the aperture function is a constant of value A_0, say. Outside the slit in the plane of the screen, the aperture function will be zero. The distribution function corresponding to the constant-aperture function A_0 is called the 'top-hat' function [Fig. 6.31(b)].

In the analysis, it is convenient to use Cartesian coordinates: one set x, y and z in the object space, and a parallel set x', y' and z' in the Fraunhofer space. For the narrow slit in the circumstances specified, the distribution of amplitude as a function of x only is required. The origin O is taken to be at the centre of the slit, so x is zero at O. In the Fraunhofer space, x' is taken to be zero at the point O', where the direct light perpendicular to the plane of the slit intersects a plane in the Fraunhofer space parallel to the screen containing the slit [Fig. 6.31(a)]. If the slit width is a, the 'top-hat' function will have the value A_0 over the interval from $-a/2$ to $+a/2$ and will be zero elsewhere. The amplitude distribution in the object space is therefore given by

$$f(x) = A_0$$

for $-a/2 < x < +a/2$ and

$$f(x) = 0$$

for $x > +a/2$ and $x < -a/2$.

The Fourier transform of $f(x)$ (see Appendix, page 362) is given by

$$f(x') = \int_{-\infty}^{\infty} f(x) \exp\left(-2\pi jxx'\right) dx$$

which, with $f(x) = A_0$ over the limits specified, becomes

$$f(x') = \int_{-a/2}^{a/2} A_0 \exp\left(-2\pi jxx'\right) dx$$

Therefore

$$f(x') = \frac{A_0}{-2\pi jx'} \left[\exp\left(-2\pi jx'a/2\right) - \exp\left(2\pi jx'a/2\right]\right]$$

Putting $\alpha = \pi ax'$, then from Equation 6.51 the expression

$$U'_x = f(x') = \frac{A_0 a}{-2j\alpha}(-2j \sin \alpha) = \frac{A_0 a \sin \alpha}{\alpha}$$

gives the amplitude U'_x at a point x' in the Fraunhofer space.

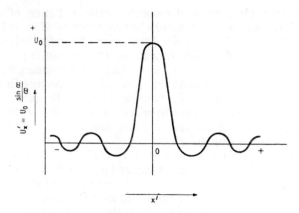

Fig. 6.32. Amplitude pattern in the Fraunhofer space when a plane wave is incident upon a narrow slit

At $x' = 0$ in the Fraunhofer space,

$$U'_x = U_0 = f(0) = A_0 a \frac{\sin 0}{0} = A_0 a$$

because

$$\lim_{\alpha \to 0} \frac{\sin \alpha}{\alpha} = 1$$

Hence

$$\frac{U'_x}{U_0} = \frac{\sin \alpha}{\alpha} \qquad (6.52)$$

and

$$\frac{I'_x}{I_0} = \frac{\sin^2 \alpha}{\alpha^2}$$

where I'_x and I_0 are the intensities corresponding to the amplitudes U'_x and U_0 respectively.

This result is the same as that obtained by a different analytical method in Section 6.11, leading to Equation 6.24. Note that $\alpha = \pi a x'$ in Equation 6.52 is the same as the α used in Section 6.11 because $x' = (\sin \theta)/\lambda$.

The distribution of amplitude in the Fraunhofer space due to a single slit as given by Equation 6.52 is shown in Fig. 6.32. It is interesting to note that conversely the Fraunhofer pattern of such a distribution will be its Fourier transform, which will be the 'top-hat' function of Fig. 6.31.

The Fourier approach to Fraunhofer diffraction described here in the case of a single narrow slit is only indicative of a powerful analytical method of particular value in problems involving diffraction and interference effects of a complexity beyond the standard of this text.

Exercise 6

1. Distinguish between Fraunhofer and Fresnel diffraction. Explain the action of a zone plate and show that the object and image distances obey the ordinary thin lens formula.
   A plane parallel beam of microwave radiation of wavelength 3 cm falls normally on a circular aperture in a conducting screen. What radii can the aperture have in order to produce a focus at an axial distance of 10 metres?
   (L.P.)

2. Explain what is meant by (a) Fresnel half-period zones, (b) a zone plate. Describe one simple experiment that can be explained in terms of half-period zones.
   A small source emitting light of wavelength 5000 Å is placed on the axis in front of a zone plate at a distance of three metres from the plate. If the diameter of the first zone is 2 mm describe with the necessary calculations what may be observed at points on the axis behind the plate.   (L.G.)

3. Give a qualitative description of the application of the Cornu spir al to the diffraction of a monochromatic cylindrical wave front by a screen having a straight edge parallel to its axis. Discuss the variation in intensity across the line of the geometrical shadow from uniformly dark to uniformly bright regions.   (L.P.)

4. Explain what is meant by a Fresnel half-period zone and use the concept of half-period zones to explain the variations in intensity occurring along the axis of a circular aperture placed tangentially to the wavefront emitted from a point source of monochromatic radiation.
   A point source of monochromatic radiation of wavelength 5460 Å is situated 50 cm from a circular aperture 1 mm in diameter, the aperture being tangential to the wavefront. Considering points on the axis calculate the greatest distance from the aperture at which a maximum of intensity occurs. Determine also the positions of the next two maxima.   (City)

5. Show that, if a cylindrical wavefront is considered as consisting of a number of narrow rectangular zones (considerably smaller than half-period zones) with uniform phase difference from one to the next, a phase diagram may be constructed from which the amplitude at a point due to any part of the wavefront may be determined.
   A source of wavelength 5460 Å producing a cylindrical wavefront is set up 50 cm from an adjustable slit whose length is parallel to the axis of the wavefront and whose plane is tangential to it. A screen is placed 100 cm from the slit, the planes of the screen and slit being parallel. Use the Cornu spiral supplied to predict the general shape of the intensity diffraction pattern on the screen when the slit is (a) 6×10^{-3} cm, (b) 7.8×10^{-2} cm, (c) 0.115 cm wide. (Detailed drawings and calculations not required.)   (City)

6. A reflecting astronomical telescope focusses light from a star on to a photo-graphic plate using a concave mirror of diameter 120 cm and focal length 700 cm. Describe and explain the photographs which may be obtained when the front of the tube is covered with (a) no screen, (b) an opaque cover with two circular apertures 12 cm in diameter and 100 cm apart, (c) a transmission grating with a grating space of 1 mm, (d) a square-mesh wire net with wires 1 mm thick spaced apart by 2 cm and (e) a mosaic screen complementary to the wire mesh in (d).   (L.P.)

7. Show that the Fraunhofer diffraction pattern of a simple one-dimensional aperture is the Fourier transform of the aperture function.

Describe what happens to a Fraunhofer single-slit diffraction pattern of monochromatic light if the whole apparatus is immersed in water.

A circular piston 60 cm in diameter oscillates at a frequency of 25,000 c/s as an underwater source of sound for submarine detection. Far from the source the sound intensity is distributed as a Fraunhofer diffraction pattern for a circular hole whose diameter equals that of the piston. Take the speed of the sound in water to be 1,450 m/s and find the angle between the normal to the piston and the direction of the first minimum.   (M.P.)

CHAPTER 7

Colour and Colour Measurement

7.1 Introductory Concepts

The reproduction of colour by physical and chemical processes in such technologies as those of colour photography, colour television, printing, fabrics, paper, plastics and ceramics has led to a twentieth-century world in which colour science has to a large extent taken over in a field in which formerly the artist was supreme. Apart from the fact that this change has probably been a main reason for the peculiarities of much of modern art, it has led to a more colourful environment and the necessity for measuring colour in a scientific manner which is, as far as possible, independent of the observer.

Independence of the observer is, however, not strictly possible, because the treatment of colour is essentially psychological or, better, psychophysical. In the first place, colour is associated with visible radiation having a given spectral distribution. But the human eye does not operate like the spectrometer: it is incapable of analysis of the component wavelengths in the spectrum; its response varies through the spectrum. The human eye is only capable of discerning three types of sensation: *hue*, *brightness* and *saturation*. Moreover, whereas radiation with a given spectral distribution produces a certain sensation in a normal observer, this same sensation—meaning that the observer sees the same colour—can be produced by a variety of different spectral distributions.

The term *hue* is, scientifically speaking, regarded as having a different meaning from the term colour in that it represents that aspect of colour which changes depending on the part of the

297

spectrum involved; hue is therefore concerned with the *dominant wavelength* present in the radiation.

In relation to sources of light, a main characteristic is luminous flux which evokes the sensation of brightness. Brightness is a measure of the total sensation; for a luminous source the more specific term is *luminous emittance;* for a body which gives out light by reflection and scattering when illuminated by a luminous source, the specific term is *luminance* (Section 6.4 of Volume 1).

Saturation is a measure of the purity of the colour. A saturated colour is pure: the monochromatic spectral radiation over a small wavelength interval in the visible spectrum is pure. Saturation decreases as the colour is mixed with white—the colour becomes desaturated.

The term *chromaticity* is used to denote both dominant wavelength (hue) and purity.

7.2 Additive Colour Mixing

One of the most fascinating results of scientific experiment is that, if three light sources of different hues are available, a whole range of colours can be produced by mixing these three different hues in various amounts. Depending on the three different hues chosen, so the ability to match a wide range of chromaticities (hue and saturation) varies. By a judicious choice of the three light sources, almost all chromaticities can be simulated. The usual choice for three primaries in additive colour mixing are red, green and blue.

This ability to match almost all colours by an appropriate additive mixture of three primaries is an established fact based on experiment. The explanation depends on the way in which the human eye works in discerning colour; this demands a *theory of colour vision*.

To explain three-colour theory, Young and also Helmholtz supposed that there are three sets of nerves in the retina of the eye, one for each primary colour. White light stimulates all three sets, yellow light stimulates the green and red nerves together, blue-green light stimulates the blue and green receptors, and similarly for other colours. These colour receptors must be associated with the cones in the retina and not the rods, which lack colour sensitivity (Section 3.2 of Volume 1).

There are objections to this theory. Anatomical examination of the eye does not reveal three sets of nerves to each sensory part of the eye. Again, this theory implies that red light will excite only red nerves, yellow will excite the blue and green nerves, and white will excite all three sensations. This was shown to be by Koenig, who experimented on the observation of

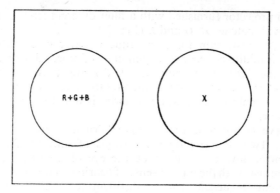

Fig. 7.1. Additive colour mixing

monochromatic radiations through the spectrum. Another difficulty is that the sensation of white light can be produced by two complementary colours. Thus if the red portion is removed from the continuous white light spectrum, the remaining colour is blue-green, which is complementary to red. A colour-blind observer incapable of seeing red may be considered simply to have the 'red' nerve sensation absent in his retina. To him, the combination of red and blue-green as complementary colours should not produce the sensation of white. But this is not correct.

Subsequent theories of colour vision have been put forward by Hering and, in recent years, much work has been done by W. D. Wright and others. The theories are useful, but not yet believed implicitly. A satisfactory explanation has yet to be evolved.

Despite the lack of a full explanation of three-colour additive mixing, the fact that it is possible remains, and it is widely used in the specification and measurement of colour. Additive colour mixing may be demonstrated simply by the use of three projection lanterns, one with a red filter over its projection lens, the second with a green filter and the third with a blue. Other colours (provided they are different from one another) can be used, but red, green and blue are a good choice.

Suppose these lanterns each projects separate circular patches of light on to a white screen. One patch R will be red, the second G will be green and the third B blue. Let each projector lamp be provided with a variac transformer control of the voltage, so that the amounts of red, green and blue light can be separately varied. The projectors are then set so that the circular patches of light overlap completely. By varying the amounts of the three colours, a very wide range of different colours can be produced, and an accurate match can be made to a separate patch of light X from a fourth projector furnished with a filter different from those concerned with patches *R*, *G* and *B* (Fig. 7.1).

This demonstration forms a crude additive colorimeter. The mixture is additive, because the amounts of reflected (or scattered) light in the three components *R*, *G* and *B* are superimposed upon one another in the total light reaching the eye. The screen has to be white simply because white material is able to scatter light of any colour.

The eye is not able to detect the primary components in a mixture. Two or more light vibrations of different frequencies when mixed give a sensation at the eye of a single frequency. This contrasts with the human sense of hearing, in which two sounds of different frequencies can be distinguished individually at the same time.

7.3 Tristimulus Additive Colour Matching

To render the simple experiment described in Section 7.2 more precise and so form a basis of quantitative colorimetry, the generation of pure spectral colours is preferable to the use of filters. Three primaries in the form of monochromatic radiations at wavelengths 6,500 Å (red), 5,300 Å (green) and 4,250 Å (violet) produced by a prism or grating monochromator may be used. The amount of each primary hue required to generate a particular colour is known as the *tristimulus value*.

In practice it is found that, however judicious the choice of the three primaries, it is not possible to generate all possible chromaticities, though a very wide range can be produced by the three primary monochromatic radiations specified. For example, it is not possible to obtain a match by such three-colour addition of saturated blue-green.

There is, however, a solution to this problem. If the light *X* to be matched by the addition of the given primaries *R*, *G* and *B* (or *V*, for violet) is outside the range producible by these primaries, a match *can* be obtained if the correct amount of light from one of the primaries is *added to X*, thus *R*, *G* or *B* is added to *X*. This corresponds to *subtracting* light from the match: the tristimulus value of the subtracted primary is then negative.

The selection of the particular red, green and blue primaries in additive mixing is not the only choice but the one which allows a wide range of colours to be matched with a minimal use of negative primaries.

An interesting illustration of colorimetry using the primary monochromatic radiations at 6,500 Å, 5,300 Å and 4,250 Å is the determination of the tristimulus values needed to produce pure

spectral hues in various parts of the visible spectrum. In the three
graphs of Fig. 7.2 are shown the number of lumens in the luminous
flux at the wavelengths 6,500 Å, 5,300 Å and 4,250 Å required to
match 1 W of radiant flux at the various wavelengths between

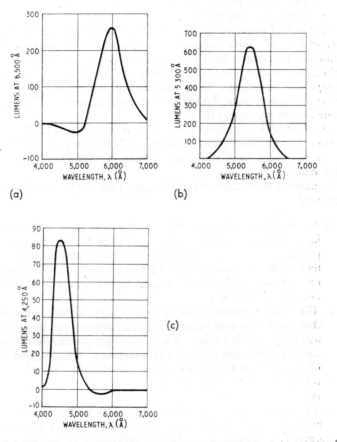

Fig. 7.2. *Matching pure spectral lines by the use of primaries: (a) at 6,500 Å;*
(b) at 5,300 Å; (c) at 4,250 Å. Tristimulus values in lumens to match 1 W
of monochromatic radiation of wavelength λ

4,000 Å and 7,000 Å marked out on the abscissae. For example,
the tristimulus values to obtain a match to 1 W of monochromatic
radiation at a wavelength of 5,000 Å are, approximately, − 20 lm
at primary 6,500 Å [Fig. 7.2(a)], 264 lm at primary 5,300 Å [Fig.
7.2(b)] and 12 lm at 4,250 Å [Fig. 7.2(c)].

7.4 The C.I.E. System in Colour Measurement

The use of actual primary colours necessitates the use of negative tristimulus values in obtaining matches to some of the chromaticities encountered in the very wide range possible. This is indicated by the negative values in the graphs of Fig. 7.2, which represent an excellent choice of primaries.

This use of negative values is undesirable in any mathematical formulation of colour matches. It can be avoided if three specified component primary lights are chosen having certain tristimulus values at various wavelengths. This can be done theoretically, though not practically. Thus imaginary primaries may be chosen for convenience, even though no conceivable sources of light are available for producing them.

The International Commission of Illumination (C.I.E., from the French 'Commission Internationale de l'Eclairage') agreed in 1931 to express all colour mixture data in terms of three specified component lights.

In making their recommendation, the following principles were observed:

1. To eliminate the effect of colour vision variation amongst human beings (which is significant even for the majority of people with 'normal' three-colour vision) and to avoid the inevitable subjective nature of colour matching, a standard observer was arrived at by averaging the responses of a large number of observers.
2. The three standard primary components chosen were such that the tristimulus values of all real colours are positive. In avoiding negative values it was necessary to choose *reference stimuli*, which are not real but 'imaginary' colours. The plots of these tristimulus values against wavelength curves for these reference stimuli (Fig. 7.3) are curves x, y and z, nominally red, green and blue.
3. The curve y (green stimulus curve) was plotted so as to be similar to the relative luminous efficiency against wavelength curve for the human eye (Fig. 6.5 of Volume 1). The maximum tristimulus value at wavelength 5,550 Å was therefore chosen to be unity. This is convenient because it ensures that the luminance of the green (curve y) primary is the same as that of the mixture, provided that it is also arranged for the luminance of the red (curve x) and blue (curve z) primaries to be zero.
4. The areas under each of the curves x, y and z are made equal. This necessitates a choice of the tristimulus values for curves x and z to agree with those selected in accordance with the

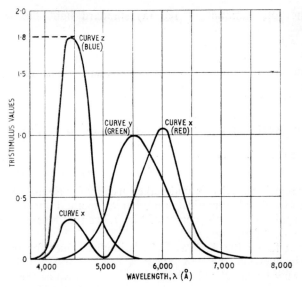

Fig. 7.3. The C.I.E. standards for colour mixing

criteria given for curve y in the paragraph above. As the
tristimulus values depend on the response of the eye at a given
wavelength times the energy radiated per second (radiant
energy emitted by the source per unit time, specified in watts),
the curves x, y and z need to be equal-energy curves; this
means that the radiant flux is the same in each and every
wavelength interval.

The symbols $\bar{x}$, $\bar{y}$ and $\bar{z}$ are used for the ordinates of each curve,
x, y and z respectively. The values of $\bar{x}$, $\bar{y}$ and $\bar{z}$ at any particular
wavelength are thus the tristimulus values of a spectral colour of
that wavelength. For example, the tristimulus values of light of
wavelength 5,000 Å are $\bar{x} = 0.0049$, $\bar{y} = 0.3320$ and $\bar{z} = 0.2720$
(these values can be seen approximately in Fig. 7.3).

Consider the C.I.E. specification of a source of light which, in
general, will not be monochromatic. This source will have a certain
spectral distribution: a radiant flux in a small wavelength interval
λ to $\lambda + d\lambda$ of $f(\lambda)\, d\lambda$, where there is a spectrophotometrically
determined graph of $f(\lambda)$ against λ. Let the tristimulus values
required for the standard C.I.E. primaries x, y, z to match the
spectral distribution of this source be X, Y and Z respectively.

As the ordinates of the curves on the tristimulus graph represent
the amount of the standard C.I.E. components required to match
unit radiant flux at each wavelength:

The total amount of red (x) standard light flux $= X =$
$\int_0^\infty \bar{x} f(\lambda) \, d\lambda$;

The total amount of green (y) standard light flux $= Y =$
$\int_0^\infty \bar{y} f(\lambda) \, d\lambda$;

The total amount of blue (z) standard light flux $= Z =$
$\int_0^\infty \bar{z} f(\lambda) \, d\lambda$.

The integration needed is undertaken usually for about 30 values of $f(\lambda)$. Graphical, numerical or mechanical methods are necessary, as $f(\lambda)$ against λ and the curves of Fig. 7.3 cannot be expressed as mathematical functions.

Having found the X, Y and Z tristimulus values for the light source in question, the *chromaticity values* x, y and z of the same source may be calculated. These values are known as the *trichromatic coefficients*. They provide a method of specifying colour independently of intensity because they are defined as:

$$x = \frac{X}{X+Y+Z}$$

$$y = \frac{Y}{X+Y+Z}$$

$$z = \frac{Z}{X+Y+Z}$$

These values could be represented on a three-dimensional diagram. However, $x+y+z = (X+Y+Z)/(X+Y+Z) = 1$, so two quantities are sufficient to define a colour. Hence, any colour may be represented on a two-dimensional coordinate system. If the same computation is undertaken for monochromatic sources, a curve called a *spectrum locus* on the *chromaticity* diagram is obtained (Fig. 7.4).

Reference is often made to 'white' light. This needs precise definition, as a wide range of sources from a tungsten filament lamp to the Sun are roughly said to produce white light. White is conveniently defined as the colour of a source emitting a continuous equal spectrum throughout the visible region: i.e. throughout the visible spectrum, the radiant flux (radiant energy emitted by the source in unit time, specified in watts) is the same in each and every wavelength interval. The radiation from the Sun forms a reasonable approximation to an equal-energy spectrum.

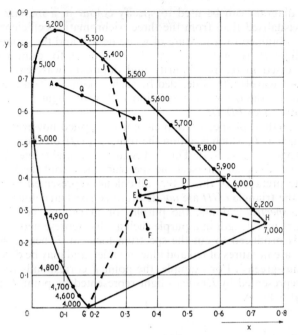

Fig. 7.4. The spectrum locus on a chromaticity diagram

If equal radiant fluxes of the primary red, green and blue lights are additively mixed, white light is generated. In the chromaticity diagram (Fig. 7.4), the values of x, y and z must therefore all be equal to 0·33, so white is represented on the diagram by point E, where $x = y = 0·33$.

The trichromatic coefficients for any colour other than mono-chromatic light lie within the spectrum locus on the chromaticity diagram. Thus, whereas monochromatic light of wavelength 5,000 Å has trichromatic coefficients of $x = 0·0082$, $y = 0·5384$ and $z = 1 - x - y = 0·4534$ and is on the spectrum locus, point E for white light (almost the same as sunlight) and point C for average daylight are inside the locus.

Let any two colours be represented by points A and B on the chromaticity diagram. Suppose these colours are mixed additively. The point representing the chromaticity of the mixture will then lie at Q on the straight line connecting A and B. The position of Q on this line will depend on the sum of the tristimulus values (not the coefficients) for each of the components A and B, which is decided by their colours and their relative amounts. If this sum is l_A for A and l_B for B, the point Q will be at a distance p from A and q from B, where $p\, l_A = q\, l_B$.

The diagram can be used to specify colour in a manner more easily visualised than from the three trichromatic coefficients. All colours obtained by a mixture of white light E and the monochromatic light P are on the line PE. The colour D, for example, can be expressed in terms of purity and dominant wavelength. The dominant wavelength is decided by such a point as P on the spectrum locus; the degree of saturation with white light by the ratio of the distances PD/DE.

This method of specification cannot be applied however to any point such as F, which is within the triangle EGH on the chromaticity diagram (Fig. 7.4). This is because a straight line from E through F does *not* intersect the spectrum locus, but the line GH. The interpretation of this is that all colours represented by points within the triangle EGH are *not* desaturated spectral colours—they are *non-spectral* colours, the purples or magentas. To find the dominant wavelength in a purple such as that represented by point F, FE is produced to cut the spectrum locus at J, near 5,400 Å. Purples are mixtures of red and blue or violet, and may be described as 'minus-greens'. For example, the point F corresponds to white light (represented by E) *minus* light represented by point J, in the green at 5,400 Å.

7.5 Reflection and Scatter of Light

So far the discussion of colour has been concerned with sources of light. Greater interest in practice is attached to the colour of surfaces illuminated by a source of light. This colour will depend on the nature of the illuminating source, as everyone will know who has seen a friend by tungsten lamp and then by sodium street lamp lighting.

It is clearly essential to standardise the luminous source by which the colour of a surface is perceived. The C.I.E. recommend three standards. These are provided by incandescent tungsten filament lamps furnished with a suitable colour filter, preferably in the form of a specified absorbing solution. The standards give a close approximation to the distribution of energy in the spectrum from a black-body. Referring to Fig. 7.4, they are A at 2,848°K (the incandescent tungsten lamp used for general illumination purposes is thereby simulated), B at 4,800°K and C at 6,500°K (an approximate simulation of average daylight). For B and C, the reddish component of tungsten lamp radiation has to be absorbed by the use of blue filters, which absorb the complementary red.

Measurement of surface colour with a standard source of illumination is then undertaken and specified in the same way as for actual luminous sources.

7.6 Subtractive Colour Mixing

In additive colour mixing, there is no light initially, and then selected amounts of the primary colours red, green and blue are added; in the subtractive colour mixing, light of all wavelengths is usual at the beginning (the frequent case being white light), and chosen amounts of red, green and blue are subtracted from the white.

If a red filter is placed over a sheet of illuminated white paper, the red light enters the eye because the filter has subtracted from

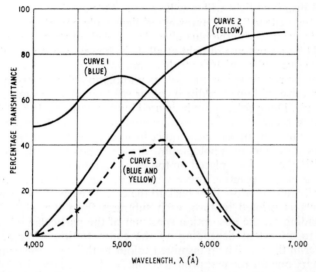

Fig. 7.5. Spectral transmittance curves: curve 1 is for blue filter, curve 2 is for yellow filter, and curve 3 is for blue plus yellow filters

the white the complementary colour to red – thus it has absorbed the blue.

Corresponding to the additive primaries red, green and blue, the subtractive primary colours will be the complementary ones to these three: *minus-red*, *minus-green* and *minus-blue*, which are blue-green (cyan), magenta and yellow respectively.

Additive mixing is concerned essentially with the addition of colour lights; subtractive mixing involves the use of absorbing filters, dye-stuffs and pigments.

An experiment in subtractive colour mixing comparable with that described on additive mixing in Section 7.2 utilises only one projection lantern instead of three. Suppose a blue filter *B* is placed over the projector lens. The colour of the light transmitted will be blue and will have a spectral distribution decided by transmittance against wavelength (curve 1 of Fig. 7.5). This colour is a consequence of the components of the 'white' light from the projector which have been absorbed by the filter: the dye-stuff in the gelatine filter subtracts the complementary colour minus-blue (or yellow). If a second filter Y which transmits yellow light with a distribution represented by curve 2 of Fig. 7.5 is placed over the first, so the transmitted light now passes through B and Y, the spectral distribution in this transmitted light will be decided by multiplying together the ordinate in the two transmittance curves. The result is a spectral transmittance shown by curve 3 of Fig. 7.5; the transmitted light will now be green.

If the yellow filter Y transmitted light truly complementary to that transmitted by the blue filter B, the result of the two together would be no passage of light at all. It is, however, not possible to obtain dye-stuffs which are truly complementary in this way.

Colour reproduction and colour photographic processes are all subtractive, although additive colour photographic processes (for example, Dufaycolor) have been used but are now obsolete. Colour printing processes utilise three coloured inks in which the colours are printed on top of one another in succession. Colour transparencies familiar in photography are three-colour with colour-sensitised emulsions placed on top of one another.

In a colour printing process on white paper, the clean paper initially reflects white light back to the eye. As each of the primary colours is printed in turn, each subtracts from the white light depending on the absorption spectrum of the particular ink used and to an extent depending on the concentration of colouring matter in the ink. The transmitted colour to the eye is the complementary one for the first printed colour, and is then decided by the products of the transmittances as the second and third colours are printed on top.

In practice, colouring materials and dyes used in colour printing and in photography cannot be produced with absorptions of satisfactory distribution in the spectrum. Ideally, sharp cut-off curves, such as that shown in Fig. 7.6(a) for a filter which transmits red, are needed; however, in practice, a curve such as Fig. 7.6(b) is obtainable. Consequently, colour printing methods are unable to reproduce good 'blacks', so four-colour printing methods are often used, the fourth ink being black. Likewise, three-colour photographic processes, though they give aesthetically pleasing results, do not reproduce accurately the colours in nature. Indeed, though much more versatile and convenient, the present-day subtractive methods are not so accurate in this respect as the older additive procedures at their best; the subtractive process in general

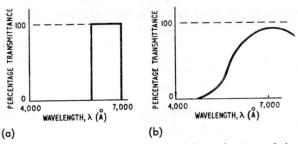

*Fig. 7.6. Spectral transmittance curves for a red dye with minus-red absorption:
(a) ideal curve; (b) actual curve*

is not capable of as good colour mixing as the additive ones, because the absorption bands of various pigments overlap to some
extent.

Colour reproductions of paintings vary greatly in quality. The
cheaper ones utilise four-colour printing: the subtractive primaries
plus black. More expensive methods utilise a greater number of
colours in the attempt to achieve verisimilitude.

7.7 The Measurement of Colour: Colorimeters

A number of instruments termed additive trichromatic colorimeters
function, as their name implies, by varying the amounts of three
component colours necessary to produce a colour match. The Ives
instrument uses filters to obtain the three components, and the
amounts of each are varied by the use of diaphragms of variable
width.

Wright described, in 1929, a colorimeter for matching any
spectral colour against three primary hues at wavelengths of 6,500
Å (red), 5,300 Å (green) and 4,600 Å (blue). The required three
beams of light of the primary hues were produced at selected
positions in a continuous spectrum. This spectrum was obtained
by dispersion of white light incident normally upon a pair of 60°
prisms in series. Within the resulting spectrum were placed, at
judicious positions, three small right-angled prisms; these returned
the three light beams of the primary wavelengths required back
to two further 60° prisms, which neutralised the dispersion in the
beams to give a single emergent beam brought by further prisms
to one-half of a field of view in an eyepiece. To enable the amount
of light in each of these three primary beams (before recombina-
tion) to be varied, a neutral wedge was placed in each of them.
The optical density of each wedge was varied depending on its
position (regulated by a drum-drive) in the beam.

The separate beam of light of a spectral colour to be matched against the mixture of primary constituents was arranged to illuminate the neighbouring other half of the eyepiece field of view. To this separate beam could be added, as required, an adjustable amount of a desaturating primary colour—thus providing the negative stimulus values needed to enable any spectral colour to be matched.

The Donaldson colorimeter (described in 1935) depends on a colour-mixing operation utilising an integrating sphere (Fig. 7.7).

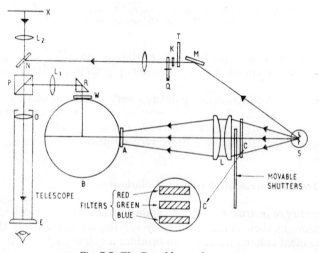

Fig. 7.7. The Donaldson colorimeter

Light from the incandescent filament lamp S passes through three primary colour filters C (red, green and blue), then traverses the condensing lens L to form an image of the light source in the aperture A of the hollow integrating sphere B, which is internally coated with white magnesium oxide. The three primary beams are mixed by diffuse reflection at this inner surface of the sphere. Consequently, light of uniform colour (a mixture of the three primaries) emerges from a separate window W in the sphere. By means of the right-angled prism R and lens L_1, this light illuminates one-half of a Lummer–Brodhun photometer cube P (Section 6.10 of Volume 1).

The other half of the photometer cube is filled with light from the specimen X, which is illuminated by a standard C.I.E. lamp (Section 7.5). The lens L_2 and the objective lens O of the viewing telescope form an image of the specimen at the eyepiece E so that the structure of the specimen is not observed when a colour match is being made. To enable this match to be made, the amounts of the three primary coloured beams reaching the integrating sphere are varied by means of movable shutters over the colour filters C or by the use of adjustable neutral wedges.

As always, for matching highly saturated colours, desaturation of the specimen colour (i.e. provision of a negative primary) is needed. This desaturation component light is provided by light from the source S reflected by the mirror M and the transparent plate N, where any one of the three primary colour filters (identical with those used at C) is inserted. These filters are mounted on a rotatable wheel T, and intensity variation is brought about by a circular neutral wedge Q, with a diffusing glass K within the beam.

In the Eastman subtractive colorimeter, a sample colour is matched by light passing through three optical wedges in succession; the thickness of the wedges in the light beam depends on their adjustable position. The wedges are minus-red, minus-green and minus-blue, forming selectively absorbing material through which light is transmitted to match the sample colour.

Exercise 7

1. In relation to terminology in the science of colour, give definitions of *hue*, *saturation*, *luminance* and *chromaticity*.
   Explain with the aid of simple diagrams what is meant by: (a) additive colour mixing, and (b) subtractive colour mixing.

2. Write an account of the tristimulus values used in additive colour matching and explain how negative tristimulus values may arise.

3. Explain the physical reasons for the reddish colour appearance of the following: (a) a piece of iron at a temperature of about 900°C, (b) a red dyestuff; (c) the red region of a spectrum produced from white light by a prism; (d) the Sun when near the horizon on a clear day; (e) a discharge in neon gas; (f) the markings of the wings of certain butterflies.

4. Write an essay on the C.I.E. system in colour measurement. The X, Y and Z tristimulus values for a source of light are 20 lm, 30 lm and 50 lm respectively. What are the trichromatic coefficients of this source?

5. Describe in detail one form of trichromatic colorimeter and explain how it is used to determine a colour match for a coloured object which is illuminated by a standard C.I.E. lamp.

CHAPTER 8

The Microscope

8.1 Introduction

The principles of the compound microscope have been described in Volume 1. The limit of resolution (Equation 12.7 of Volume 1) is given by

$$h = \frac{0 \cdot 61 \lambda}{n \sin U} \tag{8.1}$$

where h is the least separation between object points which can give rise to images distinguishable as separate in the field of view, n is the refractive index of the medium in which the object is immersed, U is the semi-angle at the vertex of the cone of rays diverging from the object to reach the objective lens, and λ is the wavelength of the radiation.

In arriving at Equation 8.1, it is assumed that the object is self-luminous and that points on it to be distinguished emit incoherent radiation. Though this is true for a telescope being used to view stars, for example, it is usually untrue for a microscope because the object is frequently in the form of a specimen sandwiched between a microscope slide and a cover glass. The illumination is from a lamp with a sub-stage condenser, which focuses light from the lamp at the plane of the object. In such circumstances, the limit of resolution is not usually decided by Equation 8.1 but by a modified equation

$$h = \frac{0 \cdot 5 \lambda}{n \sin U} \tag{8.2}$$

which arises from the Abbe theory of the microscope. Before this theory is dealt with, it is necessary to describe the sub-stage condenser systems employed.

8.2 Sub-stage Condenser Lenses

The purpose of a sub-stage condenser is to provide brilliant illumination at a selected small area of the microscope slide in order
that the field of view in the microscope eyepiece is sufficiently
bright when high magnification is used.

Two methods are used commonly: *critical illumination* and
Köhler illumination. In the former, the source of light S [Fig. 8.1(a)]
is an opal lamp or an illuminated diffusing screen. An image of S

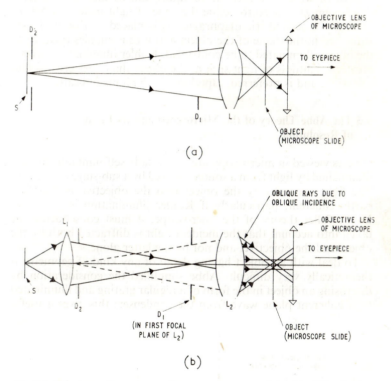

Fig. 8.1. *Sub-stage microscope condenser arrangements: (a) critical illumination;*
(b) Köhler illumination

is formed by the sub-stage condenser lens L at the object (i.e. a
small brilliant patch of light is formed in the plane of the microscope slide). Two iris diaphragms are usually incorporated: D_1 to
vary the aperture of the sub-stage condenser lens; and D_2 to
control the area of the object which is illuminated so that details
of interest in the object can be 'pin-pointed' and light from other

parts of the object can be excluded from the microscope objective lens.

In Köhler illumination [Fig. 8.1(b)], two lenses are used to form the sub-stage condenser. The field lens L_1 forms an image of the source S (often a lamp filament) in the first focal plane of the condenser lens L_2. The light emerging from L_2 is consequently collimated. These emergent collimated beams will be at angles to the axis dependent upon the angles of the incident light from L_1. The object is placed at the intersection of these emergent collimated beams, of which the extreme obliquity can be altered by an iris diaphragm D_1 placed to define the cone of light incident upon L_2 from L_1. A second iris diaphragm D_2 is placed so that its image is formed in the plane of the object and it thus enables the area of the object illuminated to be controlled. Köhler illumination gives a greater brightness of light spot at the object than does critical illumination, and is preferred, especially for high magnification.

8.3 The Abbe Theory of the Microscope and Its Limit of Resolution

Objects viewed in microscopy are not usually self-luminous but are illuminated by light from a source focused by a sub-stage condenser. The light scattered by the object into the objective is therefore partly coherent, particularly if Köhler illumination is practised. In the fuller theory of the microscope, it must consequently be taken into account that the incident light is diffracted both by the object and the objective, and not by the latter alone.

To deal with an object having detail of any kind of geometry is theoretically very difficult. Abbe simplified the consideration by discussing an object in the form of a regular grating and illuminated by a coherent plane wave from the condenser; this gives a useful

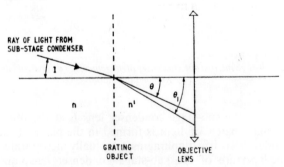

Fig. 8.2. Abbe theory of resolution of a microscope objective for an object in the form of a grating

approximation to several object specimens which have a fairly regular structure. To obtain a specification of the limit of resolution for an object in the form of a grating, Abbe advanced the principle that the microscope objective must be able to collect the direct beam and at least one of the beams in the first order of diffraction.

Suppose the sub-stage condenser produces at the grating object a beam incident at angle I in a medium of refractive index n, and that after diffraction by the grating the light emerges at an angle θ_1 in the first order of diffraction into a medium of refractive index n' (Fig. 8.2). If e is the separation between neighbouring slit centres in the grating, it follows from the well-known equation for a diffraction grating (Equation 11.20 of Volume 1) that, in the first order for light of wavelength λ,

$$e(n' \sin \theta_1 - n \sin I) = \lambda \qquad (8.3)$$

For the direct beam, Snell's law of refraction applies, so

$$n' \sin \theta = n \sin I \qquad (8.4)$$

where θ is the angle at which the undiffracted light emerges from the grating.

Applying the Abbe principle that the direct beam and one of the first order diffracted beams from the object must be able to enter the objective lens, it is clear that the limit of resolution occurs when the direct beam enters the objective lens at one extremity of its diameter and the first order beam enters this lens at the other extremity. Consequently,

$$\theta = -\theta_1 \qquad (8.5)$$

and θ must also equal U, the semi-angle at the vertex of the cone of rays entering the objective.

From Equations 8.3 and 8.4,

$$e(n' \sin \theta_1 - n' \sin \theta) = \lambda$$

Applying Equation 8.5,

$$2en' \sin \theta = 2en' \sin U = \lambda$$

Therefore

$$e = \frac{0{\cdot}5\lambda}{n' \sin U} \qquad (8.6)$$

where $n' \sin U$ is the numerical aperture (N.A.) of the microscope objective, and e is the smallest separation between adjacent lines in the grating which can be discerned.

Equation 8.6 is the Abbe equation for the limit of resolution of a microscope; it is preferred to Equation 8.1 if the object viewed is not self-luminous but is illuminated by a sub-stage condenser lens. As the angle θ can be reduced by varying the obliquity of the incident light from the sub-stage condenser on to the object, it follows that the numerical aperture of this condenser also decides the limit of resolution unless it is large enough to ensure that the limit to θ is the angle U set by the microscope objective alone.

8.4 Amplitude and Phase Objects

In microscopy, the object viewed often has variations of optical density and colour. Such an object is called an *amplitude object*. Alternatively, sometimes the object is transparent and so does not exhibit density and colour variations, but has an optical thickness which varies from point to point over its surface. Such a *phase object* will introduce phase changes in the light that traverses it, but no optical density or colour variations. The eye is incapable of discerning phase changes, though it is obviously able to respond to any density or colour variations.

In normal use, therefore, the microscope is unable to examine structural changes in phase objects. As such changes are often of importance, the techniques of dark-ground illumination and also phase-contrast microscopy have been introduced to enable them to be discerned.

8.5 Dark-ground Illumination and Phase Contrast

The basic idea involved in both dark-ground illumination and phase-contrast techniques is illustrated by Fig. 8.3. Let A, B and C be three points out of the several thousands that may be involved in a transparent phase object. The light from the sub-stage condenser incident on the object will have its electric vector in a given direction at a given point such as A at a given time. On traversing the phase object at A, this electric vector will suffer a phase change depending on the optical path difference through the object at A. In Fig. 8.3, suppose the vector AX represents the amplitude and phase of the electric vector in the light emerging at A. At the same instant of time, the corresponding electric vectors at B and C are represented by BY and CZ. The vectors will all have the same length if the object is uniformly illuminated and is uniformly transparent, but their angles of setting will be different because of the different optical thicknesses of the object at points A, B and C. The eye is unable to discern any differences between A, B and C.

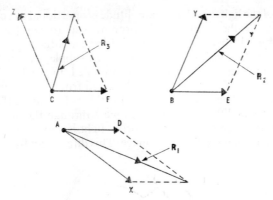

Fig. 8.3. Principle involved in converting a phase object into an amplitude object

Suppose that, by some means, light of constant amplitude and phase at a given time is added to the existing light at each of the points A, B and C. For convenience, let the vectors representing these added disturbances be horizontal in Fig. 8.3 and represented by the lines AD, BE and CF, all of equal lengths. The resultant vectors R_1, R_2 and R_3 at A, B and C respectively are now clearly of different magnitudes, and the corresponding intensities I_1, I_2 and I_3 are also different. These different intensities *can* be discerned by the eye, so variations in the optical thickness of the phase object are effectively displayed.

This concept can be expressed simply in mathematical form on the premise that the light at time t from such a point as A may be expressed as $a \sin \omega t$, where a is the amplitude of its electric vector and the light is monochromatic of frequency $\omega/2\pi$. At point B, the expression concerned will be $a \sin (\omega t + \alpha)$, where α is the phase angle between the electric vectors at A and B. If it is now assumed that light represented by $b \sin (\omega t + \beta)$ is added at A and at B, the resultant effects are determined by the following expressions: at A

$$a \sin \omega t + b \sin (\omega t + \beta)$$

and at B

$$a \sin (\omega t + \alpha) + b \sin (\omega t + \beta)$$

For simplicity, put $a = b = 1$; then at A

$$\sin \omega t + \sin (\omega t + \beta) = 2 \cos \frac{\beta}{2} \sin \left(\omega t + \frac{\beta}{2}\right)$$

and at B

$$\sin (\omega t + \alpha) + \sin (\omega t + \beta) = 2 \cos \frac{\alpha - \beta}{2} \sin \left(\omega t + \frac{\alpha + \beta}{2}\right)$$

Hence at A the light now has an amplitude proportional to cos $(\beta/2)$, whereas at B the amplitude is proportional to cos $[(\alpha-\beta)/2]$: a phase object is therefore converted into an amplitude object.

It remains to consider how the required supplementary light of constant amplitude and phase can be provided. In the dark-ground method, the same disturbance is subtracted from every point such as A, B and C. The usual technique for this is to remove that light which passes undiffracted from the object through the microscope objective; thus the direct or zero order light is subtracted, leaving only diffracted light to form the image. This direct light from a small

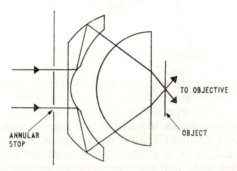

Fig. 8.4. Sub-stage condenser for dark-ground illumination

region of the illuminated object is of constant, or nearly constant, amplitude and phase at a given time. It can be removed by placing a stop in the sub-stage condenser aperture (or in the microscope objective), or by employing other means so that no direct light traverses the objective (Fig. 8.4). The image in the field of view of the object is hence formed by light in the first and higher orders of diffraction, and the object appears bright against a dark background.

8.6 Phase-contrast Microscopy

In phase-contrast techniques, a phase shift is introduced in part of the light at each point in the field of view. The direct (zero order) light is changed in phase relative to the diffracted light and not subtracted from the image-forming light as in dark-ground illumination. The phase-contrast microscope was introduced in 1935 by Zernike. A simplified version of part of his description is of interest.

In Fig. 8.5, let the amplitudes at a given time of the electric vectors in the light in the image plane due to points A, B and C in a phase object be OA, OB and OC respectively; these are conveniently drawn from a common origin O and of equal length, so A, B and C are on the circumference of a circle of which O is the centre.

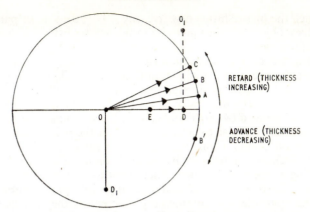

Fig. 8.5. The principle of phase contrast

For convenience, it is assumed that the optical thickness (and so the phase retardation) increases progressively from A to B to C. Suppose the vector OD represents the contribution which the direct (undiffracted) light makes at each point in the image plane. In phase contrast, the phase of this direct light is shifted relative to that of the diffracted light. Let this shift be an advance through 90°. Light of the same amplitude as the direct light, but leading it in phase by 90°, will be represented in the diagram by the vector OD_1 of the same length as OD.

Consider the effect of shifting through $+90°$ the direct part of the light which contributes to the image at point A. This is equivalent to removing from the light that due to direct illumination and substituting in its place the same amount of light advanced in phase by 90°. The removal of the direct light corresponds to subtracting the vector OD (which is equivalent to moving the origin from O to D), so that at A the effect would be represented by a vector DA. The substitution of the light advanced by 90° would then be equivalent to moving the point A downwards by the distance OD_1: but this is equivalent to leaving A where it is and instead shifting the origin from D to O_1, a vertical distance OD_1 above D in the diagram.

It follows that the resultant amplitudes and settings of the electric vectors at the given time in the light disturbances in the image plane due to points A, B and C when the positive 90° phase shift has been introduced are represented by vectors O_1A, O_1B and O_1C respectively. As the optical thickness of the phase object increases progressively from A to B to C, the amplitude of the light in the image plane decreases from O_1A to O_1B to O_1C. The thicker parts of the phase object therefore give rise to the smaller intensities in *positive phase contrast* (where the phase shift introduced is positive), which is generally convenient. It is also possible to use negative phase contrast, in which the phase shift is negative, say $-90°$; the thicker parts of the phase object will then give rise to the greater light intensities in the field of view.

In Fig. 8.5, dark-ground illumination would simply correspond to the transference of the origin from O to D. This illustrates a difficulty with dark-ground illumination, in that points placed symmetrically about OD (such as B and B') would give equal resultant intensities decided by $(DB)^2$ and $(DB')^2$. Dark-ground illumination is consequently unable to determine whether the phase is advanced by a certain amount owing to a decrease in thickness of the phase-object specimen, or retarded by the same amount owing to a corresponding increase in thickness. Phase-contrast, on the other hand, is able to do so. For points B and B', with positive phase-contrast of $90°$, the intensities are considerably different as they are decided by $(O_1B)^2$ and $(O_1B')^2$. Again, objects are frequently of mixed amplitude and phase types. For a point on such an object where the absorption is significant, the origin will not be D in dark-ground illumination but E, for example. Intensities observed in the field of view may now be due to amplitude diminution either because of absorption or because of phase. With dark-ground methods, in some instances the effects of absorption cannot be distinguished from the effects of optical thickness. This second difficulty also exists with phase-contrast methods if the phase is $\pm 90°$, but it can be overcome if a shift of phase angle rather less than $90°$ is used.

To introduce the necessary phase difference between the direct illumination (zero order) and the first and higher orders, a *phase plate* is used. A common arrangement is to place an annular aperture in the first focal plane of the sub-stage condenser lens with Köhler illumination, and the phase plate in the second focal plane of the microscope objective lens (Fig. 8.6). This phase plate consists of a disc of glass in which is cut an annular depression which is an exact counterpart of the annular aperture. The direct light through the annular aperture then traverses the annulus of the phase plate and suffers there a smaller path retardation than the remaining

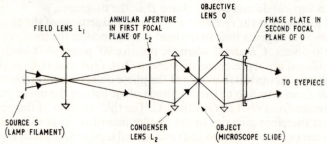

Fig. 8.6. Annular aperture and phase plate in a phase-contrast microscope

diffracted light. The phase of the direct light is therefore not retarded so much as (or rather it is advanced with respect to) the diffracted light, giving a positive phase-contrast set-up. The phase advance
introduced by the phase plate is easily seen to be $(2\pi/\lambda)(n-1)t$,
where n is the refractive index of the glass of the phase plate of
thickness t, and λ is the wavelength of the light concerned.

8.7 Interference Microscopes

Various types of interference microscope have been developed,
but only one model is described in outline here. The light is divided
by some form of beam-splitter so as to traverse two paths, one of
which is modified by the specimen. When the two optical paths
differ by $p\lambda/2$, where p is an integer and λ is the wavelength of the
monochromatic light used, the field of view in the microscope
brought about by the subsequently reunited beams will be crossed
by interference fringes of distribution and spacing related to the
structure of the specimen being viewed. Fig. 8.7 shows the optical

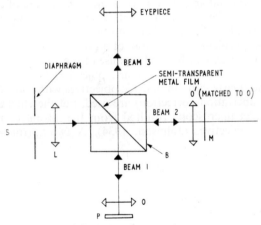

Fig. 8.7. *An interference microscope*

paths in an interference microscope used to study surface structure by
reflection. Light from the monochromatic source S is collimated by
the lens L and divided by the beam-splitter B (which consists of
a glass cube with a partially aluminised diagonal plane, the two
halves of the cube being cemented together). Beam 1 is incident
upon and reflected back by the specimen P after traversing the
microscope objective O, whereas the other beam 2 travels along the
perpendicular path to the compensating objective O' and is reflected

back by the plane mirror M. The two reflected beams, one of which is modified by the surface of the specimen, are reunited to interfere along the direction of beam 3. Beam 3 reaches the eyepiece in the field of view, in which the specimen surface topography is displayed as an interference pattern. The dark or bright lines in this pattern will be at positions corresponding to path differences of $\lambda/2$ and will correspond to contour lines in the surface of the specimen at height intervals of $\lambda/2$.

8.8 The Ultra-violet Microscope

If ultra-violet radiation of wavelength, say, 2,500 Å is used instead of visible light at 5,000 Å, then h in Equation 8.1 or Equation 8.2 will be halved for the same numerical aperture $n \sin U$. The resolving power is therefore doubled. This advantage is not so significant in practice as the fact that many substances, particularly biological specimens such as the important nucleic acids, exhibit strong absorption in the ultra-violet between 2,400 Å and 4,000 Å although they are virtually transparent to visible light. Furthermore, significant reflection and absorption phenomena which are of considerable interest in the examination of structure occur in the ultra-violet in several specimens other than biological ones.

The main problem in the design of an ultra-violet microscope is that glass optics cannot be used because of the absorption of ultra-violet radiation in glass. Fused quartz objectives (and also quartz–fluoride and quartz–lithium fluoride objectives with some degree of chromatic aberration correction) are used, but the chief advances in ultra-violet microscopy resulted from the advent of reflecting microscope objectives (Johnson, 1934). A two-mirror reflecting

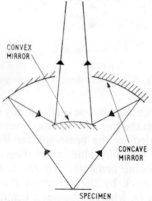

Fig. 8.8. A two-mirror reflecting microscope objective

microscope objective (Fig. 8.8) consists of a concave mirror with a central aperture concentric with a smaller convex mirror. Such a system can be designed to be free of spherical aberration and coma. The numerical aperture is limited in this design to about 0·5 because of the obstruction due to the small convex mirror. Burch designed a reflecting objective in which the concave mirror was aspherical, and this allowed the numerical aperture to be increased to 0·65 or more. To obtain significantly larger numerical apertures, such reflector systems are used in conjunction with a quartz–fluorite front-immersion lens.

The source of ultra-violet radiation used is best substantially monochromatic, so must produce well-spaced spectrum lines. Both the spark discharge between cadmium electrodes and the medium-pressure quartz-enveloped mercury lamp are employed. Filters are sometimes used to select the particular ultra-violet spectrum line of interest. These are either liquid filters in quartz parallel-sided containers or interference filters.

Some instruments incorporate an eyepiece which is either a re-fracting type made from fused quartz or a reflecting design; in other designs, an eyepiece is not used. To record the image, it may be focused at a fluorescent screen, but as the brilliance is usually inadequate, the common practice is to record the image on a pho-tographic film or plate.

Exercise 8

1. Write an account of the Abbe theory of the limit of resolution of a micro-scope in which the object is in the form of a grating illuminated by mono-chromatic light.

   Calculate the minimum separation that could be observed between parallel lines in such a grating by a microscope with a numerical aperture of 0·7 if light of wavelength 5,000 Å were employed.

2. Explain the physical principles involved in the use in microscopy of: (a) dark-ground illumination, and (b) phase contrast. What are the advan-tages of method (b) over method (a)?

   Draw a ray-path diagram showing clearly the positions in a phase-contrast microscope with Köhler illumination of the annular aperture and the com-plementary phase plate.

3. Two of the most important instruments in science are the telescope and the microscope. Write an account of *one* of these describing (i) its basic design and the features necessary to give optimum performance and (ii) how it has been developed to cover wide wavelength ranges.   (L.P.)

4. Describe, with an outline diagram, an interference microscope suitable for examining by reflection the surface topography of a metallic specimen.

5. What are the main reasons for the development of ultra-violet microscopes? Describe in outline a typical reflecting objective for an ultraviolet microscope and outline briefly the other main features of the design of such an instrument.

6. Calculate the limit of resolution in observing self-luminous objects of the following microscopes: (a) an instrument with an objective of numerical aperture 0·85 utilising light of wavelength 4,500 Å; (b) an ultra-violet microscope with a reflecting objective of numerical aperture 0·65 where the ultra-violet radiation has a wavelength of 2,400 Å; and (c) an electron microscope with a numerical aperture of 0·01 in which the electrons are accelerated through a potential difference of 50 kV.

CHAPTER 9

Coherence, Optical Masers and Holography

9.1 The Coherence of Electromagnetic Radiation

From the point of view of coherence, a source of electromagnetic radiation should, ideally, give rise to infinitely long, continuous wavetrains which are in phase and where the frequency and amplitude of the vibrations are constant at all points in the source. Such a source has not been developed; the nearest approach is the optical maser (laser), which still falls considerably short of the ideal.

Three chief types of incoherence are conveniently classified. The first results from the finite size of the source and is called *spatial incoherence*. Spatial incoherence is due to the fact that the wavefront does not emanate from an area of the source in which all points are in phase. A perfectly spatially coherent beam of radiation would thus be one in which all points in the wavefront were in phase. The second type of incoherence is known as *temporal incoherence* and results from the finite lengths of pulses of radiation produced by the source; in order to separate temporal incoherence from spatial incoherence as a phenomenon, a very small area of the source is specified. The third type is *amplitude and frequency incoherence*, which arises from perturbations in the source conditions.

9.2 Temporal Incoherence

To illustrate the effects of temporal incoherence, consider as an example Lloyd's single-mirror experiment on interference, already described in Section 8.5 of Volume 1. The two rays SP and SQP (Fig. 9.1) interfere at P to give rise to a fringe system of the 'cosine-squared' type. The visibility V of these fringes is defined by the equation

$$V = \frac{I_{\max} - I_{\min}}{I_{\max} + I_{\min}}$$

where $I_{\max}$ is the intensity at the centre of a given bright fringe, and $I_{\min}$ is the intensity at the centre of an adjacent dark fringe.

The visibility V will depend on the coherence of the source of light S and may be used as a measure of this coherence for a given path difference $\Delta = SQP - SP$. If it is postulated that the source is

Fig. 9.1. The typical interfering rays in Lloyd's single-mirror experiment

of a very small area in which the vibrations are of constant amplitude and frequency and the intensity distribution corresponds to a Dirac delta-function (see Appendix, page 366), the value of V will give a measure of the temporal coherence of the source. This is obvious in general terms, because the coherence at P depends on the degree of correlation between the electric field vectors due to the wavetrains SP and SQP. If the pulse of radiation from the source is shorter in length than the path difference Δ, the correlation will be zero and no coherence results. Generally, of course, the pulses have varying lengths and the visibility V will only have its maximum value of unity when the path difference Δ is zero because then all pulses give perfect correlation. As the value of the path difference Δ increases for a given length of pulse from the source, the visibility decreases.

9.3 The Relation Between the Spectral Line Width of the Source and the Length of the Radiated Pulse

The energy of the photon emitted by an excited atom or molecule is decided by the energy transition ΔE which an electron undergoes in moving from any energy level E_1 to a lower level E_2, where $E_1 - E_2 = \Delta E$. The frequency of the corresponding radiation is given by

$$\Delta E = h\nu$$

where h is Planck's constant.

The intensity of the spectral line resulting depends on the number of electrons per second which make such transitions. In the quantum-mechanical treatment of atomic structure, it is shown that the electrons do not occupy specific orbits but have a probability of being at a given location decided by $|\Psi|^2$, where $|\Psi|$ is the modulus of the complex amplitude of the wave function at the location in question (Section 2.15). The many electrons per second which make a transition from energy level E_1 to energy level E_2 do not therefore all undergo exactly the same energy change of ΔE, because each of the levels E_1 and E_2 has a certain natural width in accordance with the quantum-mechanical considerations. There is consequently a finite range of frequencies over the region $\pm \Delta \nu$ around a given frequency ν, and a corresponding amplitude of the energy radiated expressible as $f(\nu)\,d\nu$. This decides the natural width of the spectral line from an isolated gas or molecule. Doppler effect (Section 5.8) will cause additional line broadening.

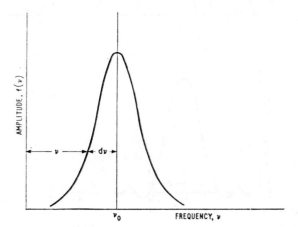

Fig. 9.2. *Curve of amplitude against frequency for light in a spectral line, indicating natural width*

For a source of very limited area, a given spectral line will therefore correspond to a small range of frequencies (Fig. 9.2). At a point such as P in the experiment illustrated by Fig. 9.1, a single pulse will now be a Fourier sum of sinusoidal components, so the amplitude of the electric vector in the radiation at P and at time t will be given by

$$E(t) = \int_{-\infty}^{\infty} f(\nu) \exp\left(2\pi j \nu t\right) d\nu \qquad (9.1)$$

The right-hand side of Equation 9.1 is the Fourier transform (see Appendix, page 362) of $f(v)$, and it must follow also that

$$f(v) = \int_{-\infty}^{\infty} E(t) \exp(-2\pi jvt)\, dt$$

because the spectral amplitude distribution is the Fourier transform of the time-modulated amplitude at the point P. It can now be seen why a *finite* pulse is inevitably radiated in practice, because

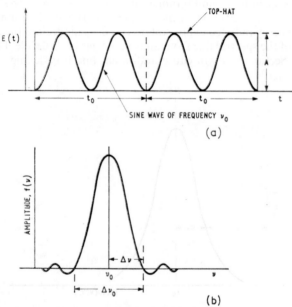

Fig. 9.3. Ideal source: (a) sinusoidal pulse modulated by a 'top-hat' waveform; (b) spectral line distribution

an inverse relationship exists between the half-width of the spectral line amplitude distribution and the amplitude modulation at point P.

The ideal source has a Dirac delta-function profile of which the Fourier transform is a constant giving a continuous sinusoidal monochromatic pulse.

Fig. 9.3(a) shows a simple hypothetical example of such a source where a sinusoidal pulse of frequency v_0 is modulated by a 'top-hat' waveform to give the spectral line amplitude distribution shown in Fig. 9.3(b).

Referring to Fig. 9.3(a),

$$f(v) = \int_{-t_0}^{t_0} E(t) \exp(-2\pi jvt)\, dt$$

$$= \frac{A}{-2\pi jv} \left[\exp(-2\pi jvt) \right]_{-t_0}^{t_0}$$

$$= \frac{A}{-2\pi jv} \left[\exp(-2\pi jvt_0) - \exp(2\pi jvt_0) \right]$$

or

$$f(v) = \frac{A \sin 2\pi vt_0}{2\pi vt_0} = \frac{A \sin \alpha}{\alpha}$$

where A is a constant and $\alpha = 2\pi vt_0$.

The width of the spectral line is proportional to $1/t_0$. As the pulse must begin at $t = 0$, the relationship between the pulse duration and the spectral frequency spread of $\Delta v_0 = 2\Delta v$ at the first zero $\alpha = \pi$ is seen to be

$$t_0 = \frac{1}{\Delta v_0} \tag{9.2}$$

Most spectral line profiles are Gaussian distribution in shape, giving rise to a pulse modulated by a Gaussian amplitude profile. The optical maser may be regarded to a first approximation as having a 'top-hat' modulation with a very broad $(\sin \alpha)/\alpha$ profile, so approximating to the ideal.

9.4 Coherence Time and Coherence Length

An arbitrary definition of coherence time may be referred for simplicity to the ideal situation illustrated by Fig. 9.3. From Equation 9.2, the coherence time t_0 is $1/\Delta v_0$, and the coherence length is defined as

$$l_0 = ct_0 = \frac{c}{\Delta v_0} \tag{9.3}$$

where c is the velocity of light. As $v_0 = c/\lambda_0$, where λ_0 is the corresponding wavelength,

$$\frac{dv_0}{d\lambda_0} = -\frac{c}{\lambda_0^2}$$

Therefore

$$\Delta v_0 = -\frac{c}{\lambda_0^2} \Delta \lambda_0$$

and

$$l_0 = \frac{c}{\Delta v_0} = \frac{\lambda_0^2}{\Delta \lambda_0} \qquad (9.4)$$

Assume that a visible spectroscopic line has this ideal shape—i.e. as in Fig. 9.3(b). A very good optical source of monochromat-light would have a frequency spread Δv_0 of about 10^{10} Hz for a frequency v_0 of 6×10^{14} Hz corresponding to a wavelength of 5,000 Å. The coherence length l_0 would then be given by Equation 9.3 as

$$l_0 = \frac{c}{\Delta v_0} = \frac{3 \times 10^{10}}{10^{10}} = 3 \text{ cm}$$

True coherence for path differences exceeding 3 cm would therefore not be expected for this source.

Optical masers (lasers) vary considerably in the stability of their output. An ideal optical maser line and the corresponding pulse shapes are shown in Fig. 9.4. The same relationship holds as in Equation 9.2, because the profiles concerned are simply interchanged. A continuous gas laser at room temperature will have a short-term value of Δv_0 as small as 10 Hz. The corresponding value of the coherence length l_0 is given by Equation 9.3 to be

$$l_0 = \frac{3 \times 10^{10}}{10} = 3 \times 10^9 \text{ cm}$$

For a pulsed ruby optical maser emitting light of wavelength $\lambda_0 = 6{,}943$ Å, Δv_0 is approximately 5×10^6, so

$$l_0 = \frac{3 \times 10^{10}}{5 \times 10^6} = 3{,}000 \text{ cm}$$

which is still remarkable, though it must be remembered that these calculations are for ideal lines.

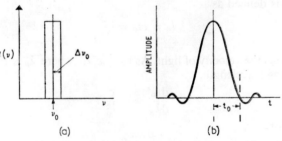

Fig. 9.4. Spectral line from an optical maser: (a) ideal spectral line; (b) corresponding pulse shape

9.5 Light Amplification by the Stimulated Emission of Radiation: the Laser Principle

Let two energy levels E_p and E_q exist in a material, where $E_p > E_q$ and the populations of these levels are N_p and N_q per unit volume of material respectively. If a transition takes place from E_p to E_q, the frequency v of the photon ejected is given by

$$v = \frac{E_p - E_q}{h}$$

where h is Planck's constant.

If this material is in thermal equilibrium at temperature $T°K$, the number of transitions per second from E_p to E_q is decided by Equation 2.69, which gives the rate of decay of the excited state. This number will be

$$AN_p + BU_T(v)N_p - BU_T(v)N_q$$

because $C = B$, $N_e = N_p$ and $N_0 = N_q$; also, the number of transitions is equal to $-dN_e/dt = -dN_p/dt$. Here, A is the Einstein coefficient for spontaneous emission, and B is the Einstein coefficient for absorption. The function $U_T(v)$ is the radiant energy per unit volume at the temperature T.

Each of these emitted photons has an energy hv, so the total radiated energy per second per unit volume of material at the frequency v is given by

$$g(v) = [AN_p + BU_T(v)(N_p - N_q)]hv$$

Equation 2.73 states that

$$\frac{A}{B} = \frac{8\pi h v^3}{c^3}$$

Therefore

$$g(v) = Ahv \left[N_p + \frac{U_T(v)c^3}{8\pi h v^3}(N_p - N_q) \right] \tag{9.5}$$

Now from Equation 2.64 with $g = 1$,

$$\frac{N_p}{N_q} = \exp\left(-\frac{E_p - E_q}{kT}\right) = \exp\left(-\frac{hv}{kT}\right) \tag{9.6}$$

where k is Boltzmann's constant. As shown is Section 2.23, $\exp(-hv/kT)$ is an exceedingly small number at optical frequencies and temperatures of about 300°K. Under normal conditions, therefore, $N_p \ll N_q$ and the right-hand side of Equation 9.5 is negative corresponding to $g(v)$ being negative; consequently, absorption of photons occurs in the material, with the number of spontaneous emissions exceeding greatly the number of stimulated emissions.

If, by some means, the electron populations can be inverted so that $N_p > N_q$ then $g(v)$ becomes positive, as is seen from Equation 9.5. The number of stimulated emissions will then preponderate, and the radiated power output from the material will be greatly increased. This population inversion demands a pumping action leading to optical maser (or laser) action. The term laser arises from the initial letters of 'Light Amplification by the Stimulated Emission of Radiation'. Lasing will be just possible when $N_p = N_q$ so that, from Equation 9.6, $hv = kT$.

Presume that $N_p > N_q$, where N_p and N_q are the populations per unit volume. Let radiation of intensity I be incident on a slab of material of thickness dx and unit cross-sectional area. This intensity I is the energy per unit area per second, and it will be related to the energy density of radiation $U(v)$ by

$$I = U(v)c \qquad (9.7)$$

where c is the velocity of light.

If $N_p > N_q$, Equation 9.5 becomes approximately

$$g(v) = \frac{AU(v)c^3}{8\pi v^2}(N_p - N_q)$$

which, making use of Equation 9.7, gives

$$g(v) = \frac{AIc^2}{8\pi v^2}(N_p - N_q)$$

But $g(v)$ is the radiated energy per unit volume of the material at the frequency v, and so for a thickness dx of unit cross-section, the radiated energy is a $g(v)dx$. This must equal the change of I by dI. Therefore

$$dI = \frac{AIc^2}{8\pi v^2}(N_p - N_q)\,dx$$

so

$$\frac{dI}{I} = \frac{Ac^2}{8\pi v^2}(N_p - N_q)\,dx$$

The intensity I emerging after a path of length x in the material, where the incident intensity is I_0, is therefore given by

$$I = I_0 \exp(\alpha x) \qquad (9.8)$$

where

$$\alpha = \frac{Ac^2}{8\pi v^2}(N_p - N_q) \tag{9.9}$$

Note that Equation 9.8 is comparable with the usual expression $I = I_0 \exp(-\mu x)$ for the absorption of radiation in a material of linear coefficient μ but where this absoprtion coefficient is *negative*. The laser action therefore amplifies the light intensity. For a helium–neon gas laser, typical values of α in Equation 9.8 are given in Table 9.1. In practice Doppler effect tends to reduce this gain.

Table 9.1.

TYPICAL VALUES OF α FOR A HELIUM–NEON GAS LASER

Wavelength (Å)	α per metre
6,328	4,342
11,523	21,710
33,913	1,128,920

9.6 The Laser as an Optical Oscillator

Population inversion is demanded in the laser. If provided, it is seen from the previous section that the laser acts as an amplifier analogous to an electronic amplifier. Pursuing this analogy, the requirements of an oscillator developed from an amplifier are positive feedback and a high Q-factor for sharpness of resonance.

In 1958, Schawlow and Townes suggested that the Fabry–Perot interferometer could be used as an optical oscillator if a suitable gaseous medium was placed between the Fabry–Perot plates in which laser action could be established. The idea is that the beam of light to be amplified in intensity (generated originally by an electron transition between energy levels in a discharge set up in the gas) is partly reflected at one of the Fabry–Perot mirrors to provide the positive feedback and totally reflected at the other mirror. The amplified output light beam emerges through the partly reflecting mirror.

In the simplest example, the Fabry–Perot etalon comprises two small flat mirrors A and B accurately parallel to each other—one at each end of a cylindrical tube 1 m long containing the gas. An arrangement of this kind (Fig. 9.5) can be thought of as a resonant cavity, analogous to a sonic cavity, containing a standing wave system of wavelength λ where

$$\frac{n\lambda}{2} = d$$

n being an integer and d the plate separation.

A fraction of the energy forms the standing wave system, and the remaining fraction is the output from the partly reflecting mirror B in Fig. 9.5. A large number of modes of the same and different wavelengths would be supported, because d is large and an infinite number of reflections are possible. If such a system were

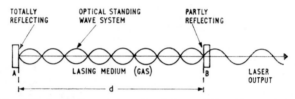

Fig. 9.5. *Optical standing wave system between Fabry–Perot mirrors in the cavity of a gas laser*

used as a laser, much of the energy would be wasted among undesirable modes. The large mirror separation confines the energy to primarily one axial mode; other modes of the same wavelength give energy lost through the sides of the cavity and hence not transmitted through the end mirror B. Such non-axial modes represent a diffraction loss of energy. Axial modes of various wavelengths could be transmitted, but in practice are unlikely to be generated because the wavelengths concerned are decided by the discrete energy levels present in the gaseous medium. As non-axial modes are lost, the resulting axial mode is highly directional. Ideally, it is assumed that over one end mirror, a uniform electric field exists in the radiation at a given time, giving rise to a uniform field at the other end mirror. In practice, diffraction losses occur and the beam spreads slightly from its perfect plane wavefront shape as it travels to and fro between the mirrors. This leads to an electric field distribution which falls off towards the outside of the plates, so the emergent beam diverges slightly.

In the ideal situation, the laser beam emerges from the plate B as a *perfectly coherent* wavefront with a constant electric field amplitude at the exit of this plate. If this plate B is a circular disc of radius a, substantially all the energy lies within the angle $\delta\theta$ (Fig. 9.6) where

$$\delta\theta = \pm\frac{1\cdot22\lambda}{a}$$

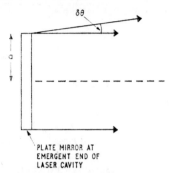

Fig. 9.6. Laser light which is emerging from a circular end plate and is subject to Fraunhofer diffraction

For example, for such a laser employing a helium–neon mixture as the gas, at a wavelength of 6,328 Å with end plates of diameter $2a = 1$ cm,

$$\delta\theta = \frac{1 \cdot 22 \times 6 \cdot 328 \times 10^{-5}}{2} = 8'' \text{ approx.}$$

In practice, the fall off of the electric field towards the edge of the end plates is equivalent in its effect to a smaller aperture than one of diameter $2a$, leading to an increased value of $\delta\theta$.

9.7 The Line Width of the Output from a Fabry–Perot Type Cavity Laser

The intensity I of the light transmitted by a Fabry–Perot etalon is given by Equation 4.15 as

$$I = \frac{I_{max}}{1 + F \sin^2 (\delta/2)} \qquad (9.10)$$

where $F = 4r/(1-r)^2$, r being the reflection coefficient, and $\delta = (2\pi/\lambda) (2d \cos \theta)$. In these equations, I_{max} is the intensity at the central maximum in the interference pattern, I is the intensity at a neighbouring position for light different in phase by δ, θ is the angle of incidence of the light at the etalon, and λ is the wavelength. Equation 9.10 is deduced on the assumption that an infinite number of reflections are at the end plates, and it is only an approximate result when the value of d is large compared with the plate dimensions. At $I = 0 \cdot 5 \, I_{max}$,

$$1 + F \sin^2 \frac{\delta}{2} = 2$$

Therefore

$$\sin^2 \frac{\delta}{2} = \frac{1}{F}$$

and

$$\sin \frac{\delta}{2} = \frac{1}{\sqrt{F}}$$

As δ is small,

$$\delta = \frac{2}{\sqrt{F}} = \frac{1-r}{\sqrt{r}} \quad \text{approx.}$$

A change of δ by 2π corresponds to a change in order by unity. Therefore

$$\frac{\delta}{2\pi} = \delta p_0$$

where δp_0 is the change in order p_0 at the centre corresponding to δ. Therefore

$$\frac{\delta p_0}{p_0} = \frac{\delta/2\pi}{p_0} = \frac{1-r}{2\pi p_0 \sqrt{r}} \tag{9.11}$$

As the frequency ν of the radiation is given by

$$\nu = \frac{c}{\lambda}$$

where c is the velocity of light,

$$p_0 = \frac{2d}{\lambda} = \frac{2dc}{\nu}$$

Therefore

$$\delta p_0 = -\frac{2dc \, \delta\nu}{\nu^2}$$

so, numerically,

$$\frac{\delta p_0}{p_0} = \frac{\delta\nu}{\nu}$$

error

Hence, from Equation 9.11,

$$\delta\nu = \frac{(1-r)\nu}{2\pi p_0 \sqrt{r}}$$

error

The half-width of the frequency band transmitted by the Fabry–Perot etalon is therefore given by

$$2\delta\nu = \Delta\nu = \frac{(1-r)c}{2\pi d \sqrt{r}} \tag{9.12}$$

because $\nu = c/\lambda$ and $p_0 = 2d/\lambda$.

For a reflection coefficient $r = 0.97$ and $d = 1.0$ m,

$$\Delta \nu = \frac{0.03 \times 3 \times 10^8}{2\pi \sqrt{(0.97)}} = 1.5 \text{ MHz} \quad \text{approx.}$$

which result is independent of the frequency ν. If, therefore, a gas laser 1 m long with reflection coefficient effectively 0.97 at the end mirrors can be constructed, the half-width of the frequency band is nominally 1.5×10^6 Hz, which is very small at optical frequencies of the order of 10^{14}–10^{15} Hz.

The line width of the spontaneous emission from a gas laser is, in fact, governed chiefly by Doppler effect (Section 5.8) and is of the order of 10^9 Hz for a temperature of 200°–300°C typically. It can be shown tht the line width $\Delta \nu$ of the stimulated emission is related to the line width $\Delta \nu_s$ of the spontaneous emission by the relation

$$\Delta \nu_s \propto \frac{\nu (\Delta \nu)^2}{P} \tag{9.13}$$

where P is the power level of the system. This gives a typical value in the visible region of

$$\Delta \nu_s = \frac{s}{P}$$

where s is an integer and P is the power output in watts.

For a gas laser, the threshold power is of the order of a milliwatt, which gives rise to an output of the order of a watt. The corresponding order of the line widths thus varies between 10^3 Hz and 1 Hz. These are instantaneous values; long-term values may not be so good because of instability. It is, however, possible to mix the frequencies of the outputs from two independent lasers and control the resonator lengths to within 10^{-3} Å, so giving a frequency drift of less than 30 Hz in the interference pattern.

9.8 Optical Pumping

Though the general idea of the gas laser has been described, it has been assumed so far that population inversion has been obtained. In fact, the basic problem in the use of any active material in which laser action is to be supported is to invert the population between the levels of a transition so that the probability of stimulated emission exceeds greatly that of spontaneous emission. This poses problems in the method of excitation and in the energy levels chosen.

The easiest way to invert the population between two energy levels E_p and E_q would be to irradiate the material with photons from an external source of frequency v equal to that corresponding to the transition, i.e. where $v = (E_p - E_q)/h$. However, this radiation would inevitably give rise to stimulated emission from the upper to the lower level, as well as vice versa. The result would be the establishment of an equilibrium of population densities. This difficulty can be overcome to some extent by making the radiation discontinuous; stimulated emission is then possible, but with very limited amplification.

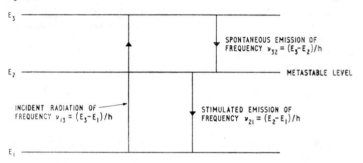

Fig. 9.7. Stimulated emission from a three-energy-level system, where metastable level E_2 becomes densely populated

A better system involves the use of three energy levels of which the intermediate one is metastable and so has a considerably longer lifetime than the outer levels. In Fig. 9.7, three energy levels E_1, E_2 and E_3 exist in the material, where $E_3 > E_2 > E_1$, and E_2 is metastable. The incident radiation from an external source is of frequency v_{13} where

$$hv_{13} = E_3 - E_1$$

so that it raises electrons from level E_1 to level E_3. The electrons in the E_3 level relax rapidly to the E_2 level and in so doing give rise to spontaneous emission of radiation of frequency v_{32} given by

$$hv_{32} = E_3 - E_2$$

As E_2 is a comparatively long-lived metastable level, electrons accumulate at this level. When this process has proceeded for a sufficient time, an incident beam of radiation of frequency v_{21} from an external source where

$$hv_{21} = E_2 - E_1$$

will give rise to stimulated emission between the levels E_2 and E_1; the population level of E_2 may also then exceed that of level E_1, because level E_1 has been robbed of electrons which go temporarily to level E_3 whereas accumulation of electrons is significant at level E_2.

This three-level system is particularly advantageous if the transition from level E_1 to level E_3 corresponds to a broad spectral line, whereas that from E_2 to E_1 corresponds to a narrow line. The light used for optical pumping (to raise electrons from E_1 to E_3) may then have a broad spectral range, while the spectral range of the stimulated emission is narrow.

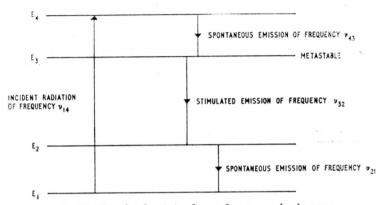

Fig. 9.8. Stimulated emission from a four-energy-level system

Fig. 9.8 illustrates a four-level system which has the advantage of producing a population inversion more quickly than the three-level system, although it still retains the advantages of a three-level system. The metastable level is now E_3, so the probabilities of the spontaneous transmissions E_4 to E_3 and E_2 to E_1 are much greater than E_3 to E_2. Hence level E_3 fills up with electrons, as in the three-level system, when radiation of frequency ν_{14} is incident. This is because relaxation is rapid from E_4 to E_3, and E_2 empties rapidly owing to the transition E_2 to E_1 as the incident radiation of frequency ν_{32} gives rise to stimulated emission from E_3 to E_2. The absorption line E_2 to E_3 will be sharp, and the absorption line E_1 to E_4 broad.

Materials with three or four energy levels suitable for optical pumping initiated by incident light of appropriate frequency include crystals, glasses, plastics, organic liquids and semiconductor materials. Doped solid-state crystalline materials are particularly suitable as they have broad absorption energy bands. Optical pumping is not generally suitable for pure gases because the absorption energy levels are too narrow; gas mixtures, such as helium–neon, are excited usually by other means than optical pumping.

340   UNIVERSITY OPTICS

9.9 The Ruby Laser

An important example of a solid-state laser with a three-energy-level system in which optical pumping is used is the ruby laser. Ruby consists of aluminium oxide (Al_2O_3) in which 0·01–0·05% of the Al^{3+} ions have been replaced by Cr^{3+} ions. It is only these chromium ions which take part in the laser action.

The energy levels in ruby which participate in the laser action are shown in Fig. 9.9. Level 1 is the ground state, the two close levels 2 are metastable energy levels, and levels 3 are in a broad energy band.

On the incidence of green light on the ruby, absorption takes place because of transitions from the ground state to the broad band of levels 3. From this excited band, electrons fall to the doublet levels 2, which are metastable and so have a long lifetime.

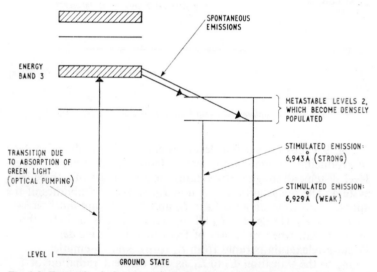

Fig. 9.9. *Energy levels for chromium ruby showing transitions involved in optical pumping, spontaneous and stimulated emissions*

As the broad band 3 can absorb a good deal of energy from the incident green light, the transitions to levels 2 bring about a high population in levels 2—greater than that of the ground state. The laser emission is primarily from the lower of the two levels 2 to ground; this is red light at a wavelength of 6,943 Å at room temperature. Transitions to the ground state also occur from the upper of the two levels 2, giving a wavelength of 6,929 Å at room temperature. This light is less intense than that at 6,943 Å, because

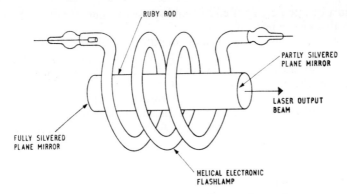

Fig. 9.10. Pulsed ruby laser (schematic diagram)

the upper level of the doublet levels 2 is less populated than the lower one.

The practical arrangement of a ruby laser (Fig. 9.10) consists of a cylindrical ruby rod of 2–20 cm in length and 0·1–2 cm in diameter, with optically polished plane-parallel ends. One end is fully reflecting and the other end is partly reflecting. This ruby rod is surrounded by a helical xenon lamp which is flashed by the discharge of capacitors through it. The pulsed ruby laser gives a laser output at wavelength of 6,943 Å of about 0·2 J for an input energy from the xenon lamp of about 5,000 J. Continuously operated ruby lasers are also made in which the flashlamp output

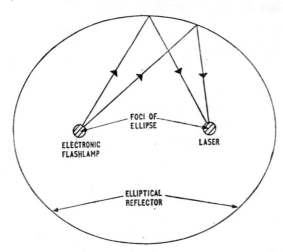

Fig. 9.11. Elliptical reflector which will focus light from a strip electronic flashlamp at a cylindrical laser

must be intensely focused by making use of internal reflectors in a small cone-shaped ruby rod.

Optical pumping is usually initiated by high-pressure xenon lamps giving a flash which lasts for 0·5–2 ms. Elliptical reflectors have been used (Fig. 9.11) with the flashlamp at one focus and the laser at the other. Unless the power supplied by the incident light is very high and well above the threshold pumping power, the output of laser light will be discontinuous or 'spiked' as a result of temporary relapses in the state of population inversion produced by the flashlamp.

9.10 Gas Lasers

Several different types of gas laser have been made. The first to be operated successfully consisted of a mixture of helium at a pressure of approximately 1 mmHg and neon at a pressure of approximately 0·1 mmHg; it was designed by Jevons and his colleagues in 1961. A more recent version of this tube (Fig. 9.12) consists of this gas

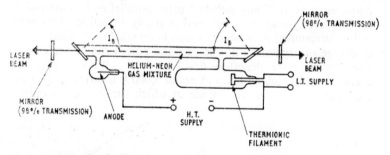

Fig. 9.12. A d.c. operated helium–neon gas laser

mixture within a cylindrical pyrex tube with optically polished glass end plates set at the Brewster angle I_B. Outside the Brewster windows are the Fabry–Perot plane-parallel mirrors of silica, each coated with multiple dielectric layers to give a reflection coefficient of 98–99% and about 0·3% transmission. It is convenient for end windows to be set at the Brewster angle to the tube, because they enable one linearly polarised component of the light to undergo very small reflection loss. The Fabry–Perot mirrors can then be outside the tube with little loss of this polarised light in the Brewster windows. These mirrors can be set in mounts for ready adjustment in 'tuning' the gas laser to optimum output. The laser tube itself is about 70 cm long, and a laser beam emerges at both ends. Fig. 9.12 illustrates a d.c. operated tube with a coated-filament source of electrons at one end and an anode at the other. High-frequency (30 MHz) operated discharges are also used (with the advantage that the electrodes can be exterior to the laser tube), but d.c. operated gas lasers seem to have a longer lifetime.

For the helium–neon gas laser, a power input from the gaseous discharge of about 50 mW is required—much lower than for optically pumped solid-state lasers—and the operation is continuous.

The energy levels appropriate to the operation of this gas laser are shown in Fig. 9.13. The neon gas is the active agent although it is present at a pressure of only 0·1 mmHg; the helium, at 1 mmHg,

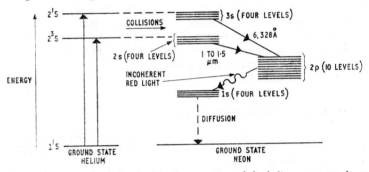

Fig. 9.13. Energy levels involved in the operation of the helium–neon gas laser

is necessary for energy transfer. The pumping in this kind of gas laser is not optical but is by electron impact. The direct current through the gas (or the excitation by a high-frequency electric field) creates the necessary electrons in the gas discharge. These electrons excite the helium atoms to the metastable 2^1S and 2^3S levels. Collisions of the excited helium atoms with the neon atoms result in a transfer of energy to the neon atoms. The close multiplet energy levels 3s and 2s of electrons in the neon thereby become populated. The probability of direct excitation of these levels in neon is very small; it is therefore necessary to populate them by energy transfer from the excited helium atoms, otherwise the mixture of gases used would be pointless.

These 3s and 2s electron levels of neon are metastable so have comparatively long lifetimes. The lower 2p levels of neon, on the other hand, are not long-lived, so depopulate very rapidly to the 1s levels. Population inversion is consequently obtained between 3s and 2p, and also between 2s and 2p. The stimulated emission responsible for the laser light is consequently $3s \rightarrow 2p$ and $2s \rightarrow 2p$. The transition $2p \rightarrow 1s$ gives incoherent radiation, which is the characteristic reddish neon discharge light. The large number of lines in the stimulated emissions (the 3s and the 2s levels are both quadruplets, whilst the $2p$ consists of 10 close levels) give rise to a corresponding multiplicity of laser lines. Isolation of particular lines in the gas laser output is therefore a problem of mode control, dependent upon the Fabry–Perot arrangement of the mirrors (Section 9.6). The wavelengths at which the helium–neon gas laser operates are 6,328 Å and in the range 10,000–15,000 Å (1–1·5 μm) with the strongest radiation at 11,523 Å.

Other gases which have been used in laser systems are pure noble gases, and mixtures of noble gases with either oxygen, carbon monoxide, carbon dioxide, nitrogen or some others gases. Optical pumping has been achieved in a caesium-filled vapour laser with a helium flashlamp. The use of a mixture such as a noble gas with oxygen excited in a high-frequency discharge operates by virtue of dissociation of the oxygen into its constituent atoms when subjected to the impact of the excited noble gas atoms. One of the oxygen atoms remains in an excited state from which it radiates stimulated emission lines.

9.11 Semiconductor or Injection Lasers

Semiconductor materials can be doped to produce an excess or a deficiency of electrons. Some lattice positions in a suitable crystalline material can be occupied by atoms containing more electrons than those in the other positions in the lattice. This process gives an n-type semiconductor. The well-known examples are silicon and germanium, both quadravalent intrinsic semiconducting materials. If silicon (or germanium) is doped with a very small percentage of pentavalent impurity (such as arsenic, phosphorus or antimony), the donor atoms in the lattice will provide excess electrons because five valence electrons are available per atom as against four for silicon.

The opposite process occurs in which some lattice sites of the semiconductor material are occupied by atoms containing few electrons: this leads to a p-type semiconductor containing positive holes. An example is silicon (or germanium) doped with a trivalent impurity such as indium, aluminium or boron. At lattice locations where an indium atom is present instead of a silicon one, only three valence electrons are available instead of four. The positions of electron deficits are the positive holes.

If a junction is made between a p-type and an n-type semiconductor, the application of a p.d. of the correct polarity will cause a flow of electrons from the n-region to the p-region. The electron surplus in the n-region occupies an energy band called the conduction band; the p-region of electron deficiency occupies the valence energy band. These two bands are broad, because each band comprises a continuous energy spread over a fairly wide region.

To obtain laser action, stimulated emission—and so a high population in a metastable level ready for transition to a comparatively empty and non-metastable state—is demanded. The process in semiconductors is very complicated and not fully understood. In outline the probable operation is as follows. A high-pulsed current (about 1,000 A cm^{-2}) is passed through a semiconductor junction from n-material to p-material. A large number of electrons may then be visualised as passing into the p-region and establishing themselves in a virtually metastable state. From this virtual state they fall to the valence level with the emission of coherent photons. The active region is very narrow: about 10^{-4} cm wide on the p-side of the junction.

An example of this process is in the gallium arsenide laser. Tellurium is added to replace some of the arsenic atoms and create an n-region, whereas zinc is added to replace some of the gallium atoms to form a p-region. Typical dimensions are 0.1 mm $\times 0.1$ mm $\times 1.0$ mm in the final cut and polished crystal (Fig. 9.14).

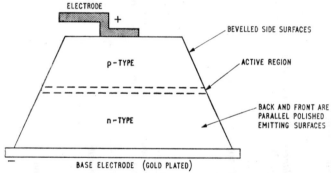

Fig. 9.14. Outline of a gallium arsenide injection laser

Semiconductor laser materials can have high efficiencies of about 50%, as compared with 5% for a helium–neon gas laser. High-power outputs with extreme brightness are possible. A significant feature as compared with other laser methods is that modulation of the light output is possible.

9.12 Q-switched or Pulsed Lasers

It is possible to increase considerably the output of a laser by a process known as Q-switching. Substantial stimulated emission is delayed until a much greater population inversion than usual is obtained. Stimulated emission is then allowed to take place suddenly, resulting in a pulse of coherent light of considerably increased

Table 9.2.

PROPERTIES AND OUTPUTS OF VARIOUS LASER MATERIALS

Source material and excitation	Power output (W)	Brightness (W sr⁻¹)	Line width (Hz)	Angular divergence (sr)	Electric field in focused spot of 5λ diameter (V cm⁻¹)	Output wavelengths (Å)
Gases (electron impact pumping)	0·05–40	10^7–10^9	10	10^{-7}	30–300	He–Ne (continuous): 6,328; 11,532; 33,900; He–Ne (pulsed): 11,177–12,066
Solid state (optical pumping)	3×10^6– 5×10^6 if Q-switched	10^7–10^{11} (Q-switched: 10^{14})	10^4–10^6 (Q-switched: 10^9)	10^{-6} (Q-switched: 10^{-5})	10^2–10^4 (Q-switched: 10^6)	Ruby (pulsed): 6,943; Neodymium (pulsed): 10,600
Semiconductor (injected)	3–10^2	10^8–10^{10}	10^5	10^{-2}	10^2–10^3	
Carbon arc as typical optical source	10	500	10^{10}	5	0·7	Continuous spectrum

intensity suitable, for example, for optical welding. In one method, the beam is interrupted by a mechanical shutter or rotating prism placed between the end of the lasing material and one of the mirrors. The shutter is connected to the flashlamp mechanism, so that the flash occurs whilst the shutter is closed. Lasing cannot take place until the shutter opens; meanwhile, the population inversion builds up to its peak value. When the shutter opens the energy is released in a giant pulse.

In another method, a bleachable solution is interposed in place of the movable shutter. For example, a cell containing phthalocyanine is used with a ruby laser. This cell absorbs strongly light of the ruby output frequency. Lasing cannot occur in the ruby until a substantial inversion has built up. Coherent light is initially faintly transmitted and bleaches the solution, which then suddenly becomes transparent allowing the passage of a large light pulse. The molecules in the solution then revert to their normal state, so the solution becomes red and the process repeats itself.

9.13 Application of Lasers

The account of optical masers or lasers that has been given is merely a survey of the more common lasing materials and methods of excitation, and is by no means comprehensive. The comparative properties of the output from the various materials used are summarised in Table 9.2.

The marked advantages of lasers lie in applications requiring a high degree of coherence in the output radiation, for example in holography. An obvious limitation is the number of frequencies at present available in the ultra-violet region of the spectrum. Stability of the output is also a problem in many applications. The applications are numerous. Broadly, they fall into five main divisions:

1. Measuring techniques taking advantage of the high coherence path length and, in some cases, the short pulse time and high intensity of the laser beam;
2. Modulation and mixing;
3. Power applications;
4. Communications;
5. Coherent-light image and data processing.

9.13.1 MEASURING TECHNIQUES

A good example of the application of a laser to measuring techniques is the use of the Twyman and Green interferometer (Section 10.4 of Volume 1) for testing optical components. With ordinary sources of light, the collimation requirements are very stringent; the use of a laser beam leads to simplification and increased accuracy. A typical set-up for testing a prism is shown in Fig. 9.15: it gives, in the focal plane of the camera, a two-dimensional Fourier distribution corresponding to the phase modulation of the reference beam by the beam returning from the prism under test.

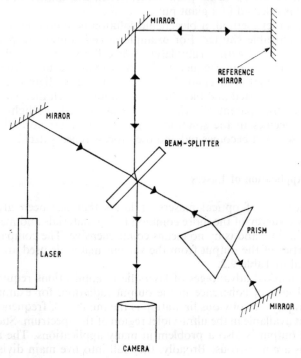

Fig. 9.15. *Arrangement for using a laser source to test a prism in a Twyman and Green interferometer*

Distance measurements in surveying can be undertaken by using a laser pulse of light and adopting the principle utilised in radar of determining electronically the time interval between the outgoing and returning pulses of light.

Ruby lasers and Q-switched lasers have facilitated several developments in high-speed photography.

The laser is not generally used as a primary frequency standard, because the laser frequency is chiefly determined by the cavity dimensions. It is, however, useful as a *relative* frequency standard. The output from a given laser can be combined with some other optical frequency (also from a laser), and the difference found to within a few hertz. It is probable that, with improved cavity tuning, the laser will become sufficiently stable to form a primary frequency standard.

There are also many possible applications in spectroscopy. The most obvious one is the exploration of the Raman effect, which presents difficulties with standard optical sources; indeed, the science of Raman spectroscopy is currently undergoing a revolution following the advent of the laser.

9.13.2 POWER APPLICATIONS

In power applications, a Q-switched laser beam is focused to a spot of about five wavelengths diameter, giving typically outputs up to megawatts at pulse rates up to 100 per second. Such intense pulses of light may be used for making very small holes in metals and other materials; for the local volatilisation of small quantities of material; for welding in engineering; for welding in position a detached eye retina; and, possibly, even for providing a sufficiently great highly localised temperature to allow a nuclear fusion (thermonuclear) reaction to proceed.

The focused beam will also probably be used in the future for the reading and writing of optical information; this will require a means of modulating precisely the position and intensity of the beam so as to produce data storable in a suitable material.

9.13.3 COMMUNICATIONS

Laser beams have obvious advantages over microwaves and conventional light sources in the field of communications: laser beams can be directed much more accurately, and have greater monochromaticity and, potentially, greater frequency bandwidths. It is possible, for example, to record a pulsed laser beam, returning after reflection at the Moon's surface, over an area of some two square miles. This illustrates dramatically the spatial coherence properties of the beam.

As an example of the potential information-carrying possibilities of the laser beam, 10^{10} channels each 10 kHz wide (corresponding to the usual audiofrequency range used in radio for modulating a carrier wave) could be accommodated on a carrier wave of frequency 10^{14} Hz. However, modulation of light beams from a laser is a difficult problem. The modulation could be superimposed at the generating lasing material or after leaving the laser. Electro-optical devices such as the Kerr cell appear to be the most promising for such modulation.

9.13.4 IMAGE AND DATA PROCESSING

The essential of image and data processing is the formation of a Fourier transform intensity distribution. For example, in Fig. 9.16, a Fourier transform of the two-dimensional transparency is formed in the second focal plane of the lens 1. This hologram (Section 9.14) may be treated in any way desired to remove, for example, offensive background detail. Alternatively, a spatial filter placed at the hologram position will give an image formed by lens 2, as shown in Fig. 9.16, with the features removed as desired. Radio

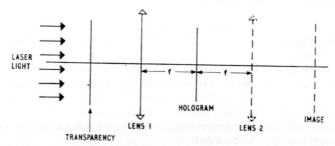

Fig. 9.16. Outline showing the formation of a hologram of an object in the form of a transparency with incident laser light

photographs usually have a background forming a regular two-dimensional lattice of spots. The hologram then shows a similar lattice with inverse dimensions. The larger scale means that a spatial filter can easily be made to remove this undesirable lattice feature from the hologram.

9.14 Holography

Suppose a plane wavefront of monochromatic light is incident upon an object. Light will be reflected (scattered) by the object, or transmitted if the object is transparent though it may contain regions of various optical densities. If this reflected or transmitted light is focused by a lens to form an image, as in a camera, the image is a two-dimensional replica of the object. If a lens is not used (i.e. a 'lensless' camera is used), implying that the light as modulated by the object falls directly upon a photographic plate or film, a diffraction pattern is recorded. This recorded diffraction pattern contains only information about the intensities in the diffracted light; it does not contain information about the phase. To put this in another way, using the concepts of Section 6.23, a Fraunhofer diffraction pattern is, to a first approximation, the Fourier transform of the diffracting aperture (the object in the present case). The record of the diffraction pattern will give no information about the phase of the Fourier transform.

If this phase information could be recorded also, the record of the light from the object would then contain all the information which goes to make up the image of the object. This data is present in the light, irrespective of whether or not a lens is used to form the usual image. To obtain in the record the necessary phase information and yet use a 'lensless' camera, the technique adopted is to direct into such a camera monochromatic light which has been modulated by the object, and at the same time provide monochromatic light of the same kind to enter the lensless camera directly. The photographic record is then of the light modulated by the object added to which is reference unmodulated light of the same wavelength.

A photographic transparency which is obtained in this way then has an optical density variation decided by both the intensity and the phase of the modulated light from the object. This photographic record is called a *hologram*.

A beam of monochromatic light is then transmitted through the hologram. A second diffraction pattern is thereby generated. A component of this second pattern on a screen reproduces an image of the original object on the screen.

Holography requires a source of radiation with a high degree of coherence and stability in time. Both these requirements are satisfied by the laser. Moreover, the intensity of the laser light output enables the hologram to be recorded in a suitable short time, so reducing the effect of any movement.

9.15 The Recording Process in Holography

As an example of holography, collimated monochromatic light from a laser is divided into two beams. One of these beams enters the lensless camera directly: in Fig. 9.17(a) it is incident on the aperture OA at which there is a photographic plate. The other beam is incident upon the object and gives rise to a scattered beam modulated in a manner dependent upon the structure of the object. This scattered light also enters the aperture OA, and the hologram required is recorded on the photographic plate at OA.

Suppose the reference collimated beam 1 of light of wavelength λ is incident normally at the aperture OA whereas the modulated beam 2 of light of the same wavelength is incident at a small angle ϕ [Fig. 9.17(b)]. The amplitude of the electric vector in the incident beam 1 will be constant over the aperture OA. Let this amplitude be E_0.

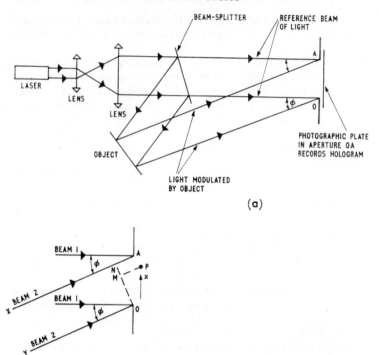

Fig. 9.17. The principle involved in holographic recording

Assuming first that the wavefront in beam 2 is also plane, the amplitude over ON drawn perpendicular to XA will be constant. For any point P in the aperture with coordinate x referred to the origin O, beam 2 will have a phase difference relative to beam 1 decided by $(2\pi/\lambda)MP$, where $MP = x \sin \phi = x\phi$, as ϕ is small. The complex amplitude of the electric vector E_2 at a point such as P in the aperture OA will therefore be represented by

$$E_2 = E_{02} \exp (jkx) \qquad (9.14)$$

where $k = 2\pi/\lambda$.

However, beam 2 is modulated by the structure of the object. Consequently, E_{02}, the amplitude of E_2 at $x = 0$, will be a function of x, taking into account only variations in the object in the x-direction (this assumes one dimension for simplicity; in practice, two or three dimensions are concerned), and therefore E_2 is put as $E(x)$. Moreover, ϕ will vary with x, because the angle ϕ depends on the direction of beam 2 which will also alter with the object structure. Hence ϕ is written as $\phi(x)$. The appropriate expression in place of Equation 9.14 for a beam 2 modulated by the object is therefore

$$E_2 = E(x) \exp [j\phi(x)] \tag{9.15}$$

The intensity of the light due to the superposition of the reference beam 1 and the modulated beam 2 in the plane of the aperture OA is therefore given by

$$
\begin{aligned}
I(x) &= \text{constant} \times |E_0 + E_2|^2 \\
&= \text{constant} \times \{|E_0|^2 + |E(x)|^2 + 2|E_0| \, |E(x)| \cos [kx + \phi(x)]\}
\end{aligned}
$$
$$\tag{9.16}$$

Equation 9.16 represents the intensity variation with x in the pattern of light that is photographed in making the hologram. This photograph is in the form of a positive transparency. As this positive transparency (hologram) is to be subsequently viewed by transmitted monochromatic light, its transmittance $T(x)$ as a function of x is of interest. The intensity of the light incident on the photographic emulsion is $I(x)$. From the data in Section 5.30 on γ of a photographic emulsion, assuming the exposure is correct so that the straight-line portion of the characteristic curve (Fig. 5.23) is utilised,

$$\log \frac{1}{T(x)} = D = \gamma \log (\text{exposure}) \propto \gamma \log [I(x)]$$

Therefore

$$\frac{1}{T(x)} \propto [I(x)]^\gamma$$

or

$$T(x) \propto [I(x)]^{-\gamma}$$

The amplitude distribution in the hologram transmittance is therefore given by

$$\sqrt{[T(x)]} \propto [I(x)]^{-\gamma/2}$$

Substituting for $I(x)$ from Equation 9.16,

$$\sqrt{[T(x)]} = a\{|E_0|^2 + |E(x)|^2 + 2|E_0| \, |E(x)| \cos [kx + \phi(x)]\}^{-\gamma/2}$$
$$= a |E_0|^{-\gamma} \left\{ 1 - \frac{1}{2} \gamma \frac{|E(x)|^2}{|E_0|^2} \right.$$
$$\left. - \gamma \frac{|E(x)|}{|E_0|} \cos [kx + \phi(x)] \right\} \quad \text{approx.}$$

where a is a constant.

As E_0 is constant for a given reference beam and γ is a constant for a given photographic emulsion and development,

$$\sqrt{[T(x)]} = b\{2\,|E_0|^2 - \gamma\,|E(x)|^2$$
$$-\,2\gamma\,|E_0|\,|E(x)|\,\cos\,[kx + \phi(x)]\} \quad \text{approx.}$$

where b is a constant; or

$$\sqrt{[T(x)]} = b(2\,|E_0|^2 - \gamma\,|E(x)|^2 - \gamma\,|E_0|\,|E(x)|\,\exp\,\{j[kx + \phi(x)]\}$$
$$-\,\gamma\,|E_0|\,|E(x)|\,\exp\,\{-j[kx + \phi(x)]\}) \quad (9.17)$$

Equation 9.17 is a mathematical representation (in one dimension, as variations of x only are discussed) of the hologram produced. It contains the phase as well as the amplitude information. The term 'hologram' was introduced in 1951 by Gabor, to whom the original process is credited.

9.16 The Reconstruction Process in Holography

If a beam of monochromatic light of constant amplitude with a plane wavefront from a laser is incident upon a hologram represented by Equation 9.17, the transmitted beam has its amplitude modulated because the incident amplitude is multiplied by $\sqrt{[T(x)]}$ on transmission.

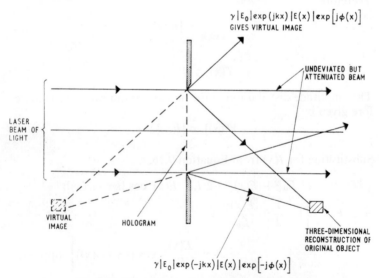

Fig. 9.18. The reconstruction process in holography

The first two terms $2|E_0|^2$ and $-\gamma|E(x)|^2$ in Equation 9.17 give rise to an undeviated but slightly diffracted beam with uniform attenuation as part of the transmitted light. The Fourier transform of a constant is a Dirac delta function (see Appendix) corresponding to the image of this beam at infinity. The third term $-\gamma|E_0|$ $|E(x)|\exp\{j[kx+\phi(x)]\}$ in Equation 9.17 gives rise to a part of the transmitted light in the form of a beam deviated upwards—Fig. 9.18 where the upward beam is $\exp(jkx)$—and is $\gamma|E_0|\exp(jkx)$ multiplied by $|E(x)|\exp[j\phi(x)]$. This upward deviated beam is therefore modulated by the original beam from the object and forms a virtual image of the object in this direction.

The final term $-\gamma|E_0||E(x)|\exp\{-j[kx+\phi(x)]\}$ in Equation 9.17 gives a part of the transmitted light in the form of a beam deviated downwards, in which $\gamma|E_0|\exp(-jkx)$ is modulated by $E(x)\exp[-j\phi(x)]$. This is the complex conjugate of the wavefront arising at the hologram from the original object.

Since the modulation is by the complex conjugate, this wave in effect retraces the steps back to the original object as it progresses. This can be seen from the example represented by Fig. 9.19. As the spherical wavefront from the point source S moves from A to B, its phase angle decreases—which is equivalent to multiplication by $\exp(-jkr)$. If, however, multiplication is by $\exp(jkr)$ (the complex conjugate), this moves the wavefront backwards in time from B [with an arbitrary phase $\exp(j\omega t)$] to A.

Thus a real three-dimensional image of the original object is formed (Fig. 9.18) from this wavefront represented by the final term of Equation 9.17.

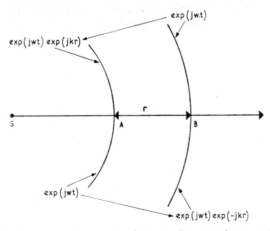

Fig. 9.19. A spherical wavefront moving from A to B is equivalent to multiplication by exp (−jkr) ; movement backwards from B to A is equivalent to multiplication by exp (jkr)

9.17 The Magnification Due to the Holographic Process

Consider two points in the object for which a hologram is made. If this hologram is subsequently illuminated by light of the same wavelength as that used in making the hologram, the separation of these points in the image formed by the hologram is the same as in the original object. The linear magnification is unity.

If, however, the hologram is illuminated by light of different wavelength from that used to make the hologram, magnification is achieved.

An expression for this magnification can be obtained in a particularly simple way by considering the hologram formed by a Young's double slit arrangement (Fig. 9.20). The incident laser

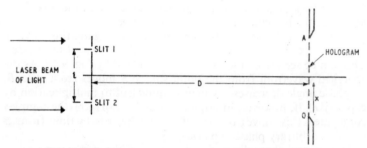

Fig. 9.20. A hologram with Young's double-slit arrangement

light may be considered to be divided into two beams by the slits, where slit 1 forms the reference beam and slit 2 the object. If the reference beam from slit 1 is represented by

$$E_1 = E_0 \exp{(jkx)}$$

then the object beam from slit 2 is represented by

$$E_2 = E_0 \exp{(-jkx)}$$

The intensity in the plane of the hologram at OA is proportional to $|E_1 + E_2|^2 = |E|^2$, say, where

$$|E|^2 = |E_0[\exp{jkx} + \exp{(-jkx)}]|^2 = 4|E_0|^2 \cos^2{kx} \quad (9.18)$$

The fringe separation is given by the usual Young's double slit expression (Equation 8.1 of Volume 1)

$$\Delta x = \frac{D\lambda}{l} \quad (9.19)$$

where Δx is the separation between neighbouring bright fringes, D is the axial distance from the plane of the slits to the plane of the diffraction pattern OA, l is the separation between the slits, and λ is the wavelength of the light.

Recording by photography to give a positive transparency of this diffraction pattern gives the hologram of the slit 2 in relation to slit 1.

Suppose this hologram is illuminated with light of wavelength λ'. The usual Fourier transform image corresponding to the last term of Equation 9.17 is obtained. At a distance D', the separation between the images of the slits will be l' such that

$$\Delta x = \frac{D'\lambda'}{l'} \tag{9.20}$$

The linear magnification m due to the process is seen from Equations 9.19 and 9.20 to be

$$m = \frac{l'}{l} = \frac{D'\lambda'}{D\lambda} \tag{9.21}$$

One application of this magnification procedure is due to Gabor, the originator of holography. The hologram is formed by illuminating the object (in an electron microscope) with electrons of wavelength given by $h/\sqrt{(2m_e eV)}$, where h is Planck's constant, m_e and e are the mass and charge of the electron, and V is the p.d. through which the electrons are accelerated. With $V = 10{,}000$ V, $\lambda = 12{\cdot}26/\sqrt{V} = 0{\cdot}01226$ Å. If this hologram is viewed by light of wavelength 5,000 Å, say, an enormous magnification of about 5×10^5 is possible.

The possibility exists also of obtaining such enormous magnifications in X-ray microscopy where the X-rays have a wavelength of $0{\cdot}1$ Å, say, and the light used to illuminate the hologram is at a wavelength of 5,000 Å. At present, however, X-ray beams with the necessary coherence are not obtainable.

Exercise 9

1. Write an essay on the coherence of radiation.

2. With the aid of a three-level energy diagram in which an appropriate level is metastable, explain how population inversion can be obtained leading to stimulated emission of radiation.

3. With the aid of suitable diagrams, describe in outline the construction and operation of a pulsed ruby optical maser.

4. Explain, in relation to an appropriate energy-level diagram, how stimulated emission results from electron impact pumping in a helium–neon gas laser.

5. Write an essay outlining some of the present and possible future applications of optical masers.

6. Without giving mathematical detail but with the aid of simple ray diagrams, describe the principles involved in obtaining a hologram of a transparent object.

7. Describe the holographic process in simple mathematical terms by reference to the formation of a hologram from either a Fresnel double-mirror system or a Young's double-slit arrangement. Explain briefly how large linear magnifications are possible in holography, indicating the limitations involved in the practical use of two sources of light of greatly differing wavelengths, where one source is used to record the hologram and the other in the reconstruction of the image.

8. An aperture is filled with a plane wavefront of monochromatic laser light of amplitude E_0 combined with light whose complex amplitude is represented by $E_2 = E(x) \exp [j\phi(x)]$; this latter light comes from the same laser as the monochromatic light, but is scattered by an object which is considered, for simplicity, to modulate this light in an x-direction only. The pattern of light formed in the aperture is photographed to produce a hologram utilising a photographic emulsion of which the slope of the characteristic curve is γ. Derive an equation which represents the variation with x of the amplitude of the light transmitted by this hologram when it is illuminated with monochromatic light. Explain how a component of this transmitted light gives rise to a real image of the original object.

Appendix

A.1 Fourier's Theorem

Let $f(x)$ be a periodic function in x with a period a and frequency $v = 1/a$. According to Fourier, such a function can be represented by a series of sine and cosine terms in the form

$$f(x) = A_0 + A_1 \sin 2\pi vx + A_2 \sin 4\pi vx + \ldots + A_p \sin 2\pi pvx$$
$$+ \ldots + B_1 \cos 2\pi vx + B_2 \cos 4\pi vx$$
$$+ \ldots + B_p \cos 2\pi pvx + \ldots$$

or

$$f(x) = A_0 + \sum_{p=1}^{p=N} (A_p \sin 2\pi pvx + B_p \cos 2\pi pvx) \qquad \text{(A.1)}$$

where A_0, A_p and B_p for $p = 1, 2, 3, \ldots, N$ are coefficients to be determined.

The values of the coefficients A_0, A_p and B_p may be found by using the orthogonality relationships of sines and cosines, which are:

$$\int_0^{2\pi} \cos p\theta \cos q\theta \, d\theta = \begin{cases} \pi & \text{for} \quad p = q \\ 0 & \text{for} \quad p \neq q \end{cases} \qquad \text{(A.2)}$$

$$\int_0^{2\pi} \sin p\theta \sin q\theta \, d\theta = \begin{cases} \pi & \text{for} \quad p = q \\ 0 & \text{for} \quad p \neq q \end{cases} \qquad \text{(A.3)}$$

$$\int_0^{2\pi} \cos p\theta \sin q\theta \, d\theta = 0 \qquad \text{(A.4)}$$

Thus, if both sides of Equation A.1 are multiplied by $\cos 2\pi qvx$ and integration is carried out over a period, then for $q \leqslant N$

$$\int_0^a f(x) \cos 2\pi qvx \, dx = A_0 \int_0^a \cos 2\pi qvx \, dx$$
$$+ \sum_{p=1}^{p=N} \int_0^a (A_p \sin 2\pi pvx \cos 2\pi qvx + B_p \cos 2\pi pvx \cos 2\pi qvx) \, dx$$

In Equations A.2, A.3 and A.4, putting $\theta = 2\pi\nu x$, the period a is equivalent to angle 2π. Therefore, in view of Equations A.2 and A.4, when $p = q$ all terms within $\sum\limits_{p=1}^{p=N}$ disappear except for the term $B_p \cos 2\pi p\nu x \cos 2\pi q\nu x$. Thus

$$\int_0^a f(x) \cos 2\pi q\nu x \, dx = A_0 \int_0^a \cos 2\pi q\nu x \, dx + \int_0^a B_p \cos^2 2\pi p\nu x \, dx$$

Now,

$$\int_0^a \cos 2\pi q\nu x \, dx = \frac{\sin 2\pi q\nu a}{2\pi q\nu} = 0$$

and, from Equation A.2,

$$\int_0^a \cos^2 2\pi p\nu x \, dx = \frac{a}{2}$$

Therefore

$$\int_0^a f(x) \cos 2\pi q\nu x \, dx = \frac{B_p a}{2}$$

so

$$B_p = \frac{2}{a} \int_0^a f(x) \cos 2\pi q\nu x \, dx \qquad (A.5)$$

Similarly, multiplying both sides of Equation A.1 by $\sin 2\pi q\nu x$, it follows that

$$A_p = \frac{2}{a} \int_0^a f(x) \sin 2\pi q\nu x \, dx \qquad (A.6)$$

To find A_0, integrate Equation A.1 from 0 to a to give

$$\int_0^a f(x) \, dx = \int_0^a A_0 \, dx = A_0 a$$

because all other terms in Equation A.1 become zero in view of the relationship

$$\int_0^{2\pi} \sin p\theta \, d\theta = \int_0^{2\pi} \cos p\theta \, d\theta = 0$$

Therefore

$$A_0 = \frac{1}{a} \int_0^a f(x)\, dx \qquad (A.7)$$

Equations A.5, A.6 and A.7 are used to evaluate the constants B_p, A_p and A_0 respectively.

A.2 The Complex Fourier Series

As

$$\cos 2\pi pvx = \frac{1}{2}[\exp(j2\pi pvx) + \exp(-j2\pi pvx)]$$

and

$$\sin 2\pi pvx = \frac{1}{2j}[\exp(j2\pi pvx) - \exp(-j2\pi pvx)]$$

a pair of terms in Equation A.1 such as $A_p \sin 2\pi vpx + B_p \cos 2\pi pvx$ may be written as

$$\frac{A_p}{2j}[\exp(j2\pi pvx) - \exp(-j2\pi pvx)]$$

$$+ \frac{B_p}{2}[\exp(j2\pi pvx) + \exp(-j2\pi pvx)]$$

$$= C_p \exp(j2\pi pvx) + C_{-p} \exp(-j2\pi pvx)$$

where

$$C_p = \frac{1}{2}\left(\frac{A_p}{j} + B_p\right) = \frac{1}{2}(B_p - jA_p) \qquad (A.8)$$

and

$$C_{-p} = \frac{1}{2}\left(-\frac{A_p}{j} + B_p\right) = \frac{1}{2}(jA_p + B_p) \qquad (A.9)$$

Equation A.1 can therefore be written in the form

$$f(x) = \sum_{p=-N}^{p=N} \{[\exp(j2\pi pvx]C_p\} \qquad (A.10)$$

where $p = -N, -(N-1), \ldots, -1, 0, 1, \ldots, N$, and where it is seen from Equations A.8 and A.9 that the values of C_p are, in general, complex.

To find the coefficients in Equation A.10, the orthogonality relationship used is

$$\int_0^{2\pi} \exp(jp\theta)\exp(-jp\theta)\,d\theta = \begin{cases} 2\pi & \text{for} \quad p = -q \\ 0 & \text{for} \quad p \neq -q \end{cases}$$

Multiplying both sides of Equation A.10 by $\exp(-j2\pi pvx)$ and integrating over the range 0 to a gives

$$C_p = \frac{1}{a}\int_0^a f(x)\exp(-j2\pi pvx)\,dx \qquad \text{(A.11)}$$

The coefficients in Equation A.10 may be represented by a Fourier spectrum (Fig. A.1) making use of Equation A.11.

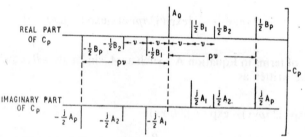

Fig. A.1. A Fourier spectrum (p is positive or negative)

If the function $f(x)$ is real, then

$$C_p = \bar{C}_{-p}$$

where $\bar{C}_{-p}$ is the conjugate of C_{-p}, giving a series of real terms $C_p \exp(j2\pi vpx) + C_p \exp(-j2\pi vpx)$.

A.3 The Fourier Transform

Suppose that the range of the function to be represented by a Fourier series is very large. The period a in Equation A.11 then tends to infinity, and v (the interval between the coefficients C_p in the Fourier spectrum illustrated in Fig. A.1) tends to zero. The amplitudes of the various terms are now represented by a continuous function, in the limit (Fig. A.2). The coefficient C_p represents the contribution to the amplitude between frequencies pv and $pv \pm \delta v$ and is expressed by

$$C_p = F(v)\,\delta v$$

Equation A.11 is therefore written in the form

$$F(v)\, \delta v = \frac{1}{a} \int_0^a f(x) \exp{(-j2\pi p v x)}\, \mathrm{d}x$$

Let $\delta v \to 0$ and $a \to \infty$, representing a range from $-\infty$ to ∞. Also, write pv as a general frequency v. Then,

$$F(v) = \lim_{\substack{\delta \to 0 \\ a \to \infty}} \left[\frac{1}{\delta v(a)}\right] \int_{-\infty}^{\infty} f(x) \exp{(-j2\pi p v x)}\, \mathrm{d}x$$

or

$$F(v) = \int_{-\infty}^{\infty} f(x) \exp{(-j2\pi v x)}\, \mathrm{d}x \qquad (A.12)$$

Note that both $f(x)$ and $F(x)$ are generally complex.

Equation A.12 is true if the functions and their first and second derivatives are continuous. The function $F(v)$ is called the *Fourier*

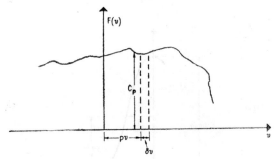

Fig. A.2. *Diagram of the Fourier spectrum where the interval between coefficients tends to zero*

transform of $f(x)$. The Fourier transform of any function is therefore simply the amplitude distribution of the continuous Fourier series which represents that function. The converse is also true, i.e.

$$f(x) = \int_{-\infty}^{\infty} F(v) \exp{(j2\pi v x)}\, \mathrm{d}v \qquad (A.13)$$

where the exponential sign is strictly reversed but, in practice, this is arbitrary.

The functions $f(x)$ and $F(v)$ are known as *Fourier mates*, and $f(x) \rightleftharpoons F(v)$.

A.4 Examples of Fourier Transforms

A common example is the Gaussian function [Fig. A.3(a)]. It is given by

$$f(x) = h \exp\left(-\frac{x^2}{\sigma^2}\right) \qquad \text{(A.14)}$$

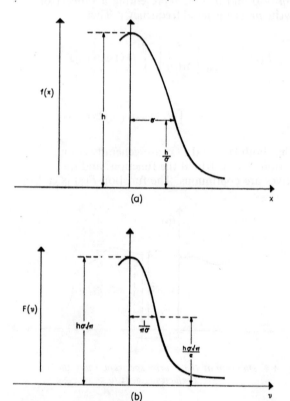

Fig. A.3. *The Gaussian function and its Fourier transform*

Therefore, applying Equation A.12,

$$F(v) = \int_{-\infty}^{\infty} h \exp\left(-\frac{x^2}{\sigma^2}\right) \exp\left(-j2\pi vx\right) dx$$

$$= h \exp\left(-\pi^2 v^2 \sigma^2\right) \int_{-\infty}^{\infty} \exp\left(-\frac{x}{\sigma} + j\pi v\sigma\right)^2 dx$$

As

$$\int\limits_{-\infty}^{\infty} \exp(-z^2)\, dz = \sqrt{\pi}$$

therefore

$$F(v) = h\sigma\sqrt{\pi}\,[\exp(-\pi^2 v^2 \sigma^2)] \qquad (A.15)$$

Equation A.15 is also a Gaussian function [Fig. A.3(b)], but note that the width parameter is proportional to $1/\sigma$, which is generally true of Fourier transforms.

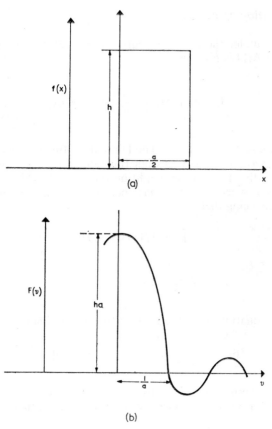

Fig. A.4. The 'top-hat' function and its Fourier transform

Another example is the 'top-hat' function [Fig. A.4(a)], where $f(x) = h$ for $-a/2 < x < a/2$ and is zero elsewhere. Therefore, from

Equation A.12,

$$F(v) = \int_{-a/2}^{+a/2} h \exp(-j2\pi v x) \, dx = \frac{ha \sin \phi}{\phi}$$

where $\phi = \pi a v$.

The function $F(v)$ has a first minimum at $\phi = \pi = \pi a v$; hence $v = 1/a$ [Fig. A.4(b)], so again the inverse width relationship has been obtained.

A.5 The Dirac Delta-function

The area under the Gaussian curve [Fig. A.3(a)] represented by Equation A.14 is given by

$$A = h \int_{-\infty}^{\infty} \exp\left(-\frac{x^2}{\sigma^2}\right) dx = h\sigma\sqrt{\pi}$$

Hence if $h = 1/\sigma\sqrt{\pi}$, $A = 1$. The Dirac delta-function $\delta(x)$ may be defined as the limiting Gaussian function when $h \to \infty$ and $\sigma \to 0$, subject to the normalising condition that $A = 1$. This function is zero except when $x = 0$. It has special properties, a particularly useful one being that

$$\int_{-\infty}^{\infty} \delta(x) f(x) \, dx = f(0) \tag{A.16}$$

and

$$\int_{-\infty}^{\infty} \delta(x-a) f(x) \, dx = f(a) \tag{A.17}$$

From Equation A.15, the Fourier transform of $\delta(x)$ is

$$\lim_{\sigma \to 0} \left(\frac{1}{\sigma\sqrt{\pi}}\right) \sigma\sqrt{\pi} \, [\exp(-\pi^2 v^2 \sigma^2)] = 1 \tag{A.18}$$

In general terms, therefore, the Fourier transform of the delta-function is a constant, and vice versa. So Dirac delta-function $\rightleftharpoons$ constant.

Numerical Values of Constants

Atomic mass unit (a.m.u.) = $1\cdot6598\times10^{-27}$ kg
Avogadro's number (N) = $6\cdot02486\times10^{23}$ molecules mol^{-1}
Bohr magneton (β) = $1\cdot16544\times10^{-29}$ Wb m
Boltzmann's constant (k) = $1\cdot38044\times10^{-23}$ J deg^{-1} C
Electron, charge of (e) = $1\cdot60206\times10^{-19}$ C
Electron, rest mass of (m_e) = $9\cdot1083\times10^{-31}$ kg
Electron, specific charge of (e/m_e) = $1\cdot7589\times10^{11}$ C kg^{-1}
Electron volt (eV) = $1\cdot60206\times10^{-19}$ J
Hydrogen atom, mass of = $1\cdot6733\times10^{-27}$ kg
$\qquad\qquad\qquad\qquad = 1\cdot008142$ a.m.u.
Permeability of free space (μ_0) = $4\pi\times10^{-7}$ H m^{-1}
Permittivity of free space (ε_0) = $8\cdot85424\times10^{-12}$ F m^{-1}
Planck's constant (h) = $6\cdot62517\times10^{-34}$ J s
Proton, rest mass of (m_p) = $1\cdot67239\times10^{-27}$ kg
$\qquad\qquad\qquad\qquad = 1\cdot007593$ a.m.u.
$\qquad\qquad\qquad\qquad = 1{,}836\cdot12\ m_e$
Rydberg constant for infinite mass (R_∞) = $1\cdot0973731\times10^7$ m^{-1}
Velocity of light in free space (c) = $2\cdot99793\times10^8$ m s^{-1}

Answers to Numerical Exercises

Exercise 1, Page 32

7. Reflected intensity 0·1722 times incident intensity
8. 1/9
11. 109·5 V m⁻¹

Exercise 2, Page 90

2. (a) 3×10^{-7} m = 3,000 Å; (b) 8.486×10^5 m s⁻¹
3. (a) 6.546×10^{-7} m = 6,546 Å; 4.854×10^{-7} m = 4,854 Å;
   4.339×10^{-7} m = 4,339 Å; (b) 13·67 eV
4. 5.3×10^{-11} m = 0·53 Å
5. 13·67 eV; 5.3×10^{-11} m = 0·53 Å
7. 1.8×10^{11} C kg⁻¹
9. 2·15 Å in wavelength on either side of the line of wavelength 5000·0 Å

Exercise 3, Page 147

3. 1·732
5. 1.64×10^{-3} cm
6. Light is plane-polarised
9. $1/\sqrt{3}$; 30°
10. (a) plane-polarised; (b) elliptically polarised
11. 7·2 mm; 2·4 mm
13. 4180 Å, 4500 Å, 4910 Å, 5460 Å, 6090 Å and 6920 Å
15. 130
18. 1·3°; 3.6×10^{-8}
19. For left-handed rotation: rotations of 36°, 216°, 396° and 576° correspond to one-third previous concentration. Estimates of rotations for full concentration are therefore 108°, 648°, 1188° and 1728°; these are the same as 108°, 288°, 108°, 288°, of which 288° ≡ 72° right-handed rotation. Therefore a left-handed rotation of 36° is, in fact, 216°, corresponding to 648° ≡ ≡ 288° ≡ 72° right-handed. To avoid ambiguities, alter tube length by a small amount.

Exercise 4, Page 177

5. 10 cm
7. 25·46 days
8. $1·25 \times 10^{-10}$ cm
9. $2·02 \times 10^{-5}$ cm or $4·04 \times 10^{-5}$ cm

Exercise 5, Page 246

5. Mean wavelength = 5788 Å; range of wavelengths = 68 Å
11. 6235 Å and 6061 Å
16. 50 cm length in first order; 25 cm length in second order

Exercise 6, Page 295

1. 17·32 cm or 17·32 $\sqrt{n}$ cm where $n = 3$ or 5
2. Bright image at distance beyond zone plate of 31·6 cm, with fainter images at 19·4 cm and 14 cm; much fainter images in between these positions.
4. 543 cm; 45·5 cm; 11·22 cm
7. 6·65°

Exercise 7, Page 311

4. 0·2, 0·3 and 0·5

Exercise 8, Page 323

1. $3·57 \times 10^{-5}$ cm
6. (a) $3·23 \times 10^{-5}$ cm; (b) $2·26 \times 10^{-5}$ cm; (c) $3·35 \times 10^{-8}$ cm

Index